Cutting
Teeth

ALSO BY CHANDLER BAKER

Whisper Network
The Husbands

Cutting Teeth

▼▼▼

CHANDLER BAKER

FLATIRON
BOOKS
NEW YORK

CUTTING TEETH. Copyright © 2023 by Chandler Baker. All rights reserved. Printed in the United States of America. For information, address Flatiron Books, 120 Broadway, New York, NY 10271.

www.flatironbooks.com

Library of Congress Cataloging-in-Publication Data

Names: Baker, Chandler, author.
Title: Cutting teeth / Chandler Baker.
Description: First edition. | New York : Flatiron Books, 2023.
Identifiers: LCCN 2022060815 | ISBN 9781250839787 (hardcover) |
    ISBN 9781250839794 (ebook)
Subjects: LCSH: Love, Maternal—Fiction. | Mother and child—Fiction. |
    LCGFT: Paranormal fiction. | Detective and mystery fiction. | Novels.
Classification: LCC PS3602.A5855 C88 2023 | DDC 813/.6—dc23/eng/20230104
LC record available at https://lccn.loc.gov/2022060815

Our books may be purchased in bulk for promotional, educational, or business use. Please contact your local bookseller or the Macmillan Corporate and Premium Sales Department at 1-800-221-7945, extension 5442, or by email at MacmillanSpecialMarkets@macmillan.com.

First Edition: 2023

10 9 8 7 6 5 4 3 2 1

To my son, Colin, the jolliest class biter around—your taste for human flesh may fade, but my love for you will never

Cutting
Teeth

PROLOGUE

▼

It's not true that nothing bad has ever happened at Little Academy. Not entirely. There was the boy last year whose hands slipped off the monkey bars. Next thing the mother knew his collarbone was popping clean out of his skin. (His father right there, he could have caught him!) At least once a school year, when the temperatures still reach well into the nineties, some mom or other accidentally locks her keys in the car along with her baby. The school is just around the corner from the fire station and the truck arrives within minutes, but the mother still sobs, unable to believe she's been so careless; it could have been worse. Not that it ever is. Not here. Not at Little.

Maybe all preschools are designed to be adorable, but Little Academy is particularly so. Children's handprints outline a cement walkway where on a typical day the baby classes ride around in covered hippo wagons. The children help to maintain a garden; in it grows an impressive display of knockout rosebushes and jasmine and other sorts of flowers that attract real, live butterflies. To step on campus is to feel your heart lift just the slightest bit in your chest, almost as if there's less gravity there. A shrine to these final few glimmering months when none of the kids are too old for enthusiastic hugs at pickup, when big, fat tears are still cried while waiting for mommies.

Inside, the walls echo with the shrieks of tiny voices, muffled behind closed pony doors. Teachers clap—one, two, three—and announce that it's time to change centers, to clean up, to keep hands to yourselves.

It smells like graham crackers. The memory of chubby wax crayons white-knuckle pressed between small fingers. That's how it looks, actually—melted wax creeping shadowlike from beneath the door, out into the empty hall. The reflection of a fluorescent ceiling light wavers uncertainly on the puddle's slick, red surface.

The door at the foot of the corridor hasn't been closed properly. The way it hangs ajar feels lazy; somebody should put up a note, ought to be more careful. The supply room is where all the pointy things live—grown-up scissors, industrial paper cutters, letter openers. With all the tiny curious hands, it's a bad situation waiting to happen.

The soft sound coming from the other side of the door is hard to place. A gentle wet sopping noise, like a puppy trying to suckle. A too-wet tongue. The smell of saliva like mouth sweat in the air.

The light flips back on, motion activated.

There is blood everywhere, but on the gray-flecked tile most of all. Viscous and slippery, it squelches and slides. Heat leaks out along with it and the room feels dank. Used up.

But even here, cold creeps across skin, puckering it into goose flesh. An electric current charged with disbelief hums in the deafening quiet. The wrongness of it, plain as day. Car seats, child-proof locks, *Consumer Reports*, swim lessons, they've worked so hard to avoid danger, to ward it off, and yet somehow, some way it's snuck right past them.

First comes love, then comes marriage, then comes the baby carriage. And now, now at last, the fear arrives.

ONE

▼

The blood kept coming out of her. She was going to die. People died. She knew that intellectually and yet she couldn't believe it was going to be her.

Rhea's teeth rattled around in her skull like one of those wind-up chatter-jaw toys with the little feet.

"It's going to be okay. You're going to be all right now." Behind her, the orderly with the James Earl Jones voice tapped the rubber grip on the wheelchair handle. She hadn't seen his face before he whisked her down the corridor, following the intake nurse's instructions.

How much blood was in her body? How much could she stand to lose? Of all the stupid things she'd been forced to learn in school, shouldn't this at least have been one of them?

The elevator lurched up and Rhea felt her vision narrowing to pinholes, the whole world shrinking. When the orderly asked if she could stand to get into the hospital bed, she wasn't sure her legs would hold her. He took her beneath an armpit and an elbow. As he lifted, she felt sure the bottom of her would fall out like the base of a soggy brown grocery bag and what would spill out was her own insides.

A new nurse came in and immediately started messing with the cords and tubes behind Rhea. Her back was on fire. Her body felt like it was begging her to evacuate, get out, leave now, before it was too late, but she found all exits blocked.

"How long have you been bleeding?" A female doctor looked deep into her eyes. She and Rhea were about the same age and Rhea had never seen this doctor before in her entire life.

Spit flew out from the corners of Rhea's mouth as she forced the words through her teeth. "A couple of hours. I came as soon as it started, but I've been waiting."

The doctor pressed a jellied ultrasound wand to her belly now. "Has it been about this rate since the bleeding began?"

A warm gush flowed between her legs. Rhea moaned. Her Walmart maternity joggers stuck to the inside of her thighs.

The doctor stopped moving the wand and looked gravely at the screen. "The placenta has completely separated from the uterine wall, Rhea, and I can see you're hemorrhaging. You're going to need a blood transfusion." The doctor reached for a blue button on the panel above Rhea's head and pressed it. "And we need to deliver that baby. Now. Do you understand?"

"I'm only thirty-six weeks." She clawed at the nubby hospital blanket beneath her. Copper and earth tinged her nostrils and she registered, impossibly, that the smell was her.

More people filled the room. She could suffocate. She wasn't even sure if she was breathing. "What are you doing?" She panted. "What's happening? Wait. You have to stop. Wait."

The nurse, who'd at some point stabbed her with an IV, now buzzed around her head. "I'm going to slip this mask on over your mouth and nose. Nice and easy. Very gentle." She adjusted the rubber band behind Rhea's ears. "How's that? Comfortable. Breathe normally."

Pain lassoed her stomach. Another giant gush of blood. She screamed into the hollow plastic.

"The baby doesn't have oxygen." The doctor moved so quickly around her. It was as if everyone were paying attention to Rhea and also no one at all. "We have to do a crash section." This didn't feel right. Wait. Wait. "We have seconds, not minutes, *seconds.*"

Rhea could feel her body shutting down. She hadn't even asked about her baby yet. The fire burned up and down her spine, tearing through her ass muscles.

"No time for an epidural or painkillers. Rhea, you'll be put straight to sleep. Do you understand?"

No. She was trying to tell them. No. No. She'd miss it if they put her to sleep. She would miss this thing, she would miss everything, everything she was promised. She would miss him. Hers.

"Take a deep breath." She gasped, more a death rattle than an attempt to cooperate, but the world dissolved around her anyway. Down she sank. Down, down, down, down. Into a deep, salty darkness. Into a rotting cavity with no bottom, a medically induced black hole, bitter-tasting, like Advil with the sweet casing dissolved; she was swallowed alive. Rhea was plunged into motherhood the same way a cat's drowned in water.

Some days she feels like she went to sleep on that hospital bed and woke up where she is now, with Bodhi four years old. Her eyes travel his classroom as she waits impatiently for his teacher to join her.

When she woke up at the hospital, it was to find that not only was she no longer pregnant but that her heart had been extracted, taken out of her chest, and transplanted into this beautiful little boy. She now watches her heart play trucks with two other boys his age. Her moon baby. Her wildflower. Her ocean soul.

Around her, the classroom is a museum of enthusiastic art displays: colorful handprints, a kindness tree, a guess-the-smell chart on which one little girl answered "wine," and tissue collages. The colorful rug at the center of the room has all the letters of the alphabet and ten wooden cubbies house ten individual lunch boxes—hearts, superheroes, princesses—each a little dingier than when they were so lovingly selected at the start of the year.

It wasn't that long ago that Rhea's experience at this school had been not as a parent, but as a nanny, though she doesn't advertise that. To a little blond girl who, at just three years old, attended Kumon for tutoring, loved sloths, and hated the smell of yogurt, and Rhea thought, as she took in the sparkling school, slightly dumbfounded, slightly awestruck: *If I ever have a baby, this is it.*

This is Little Academy, a small, private preschool on the campus of RiverRock Church. Rhea's not religious, but she sees the value in a strong moral upbringing at this age, good versus evil, wrong and right, and all that.

Over by the sink, Bodhi's teacher, Miss Ollie, helps Noelle Brandt unscrew the top of an Elmer's glue, then comes over to join Rhea.

"I'm glad we could connect finally," says Miss Ollie, dusting her hands off on a bright yellow maxi skirt as she sits. The tails of a chambray top are tied at her waist. She looks like a Disney princess, with her candy-apple cheeks and pearly pageant teeth. "It's been hard to reach you by email."

Rhea runs her fingers through her long strands of inky black hair, interlaced with a few subtle streaks of mauve. A gorgeous willow tree tattoo with deep, intricate roots appears to sway on the pale inside of her forearm. It's not easy to look dignified while squatting on a tiny chair made for tiny-assed children, but she's making it work.

"I must not have gotten them," says Rhea, which might be true, who knows. She gets hundreds of emails a week. Her burgeoning business, Terrene, a curated essential oil collection (super easy to use *and* accessible) is a one-woman show and she's that woman.

"Or phone."

"I'm here now." Though only because Miss Ollie waylaid her at drop-off this morning.

There was a big fuss amongst the other parents when Miss Erin Ollie joined the staff of Little Academy. She has a PhD in child development and Rhea doesn't have one clue what she's doing here teaching toddlers like some kind of Preschool Poppins, but you do you.

Out of the corner of her eye, she sees Bodhi pick up a toy bus and move out of her line of sight. She resists the urge to keep her eyes on him. The instinct to watch over him is nearly impossible to turn off in his presence. She missed his first cry, his first breath. She doesn't know what the first thing her son experienced in this world was, but it wasn't her. Maybe it's because she was still asleep when the umbilical cord was cut that she still feels it tying her to Bodhi like a phantom limb.

"Bodhi's looking a little thin," says Miss Ollie. "For his age, I mean."

"Okay," Rhea answers carefully. "He was a chunky baby. Now he's growing like crazy." Her son has beautiful brown skin and thick, brown shoulder-length locks. If Rhea had a dollar for every person who asked if he's adopted, she could afford the down payment on a house.

"For sure. One hundred percent. I just wanted to point out that it's noticeable compared to the other children and I—" Miss Ollie wrings her hands like she's getting ready to break up with a boyfriend, but feels really badly about it. "Restrictive diets can have a number of health benefits, I know—but in adults."

"Excuse me?"

"I see his lunches. The dried seaweed and purple cauliflower and vegetable grits. He's hardly eating any of it. I know you want him to eat healthfully. I just wonder if it would be better, you know, for Bodhi, if he had a few more normal, higher-calorie options day-to-day."

"Better . . . for Bodhi?" Rhea's not hard of hearing, she just wants to give this twentysomething a chance to run that back. *Better for Bodhi.* Did she really just say that?

Rhea gives nothing away. She is the still pond. She is the tree trunk, unruffled by the wind. She is the horizon in the distance. But underneath, Rhea feels undulations of rage crashing at her seams. Who the *fuck* does this woman think she is?

"You know," Miss Ollie continues like this is all just occurring to her, "it might be worth including Bodhi's father in this conversation."

"I can talk to Marcus just fine, thanks."

She knows most people, her friends included, refer to Marcus as her "ex," though ex-what she has no idea. When she got pregnant with Bodhi, she had only just started a new type of birth control, a last-ditch attempt to curb the chronically vicious menstrual cramps that had been wrecking her world. She chalked up her missing period to the new pills for longer than she might have otherwise. She didn't get cramps anymore. But she got a baby.

And mostly, single motherhood suits her. She makes what she wants for dinner. She decorates the apartment to her taste. Lets Bodhi watch television or doesn't, her rules. She starts a business, her money.

"Right." Miss Ollie chews her lip, waiting for Rhea to make this less awkward. She's going to be waiting awhile. "I could provide a list of easy lunch ideas. I just want to be a—" But right at that moment, it's as though the ground beneath her sentence crumbles. Her whole demeanor transforms. "No!" she bellows, jumping from her chair. "No! No! No!"

Rhea whips around at the same time as a single, panicked cry of agony splits the room. A small pile of children writhes on the story mat. An empty shoe flops out of the mess. Rhea's eyes dart to every corner— where's Bodhi? *Where* is Bodhi?

"Where's my son?" This time out loud.

A girl whines. Then— "You're hurting him."

"Mommy." His voice is small and muffled. The word throbs inside her. "Mommy?"

"Bodhi? Bodhi!" Rhea drops to her hands and knees and crawls toward the fray. Her own sandal loses its grip between her toes and she slips out of it. The stiff carpet dimples the thin skin over her kneecaps as she stretches an arm into the tangle of tiny limbs. The willow tree disappears within.

A distinct growl from somewhere in the broil and Miss Ollie's face goes red as she heaves a toddler by the armpits. "Off! Off! There are grown-ups here!"

The two kids remaining scatter, but the bottom one stays put, shaking uncontrollably with silent sobs.

Bodhi.

His long hair fans out around his head. He still clutches the large plastic bus in his arms as blood soaks through the cotton collar of a sky-blue T-shirt. Rhea drags him up and pulls him tight to her chest. "Shhhh, shhhhh, shhhhhh," she soothes. "Mama's got you."

"Teeth are *not* for biting." Miss Ollie's voice seesaws as she crouches down to eye level with Zeke Tolbert, a chunky biracial boy with a tight fade and striking, crystal-blue eyes. "You know better."

"I didn't do anything," says Noelle as she plucks her giant pink bow from the floor and clips it back in her curly blond hair. "I told Zeke he better stop it. Also I need a Band-Aid." She holds up her fingers, which are red from being squished.

"Bodhi wouldn't share his bus and he's gotten a super long turn. Like, super long." George Hall, who is always dressed like a tiny golfer, limps to retrieve his lost club loafer.

Rhea feels an earthquake coming on. Her hands tremble as she pulls her son from her body to examine him. A ring of puncture wounds where Bodhi's neck meets the curve of his shoulder leaks an angry shade of red, leaving behind a Rorschach test of spots on her linen tunic.

"Oh-kaaaay" is all Miss Ollie manages for a handful of seconds. "That's—okay. We'll—everyone's okay."

Rhea glares over the top of her son's head. "I'm sorry, what now?" She feels the heat in her hands first, that sensation of warmth spreading through her veins, shooting up toward her head. Her voice trembles; the sight of her son, her sweet, wouldn't-hurt-a-fly baby boy oozing blood from an attack in his own classroom makes her feel as though she's been sliced open herself. She's waiting for Miss Teacher-of-the-Year over here to show the same degree of horror she'd reserved for Rhea's cauliflower just two minutes earlier, but look who's all laissez-faire now. Maybe *she* deserves to get bitten, see how "okay" she feels about it then.

"It's definitely *not* okay. Okay?"

The teacher stares, open-mouthed. Some of the other children have already resumed playing with blocks and plastic food items and pretend cash registers. George tries to pull a picture book off the overstuffed Read-with-Me shelf and the books that fall off make the sound of dead birds slapping the ground. Miss Ollie's eyes dart over then back. "I'm sorry, I don't know what's been getting into them." She takes Zeke's hand in her own.

"What's been getting into them? Like this has happened before? Like this is a normal occurrence?"

"No." Miss Ollie swallows. "It's not that— I'm sorry, I'm not allowed to discuss incidents involving any of the other children. But I take it very seriously. We're working through it. Rhea, I understand you're upset. I'm upset, too. These are like my children."

"Yeah?" Rhea says. "Except that's the difference, isn't it? They're not."

TRANSCRIPT OF INTERVIEW OF WITNESS, BODHI ANDERSON

APPEARANCES:

Detective Wanda Bright

PROCEEDINGS

DET. BRIGHT: Do you know what detectives do, Bodhi?

BODHI ANDERSON: Beep when there's smoke in the kitchen.

DET. BRIGHT: Beep when there's sm— Oh, no, those are detectors. I'm a detective. I solve mysteries. Mysteries are stories we don't know the ending to yet.

BODHI ANDERSON: I don't want to be that. I want to be a teacher and a veterinarian.

DET. BRIGHT: Sounds like you're going to be pretty busy. Do you think for today, though, you could help me solve a mystery?

BODHI ANDERSON: What's the other choice?

DET. BRIGHT: What do you mean?

BODHI ANDERSON: Do you want to color for five extra minutes or would you like to hear the end of this story? Like that.

DET. BRIGHT: Oh, um, you can help me solve a mystery or you can answer some questions. Which one do you want to do?

BODHI ANDERSON: I'll do the mystery.

DET. BRIGHT: Okay, Bodhi. Can you tell me whether anyone was in your class that day that wasn't usually in your class?

BODHI ANDERSON: No.

DET. BRIGHT: Even for a second.

BODHI ANDERSON: I guess one person.

DET. BRIGHT: Who was that, Bodhi?

BODHI ANDERSON: Just my mommy.

TWO

▼

S he did seem like she felt really bad about it," says Darby Morton, who had returned to drop off Lola's forgotten water bottle—there has been a lot of drama around that water bottle—and had therefore witnessed the immediate aftermath in Miss Ollie's classroom. Darby has one of those pleasantly round faces with bright skin that makes her nearly impossible to get irritated with, which, in itself, can be a bit irritating, Mary Beth finds, if she's being honest. "She went pale," Darby relates, dramatically. "Like a ghost."

"I don't care how she feels. It shouldn't have happened," Rhea shoots back. There is a lovely tattoo of a hummingbird just below Rhea's collarbone that Mary Beth finds oddly uplifting at a time like this, which one might not expect to be her official opinion on the matter, but there it is.

The thing about Rhea is that she is granola, which is the polite term Mary Beth's mother would have used for *hippie*, and Mary Beth hoped that the mere proximity of fresh-pressed juices and ancient grain bowls at this aggressively healthy café where the three mothers have agreed to meet would have helped to ease her off the ledge.

"Right." Mary Beth sets down her tea. "Of course. But she's a fantastic teacher. I think we can all agree, we're lucky to have her."

Rhea makes a noise that suggests they cannot all agree.

Mary Beth has yet to remove the large, buglike sunglasses from her face as she sips hot tea while nursing the tail end of a forty-eight-hour migraine. A nasty one, too.

The headaches started sometime after her last pregnancy, though one has nothing to do with the other, according to doctors. After one of her episodes, she invariably craves carbs, ideally in the form of french fries. She imagines the look on the waitress's face if she were to try ordering some, just for kicks. Perhaps it will be similar to the look she gives when Mary Beth vomits all over this gluten-free menu.

She really does try not to take Rhea's perspective personally, but if Rhea only fully grasped the number of envelopes Mary Beth stuffed, the scope of fundraising meetings she attended, the Edible Arrangements she delivered just to ensure that the three of them had first pick of teachers this year of all years—the fours.

Less discerning mothers might have been put off by the fact that this is Miss Ollie's first year teaching at Little, but not Mary Beth. Her résumé alone separated her head and shoulders above the rest. But also, it's more than that. Miss Ollie seems to prefer the children, teaching them knock-knock jokes, crawling through chair tunnels on the floor, never getting sucked into adult conversation with parents. She's like magic.

"The dads definitely agree with you on that front. *Fantastic* is absolutely one of the words they'd used to describe her, I think," says Darby.

"What's that supposed to mean?" Mary Beth lifts her sunglasses to wipe the beads of sweat copulating on the bridge of her nose.

"Oh, come on. All the moms are talking about it. The dads are *ogling* Miss Ollie. Asher's dad told his brother—you know, Asher's uncle—and now that uncle volunteered to pick Asher up from school just to catch a peek for himself. Katia probably doesn't mind the extra help, though."

"Stop it." A phantom wisp of pain echoes around Mary Beth's head, and she winces, but barely. "That's got nothing to do with it. Doug volunteered to do drop-off a couple times last week." She hears how it sounds as soon as she's said it.

"That's very generous of him." Darby feigns wide-eyed innocence.

"She's not his type," says Mary Beth, not minding if she sounds clueless.

The three of their kids—Noelle, Lola, and Bodhi—were in the same infant class, and they've grown up together ever since, year after year, lockstep, the best of friends. Or at least that's the way it *has* been up until recently.

The waitress with the nose ring pierced through her septum comes to collect their orders, and Darby takes the opportunity to pick up her phone and scroll through work email. She's from Los Angeles and has a background as a high-powered PR executive but took a step back when she had Lola. Now she's overqualified for her job as a crisis manager for the county, where Mary Beth can only assume there are no pressing crises to manage today.

Rhea's background, on the other hand, has always been more of a mystery. She pulls a gauzy orange wrap around her shoulders, obscuring the little hummingbird from view.

"If Miss Ollie spent half the amount of time and energy she spends nosing into how I parent my kid on her own teaching," says Rhea, "then she might be able to control what goes on in her class. It makes me question whether our kids are even safe." She levels her mossy green eyes at them. "I'm thinking about filing a formal complaint with the school."

"Rhea." It comes out more chiding than Mary Beth intends and indignation flashes across Rhea's face.

"What?" Rhea blinks hard. "You think because maybe I don't pay as much tuition as you I don't get as much say?"

"No," Mary Beth stammers. "Of course not." She feels her face flush. She knows Rhea accepts some sort of financial aid package from the school even though, as she understands it, Bodhi's father, Marcus, offered to pay the difference, no problem. For whatever reason, Rhea preferred to take out the loan instead and so naturally Mary Beth hadn't been thinking about money when she made her comment. Anyway, she thought maybe Rhea's business was doing quite well these days. Terrene. You've got to extend the *e* when you say it, like *serene*.

"I just think being a teacher is a really challenging job," Mary Beth says gently.

"And maybe not everyone's cut out for it."

Mary Beth presses her lips together. She tries very hard to see it from Rhea's point of view. Rhea's feelings are . . . valid. Her child was harmed. Emotions are high. Of course they are.

"Care to jump in here, Darby?" Rhea sets her water down too hard and the ice tinkles against the glass. "Anything to add?"

Darby glances up from her phone. "Sorry, what are we talking about?"

Rhea rolls her eyes. They both know Darby has a tendency not to pay close attention, though Mary Beth sometimes suspects it's a selective strategy more than a condition.

How long can it take to make raw food? she wonders a tad miserably.

"I'm *talking* about how I saw Griff at school." Rhea leans back in her chair like she rests her case.

Darby puts down her phone. "I doubt that. What would he be doing there?"

Not that it would prove any point, but Mary Beth would like to know the same thing. Of all her friends' husbands, Griff Morton is, by far, her least favorite.

Rhea purses her lips, like she's not sure how much she should say, but now that she's started, the lid has been good and lifted and what else can she do? "I only bring it up because he didn't look too happy with Miss Ollie. He was, you know . . . They were arguing." She watches Darby, they both do, searching for a glimmer of recognition. *This is ringing a bell, right? You know about this, surely?* But Darby's face remains disturbingly blank. "I figured," Rhea presses, "that something must be going on with Lola."

Yes, Mary Beth thinks. There. Finally. Something *is* going on with Lola Morton. And now someone has finally had the guts to say so.

After dinner, Mary Beth takes an Oreo out of the package. Then she takes three. She eats them standing over the freshly wiped counter in her modern farmhouse.

Sooner or later, she and Darby will have to face the conversation about their daughters head-on. Of course, Mary Beth will be exceedingly gracious; she's already been practicing in the shower how gracious she'll be because it's important not to gloat, *never* to gloat. It's not her own daughter who's been turning into a little monster (no wonder Noelle no longer wants to be friends with her), but it just as easily could be.

Well, maybe not just as easily. No judgment (Verse 7:1).

She scrapes the crumbs from the countertop and dusts them from her palms into the sink. Then she climbs the stairs to her master bedroom and rustles in the back of her closet for a shopping bag. Out from it, she pulls what the saleswoman called a red "cocktail lace playsuit," which sounded promising.

She musses her hair, the way the models do in Victoria's Secret ads. Better.

Swear on the Holy Bible, she never would have thought to buy lingerie if it weren't for Pastor Ben.

Pastor Ben is new. Pastor Ben has tattoos. And wears hats indoors. She wasn't even intending to pay *attention* to the sermon. Many Sundays, she tunes out, enjoying the forty-five or so minutes of her week during which no one is asking for chocolate milk at the exact same moment she sits down, or wondering whether she's seen the remote, or talking to her while she's on the toilet, asking her what smells.

Pastor Ben came onstage to the tune of "SexyBack" and Mary Beth was alerted to the movement of his firm biceps, his swaying hips, and his lack of forehead wrinkles. The point of the talk was to encourage married couples to have sex and, at the end of it, he announced the 30-Day Challenge with a zingy exclamation mark.

A spark plug shot off inside Mary Beth. When *was* the last time that she and Doug had had sex? Three months ago? Four?

But now, as she stands in front of a mirror in desperate need of a good Windex, wearing some unmentionables, a swell of pride rushes into her rib cage. She can do this. A starting point. A fighting chance. Carve out a place for herself, away from her crippling headaches and her nibbling volunteer work and her adorable children. She can take back her life.

Y ou didn't need to do all that for me." Doug's put the kids to bed and, finally, the house is quiet. He peels off his socks and drops them into the hamper.

And suddenly, Mary Beth feels silly, and silly is not what one wants to feel in a cocktail lace playsuit. "I know." She sounds dull, not vixen-y at all.

But *need* had nothing to do with it. Of course she didn't *need* to wear new lingerie. What she's after is desire. Now she doesn't know what, exactly, she was expecting.

Or maybe, worse, she does.

She hoped her husband's eyes would widen, caught by surprise, like a camera flash had gone off two inches from his nose. She imagined him crossing the room without a word, wrapping his fingers in the hair at the base of her skull and tipping her head back so that he could lower his mouth onto hers. That had never happened to her before and it sounded nice, like something she should experience at least once.

Instead, Doug stares at her, flat-footed, in his rumpled khakis and flannel shirt. He's a regular guy, her husband. A dad sort, and that is not a knock. He enjoys putting up Christmas lights and coming up with family itineraries for the weekend and talking hypothetically about the dog he plans to get when "things slow down."

"Pastor Ben told us we should have fun with it." She evokes the pastor's name like a shield: *Don't blame me, this wasn't my idea.*

Mary Beth could have sworn she was warned—many, many times, in fact—that she would spend much of her married life concocting sorry excuses to stave off the unwanted advances of a pawing husband. She thought that once there were no longer sleepless nights with babies in the house, the space in their minds and bodies would open up naturally, but perhaps they needed a jump start. Enter Pastor Ben.

"It was on sale," she says. It wasn't.

"I mean, I like it." Doug can't seem to sort out what to do with his hands. He scratches behind his ear, pets the back of his neck, checks the buttons on his shirt.

"You do?"

"I haven't seen you wear lingerie since our wedding night." He grins now, his turn to look silly.

"But that was just yesterday," she says, which they both know is the most ridiculous thing of all. Their wedding feels like eons ago. Recently, in a morning breath fog, as she fumbled for coffee, she had the thought: *Wait, does the Earth go around the sun once a year, or is it a day?*

It takes something like five or six or fifteen seconds for Doug to cross the room to her, and though his fingers do not twine through the roots of her hair, what they do instead is quite nice.

An absurd number of throw pillows rains down onto the floor and the playsuit soon becomes irrelevant as Mary Beth forgets all the things she's been forgetting lately and time swirls in a way that doesn't feel draining and she is very thankful for her soft, cushioned mom body, which is rarely if ever ogled when—ouch! *ouch!*—there's an alarming pinch on her heel.

"Did you do that?" Her head picks up from the mattress.

"Do what?" He hovers over her, a sheen of sweat slicked across his wiry chest.

She rolls him off the top of her, and then emits a bleat of distress when she sees the blond top of her four-year-old's head sticking up over the edge of the bed.

"Honey!" she shrieks, unsure to which member of her family she's speaking. "Noelle! Noelle, sweetie! What are you doing up?" Mary Beth huddles her knees into her chest while Doug's busy pulling pillows over his most sensitive areas.

"I couldn't sleep." Noelle has a sweet, high-pitched voice that reminds Mary Beth of angel bells.

"Okay. Well . . ." She trails off.

The door. They should have locked the door.

"Watch it." Doug points. "You're dripping."

She is momentarily horrified by his implication before she sees what he means.

Blood slowly bubbles up in the spot on her ankle where she'd felt the pinch. A bright bead falls onto her white duvet spread. "Shit." She scoops her hand underneath her heel.

"Language."

"Sorry." She takes a closer look and counts. There are six separate puncture wounds. "Did you . . . did you bite Mommy, Noelle?" There it is, that absurd third person, which, for whatever reason, has come to sound completely natural to her ear, as though that Mary Beth—Mommy Mary Beth—is her own person. As though she lost the *I* of it all once she became somebody's mother. If witness protection really wants to know the quickest way to make a woman disappear, just make her a mom.

Noelle gives a wide-eyed nod. Tears are welling in her little-girl eyes. "I'm sorry, Mommy. I—"

Mary Beth scoots her bare ass off the end of the bed and, in a few quick strides, wraps herself in her plush, white robe.

"It was probably just a reaction to—well—to what we were doing." Pink blotches have erupted at the tops of her husband's cheeks. "She's traumatized."

Mary Beth sinks to her daughter's level. "Did we scare you?" Noelle shakes her head. "Were you not able to get our attention? Was that it?" Noelle shrugs.

"Oh my god," Doug says, but there's a hint of a chuckle in his voice. At least bewilderment. "Should I phone the child psychologist now or wait till morning?"

"Shhh. She doesn't know. She's too young." Then to Noelle— "Mommy and Daddy were just play wrestling, that's all. We're so silly, aren't we?"

Come to think of it, Mary Beth herself feels a tiny bit traumatized.

She uses toilet paper to blot the spot on her heel, which continues to ooze. What on earth got into Noelle? That *hurt*.

She feels sorry now for her discarded playsuit and its truncated spin around the block—so much for adult time. What's the etiquette of wearing it again, anyway?

As she leads her daughter back to her bedroom, Mary Beth wonders if, given everything, it still might be perfectly honest to successfully check off day number 6 in her challenge. She's not one to bend the rules, but just this once it might be harmless. They can always do better tomorrow.

THREE

▼

Darby hit her child. *Hit* her. The things you say you'll never do as a parent, and yet. Is a "bop" a hit?

Griff screamed, "You can't hit her!"

That was all her husband did, though.

All he did as she shrieked bloody murder. "She's got me! Let go! You're hurting Mommy!" *Bop, bop, bop.* Panic climbing her rib cage like a ladder.

Her wrist now has a visible heartbeat. The surface puddles of eight wounds—a top row and a bottom—ooze in rhythm with her pulse. The two holes where the little incisors pierced remind her of natural hot springs, their depths ominously unknown, mystically terrifying.

What was she thinking moments earlier? What was it? She feels like her earth has been scorched, razed in the rush of searing pain, shocking and distressing as her daughter bit the shit out of her.

Moments before the bite, Griff was rubbing his whole face with his palms, ruffling the boyish mop of chestnut hair that hangs down over his forehead. "This just—this can't be normal! What if there is something *wrong* with her? Like, psychologically? But we don't know! Because you're so against the idea of asking the school to do a workup with the counselor for no reason! Except that it wasn't your idea, probably."

Lola's cartoonishly red face dripped with snot and tears, lubricating her cheek as she slid it over the hardwood floor like a wonder mop, knees tucked underneath her, tiny bottom spiked in the air, knuckles wrapping around her hair as she screamed and sobbed, then screamed some more.

And Darby shouted back, "It is *normal*. Four-year-olds have tantrums. *Normally.*"

But the violence of Lola's fits has been getting incrementally worse lately.

Griff went for the stern-dad voice. "Lola, if you don't stop crying in five seconds. One . . . two . . ." The volume of her cries only increased.

"No! No! No! No! *Noooooo!*" she shrieked.

"Three . . . four . . . five." Griff finished the pointless exercise.

"And?" Darby looked at him, expectantly. "If she doesn't stop crying in five seconds then . . . what?"

He rolled his eyes. She and Griff are as bad as the kids.

"That was the entire plan? That was it? That's as far as you got?"

At which point, she consigned herself to carrying Lola to her room, where her daughter could remain until her soul returned to her body. She reached for Lola's armpits to scoop her up like a kicking, screaming rag doll and that's when she got bitten, bitten so deeply Darby felt the scrape of bone on bone, and tasted iron on her tongue.

Her own mouth contorted into an ugly, silent scream as she pressed her thumb in the spot between Lola's eyebrows and slowly, painfully pushed—with the excruciating care of one pulling a nail from her foot. Chin tipped back, her daughter's bangs, which are cut straight across and styled into a short, 1920s flapper bob, swept from her darling forehead. Her tiny jaw released and Darby thought: *Every year, every month, every day; it's supposed to be getting easier!* And then Lola's tongue, washed bright red, slipped out and licked the cupid's bow of her precious, heart-shaped mouth.

That was two hours ago. Now Griff accepts the glass of pinot noir that Darby hands him before setting it down on the coffee table, untouched.

A couple days ago, there was a shooting at a Midwestern school and you know what Darby thought while sobbing at her computer screen? She thought: *I'm going to cherish every moment with my children from now on.* The next day, she set a timer just to get herself to play Star Wars toys with Lola for twenty minutes without glancing at her phone. And now imagine how she feels today, the self-loathing of it all.

The hallmarks of motherhood are already written over Darby's body, like a cautionary billboard. She remembers that ad campaign, the one with the egg frying in a pan—*This is your brain on drugs.* That's Darby: *This is your body; this is your body on motherhood.* Terrifying. Utterly terrifying.

She really committed to pregnancy, at least insofar as it involved eating for two. It was the one time—okay, two—in her life that she stopped worrying for a goddamn second about counting calories or exercising properly or how she looked naked. She ate ice cream daily, *with* toppings, and it was cute. People told her what an adorable pregnant lady she was. She felt like a jolly panda bear. Of course, no one warned her there would be consequences. Or if they did, she pretended not to hear—she does have a habit of doing that occasionally. But that changed instantly after her babies were born and suddenly she was surrounded by advice on how she could lose the baby weight. The emails she once so loved to receive, the ones that used to track her baby's growth in terms of fruit size, instead started sending her strength-training programs.

In her defense, she developed a bad case of diastasis recti, the condition, which she previously believed was fake, where a woman's abdominal muscles fail to knit back together properly postpartum, meaning that more than a year after having Jack, she's been asked on more than one occasion when her baby's due.

Did you gain a lot of weight during your pregnancy? The physical therapist asked when she went in to learn exercises to address the issue. She never went back.

She has stretch marks, too, silvery veins that crawl across her hips and ass. It's in vogue to call them her "tiger stripes." Apparently, she's supposed to love them, they're supposed to make her feel fierce. Look what her body has done. It has birthed two small human beings.

She hates those stripes, has no interest in making peace with them. And this is to say nothing of her breasts, which used to be quite nice before her kids literally ate them. Lately, she's been able to crunch them up in her fists like stress balls. They didn't use to do that.

When Darby looks at her body, she doesn't recognize it. She feels like it belongs to someone else, mostly because it does.

"What if she has rabies?" Darby asks her husband. "You can't cure rabies."

"Rabies is already cured."

"Not once you show symptoms." Darby takes a long pull of wine. It's not from one of their better bottles. "Google it. What if there was a bat in her room? Or a rat."

Lola bit her. Not just bit but—and this is unpleasant—*chewed* on her. She distinctly felt grinding.

Fine, she'll admit, she felt a little smug when Zeke Tolbert had been the culprit today in class. It felt good. For once, on the right side of things. It's just that Lola isn't an easy child and, as such, Darby gets a perverse sense of satisfaction when somebody else's kid is the problem. Allow her this small pleasure.

Griff hunches over his phone, scrolling. "You're right," he says. "How did I not know that? She can't have rabies. We don't have *rats*. I think we'd know."

"I'm going to be up all night thinking about whether she's contracted rabies," Darby says. "Should we put her in our bed?"

"We just got her to sleep." He sighs.

There are so many things she would never have expected to fret over as a parent, pinworms chief among them. But others include time changes, teaching her kids their home address in case of emergency, flying on the same plane as Griff without their children, stem cells, wills, whether other parents own guns, constipation, the proper age for ear piercing, Elf on the Shelf, and now rabies.

"Maybe you can at least check to see if there are any cracks in her walls. Or in the vents?" she suggests instead.

"Right now?"

"Yes, right now." Darby can be bossy. Just thirteen years earlier, which isn't really that long ago if you think about it, she was captain of the varsity volleyball squad at UCLA, one of the best volleyball programs in the country, and she was very physically fit, a fact that, though not actually relevant to this situation, bears repeating because, to reiterate, it wasn't that long ago and she could be in good shape again, it's not out of the question.

"But I'll wake her up."

"Never mind. I'll just stay in her room tonight." She isn't looking forward to having her stomach, thighs, and rib cage poked and kicked through the night, but at least maybe her mind will be at ease.

Griff pinches his earlobe. "I have to head back to the office."

"Tonight? Are you sure?"

He's spent his entire career working in the IT department of a large law firm, where he's now the manager. It's a thankless job and Darby has been telling him to find a better one for ages, but that would require interviewing, which would require talking to people, which means Griff won't do it.

"Hardware update."

"How late will you be?"

When Lola was born, Darby went from senior publicist at a brand management agency to working completely from home as a crisis manager for the county. She thought she should be more available, the way her mother was for her growing up. Now she manages just enough to keep from getting fired and begrudges Griff the freedom to walk out the door and wind up at a place where only grown-ups need him.

"Should be back by eleven or so."

As she mounts the stairs, her knee cracks from where she had ACL surgery years and years ago. "Oh." She stops midway and leans over the banister, a scenic overlook from which to appreciate a living room she once quite liked before her daughter used marker on the green-upholstered chair and stuffed animals overflowed from three separate boxes next to what should have been a wet bar. "I meant to ask. You didn't go to school the other day to talk to Miss Ollie, did you?"

The thought has been prickling the back of her mind since lunch. It seems like she and Griff agree less and less about the best way to parent their daughter with each passing day, but he wouldn't go behind her back. Would he?

He thumbs through his phone, a terrible habit they share equally. "No. Why?"

"Never mind." She shakes her head. "That's what I thought."

And that, she reminds herself, is one of the many perks to being married to Griff: She never has to worry.

FOUR

▼

I'm hungry." Bodhi is already wearing his coat, the hood pulled up over his curly black hair.

By evening, Rhea's managed to climb back into her skin. She's applied honey and garlic to the bruised area across Bodhi's collarbone and told him not to try licking it off unless he wants to have nasty monster breath. He pulled one of his scary faces and made her laugh from deep down in her belly, despite herself. That's the magic of Bodhi, her alchemist. Takes a bad situation and, just like that, turns it around in ways big and small, the same way he did with her whole life.

"Your father will be here any minute." She dumps the crumbled ash from her incense plate into the sink and checks the clock. Marcus is ten minutes late.

She keeps busy, running a cloth over a few plates and adding them to the drying rack. As soon as he walks in, she'll tell him about the conversation with Miss Ollie and it'll be no big deal, just wait, she'll see. Marcus trusts her instincts as a mother. He's always let her take the lead, never stepped on her toes, not once. As a father, he's both present and enthusiastic, but not overly confident.

Rhea's own father was a wet blanket of a man, not mean or cruel or temperamental, but he chewed up dreams in the same plodding manner that he chewed his breakfast cereal. He liked to dispense life advice like *Lower your expectations and you won't be disappointed*, and *You can take the girl out of the trailer park, but you can't take the trailer park out of the girl*, which was the closest she ever heard him come to making a joke. Her mother was kind but busy. She worked as a call center agent, long hours, lining somebody else's pocket, leaving Rhea to fend for herself, surviving off Chef Boyardee and Ritz crackers. So, yeah, everything Rhea knows, she learned from her parents.

"Can I have a snack, please?"

Rhea smiles at her son's impeccable manners, another sign she's doing a good job. Take that, Miss Ollie.

Rhea still breastfeeds Bodhi before bed, but only when he asks. His diet is whole-food-centric, no gluten, GMO-free, and she avoids as many over-the-counter drugs as she possibly can. Does this make her life harder on occasion? Yes. But how could she forgive herself if she didn't offer her child the best, the healthiest, the free-est? The last thing she needs is anyone looking at Bodhi sideways, feeling sorry that he got stuck with a single mother. And so she can't just be good; she has to be superior.

"He'll be here any minute," she repeats. But the minutes are ticking slowly, slowly by, as they always do in the span before Marcus's arrival.

The doorbell to her duplex rings. "What'd I tell you?" She cuts through the living room, which has been transformed into a fulfillment center—boxes, packaging labels, tissue paper—piled high with her jars of oils and special blends. Tea tree oil helps with acne and athlete's foot. Peppermint supports digestion and relieves headaches. Lemon oil kills bacteria and reduces anxiety. Orange for pain. Rosemary for joint inflammation. Bergamot to lower blood pressure. Rhea feels like a witch, mixing and matching, finding just the right recipes to create unique potions for her customers' particular ailments.

"Sorry I'm late." Marcus rubs the soles of his shoes on the doormat. Rhea's tall, but Marcus is taller. Deep brown skin and broad shoulders and a groomed beard. Rhea's got good taste in men, always has, but it's a gift that's mostly wasted on her.

"You're not that late."

He gets that stupid dimple in his left cheek like he knows she's giving him a free pass. He must not have a girlfriend at the moment. She can always tell.

"How's the walking wounded?" Marcus teases. Kneeling down in front of his son, he gently peels back the bandage Rhea freshly placed. "Oh, it's not that bad." He grins up at her. "I think he'll live."

Rhea doesn't see what's so funny. "He was bleeding." Is Marcus blind? Why is everyone minimizing this? Her son—*their* son—was attacked. Viciously attacked. At school. He cried out for her.

"Kids bite." Marcus palms their son's sweet head. "It happens. Can't roll him up in bubble wrap." As if that's what she's implying.

"You weren't there," she says.

"You *were*?" He frowns, surprised. "Why?"

"I—" It's not actually that hard to lie once you've had a bit of practice, and Rhea has had some. "I was just dropping off some supplies."

It hangs there between them. *Fix it*, she thinks. Explain. Tell him what Miss Ollie told her and let him offer his two cents. He pays his child support, on time—usually a few days early, if she's being honest—every month, without fail; this is the deal. The moment balloons.

"Where y'all headed?" Her breath spills out. She kneels to tie Bodhi's shoe and looks down at the floor, brushes the whole thing off.

"Fresa's."

She gives Marcus a look. "No flour tortillas, remember?"

"Yeah, I know." He cranes his neck to peer into her living room, all nosy. "Looks like you're running Grand Central Station. How many orders are you sending out these days?"

Her cheeks plump as she tries not to look too pleased with herself. "About two hundred a day." It's been five whole months since she put in her notice at the property management company where she was working as an executive assistant to the owner, her latest in a long stream of meaningless jobs.

"I hear you're looking for investors, Rhea," he says, putting his hand on Bodhi's shoulder.

"I don't need your money." She folds an olive-colored dish towel and hangs it on the oven handle out of habit. She keeps her duplex cozy but neat. A macramé fruit hammock hangs from a nail in the low popcorn ceiling. She likes the feeling of the clean wood-grain tile beneath her bare feet and the butcher-block countertop under her palms when she prepares fresh food.

"Maybe I want to give it."

"I'm not looking for gifts. I've got a prospectus and everything."

"A prospectus?"

She sighs, half wondering what happened to that law student he was dating. Laurie, was it? "Yeah. Investor literature. I went and got a business accountant."

Marcus whistles low. "Okay, I see how it is." He winks. "We got a girlboss here." For the record, Rhea hates that term. "Well, come on, Bode-Man. We better get out of here. Oh, hey, you catch that email from the school?" He turns halfway out the door. "What's that about?"

"What email?" she asks.

"You gotta check your emails, Rhea." Jesus, she knows, she knows. Marcus treats every email from the school like it's mission critical. "The one sent about half an hour ago." He starts to pull out his phone to show her.

"I'll check it out," she cuts him off.

He looks hard at her. "You okay? You seem, like, stressed or something."

"I'm fine. I'll see you tomorrow after school, Bodhi—love you." Her heart jams up in her chest.

Marcus lingers another beat and, for a second, she wonders: Does he know? Is he testing her? Is she failing by not communicating about Miss Ollie and the lunches? She holds her breath, unsure of what to do or why this thought has even occurred to her.

"Later, Rhea." He pulls the door gently closed behind him.

Dear Little Academy Parents,

I hope your weekends have been restful. I'm writing to keep you apprised of a few developments in our classroom. While I would never discuss any particular child's health status or concerns, I do want to mention that a number of parents have informed me that something seems to be going around, the first instance having been reported to me right around

Thursday morning. We don't currently know the cause, so for now, if your child is acting "off" or doesn't seem like him- or herself, please do take them to see their pediatrician as soon as possible. Thank you for your cooperation.

Yours truly,

Miss Ollie

By morning, the pads of Rhea's fingertips are raw from pulling at packing tape and wrestling cardboard boxes into submission. She put together each shipment of Terrene by hand, finishing the latest batch sometime around three in the morning and realizing, at that point, that she'd hardly get any sleep anyway, so she might as well spend the wee hours putting together the pitch deck for the angel investors.

Two weeks ago, she hired a brand consultant and paid 500 of her own hard-earned dollars to meet with her for an hour. It turned out mostly to be a crock. A bleached-blond lady with hot pink crocodile-leather shoes and a turquoise portfolio who suggested Rhea become the Earth Mama version of Gwyneth Paltrow—effortless, aspirational, more design-forward, less folksy.

Last night, she stared at profit-and-loss statements, at account numbers, and at scaling projections until it felt as though her eyes would bleed, praying that her numbers weren't wrong. Almost everything she knows about running a business has come from a mix of Google and trial and error. Each slide preparation, each calculation takes Rhea twice as long as it would someone with formal training. Investors would change that. She could get an assistant, a bookkeeper, a warehouse that wasn't her living room. But not today.

Today, her insides feel like a growl. In and out, that's all she's got to do. Grab Bodhi and go.

On her way onto campus, a group of old church ladies wave from the Mobile Loaves and Fishes truck—"Good morning!"—back from their morning rounds feeding the community's homeless. Rhea smiles back at them, tight-lipped.

She presses the passcode into the preschool hallway keypad and holds the door open to enter the upper-age-range hall. Everything smells like apple juice, but not how Rhea makes it. No, the kind with "made from concentrate" stamped across the box. Surely parents wouldn't choose to rot their children's teeth with that junk if they knew what kind of pesticides and growth hormones went into it, but, then again, she's always surprised what parents will and won't do.

Rhea joins the other parents in line to pick up their children. She watches the class through the doorway and, for a moment, she forgets herself, forgets her foul mood, forgets that she's avoiding Bodhi's teacher. She loves the time at the end of Bodhi's school day when she gets to watch him play, stolen seconds before he senses her presence.

She scribbles gibberish across the sign-out sheet and, when Miss Ollie's back is turned, waves to get Bodhi's attention. Miss Ollie helps one of the little girls gently collect a stack of not-quite-dry art projects.

Come on. Rhea gestures to her son enthusiastically. And you know, she's about to get away with it, too. Other parents collect their children, other parents leave. And Bodhi moves slowly.

Like he's got some kind of Mommy's-in-a-hurry radar that taps his internal brakes upon detection. The boy can mosey. Mosey to gather his artwork. Mosey to retrieve his backpack. Mosey to locate his water bottle. Easy like Sunday morning.

And here's Rhea, losing her mind.

"Rhea?" Out of nowhere, Miss Ollie turns and registers her. "I wanted to say again how sorry I am about what happened to Bodhi. It looks like it really hurt. He seems to be doing much better today, though. I'm sure you saw my message," she continues. "If it's any comfort, I'll just say that Bodhi isn't the only one, and we're working on the biting behaviors. We'll be talking about it in class—"

"That's all right." Rhea leans in, looking for Bodhi again.

"Also." Miss Ollie pushes back into Rhea's line of vision. "I was thinking that I really would like to speak with Bodhi's father about what we discussed last time."

"Not necessary," says Rhea.

"I know." She gently touches Rhea's arm; Rhea's whole body goes rigid. "I would just feel more comfortable. I wanted to give you a heads-up and make sure you had the opportunity to catch up with him first if you wanted." Miss Ollie beckons and Bodhi comes trotting over. The teacher helps him loop his skinny arms through the straps of his backpack. "Please feel free to have Marcus contact me. If I haven't heard from him by Friday, then I'll go ahead and reach out directly."

Finally, Bodhi rushes out the door, headlong into his mother's body. He wraps his arms tightly around her waist, pressing his face into her belly button. Her fingers find the familiar flat spot on the back of his skull. Ears ringing, her feet feel like they've been planted there and put down roots.

Miss Ollie busies herself with the other children. A hot flush rises between Rhea's breasts, sweat building in the pockets beneath her arms. Is it because of what Rhea said, about none of the children being hers? Could Miss Ollie, a whole-ass adult, really be that petty? Is this some kind of power trip? Is this because Rhea is the only single mother in the class? Would she be making a thing about contacting the father if Rhea and Marcus were together? Or how about if Rhea looked more like one of the Lululemon moms, the PTA moms, the moms who wear Tom Ford lipstick and consider drag queen brunch a wild girls' outing, and who are not "alternative," as Mary Beth once described Rhea?

"Mommy? Mommy?" Rhea feels the tug on her skirt and understands her son has been trying to get her attention. Mommy. *Mommy.*

The world and its sounds come crashing back in, fast and loud.

"What, honey?" She takes his wrist gently in her hand. Mommy. *Mommy.*

The spit that hits the back of her throat feels tacky. She tries to let the name soak in—*Mommy*. What business does Erin Ollie think she has stepping between her and *her* child? She has half a mind to—

"Can we go?" Bodhi whines.

Rhea looks down at her beautifully innocent son and sees how rare and precious a thing that is.

Adults, in comparison, are garbage. If Erin Ollie doesn't understand the line between doing her job and meddling, then Rhea will have to show her.

TRANSCRIPT OF INTERVIEW OF WITNESS, GEORGE HALL

APPEARANCES:

Detective Wanda Bright

PROCEEDINGS

DET. BRIGHT: So it was sudden? One day friends just started biting; is that right, George?

GEORGE HALL: Yeah. But Zeke said sorry and it's not nice to stay mad at people, Miss Ollie says.

DET. BRIGHT: I agree. Do you have any idea why they were biting?

GEORGE HALL: Over the bus usually. Sometimes the big elephant because there is only one big elephant. Their tusks are actually teeth and they can use their trunks to snorkel.

DET. BRIGHT: Right, yes, the elephant. But did anything happen? Did anything change that gave kids the idea to start biting?

GEORGE HALL: I don't know. Mommy says you've got to bite when it's stranger danger.

DET. BRIGHT: That's true.

GEORGE HALL: If you see a stranger you can kick and punch and bite and pull down their underwear and you won't get in trouble at all, it's allowed.

DET. BRIGHT: Sure. But the first time—

GEORGE HALL: Mommy told me even my old man neighbor can be a stranger and that he might try to take me.

DET. BRIGHT: George, did you see a stranger?

FIVE

▼

Pastor Ben?" Mary Beth blurts his name without thinking when she passes him in the preschool hall. It's a Tuesday morning and she's just dropped off Noelle. The blip of recognition electrifies her, as though she's spotted a minor celebrity somewhere unexpected, like in her local Starbucks.

He has the dark waves of a nineties heartthrob and a V of back muscles to fill out his white T-shirt to go with it. He probably does CrossFit or some newer, cooler workout Mary Beth hasn't even heard of yet.

He stops mid-stride, confused. Sheepishly, she waves. "Sorry, that was me."

"Hi."

She's surprised to learn that he also has eyes the color of a Christmas tree, and that when he turns to look at her, the lights twinkle on. A mischievous sort of grin plays at the corners of his mouth as though he's listening to a good joke.

That's her cue. *Say something.* She's usually so good at this.

"Hi, no, sorry, you don't know me. I just—I wanted to tell you that I loved your last sermon." You can never go wrong with a compliment, that's Mary Beth's motto.

Once a week, Mary Beth attends RiverRock for church service. Partly for the forty-five minutes of quiet time, but she also considers it an act of spiritual exercise, a time to reflect on "her *why*," an expression amongst her Bible study group best defined as the reason she does all the back bending and self-sacrifice her daily life requires. A mother's why should always be her kids. Always.

That's why she's an involved mother. On Mondays, she volunteers at the library. On Tuesdays and Thursdays, she shows up as a lunch aide at

Angeline's elementary school. She chairs the silent auction committee for the school's annual Spring Fling and the Fall Gala at Little Academy and she never misses a chance to sign up as one of the "read-aloud" parents in her children's classes.

The Bible is filled with really good mothers. There was Rebecca and Leah and Jochebed, not to mention the Virgin Mary, all women who did far more than Mary Beth and without the benefit of arch support. Sometimes she asks Noelle what mommies she learned about in school, but it's always Jonah and his whale and David and the lions that stick in children's minds. God should have given biblical women more stories involving animals.

"So glad you liked the sermon." Pastor Ben has a slow southern lilt that makes Mary Beth imagine him standing whenever a lady gets up from the table. "Now, do you mind going back and telling that to my public speaking professor at divinity school? I got a D in that class." He puts a finger to his lips; their little secret.

"Stop, you're very inspiring." She touches him, actually *touches* his forearm where a diamond-shaped freckle dots the outside of his elbow, touches him like her own hand isn't part of her body. She slides it away, but she can still feel it like an indelible mark between them. "My *husband* and I—" She invokes Doug for obvious reasons. "—we're actually doing your challenge, the having sex one. Some nights have been harder than others, but we're keeping at it." Oh dear. Did she really just say that?

"Tell your husband I accept thank-yous in the form of chocolate and Chick-fil-A." He scratches the scruff on his cheek; he must only shave on Sundays.

She notices they have naturally begun talking in hushed voices. It feels sort of weirdly intimate, but also, if she's being honest, not weird at all. The school hallways are remarkably quiet at this time of morning as classes begin emptying out onto the playground for the first recess of the day. There's no one volunteering in the little square room a couple doors down that passes for a school library, with its Adirondack rocking chair and assortment of puppets that can be checked out to children's homes right along with the tattered old books.

"It's more me, actually." She laughs. Lord Jesus. "I mean—"

"I didn't catch your name," he says.

"Mary Beth Brandt." She extends her hand to shake, touches him for the second time. His hand is warm in hers and he gives it a knowing squeeze. *Oh. Ohhhh.* And just like that, her buzzing, busy-lady thoughts are replaced by a new awareness of a gentle sensation that's taking root between her legs, a familiar but long-lost tingle, like an old friend she hasn't seen in ages, though now that they're together, it seems they've still got plenty to talk about. She clears her throat, self-consciously. "Ah. Well. What brings you to this side of campus?" she asks.

"I'm reviewing plans for the new youth center I've been spearheading. Exciting developments. Doing the Lord's work."

"I had no idea." Though she's not surprised. In general, the church does beautiful ministry. Teen mission trips to Yucatán, backpack drives, and the important work of preventing human trafficking. "I have a daughter who still attends here."

"You know, I had a hunch," he teases.

"Right. Duh." She palms her forehead. "She's in the fours. I'm on the parents' committee actually and chaired the gala last year, so if I can ever be a resource, please don't hesitate to—"

"You know." He snaps his fingers. "Maybe you're the person we should be roping in to help fundraise."

"I mean," she stumbles, "I guess I could."

Ben crosses his arms, biceps forming small hilltops. She can't tell what the tattoo is that peeks from his T-shirt, some kind of forked tail, maybe a sparrow or perhaps a mermaid.

She loves her husband and not in, like, a familial, we've-been-married-so-long type way. Doug's cute. He has a baby face that's hardly aged a day since they met; he looks the same, other than the few new pounds around his neck and jowls. She likes to back her body into the curve of his chest and stomach in bed. She enjoys the touch of his nose in the crook of her neck. All this to say there's no harm in a crush. She's not worried when that feeling in her vagina unexpectedly drops in for a visit and unpacks its bags and decides to stay awhile longer.

"Think of the children." He winks.

"Well, when you put it that way," she says. "I guess I have no choice. I'd do anything for our children. Absolutely anything."

Maybe that's Mary Beth's problem.

Hello, Mary Beth?" It's soft-spoken Charlotte Higsby, George's mom, on the phone. "I just wanted to check to see if you were aware of what happened in the parking lot this morning?"

The parking lot . . . the parking lot. She doesn't like the sound of that. An uneasy feeling leaks into Mary Beth's stomach, instant visions of a child being run over by a member of the army of mothers reversing their three-row SUVs.

"Not specifically, no," she answers uncertainly.

Charlotte isn't a fussy mom. She pays on time to the teacher gift fund, usually sending in a little extra. She asks Mary Beth how she can help. She's the type of mother who will be her son's first and maybe last love. And that's why Mary Beth knows that if Charlotte Higsby is calling it must be for a very good reason.

"Another biting incident." An audible wince in her milk-sweet voice. "Bex bit her mom—sorry, I'm trying to remember her name—?"

"Lena," Mary Beth supplies.

"Right. Bex bit Lena. Badly."

"Oh gosh." Though there's more than a little relief for Mary Beth. "I'm so sorry to hear that. Is she okay?" The nip on Mary Beth's own ankle is already just a circle of itchy scabs. She understood Miss Ollie's cryptic email last night to be somehow related to Zeke's biting incident and heard rumblings of a small uptick in class bites. A sibling had been uncharacteristically bitten over the weekend. A nip last week in class that nobody thought much of. One of Lincoln's moms said something about nearly losing a toe. The rhythm of life with tiny humans.

"Um, well, yes, mostly. It was the weirdest thing. Bex got agitated and then, you know, out of nowhere, practically, she bit Lena on the thigh and . . . okay, I'm just going to say it: I think she licked it."

"Licked what?" Mary Beth asks.

"The blood. She licked the blood."

Silence because, well, what really is there to say to that? A child who licked blood. Licked her mother's blood? Mary Beth has the intense urge to say, "No, but thanks for calling," and hang up.

"Zeke's mother, Megan, is a nurse," Charlotte continues as though Mary Beth doesn't know. "She applied a butterfly bandage and said she didn't think it would require stitches."

"Poor Lena." Mary Beth makes a mental note to add Lena to her prayer list tonight; it isn't fun when your child acts out, let alone in public. Maybe she should send a note of encouragement. On second thought, that might make things worse. "Is there something I can do to help?"

"The other parents agreed we should be keeping a record. Of the biting. I understand there have been seven total from our class. Maybe a couple in others across the hall, but that was just something I heard."

Seven. Seven instances of biting seems excessive, doesn't it? Or does seven seem normal? It feels like Mary Beth should know the answer one way or the other, and yet she could be convinced either way. Seven.

"We figured," Charlotte continues, "as our Room Mom you might be able to help keep a record, you know, just in case."

It will be another sixteen minutes before the obvious question pops into her head: *Just in case? Just in case what?*

Mary Beth sits in the over-air-conditioned church meeting room, with its violent bright-white lighting, the sort almost always head-scratchingly reserved for swimsuit fitting rooms. Pastor Ben is running late, giving her mind a chance to wander in all the wrong directions.

"Oh good." Miss Ollie slides into the chair beside her. "We haven't started yet."

"I didn't know *you* were on the youth center committee," says Mary Beth. "I would have joined sooner." As if there'd been arm-twisting.

Miss Ollie shrugs. She so rarely shows her twenties, but, here and there, a peek. "I think it's important for the preschool to have representation. There will be a lot of overlap. Design input. Construction. Logistical hang-ups."

"Mm, yeah, of course." Mary Beth feels a sense of maternal protectiveness over Miss Ollie, the way she does for all of Noelle and Angeline's babysitters. She enjoys hearing their plans, their goals, their relationship drama. "Did you hear Bex bit Lena? George's mom called me a few minutes ago to tell me."

She has big girl-next-door eyes. Probably very popular in high school. And college. "Really? That's number seven."

"You're keeping track?"

"I think it's important to." Miss Ollie reaches into her canvas tote and pulls out a notebook. She uncaps a pen with her mouth. "I come from a research background. Data points are my love language." She flashes a grin; her bottom teeth are a little crooked. Mary Beth never noticed. Probably didn't wear her retainer religiously. Mary Beth will definitely make her girls wear theirs every single night until she's dead.

Miss Ollie leafs through the pages of her notebook and begins printing Bex Feinstein's name along with the date on a fresh line. "I've been doing my own research." She talks as she writes. "There's a syndrome associated with biting. It's called Renfield's syndrome. It's a psychological condition that causes those afflicted to crave blood the way some pregnant women want to eat clay, and there are documented pediatric cases going back at least fifty years. It's kind of amazing."

Amazing. The word rolls around in Mary Beth's head. She blinks. "Um, are we sure we shouldn't be looking into something a little more, you know, run-of-the-mill first? Like, could it be something the kids are picking up at school?" Seven bites. Seven—eight, actually, because she hasn't mentioned Noelle's—and counting. And that actually is a lot, yes, Mary Beth sees that now, and yet it feels like she's treading water against the current. The children are in the same class, so she starts there. "They're learning about dinosaurs this week, aren't they?" she asks. "Maybe if we laid off the dinosaurs, just a thought?"

Miss Ollie looks at her with tremendous gravitas and says, "We've been keeping it to non-scary dinosaurs. Herbivores like the stegosaurus and the brontosaurus."

"Right." Mary Beth chews the calloused side of her thumb.

"Kids love dinosaurs. Barney is a dinosaur. Barney is a *T. rex*. I don't think dinosaurs are the problem."

Mary Beth presses her lips together. They're the youngest committee volunteers by a landslide. Across the room sit a couple blue-haired ladies and men with thick-soled orthopedic shoes and brown, pilled socks.

Miss Ollie scribbles a final note and flips the cover shut. "I plan on sending some literature home this weekend. I really do care about this class. They're some special kids."

On the worktable in front of them, Miss Ollie's phone screen illuminates with a text. The background of her lock screen shows a guy in his early twenties—tanned, outdoorsy, kissing a scruffy terrier mix in his arms.

Mary Beth smiles. "Is that your boyfriend?" Changing the subject.

"My brother."

"That's sweet. I hope Noelle and Angeline are close like that when they grow up. You know, this might be too personal," Mary Beth says in her best big-sister tone, which is exactly how she'd like Miss Ollie to see her, like a cool, laid-back, but very nice and popular big sister. "*Do you want kids of your own some day?*"

Erin brightens. "I can't wait to be a mother."

The perfect answer, at least for Mary Beth, who loves baby showers, loves visiting new moms and offering to hold their infants while the new mother sneaks a quick nap. She loves getting soft blankets monogrammed. She loves the way in which every daughter is suddenly open to her mother's advice.

But right then, Pastor Ben arrives and both of their eyes slide over to him. For a moment, Mary Beth is fully lost in the presence of the man, like a silly middle school student daydreaming about her crush. He's like a work of art. She keeps noticing something new about him to appreciate. He looks vaguely like someone she knows, an actor maybe, but after a second or two of not being able to place him, she's forced to give up. She's never been good at this game.

"I want to start today's meeting by talking to you about a troubled young kid I knew." He folds his hands behind his back. "This kid came from a good family. Grew up middle class, mom and dad were kind, committed parents. But this kid had a wandering eye. At fourteen, he started drinking at friends' houses. Not even beer. He went straight to the hard stuff. At first he got hangovers and then, sure enough, he could hold his liquor. Though that was just the start, as it turned out. He discovered pornography shortly thereafter and pretty soon he was obsessed with it." A murmur hums through the committee members at the mention of such a naughty word in a church space. "That led to girls, which led to parties, and by sixteen he started taking prescription pain pills. He even sold them when he could. This kid barely graduated from high school, skated through college by the skin of his teeth. He even saw a close friend die in a terrible accident while driving under the influence that he, himself, was lucky enough to survive." A small sound escapes Miss Ollie beside her. Everyone in the room appears to be deeply moved by the story. "Even still, he didn't wake up. Not until he was twenty-three years old and he overdosed. He was found, you see, with vomit caked in the corners of his mouth." He demonstrates. "Barely breathing, by one of his so-called friend's parents, and he was rushed to the hospital, where he was resuscitated by the grace of God. After that, he found Jesus. Or maybe Jesus found him. He went to seminary. And he became . . . the church pastor you see standing before you today."

A murmur of appreciation. Mary Beth glances over at Miss Ollie again to see if she'd guessed the punch line. Erin stares, rapt, yes, genuinely emotional.

"Children are our future," he says, easing back into his slow-honey cadence. "But when I tell you the most shameful part of my past was seeded in my childhood, you've got to believe me. And that's why it's our responsibility, our duty, to take our youth in our arms and carry them across the finish line to adulthood, so that they can arrive unscathed." With a flourish, he unveils the blueprint. "Many of you know I've been spearheading this initiative almost since my arrival, and that's why I'm overjoyed to have something concrete to share with our committee today, never before seen. It's going to take a lot of time, effort, and, frankly, expense," says Pastor Ben. "But I believe our children are worth every penny." He receives a hearty *hear-hear* from the group.

After, he shares the figures that have been set aside by the church so far, numbers already reaching into the six figures, but they'll need more. A lot more if they're going to build it. That's why they're gathered, to float ideas. Where will the money come from?

"We haven't chosen a cause for this year's Trike-a-Thon," Mary Beth points out. "If she agrees, Miss Ollie and I could suggest it. I actually think parents might be even more generous than they are with children's hospitals, though those are very worthy causes as well."

Pastor Ben claps. "Yes! Now those are the kinds of ideas I'm talking about."

Mary Beth blushes. Before the end of the meeting, she's more than earned her keep. "Easy," she tells the group. "People, especially parents, want *easy*. Make it so they can just sign a form and they're automatically billed as part of their tuition and—bingo—they're in. Maybe even a QR code. Point and click and the money pours in." She beams.

Miss Ollie doesn't say much, but at least she agrees with everything Mary Beth proposes. After the business of the meeting wraps and Mary Beth is flush with visions of dollar signs dancing in her head, Pastor Ben lopes over and offers her a high five. A high five!

When she slaps his palm, he grips his fingers around her hand, again, the second time today, and they wind up in a secret handshake of sorts. Her nervous system *reacts*. "Good chat," he says.

After, Mary Beth packs up her day planner and ballpoint pen. "I've been wanting to talk to you about Lola and Noelle when you have a minute," she says to Miss Ollie, scooping the strap of her purse onto her shoulder. She feels emboldened. "Doesn't have to be now."

Miss Ollie's eyes are unfocused, her mind elsewhere. Mary Beth can see her dragging her attention back from wherever it went.

"I think that's—that's a good idea." Miss Ollie runs her fingers through her glossy hair. "Actually, I asked Darby to come in Thursday before pickup. Can you make it then?"

Mary Beth hesitates. "For us all to meet together, you mean?"

Erin scratches her arm, leaving white nail lines across the pink bump of a mosquito bite. "It's easier if we're all on the same page."

"It'll be picture day." Mary Beth already has Noelle's outfit laid out—a blue-and-white-striped dress with a Peter Pan collar from Mini Boden. A splurge, but she would always prefer to spend money dressing her girls than herself.

"That never takes long." Erin reaches her arm over her head, stretching for a spot between her shoulder blades. Her shirt lifts, exposing her belly button and the taut skin just beneath it.

"Here, let me get that," says Mary Beth. She eases around Miss Ollie's side and digs her nails through the fabric as best she can. "Better?"

"Much. Thanks." Miss Ollie nods and relaxes finally. "Do you mind if I ask what you think of Ben?"

"Ben?" Mary Beth's fingers freeze on the young teacher's back. "Oh," she says. "Pastor Ben, right. I . . . think he's a good speaker and he's doing great work in the church."

Miss Ollie frowns but adds nothing.

Oh. My. God.

She's starting to feel very itchy herself as the revelation that single, twentysomething Miss Ollie would have her eye on Pastor Ben—sorry, just *Ben* to her—breaks over her.

"You know what?" Mary Beth says. "I think I need to visit the ladies' room on the way out. I'll see you tomorrow."

Without waiting for a reply, she flees to the bathroom, which is bare-bones and reminds her of middle school, with its dirty grout and penny-round tiles the color of pink Tums. She slumps down onto the toilet seat and drops her sweaty forehead into her open hands.

It's not fair. She can't even be mad properly. She can only feel stupid. Her children deprive her of any ability to feel remotely sexy and the moment she does feel the slightest bit hot and bothered, sensuous, flir-tatious (fine), in waltzes their teacher.

Pain has started to shish kebab her right eyeball. *Go away*, she wills it. *Not now.*

She removes a fistful of toilet paper and dabs at her nose and around her eye.

The socket throbs, agony dancing around the rim of bone. She feels like she's brought it on herself somehow. It's not full-blown yet, this terrible head implosion with which she's becoming all too familiar. *Nevertheless, she persists*, she thinks, with only a touch of irony. Because isn't that what motherhood is? Tiny acts of heroism and daily sacrifice. Where is *her* Purple Heart?

She takes stock. She feels like she's crash-landed into this tiny rest-room stall that stinks of blue toilet bowl disks and urine, bottom first, right back into her life as Mom. Not enough fuel in the tank to go or be anywhere else; she's marooned here. So she grants herself one last heaving, dramatic sigh because it's both that bad and not really that bad at all being Mary Beth Brandt. What she's got to do now is get ready for Thursday and figure out how to break the news to Darby that, difficult as it may be to hear, Lola needs help before she gets completely out of hand.

SIX

▼

ola is on her best behavior as Dr. Meckler crab-scuttles around on his rolling stool, listening to her heart and pointing an LED light up her nostrils. The examination room is haphazardly decorated to the theme of *fish* with peeling vinyl stickers—seaweed, bubbles, blowfish—stuck to the walls. Of all things, this has deeply impressed Lola, who loves marine life with the sort of reckless abandon most children reserve for candy.

"Kids bite," he says, bumping Darby's knees again as he rolls past. "It's a way of testing their limits or expressing feelings."

"She's four. She's never bitten before. Never."

"It's a normal part of childhood development. Probably just a very brief but frustrating phase. And it can start even as old as four."

She chose Dr. Meckler that many years ago because he had jovial wrinkles around his eyes and a very comforting look about him, probably a favorite grandpa, a man who reads Mitch Albom novels by the fire, but "comforted" isn't what Darby's feeling right now. She's actually frightened of her daughter, if she's being completely honest. It's like she's built her home on an active minefield.

"It wasn't normal," she insists. "She came after me like I was prime rib." Something thick and hard swims up her throat. "I think she might have actually . . . swallowed blood."

A flicker of a frown for Dr. Meckler.

Her search history from last night was the work of a masochist. A litany of every horrible, unthinkable malady that could have befallen her daughter. Darby may not always love the grind of motherhood, but she's still spent every year since entering it mentally running through each terrifying potential calamity like a pilot through a flight simulator. How she could throw her body in front of a moving vehicle, what she would do in the event of a home intruder or choking incident, the complete inventory of precious items she'd sell off in a heartbeat if she ever needed to pay for her children's medical bills.

"You're sure it's not rabies?" She tries again when he doesn't immediately snap into problem-solving mode. Her daughter's lips had glistened with blood.

"There's no sign of a bite mark on her anywhere. She doesn't have a fever, no headache, no vomiting. She's swallowing perfectly, doesn't seem confused. I can promise you, this isn't a kid with rabies. If it makes you feel better, I'm happy to order tests. Blood, saliva, skin biopsy, the works, if it's what you need."

His suggestion makes her feel dippy.

When it comes to parenthood, people love to tell you that everything that happens along the way is so *normal*. As though that makes it better. Your feet have grown a size during pregnancy—normal! You need to go on bed rest for four weeks—normal! Your baby has acid reflux—normal! You haven't slept for ten months—normal! You pee when you sneeze—normal! Your child still isn't talking at two, you had a miscarriage, your toddler still wears pull-ups at night—normal, normal, NOR-MAL!

But the worst part, the absolute shittiest bit about the word *normal*, is how the word itself gives permission to take whatever it is that's *normal* for granted. Why not? Who needs to appreciate the unremarkable?

"Could she be sick?" Doesn't hurt to brainstorm. "Can't pets become aggressive when they've injured a leg or something?" What if Darby missed some vital sign related to Lola's health and now it's too late? That would be so infuriatingly like Darby, who feels like she's missing whatever gene moms have that helps them remember to schedule their children's dentist appointments.

Dr. Meckler ropes his stethoscope over the back of his neck and Darby steels herself. "She's fine, she's healthy."

"I know—I just—" She doesn't mean to be rude. It's simply occurring to her that she's never seen a pediatrician do anything other than press on her children's bellies and stick flashlights up their noses. It seems like there should be a level two for bigger emergencies. "Then what about something . . . mental? My husband and I, well, we have different opinions. That's putting it lightly, actually. We've been arguing—not in front of the kids, or at least not loudly—about whether we need the school counselor to do a full evaluation. I think maybe he's just being impatient—she's a kid, you know how men are sometimes, sorry, Dr. Meckler, but you must know and I guess, though, I'm asking you: Does she need help?"

She holds her breath. Darby will admit that Lola is more sensitive than other children, that she likes things a certain way, that she struggles with transition, but she's always believed in her heart that Lola is a good person. She just needs direction. A bit of guidance. And patience. A lot of patience.

He types notes into her daughter's chart. "I know it's hard as a parent not to feel anxious over every little thing."

Darby rubs the spot on her arm, which doesn't feel little. She's not one of those parents whose children act as socially acceptable outlets for their varying neuroses. Depending on the day of the week, Darby can either feel proud or negligent for being one of the "laid-back moms," but always one or the other, as if her brand of mothering is a choice and not mere survival.

She doesn't agree with Griff, but that doesn't mean she automatically agrees with Dr. Meckler either.

"I think I'd like to go ahead and order those tests, please." And she resigns herself to saying goodbye to the rest of her morning.

I'm thirsty, Mom." From the back seat, Lola stares too hard into the rearview mirror through her fringe of bangs. Darby doesn't like this "Mom" business. None of the other four-year-olds call their mothers Mom. It's weird.

"Where's your water bottle?"

"Gone."

"What do you mean it's *gone*? The one with the whales on it?"

Lola had not wanted the cute sparkly water bottle that Darby picked out to replace the one that got squished beneath her tires when she accidentally left it on the roof of her car. She also didn't want the purple unicorn water bottle that matched her backpack.

Lola isn't prone to suggestion. She doesn't go with the flow. Darby can't present Lola with a surprise and expect happiness. Her daughter doesn't work like that. And so they returned to the store where Lola picked out whales. That was five days ago. And the whales are now gone and Darby thinks she might—probably will—scream.

"It's stolen." Lola is defiant for no reason.

Darby beats the heel of her hand—the one that was recently spattered with pee while helping collect her daughter's urine sample—gently against the steering wheel. "It's not *stolen*, Lola. It's misplaced. There aren't water bottle burglars. That's not a thing."

Lola pouts. "I'm thirsty," she repeats. "I wish I could bite you."

The meanness of her little girl's words pierces Darby. She gave up her whole day to take Lola to the pediatrician. And she feels like a bag lady in her shapeless tan dress that looked sort of chic on the mannequin but not on her. And she can spot pretzel bits and goldfish crumbs in the space between her seat and the console. She's not even mad at Lola. It's worse. She's annoyed. Her daughter is bugging her. For a split second, she can see the appeal of Lola's tantrums. It would feel so good to throw her sunglasses into the windshield and pull her hair and scream at her daughter to *shut up, shut up, shut up.*

Instead, she sits very still, growing angrier and more exasperated both with Lola and with herself. She should feel relieved. They've dodged at least one potential catastrophe. If it were an emergency, she could call Griff on his office line and speak to the receptionist, but it's more like the opposite of an emergency. What about that? Does that still warrant a call?

She'd done the thing so many mothers had done before her, put herself on the Mommy Track in her career. She didn't want to miss her children being little. She wanted to experience childlike wonder through their eyes. Except that's the problem. It's *their* wonder. She thought she was giving up her big, fancy job for something more exciting, but watching kids is pretty mundane stuff.

She tries calling Griff. His voice mail recording picks up immediately. Her husband has turned off his phone.

TRANSCRIPT OF INTERVIEW OF WITNESS, BEATRICE "BEX" FEINSTEIN

APPEARANCES:
Detective Wanda Bright

PROCEEDINGS

DET. BRIGHT: What's your favorite part of the school day, Bex?

BEX FEINSTEIN: I'm tired of talking. I don't want to talk about school. I hate talking about school because it's boring.

DET. BRIGHT: We just started, Bex.

BEX FEINSTEIN: Why do you keep calling me that? Bex Bex Bex.

DET. BRIGHT: That's your name, isn't it?

BEX FEINSTEIN: Well, yeah. Okay. How about it's my turn to choose what we talk about, then?

DET. BRIGHT: I have a few questions I need to—

BEX FEINSTEIN: But that's not fair because you had a turn already.

DET. BRIGHT: Actually, I didn't.

BEX FEINSTEIN: Do you have any pets?

DET. BRIGHT: I have one cat.

BEX FEINSTEIN: What's your cat's name?

DET. BRIGHT: Stabler. Bex—

BEX FEINSTEIN: You said my name again! That's kind of weird!

DET. BRIGHT: At the end of the day, when it was almost time to go home, can you remember noticing anything different? Maybe close your eyes. Imagine that you're back in your classroom. Do you notice anything, anything at all?

BEX FEINSTEIN: There was one thing. I smelled blood.

DET. BRIGHT: Okay, okay, good. How did you know it was blood?

BEX FEINSTEIN: I can always smell blood now.

SEVEN

▼

I've tried everything." Mary Beth declines to sit on the exam table at the clinic. Not necessary. It's just her head. Just blinding pain that lights up her entire skull with absolutely no warning or regard for her schedule. Only a silly thing like her brain.

And thank God she doesn't *work*, doesn't have a real job. Thank heavens she's so fortunate that she can turn off the lights and nap when she feels one coming on. Another doctor had said those words to her. Those very words. And Mary Beth had blessed his heart.

"It could be anxiety," says the doctor, liver spots speckling his cheeks. "That's usually the trigger for these things. Are you under a lot of—" His cough is phlegmy. "Stress?"

"Isn't everyone?"

"But the migraines have been relatively manageable until now?"

"No." She wrote that on her intake form, which he obviously didn't bother to read. "That's why I'm here. They're terrible. A ten out of ten on the pain scale. Right now. I feel like I'm going to be sick. And then I start to panic because I have no idea when it will stop. They can last days and days and days."

Hope. That's what she feels every time she enters a new doctor's office. Here she is giving this new medical person the chance of a lifetime, the chance to be a hero. That's what she wants to tell him. *Be my guest! Save my day, Dr. Whatever-Your-Name-Is!*

But she recognizes the signs. The aloof expression. The interminable time in the waiting room. He came highly recommended by the friend of a friend of a woman in her Bible study. (This is *the* guy!)

She's willing to try anything. Already she's sampled acupuncture and Botox at the top of her neck. She took magnesium supplements and went cold turkey off of coffee, then tried to drink even more of it after hearing conflicting advice. She takes topiramate at night and whatever triptan is currently on trend at the outset of her symptoms. And still they come for her.

"I hear you," he says. "That panic may actually be contributing to the severity of the pain. It's incredibly frustrating, I know, but I see this in my office every day with women."

"And?" Her entire face feels like a rotting bruise on an apple. Driving herself here felt borderline dangerous.

"Nine times out of ten it's a nasty cocktail of anxiety, depression, and hormones. I know that probably isn't what you want to hear."

"It's just that I don't feel anxious or depressed." She carefully measures out her words, trying to sound like a person who should be taken seriously, not like someone who barely graduated from college. "Or hormonal."

She thinks vaguely of Miss Ollie and what she'd said about the reasons the children may be manifesting a physical urge to crave blood based on psychology. Or something like that. Mary Beth doesn't really understand the details, but she could swear she did see a smear of red across little Asher's cheek this morning that could have been jam, but looked distinctly, she feared, like blood.

Is that this doctor's point? Psychology and anatomy and whatever else all conspire to make the human body go haywire?

"Maybe you don't. But your body is telling you otherwise. It's flashing the 'check engine' light. You're a busy mom of . . ."

"Two," she supplies obediently.

"See? That's the hardest job in the world." Is he being condescending? Does he mean it, or, worse, only *wants* to mean it? She can never tell. "And a lot of times, this is the mind's way of saying *enough*. The good news is I can prescribe something that should help take the edge off. Have you tried a triptan before?"

She feels murder pumping from her heart. By the grace of God there are no sharp objects within reach because otherwise she couldn't guarantee his safety. The pain borders on violence and she wants it out, out, out.

Off her look, he gives a casual wave of his hand—yes, yes, he gets it, no worries. "I can use an alternative. Not a problem. But." His fingers hover over the keyboard. "Remember that's just going to treat the pain, and the pain is the symptom. Not the cause."

"You're sure it's not something—" She's choking down the desire to leap at his throat and shake him. Her molars smash together. She will stay polite. She will hold it together. She will show this man mercy, for he knows not what he does. "I'm worried when I look online that—"

"Dr. Google. Well."

It must be frustrating having laypeople like Mary Beth believing that WebMD is as valuable as a very expensive and hard-to-achieve medical degree. But it is also frustrating, she would like to point out, to feel as though your brain is going to ooze through your eye sockets. "I just mean that you're sure it's not something more serious?"

The doctor puts his glasses on his nose. "It depends what you mean. There have been new studies showing a statistically significant link between certain mental health disorders and migraine headaches. If you're serious about this, then personally, as a next step, I'd suggest being evaluated by a psychologist as soon as possible. But for today, go home, get some rest, take a nap."

Again with the naps! In the middle of the day! That's the prescription, that's the treatment plan? Sure, doc, seems reasonable. Not like she has things to do. Has he ever stopped to wonder why being a mom actually is the hardest job in the world and not just something thoughtless people say?

It's because there's never a day off—not just a day, but an hour, not so much as a minute. Is she sick? Is she feeling under the weather? Too bad! There's no one to cover her interminable shift; she'll get off when she dies. *She* is non-fungible. Doctors may be replaced eventually through artificial intelligence, and last time she checked there are robots that can do surgery, but mothers' jobs are never, will never be, in danger.

There isn't *time* for a nap. There is *never* time for a nap because of a mother's Forty-Five-Minute Rule. That's what she wants to shout in his pruned face. She is always supposed to be somewhere in forty-five minutes. Not enough time to go home and take off her too-tight pants and watch an episode of *Love Island*. Take any point in her day and the same will be true. And today that somewhere is Noelle's school, where she's supposed to be meeting with Darby and Miss Ollie. In forty-five minutes.

EIGHT

▼

On the drive, Rhea listens to *Bitch, Please*, a motivational audio-book by Zazzy Tims, recommended by her new investment advisor. A little grabby for Rhea's usual tastes, but she tries not to hold that against it.

Zazzy—a sassy white Midwestern lady with an inverted bob on the thumbnail image—walks women through the ten most common ex-cuses they make for themselves, the ones that keep them from realizing their dreams, and answers each excuse with a resounding "Bitch, please!" coupled with a humorous essay about her own rise in the business world.

Rhea cuts the ignition, snapping Zazzy off mid-sentence and filling her little lime-green Kia with bloated silence. Beyond the windshield, a bluebird day unfurls over the Little Academy campus, fucking with her whole vibe.

She goes over it again in her head because once she steps foot on that pavement, there's no turning back.

Yesterday she put in a formal request for Bodhi to change classrooms and was rejected flat out. Some kind of freeze on all transfer requests, the front office said, thanks to this crazy situation with kids biting the bejesus out of each other. That was Wednesday. Today is Thursday, to-morrow Friday. Tomorrow Miss Ollie emails Marcus and gives him ideas about how things ought to go with her son.

Rhea runs her fingers along the border of the thin manila envelope in her hands. Is she really going to do this? Is she prepared to ruin a woman's life? Her breathing is even, her pulse steady. She's not flying off the handle. This is not the Rhea of seven or eight years ago. The one who made a stupid snap decision that nearly ruined her whole life. Even though she knows *that* Rhea is in there, waiting, biding her time, this one has thought it through. This is different. This is about her child.

She unbuckles her seatbelt and climbs out.

NINE

▼

Darby's stalling. It's amazing how easy it is to stall with a smart-phone; she used to have to get creative. When she received Miss Ollie's very nice, very nonthreatening request for a meeting to "touch base," her first thought had been: *Can we not?* Though you're not allowed to say that when it comes to your kid. You have to *care.* You have to care so much and you have to do it all the time. You have to care which school to send them to and about the evils of You-Tube and whether they're sharing and the changing consistencies of their diaper contents and high-fructose corn syrup. All of it matters be-cause apparently every parent is one wrong move away from raising a serial killer.

But sometimes—only sometimes—Darby would appreciate a time-out from all the paying attention and keeping an eye on, just a month or two break from giving a shit. Maybe it's one thing for the parents with easy children, who frankly ruin it for everyone, but Darby has a wonder-ful but difficult daughter.

So she will show up and listen and not get defensive at this meeting. She will lean forward and ask questions. She'll welcome an outsider's perspective. Anything to understand what makes Lola tick. Because Darby is realizing more and more that she has no idea.

And she especially doesn't know what any of this has got to do with Noelle and Mary Beth. She hopes it's not the biting. Please, anything but that.

I wish I could bite you. Lola had sounded so cold and calculating yes-terday in the car; she can be sweet, she really can be. But Darby knows better than to say this in the meeting. She sounds like a crazy person, even to Griff, who just this morning suggested they send their four-year-old to some kind of experimental group therapy he'd read one stupid article about. Sometimes, Darby feels like she's seeing someone who isn't really there. A different version of her little girl.

Whatever it is, she's glad Mary Beth will be there. Mary Beth is a world-class carer.

As if on cue, a text pings her phone from Mary Beth. *Bad news*, it reads.

TEN

▼

In her car, Rhea's hands still tremble in her lap, where no one would know they've been trembling for a full fifteen minutes before the first responders ever got there. An ambulance, three police cars, and a fire truck.

She's now been staring at the vehicles blocking the pickup lane, her pulse booming in her ears. A hard *thwap* on the driver's-side glass startles her.

"Bodhi's fine," another mother—her name's Roxy—calls through the window. "The kids are all fine." She gives a thumbs-up and Rhea nods dumbly.

"Yeah. Yeah. Okay," she mumbles through the glass, realizing too late she's forgotten to thank Roxy. Rhea would never have thought to do that, and knowing this about herself makes her feel lonely, like maybe she needs to examine some stuff.

"Bitch, please!" Zazzy Tims exhorts through the car speakers. She can't remember turning the ignition back on, hasn't caught a single word of the chapter in this ridiculous audiobook since she made her final decision, stepped out of the car, and walked across the promenade to change things.

Things did change. Plans changed. She changed. She looks at her big green eyes in the mirror and tries to figure out whether she recognizes the woman she sees there.

Meanwhile, Roxy moves on to knocking on the windows of other parents as they pull into the parking lot: *Your child is fine. All the kids are fine.* She disarms each bomb, one by one.

And, of course, everybody's got to be figuring it out by now: The emergency trucks aren't going anywhere.

Bodhi's fine, he's fine. Thumbs-up. Okay. She goes to unclick her seatbelt, only she's not wearing one.

An amorphous blob of parents gathers near the Charity Fountain or whatever the fuck it's called.

Darby finds Rhea in the crowd. "Roxy says the kids are fine."

Rhea can already feel her opinion of Little Academy souring. "Yeah, she told me." At her sides, Rhea's fingers move to the gauzy fabric of her skirt.

Nearly four years she and Darby have been friends now. She remembers when they met at their very first teacher's meet and greet. The teacher's name was Mrs. Louise. On a card table outside the babies' new classroom Mrs. Louise had prepared the parents' name tags, handwritten in the kind of permanent marker Rhea liked the smell of. She peeled the backing off the sticker that read *Bodhi's Mom* and pressed it over her heart. Six months after their babies were born, most of the mothers were still swollen, heavy breasted, and round bellied. They all wore lotion and perfume and tried to sweep their hair into ponytails and buns beneath headbands to mask greasy roots, but who were they fooling? They were all So-and-So's Mom now. They asked questions about classroom ratios and choking hazards and sleep schedules and soothing philosophies as if they weren't all prepared to leave their infants with the first warm body to walk through that door.

Darby raised her hand and said, *Mrs. Louise, do you have a spare marker or pen I could borrow?* She used it to write *Darby Morton* over *Lola's Mom.* Then she asked if anyone else needed to use the Sharpie. Rhea liked Darby after that. She wasn't afraid to do her own thing. Kind of like Rhea.

So they could be friends as long as Darby swore off referring to them as "mommy friends." The thing about mommy friends, though, because there actually isn't a better term for it, is that more than once, they will change your child's diaper without asking, even the really dirty ones.

They will offer to hold your baby so you can eat. Your child will come to know them by name and they will know if your child loves monsters or princesses or horses. They will notice when your kid grows taller and recognize when he gets a new backpack and offer to pick up school supplies when you're busy.

But what you don't know is whether the "mommy" part of "mommy friends" is load-bearing, whether the friendship is structurally sound apart from the children.

"I hope everything's okay," Darby says. All the parents are staring at the school building like they've got X-ray vision.

"I just want to get Bodhi and get the hell out of here." Rhea shifts her weight, searching for her center.

"You don't think anything happened to—" The tendons on Darby's throat turn to hard wires racing up her neck.

"She said the kids were fine," Rhea says evenly. There's no sense in getting worked up before someone gives them a reason to. She is a steady oak in a grassy knoll. She is a falcon, strong and still, floating on the breeze. She is the lake at dawn, she reminds herself.

"Right. Yeah." Darby nods. "Though, what else would they say?"

"Where's Mary Beth?" Rhea asks.

"She texted me that she had to pick up Noelle early today from school."

Just then Lena Feinstein, with her small bones and big hair, flits over to their two-person clump. "We're hearing that she's dead." Lena can't seem to control her face and it keeps wavering between hot gossip she clearly can't wait to share and genuine grief. But then, that's how it is sometimes. "It happened so close to the end of the day, they didn't have time to notify the parents."

"Who?" Darby asks.

"You don't know? Oh my god, I'm so sorry. We've got ears in the office building. One of Megan's babysitters is a niece or a daughter or a cousin of someone. Anyway, the ambulance and everything are here for Miss Ollie."

"Oh damn." Rhea can't help herself.

"No," Darby says. "She's not dead. Dead? She's, like, twenty-six."

Of the mothers, Megan, Charlotte, and Robin have all started crying. Rhea thinks: *I should do that, I should show more emotion, I should feel bad.* She needs to act right.

"Where are the kids? I want to see Lola. I want to see her right now."

"They're treating it as a crime scene." Asher's dad leans over, his hand over the mouthpiece of his cell phone. "I'm on with one of my friends at the DA's office," he explains, sounding like a lawyer. Lawyers, Rhea finds, always want to sound like lawyers. "He reached out to his connection on the force and— What's that? Sorry."

Rhea swallows, mouth drying. A crime scene, an active crime scene investigation at Little Academy. Her body bristles.

In her pocket, she rolls a small piece of silver in her fingertips, pushing the pointy edges into the pads, feeling its shape. The familiar urge to squeeze the life out of something, not to hold back. The small, brutal satisfaction when a silver corner breaks skin; she flinches. Just over half an hour ago, before returning to her car, it had made a scraping sound against the linoleum tile when it caught beneath her shoe. Where she found the small metal letter just outside Miss Ollie's classroom.

TRANSCRIPT OF INTERVIEW OF WITNESS, NOELLE BRANDT

APPEARANCES:

Detective Wanda Bright

PROCEEDINGS

DET. BRIGHT: There's no reason to be nervous. I'm going to ask you a few simple questions and I bet—I *bet*, you'll be able to get them just right. Sound good?

NOELLE BRANDT: Okay.

DET. BRIGHT: And if at any point, you get worried or anxious, you can just look at your mommy and she'll be right here the whole time. Got it?

NOELLE BRANDT: Yes.

MRS. MARY BETH BRANDT: Yes, *ma'am*.

NOELLE: Yes, ma'am.

DET. BRIGHT: We can keep it relaxed. That's fine, just fine. First of all, can you tell me your name?

NOELLE BRANDT: Noelle. N-O-E-Double-L-E. Noelle.

DET. BRIGHT: Whew. Good. See? I had a feeling you'd do a great job. And how old are you, Noelle?

NOELLE BRANDT: I'm four and a half.

DET. BRIGHT: Wow, four. That's big. Where do you go to school?

NOELLE BRANDT: Little Academy.

DET. BRIGHT: Do you like your school?

NOELLE BRANDT: Yes. Ma'am.

DET. BRIGHT: What do you like about it?

NOELLE BRANDT: The playground.

DET. BRIGHT: The playground does look really cool.

NOELLE BRANDT: I like the slides because I can go down on my tummy and climb back up the wrong way by myself now.

DET. BRIGHT: Wow, that's impressive. Noelle, do you know what happened to Miss Ollie?

NOELLE BRANDT: Yes. I do.

DET. BRIGHT: You do? That's very helpful. Can you tell me?

NOELLE BRANDT: Miss Ollie's an angel.

ELEVEN

▼

Miss Ollie is dead, that much Mary Beth has ascertained. Mary Beth felt it—this breakthrough—so acutely it was sensory, almost physical, reaching through the fog of her insane headache, clawing at her to pay attention, snap to it, Mary Beth. She watches the ceiling fan in her bedroom go around and around, a sort of meditation.

If she thought she knew how she would react in a catastrophe, if she thought it would be logical, then, turns out, she was wrong. Because in response, she returned home, put the kids in front of a movie, and dragged Doug upstairs, where she attempted to screw her brains out—literally.

The strategy worked, somewhat.

Her head hurts less, her animal instincts for survival—survival of her family, but more importantly survival of herself—are satiated, but Miss Ollie is still dead. She tries to find room for that knowledge in her swollen brain, but it keeps resisting, pushing against facts like an overstuffed closet. The death of her daughter's preschool teacher floats outside of her. She knows this because if she swallowed it, made room, let it in as something to be digested, she would feel wildly different by now. She would comprehend that her daughter was no doubt in grave danger, that nowhere was safe, not even a preschool. She would think about how just yesterday she'd seen Miss Ollie: healthy, young, alive, *present*. And now she doesn't even have a heartbeat.

"How many days is that?" Doug rolls over, probably a tad shell-shocked, poor thing.

"I'll have to check the calendar." She sounds robotic. The air from the fan whips her sticky cheeks and the thick, slippery sweat pooled beneath her boobs.

Doug props himself up on his elbow. She hasn't shaved her bikini line in ages and it's nice that this no longer embarrasses her.

"How does Noelle seem, considering?" he murmurs. Did he think of their daughter's dead teacher while he was fucking her? Was he waiting to ask this question the whole time?

Her heart thumps, most likely an aftereffect of the sex.

"Fine." She pries herself from the bed, locates a clean towel, and rubs it between her thighs. "I think I better go call the other moms, speaking of. Can you get the girls to bed?"

Doug still goes through the motions of running his fingers through his hair even though he hasn't had enough hair to run them through for years. "What if Noelle wants you? She's going through a real mommy phase, I think." He makes no motion to go do anything as she pulls on the droopy sleeves of her robe.

"She won't," answers Mary Beth.

"She keeps saying she's—"

"I don't know," she snaps. Mary Beth never snaps. "Figure it out. How should I know any better than you?"

She's a tiny bit satisfied when his lower lip drops.

At Mary Beth's bridal shower, she received all kinds of advice related to her impending marriage. Never go to bed angry. Always kiss good-night. Say sorry even when you don't mean it. Children will make you happier. And for the most part, she believes these kernels of wisdom are clichés for a reason. They are good and true and occasionally, like now, totally irrelevant.

Megan, *hi*, it's Mary Beth." Her practice of entering the contact information of every parent in her daughters' classes does come in handy more than one would think. "I'm not great, how are you?"

Megan is one of the better-liked mothers in the class, not quite as overtly friendly as Mary Beth, but she doesn't avoid eye contact at pickup the way, say, Rhea does.

"Shaken." Megan sighs. "I can't believe something like this could happen at our school. Zeke's been going there since he was sixteen months old."

Mary Beth paces at the foot of her bed. She's locked the door, for privacy. "Someone must have seen something, right?"

She hates that she was gone by the time it all went down. She missed everything. She should have been there. She could have helped. It's not her fault that she has migraines. She does wish she had communicated with Darby earlier about the meeting, it would have been preferable, but she wasn't *planning* on missing it.

"That's what I'm afraid of. Think of what our kids might have witnessed. It's making me sick. This is just—unbelievable. I really can't believe it."

"It doesn't make any sense," Mary Beth agrees.

"Miss Roberta across the hall was keeping tabs, but apparently there was a potty emergency and she can't be totally sure on the timeline."

Mary Beth paces on the bedroom carpeting she's said she's going to replace for the last three years. "That's unfortunate."

"Everything was fine, though, when you picked up Noelle, wasn't it?"

"Yes, completely."

"And you spoke to Miss Ollie?"

"Just briefly." Mary Beth should have a reason for calling other than stirring up chatter. "It's unfathomable," she says. "Miss Ollie's family is in my prayers. I thought I might organize a meal train for her—well, for whoever her next of kin is. I think we should do something."

It's seamless getting other mothers to agree to help. Everyone wants to do something, and so once Mary Beth has taken up the mantle of the meal train, she experiences zero friction as she slips in and out of telephone calls.

"Lena? Hi, it's Mary Beth Brandt. I'm calling around to organize a meal train for Erin Ollie's family," she says. "And I'm curious—have you heard anything more about what they think happened?"

"Mary Beth. *God.* Sorry. Gosh. My husband and I are freaking out. Have you talked to Asher's dad, the lawyer?" Now Chelsea is on the phone.

Mary Beth is trying to keep up. "Our kids might be called in as *witnesses*. They're only four. Four-year-old criminal witnesses. Who's ever heard of such a thing?"

"That seems way too young," Mary Beth agrees. "Isn't there some kind of age minimum for that sort of thing? I mean, what could they really know?"

"I don't know. I'm trying to get it out of Lincoln, you know, what might have happened, but—"

"But what?"

"He's four."

"Right." A small laugh. If nothing else it helps Mary Beth to evacuate the hot, stagnant air from her lungs. She hangs up. No one mentions the biting. Not one single person.

TWELVE

▼

Lola is screaming her head off.

Not actually, Darby concedes, but give it ten more minutes, then check back and who knows.

In the background, Jack watches his sister from his high chair, where he regally munches on soggy noodles and canned green beans like: *What's the fuss.*

"Deep breaths. Let's try to calm down." Darby channels the lessons of a certain cartoon tiger. "Can you count to four with me? One . . . two . . . three . . ." Lola's tantrums trigger a diarrhea of energy in Darby, the final reserves of vitality and resolve slowly squirting out her ass.

She wonders if there's some safety precaution she ought to be taking on behalf of her daughter, the way you're supposed to roll someone onto their side in the event of a seizure.

The back door beeps. She can literally see the moment Griff's face hits the tantrum air.

"Who died?" he asks, glumly dropping his car keys onto the kitchen counter.

"Miss Ollie!" she screams, but mainly because it's very, very loud and she is very, very close to losing her shit.

There was a time, she remembers, when she used to feel like they really had their shit together, by the way. But ever since having children, they've let their shit get everywhere. Filling up trash cans, in the bathtub, sometimes even in her hair.

She watches his face carefully. "Wait, what?" She tries to decipher what she sees there. Shock? It definitely seems in the shock family. God, but maybe she needs to get her eyes checked. She could have sworn she saw . . . for an instant . . . just in passing . . .

One thing's for sure: She should never have gone into that school without Mary Beth.

"Lola's teacher," she says in a tone that implies this is somehow, some way, his fault. "Miss Ollie died during school today, which you would *know* if you were answering your *phone.*" *Or if you were there,* she thinks grimly. But why would he be? It certainly has been a day. A long, terrible day.

"I'm sorry it . . . died . . . too." Perhaps, and this is just a thought, there should be a different word for what happens to cell phones when they stop working temporarily than the one for people who cease to exist permanently. "Jesus, what happened?"

"I don't want to say." She makes eyes at the children. Jack shrieks, could be happy, could be mad, they'll know in a minute.

Griff follows her look, nods. Then he grips her arm, fingertips digging into her bicep, and drags her roughly into the pantry.

"Ouch, Griff, too hard." She shrugs him off.

Surrounded by all of the junky stuff from the middle of the grocery store that health magazines tell you not to buy, they're forced to stand close enough together that she can spot all the gray flecks in her husband's stubble.

"Sorry." He runs his palm down his cheek and he does look apologetic, more like the adorably sheepish man she first met when watching him get repeatedly and flagrantly passed over again and again while trying to order a drink at a crowded San Antonio bar all those years ago. He was the least pushy man she had ever met. "What happened?" he repeats.

She imagines the inevitable newspaper reports: "Teacher Slain at Local Preschool." Only the local preschool will be their preschool. Little Academy.

"My impression is that it wasn't of natural causes."

"Suicide?"

She takes a shaky breath. "Supposedly two of her fingers were sliced off, so that seems . . . unlikely."

She's already been warned not to expect an official cause of death to be released possibly for months, but other tidbits have reached her over the course of the afternoon. The director and assistant director of both Little Academy and RiverRock Church have been notified on an "as-needed basis" about the extent of the damage to the preschool supply room. *Blood. There was a lot of blood spilled on scene.*

For the first time, the realness is crashing in on her, what happened, what it means.

He looks away, unfocused eyes trailing off in the direction of the Pirate's Booty, may the sight give him comfort. "And that's why Lola's freaking out?"

Outside the pantry, Lola's pitch and volume remain remarkably consistent.

"Not exactly." She's begun to feel claustrophobic. She'll need to get out of this cramped space that smells like stale crumbs and long-since-spilled marinara sauce soon. "I don't know. It's been a long day. We have no idea what the kids might have seen or heard or—"

"Well, have you asked her?" He surprises her with his emotion.

"Yes, Griff, obviously I've asked Lola," she responds calmly—not usually her role, but fine. "But, you know, she doesn't really like to talk about school. When I tried, she asked me if triceratops have nipples." He pinches the bridge of his nose like he's getting a headache. "Do they?"

He glowers at her and, for a moment, she feels like she doesn't recognize him. He looks *mean*—no, *cruel*. "Does she even know?" he asks.

"In so many words." Darby pokes her head out to check on the kids. Jack is arching his back in the high chair; he wants down. Lola kicks her feet into the hard floor.

Griff's Adam's apple bobs. "Sorry," he repeats. "I just don't know how to handle this." He means *her*. Lola. He doesn't know how to handle his daughter. It's a long-running source of conflict between them, their competing theories on the best way to parent. Darby believes their daughter's behavior is a family matter without a silver-bullet solution; it will be improved gradually through firm boundaries and a consistent, united front. Meanwhile Griff often prefers the path of least resistance in tandem with a half-assed strategy of outsourcing the issue to "professionals who can handle it." Neither theory has been proven in their household, barely even tested.

Together, they emerge from the pantry to face their children. Darby removes the high-chair tray and begins unbuckling Jack, reluctantly freeing him from his confines. Lola lifts her chin off the ground and Darby is afraid that one of these days Lola's going to seriously injure herself. "Mommy, please, Mommy."

Please what? What, Lola!

"I've been hearing things," Griff says softly.

"What things?"

"On the text chain with the dads in Lola's class."

"There's a text chain?" she asks. "And *you're* on it?"

"I didn't ask to be." He walks in a slow circle, hands on his hips. Jack eats food off the floor. "The biting. Some of the dads have said, you know, it's a thing in their house." She looks questioningly at him. "Like they're starting to allow it. Like, I don't know, like maybe it's some kind of—okay, one of the dads who is some kind of doctor I think said it might be a vitamin deficiency or a perceived one or I can't remember exactly what he called it."

"What are you saying?"

He shakes his head, regrouping. "A lot of the kids are biting in this one class at this one school, all at the same time, and there's something there, some conclusion to draw, I mean, don't you think?" Is he hoping for this to be true? Whatever *this* is. Because that would mean maybe the thing that's wrong isn't with their daughter specifically, but with all the kids, is that his thought process? Parenting should be fucked for everyone, not just them.

"Lola, honey," she says more firmly. "We need to calm down."

For the first time since the start of this particular meltdown, Lola sits up, rubbing her eyes. Her chest still heaves. Tears hurtle down her face. But there's movement. "I won't," she shrieks at a pitch that literally hurts Darby's eardrums. "I won't! I won't! I won't!"

"Maybe you should let her." Griff keeps his voice low.

"Let her what?"

"You know, bite you? I mean, just this once."

"She lost her teacher today, Griff. I'm pretty sure that probably has something to do with all this."

"Exactly. That's what I mean. Given what happened."

They stare down at Lola, this tiny hijacker of their lives.

"The dads have said it can help. It's comforting. One of them has done some research and this isn't even unprecedented. You said yourself that Dr. Meckler called it a normal phase of childhood development, so, you know, thinking of it like that, but just veering off in a different direction it's—"

"No."

"Why not?"

"Because it *hurts*. If you're so sure, then you do it."

"Okay. Yeah. No problem." He squats down and pushes up the sleeve of a black sweater that Darby doesn't recognize. "Lola, sweetie, do you— I mean, would it help do you think if you—are you having the urge to bite, because it's okay if you are and maybe I can help you with that?"

The decibel level drops, just a little, just enough not to make Darby wish she were dead.

Lola looks at Griff. "It's okay," he encourages. "It's okay."

Lola leans into him, sniffs—does she sniff or sniffle?—and cautiously wraps her mouth around the base of his meaty man thumb. A fresh set of tears runs like bathwater from a faucet. Nothing happens.

"I want my mommy." A wail. She leaves behind a slug trail of saliva on her daddy's hand. "I want Mommy!"

Griff looks up at Darby expectantly, like he just *knows* some maternal instinct inside her is about to click in. The sheer entitlement they all have to her, from Jack all the way up to Griff, is a joke. Does no one here remember the last year of her life that she sacrificed to breastfeed Jack, who was allergic to dairy, soy, eggs, wheat, nuts—everything? She lived on plain chicken and rice for months and cried when Griff ate a cookie. Every day felt as though it would never end. But she'd done it. Because the pediatricians and the mommy groups said it would be best and what was a few months of not eating anything that made her happy compared to doing what was best for her child? Except that Darby also had a very real need—for brownies—every so often and she hadn't eaten them, not once.

The wonderful thing about breastfeeding is that it's free, she had read. But was it? Did it cost her nothing? Because if so, her time and energy and mental health must be valued at zero, in which case, in everyone else's opinion, she hadn't made a sacrifice at all. She hadn't given anything.

But less than a year later, here they are, coming back for more: more sweat, more tears, and, more to the point, blood.

"She's asking for you," Griff says as though he's the expert. *He is on a goddamn text chain, everyone!*

"I'm sorry, I guess I missed this chapter in *What to Expect When You're Expecting.*" She crosses her arms, angles her body away. Why does no one tell you what it's going to be like as a parent? Why did nobody explain that she and her husband would argue over who got to run out to buy AAA batteries like it was a free ticket to Bora Bora?

"I'm not saying—I'm just—" Griff pleads. "Let's just try it, that's all." It's kind of amazing, the way their daughter's tantrums instantly age her husband. "Her favorite teacher, Darby. You've said they have—*had*—a very special bond. Please."

She gives in, as if there's another option. She cries when Lola draws blood and not just because it hurts, that's not even the half of it.

I'm sorry, but I have to go back to the office tonight again," he says, stripping off his sweater and wrestling his arms and head through a midnight-blue T-shirt. He doesn't turn away; he's not self-conscious. *He doesn't even appreciate that there isn't a spot directly above his belly button that will always sag no matter what.*

"Tonight?" Lola crashed soon after she finished drinking.

"Yes. The litigation partners are getting new desktop computers." Head down as he rifles through his sock drawer.

"Okay. But like you said, Miss Ollie died and Lola liked her."

"But you weren't that close to her, were you?" His interest is genuine, curious. He'll stay if she wants him to because he's her husband, her sweet, clingy husband, who, yes, likes computers as much as people, but there are worse things.

She doesn't know how to answer the question. There's so much to explain—what she thought, where she was, what she saw, and how close she really got to Miss Ollie in the end. She pushes herself up onto the big bed. She's tired and her brain is mashed potatoes and she really should get a good night's sleep before jumping to any rash conclusions.

"Go," she tells him. "I'm fine."

Earlier that day, she had followed the paths through the church campus, past the Charity Fountain, by the Remembrance Gardens. The memory is already growing hazy. Between the chapel and the stone auditorium building to the place where the sidewalk ended, to an empty foyer, chasing what must have been a mirage. The forest of her mind feels thick with stress and fogged up by flagging adrenaline.

That night, Darby calls out from work for the next day because that's what you do after your child's teacher is brutally murdered on school grounds. She goes to bed alone and dreams of a school full of little vampires, only when she wakes up it's still true.

Mary Beth texts her early that morning: *We're meeting at Sun Tree Park to let the kids run off some energy.*

Darby bangs her shin while opening Jack's stroller in the parking lot and asks Lola to help her carry the water bottles. Lola says no and heads straight underneath the bright blue fort to play with mulch.

Nearby, the mothers gather on a set of picnic tables, diaper bags clumped together on the ground. Six mothers total, more than half the class. Darby scoots in beside Mary Beth, always a tiny bit proud to have her as her closest mommy friend, like their relationship must be proof of something, namely that Darby is a better mother than she seems. Noelle always says *please* and *thank you* and sits still during story time; it's very aspirational for Darby.

"Does anyone have any picture book recommendations that cover coping with grief?" Megan's black hair is barely long enough to pull back into a nub of a ponytail. She wears Hoka running shoes with clean purple hospital scrubs and no makeup.

"I asked my neighborhood mom text chain the same question last night," Charlotte Higsby says. She's George's mother, though they have different last names, Darby recently realized, and she's still married, which is actually fairly modern for a woman like Charlotte, who loves— like, truly loves—Lilly Pulitzer dresses. "I can send some titles to the group if that would be helpful."

They all nod like this is the best idea ever. Darby wants to ask all the wrong questions, like if anyone knows what killed Miss Ollie—a gun, a knife, strangulation. She wants to ask who called Miss Ollie's parents and if they screamed when they found out. She wants to know if Miss Ollie secretly did drugs or had a lot of sex.

"Where's Rhea?" she murmurs to Mary Beth.

"She wasn't answering her phone." Which is pretty par-for-the-course Rhea behavior, so at least one thing is normal.

"She really should be here," muses Mary Beth absently. "We need to be *in* community."

"Yes, well." Darby shrugs. Rhea's a bit of a lone wolf, which is why she and Mary Beth don't always get along. Darby understands both sides, probably because she's got Griff and he hates people, so it evens out.

Chelsea Sawyer twists the top off an applesauce pouch for Lincoln. Less than ten minutes in and the snacks have already started flowing.

"I called my therapist yesterday," says Roxy, one of the younger moms, with too much filler in her lips and a husband who's some kind of surgeon with vanity plates on his Porsche. "She said they're probably too young to really understand and that we only have to explain as much as we want to. It's perfectly fine if we prefer to make something up."

"Like say Miss Ollie went to the farm?" asks Darby.

"Exactly." Roxy tousles her hair with long acrylic nails, which make a satisfying scratching noise against her scalp.

"Okay." Darby tries not to let on that she thinks this is a stupid suggestion, no offense to Roxy's therapist. "But I think that's ignoring the fact that they were *there*." She looks around to the other mothers for support. "There's a certain amount of time that is completely unaccounted for. We don't know what happened, what they witnessed. Miss Ollie was murdered literal steps away from her classroom. You're telling me you don't think any of them saw anything relevant?"

She leaves out her own whereabouts and whether *she* might have seen something relevant because that's not really what this is about right now. Is it?

The beautiful Charlotte Higsby, who has probably never once raised her voice at her children, shifts her weight between her bony ass cheeks. "Don't you think one of the kids would have said something by now? They're four. They aren't exactly known for their secret-keeping skills."

"That's true." Darby sits on her side of the picnic bench with bad posture. Something weird is happening amongst the women gathered here. They're both very upset and also trying to *seem* very upset. You wouldn't think the second would need to be true when the first is, and yet she, too, feels the pressure to perform this unfamiliar ritual properly. She would even welcome a few tears, if they were to flow.

Zeke comes over to hang on his mother, tugging on her arm, asking her to come push him on the tire swing. *Mommy, mommy, mommy.* Darby watches Megan's body lurch as she strains against the forty-odd pounds of her son. *Not right now, maybe later. I would love to play with you, sweetie. Grown-ups are talking.* Her whole voice changes. Darby watches, wondering if this is how Megan sounds when she and Zeke are alone or if this is just the parent she is when she has an audience.

"This is just awful," says Chelsea. "Genuinely awful. I can't believe how awful, and it's going to get worse. Robin says there's bound to be media coverage. She was so young and—"

"The kids," says Bex's mother, Lena.

"What about them?" asks Charlotte.

Lena's eyes travel over all of their faces. "They're biting," Lena prompts. "Oh, come on. I know I'm not the only one. The . . . licking blood. They're drinking it now, more or less."

Darby had no intention of discussing what she'd done the night before, the way she closed her eyes and let Lola open up the wounds on her hand, the mix of disgust and perverse pleasure that her pain calmed her daughter, that it worked—what was that?

"The dads have a text chain," says Darby. She watches her son climb the slide while Lola jumps out from underneath it and makes him giggle. Why won't she play with kids her own age? Normally, she would commiserate with Griff, give him a play-by-play of what their daughter did and didn't do on the playground, but not today, she won't tell him a thing.

Yes, the other moms know about the text chain. Yes, they all find it annoying.

"I talked to Miss Ollie before," Megan says, as if the "before" time frame isn't obvious. "And she mentioned a thing I'd never heard of because, you know—because of what happened with Zeke and Bodhi Anderson and how it all played out."

Go, Megan says to Zeke with her eyes, stopping him before he sets foot again on the concrete slab where the picnic benches live. Play.

"Renfield's syndrome?" Darby is shocked to hear Mary Beth speak up, a small but discernible quiver in her voice.

"Yes!" says Megan. "That's it. Pediatric Renfield's syndrome. I'm not saying I buy it necessarily . . ." After that, Megan explains the gist of the condition as Miss Ollie explained it to her; none of which has been mentioned even in passing by Lola's pediatrician, so what is Darby to make of that? On the one hand, Dr. Meckler was dismissive of Darby's best mom instincts. On the other, Dr. Meckler's version was much simpler.

Roxy shivers. "That sounds sick, like, seriously disturbed."

"It makes sense to me." God, Darby will say almost anything to contradict someone she doesn't like; she will even say that it makes perfect sense that small children would want to suck blood. Even hers.

"I don't know what we should do," says Lena. "I'm at a loss. I'm crushed over what happened to Miss Ollie, of course." *Of course*, they all agree. "But our kids. I don't want our kids to be psychologically damaged once the press sinks their teeth—sorry—into all of this. That's our responsibility."

"And we have to keep them safe," Charlotte continues. "We have to be realistic about who might have done this. Someone with access. A staff member, a teacher, a boyfriend, a parent. Which means our kids might have been exposed to violent behavior, and not just yesterday."

Darby is suddenly very aware of the stillness of the air, which feels as though it's sitting on her skin, like hot breath on the back of her neck. She's having trouble breathing. She needs a stiff breeze, or a stiff drink, preferably both. Maybe it was a mistake coming here to speak with the other moms. *A parent*, Charlotte said.

"Darby." Mary Beth puts her hand over her knee. Not helping matters. "I can't believe I'm only just thinking of this. You could help us." No one is more surprised by this news than Darby, who isn't exactly what one would call the "likely candidate." She tries gingerly to scoot away from Mary Beth's hand; the touch of skin on skin is making her woozy. "You could help us to navigate all of this. Darby was in PR and now she's a crisis manager," she explains to the group, which doesn't seem all that comforted by the news. She hears Mary Beth's voice coming from far away. "And this is a crisis."

THIRTEEN

▼

1962: That's the earliest record of Renfield's syndrome that Mary Beth has come across. A group of kindergarteners in Columbus, Ohio, smiling together in a black-and-white school portrait. Bibbed dresses, tapered trousers, plaid sweater-vests documented in a head-scratching yearbook entry for the district's elementary school, the picture captioned: "Ms. Linda's Little Leeches." Did they think it was funny back then? The true start of the sixties, anything goes?

In 1975, two pediatricians from Oklahoma collaborated on a joint article when a group of parents in a suburban neighborhood outside of Ardmore began complaining about a series of violent biting incidents. The ages of the affected children ranged from three to seven and some of the parents reported that if the children were allowed to drink small quantities of blood, they would no longer bite. The doctors hypothesized it might have something to do with the high iron levels that gave the dirt on which the neighborhood was built a red appearance. But no conclusion was reached and the study devolved into quackery when one doctor insisted the number thirteen—the number of children afflicted—bore significance. No photos were taken of the group.

Mary Beth hasn't been sleeping well. She's been walking around since the day of Miss Ollie's murder feeling hopped up on caffeine, though she doesn't even drink coffee. She's always excelled in times of adversity. What she lacks in book smarts, she makes up for in life skills. That's why she's Room Mom. That's why she chairs countless galas. She tackles projects like a linebacker. Mary Beth Brandt gets stuff done.

She reviews the neat lines of handwritten notes in her journal.

By the eighties, a few medical schools included "pediatric Renfield's syndrome," or the urge to ingest blood, in their list of novelty case studies. Though by 1988, a preschool class was the subject of a nasty bout of angry protests during the height of Satanic Panic, and the tiny bloodsuckers were shortly thereafter expelled. Parents were advised to refuse all urges and to instead employ the use of palatable substitutes such as ketchup. A short newspaper article mentioned behavioral issues amongst the children, but no evidence of anything serious.

After that, a gentler, more clinical approach was adopted in some psychology circles, though there does still seem to be room for plenty of debate about whether pediatric Renfield's syndrome is even real, and this includes the opinions of doctors who have cared for some of the young patients.

Toddlers in Ontario. A playdate group in Fresno. Eight second graders—the oldest children on record—in Washington, D.C. A day care in Atlanta. And now Little Academy, now Mary Beth's daughter.

Ten documented cases in the last fifty years. The odds are astronomical.

She recalls a group of students in upstate New York in the early 2000s. Dozens of high school girls developed an odd tic, almost simultaneously. They were on the *Today* show. Last night, she checked back on those long-forgotten girls. What had become of them? Who were they? Experts never discovered what prompted the tic. They never even agreed whether or not the girls were faking it. And yet twenty years later, plenty of those girls still have tics.

It doesn't matter. Noelle is four. Four-year-olds can't fake it.

She keeps snatching glances of Noelle as though she's stealing them and stuffing them under her mattress. Noelle with her tongue out as she tries to color inside the lines of an *Encanto* coloring book. Noelle practicing beginner ballet. Noelle pumping her knobby knees on the swing set. Noelle as she bows her curly head to pray before bed; she always comes up with the funniest, most earnest little prayers. *Dear God, please make Daddy not allergic to cats or, if that's too much to ask, find him a new home to live in next door. Dear God, I'm sorry I don't like carrots. Did you ever have to put Jesus in time-out when he was my age?*

She will see her daughter through this crisis. That's what mothers do.

They protect their young. They lift cars off children with their bare hands. They push through the pain. Mary Beth will power through, which, after all, is basically her whole vibe. Whether it's a family vacation, a terrible head cold, a sleepless night, packing for summer camps, making home-made Valentines at 9:00 P.M. on February 13, pay no mind, she will power through.

She inventories the three Amazon boxes she's collected from her porch, setting the contents out on the kitchen countertop. Twenty-pack of syringes. Catheter tips. Fluid bags. Tubes. Vials. Biohazard disposal container. Spring-loaded lancets. Cotton wool. Alcohol pads.

This morning, she found Noelle licking a used Band-Aid Angeline had left in the girls' wastebasket after she scraped her knee riding her scooter, and would anyone believe Mary Beth didn't vomit?

The first few steps of the process are easy. She washes her hands and gathers her supplies. After cleaning the pale part of her inner arm with one of the alcohol swabs, she straightens it and studies the blue lines running beneath the surface. She could have used help tying the tourniquet above her elbow, but with a few tries she's able to use her teeth to squeeze it tightly enough. Now she threads the needle into the holder. It takes a few tries, too. And she taps the tube. No explanation as to why, but that's what the instructions say, so probably best to follow it to the letter.

Her mouth tastes sour. She hesitates with the needle hovering over her skin. It can't be anything compared to childbirth, which she's always known she would do a thousand times over if it meant getting her two girls. However, she would prefer *not* to do it a thousand times over, if she has a choice.

When Mary Beth first became a mother, she used to tear up watching the terrible sacrifices mothers in developing nations made for their babies and thought with her hand over her heart in solidarity: *I would do the same thing.*

And now, she hesitates with a sterile needle poised over her arm. She bites her tongue as she sinks the needle into the skin—*ouch*—it stings.

She doesn't know if it's worse or better for being self-inflicted. The first time she pushes too deep, the next too shallow, and the third she misses a vein entirely. It takes six tries to get a good line, one where the blood begins to flow into the big tube. Oh! And boy does it flow. She watches with sick fascination. There's a current to it. Is there supposed to be a current? The tube fills and she remembers at the last moment that she's supposed to switch to a new one.

There. Better.

It fills and fills. The crimson rivulets feel completely separate from Mary Beth.

Oh wow, that's a lot of blood. It's like a very well-organized murder scene. She chuckles at her own sick sense of humor as she pulls the last tube and plugs the stopper over it, careful not to spill a single drop. Finally, she slides the needle catheter from her vein—not as carefully as she intended. Four full vials are lined neatly on her white marble countertop. Where were all these gizmos on her baby registry, huh?

In another year or so, she imagines a line of blood containers marked up to three times the price, but with cute little lions and sloths printed on the cylinders. How adorable.

She labels three with a black sharpie and pours the fourth into a plastic cup. She is a good mother, she thinks as she makes her way, stumbling ever so slightly sideways, back to a daughter who is waiting for her. A good mother, but also—*oh*—a dizzy one.

At least she can look forward to tomorrow, when they'll attend the school's memorial service for Erin Ollie. Not that she's looking forward to the service itself per se, but what it signifies: the ability to move on, to get past this together. That will be positive. Twenty-four hours. It might not be easy, but it will be over. She just has to power through.

FOURTEEN

▼

R hea feels like it would be a mistake to stop moving. She spoons her breakfast of overnight oats into her mouth while at the same time tidying the living room, moving throw pillows back into place, pushing down the corner on a rug, pulling an empty mug off the coffee table.

"Bodhi!" She sticks her head down the hall. "What's taking so long in there?"

"Privacy," he calls through the bathroom door.

She retreats back into the kitchen, where she tosses the dirtied mason jar and mug into the sink and runs the water over it, returning to find the door to the bathroom they share locked. "We're going to be late." She leans her shoulder against the frame, waiting. She doesn't even like the black dress she pulled from the back of her closet. The hem bubbles and the seams itch around the armholes. She pulls her hair into a sleek bun at the nape of her neck and feels like a fraud, like a Stepford version of herself.

"Privacy!" he repeats.

"You know that door's not supposed to be locked."

A pause. "Daddy lets me."

"Bodhi," she warns. "I'm just trying to get out the door. Darby and Lola are going to be here any minute. Please don't make it harder than it needs to be." She taps her phone screen to check the time. Her blood pressure blips upward.

Miss Ollie's family had opted for a private ceremony, but apparently everyone (except for Rhea) agreed that the kids deserved an opportunity to say goodbye. It would be rude to miss, Darby insisted when Rhea broached the subject, as if Rhea is particularly afraid of rudeness.

We're coming together as a community. Mary Beth sounded like a broken record. *To process as one.* In the end, it was all decided and out of Rhea's hands, more or less.

At home, she twists her big toe into the carpet. It's way too quiet on the other side of the door. "Bodhi!" She bangs on it with her fist and, finally, it opens. Bodhi grins up at her, wearing the pint-sized black suit she bought him for the occasion. "Did you wash your hands?" He nods.

She goes to grab to grab his silver clip-on tie off the top of his dresser, then kneels down in front of him. He smells like toothpaste.

"I want to look handsome for Miss Ollie," he says, puffing out his chest.

Her face crumples. She presses her eyes closed and feels for his hand, still damp. "Honey," she says. "You know Miss Ollie won't be there."

And here it is. She knew she shouldn't have stood still, not for a second, not today. No time for thinking, no time for questioning past choices. But she knows now. It's all there, pooling in her insides. Biding time.

"Why not?" he asks. Her breath takes on weight in her chest. Not again. They went over this.

What she wants to say is: *Because Miss Ollie doesn't exist, Bodhi, because Miss Ollie* never *existed.* But she can't for obvious reasons, plus a few that are less so.

"Miss Ollie died, Bodhi. She's not coming back. Unfortunately." She forces herself to add that last bit. "Her soul is at peace. She's resting, but permanently. I'm sorry."

"Forever?" There is real sorrow in his deep brown eyes. She wants to take it from him, to say, *Here, I'll hold that,* the way she does when he hands her an empty snack wrapper.

Miss Ollie wasn't real, that's true. As far as she's aware, Rhea is the only parent who knows about the legal name change. Just over a year ago. No marriage. No divorce. No discernible reason. The origin story of the woman now known as Erin Ollie remains a mystery.

But whoever she was, she was real to Rhea's son, and that's why Rhea has agreed to go today. For Bodhi. Her fire keeper, her wild darling, her earth soul. Her forever reason. What won't she do for him?

The doorbell rings, followed by a quick rap on the front door. "They're here." She gives Bodhi a quick kiss on his forehead. "Don't worry. I'll be with you the whole time. Why don't you go answer that while Mommy grabs her purse?"

She disappears into her room, where she examines her reflection in an old vanity she found discarded in an alleyway and fixed up with chalk paint and a set of knobs she bought at the craft store. She stares hard, looking over the sheen of her washed-out complexion, the freckles on the bridge of her nose that fan up to her temples, and tries to look for any sign someone might pick up on that something's not right with her.

Then, she steps out of her bedroom as though stepping onto a stage, ready to perform. "Hi, Darby, thanks for— Oh. Griff. I—" She clears a cough from her throat and tries to work her mouth into a pleasant expression, at least for Lola, who looks sort of tragic in a full-skirted black tutu and black T-shirt. "I didn't know you were coming."

Griff presses his lips together and shrugs. His eyes float around the room, judging.

"He wouldn't miss it," Darby says with a perfunctory coolness to her tone.

"Right. I figured he had to work," Rhea says. While Bodhi shows Lola a Hot Wheels car, the three grown-ups just stand there uncomfortably, somehow finding themselves stuck in a Bermuda Triangle of conversation. For once, Rhea could use Darby's usual font of chatter. Of all the times for it to run dry. "Are you sure there's room for us?" Rhea asks hopefully. She doesn't know what Darby sees in Griff Morton. He's the sort of lousy husband that women have to make excuses for. *Sure he likes you, he's just reserved. He doesn't mean to come off that way, he's just socially awkward.* Rhea's known plenty of middle-aged dudes just like him, ones who get by on their good looks and their height and their college education. "We could drive ourselves, really, I don't mind."

"Don't be silly." It comes out more like a barked order, and in its wake, the sounds of the surrounding neighborhood feel embarrassingly loud—a car honks at the light, somewhere down the street a mower chainsaws up and down a grass lawn, squirrels chatter in the oak outside. Darby winces. "I just mean I left Jack with a babysitter and we can all squeeze in just fine."

"Yeah, but we don't have to squeeze at all. You guys look, you know, fancy," Rhea says, searching. "I don't want you showing up looking all rumpled on account of us. It's no big deal."

"Rhea." Darby puts her hands on her hips as though Rhea's being a child who refuses to cooperate.

"What?"

"Well, you know." She sounds exasperated and taps her foot on the floor. "I couldn't bear the thought of you going alone."

"Marcus will be there," Rhea answers. Griff still won't look at her. She wonders if he's secretly hoping she'll insist on driving herself and whether that makes her more or less likely to. "And Bodhi." It's amazing how terrified other people are of her being alone.

"You know what I mean," says Darby, skirting a glance at Griff. "Please." And Rhea has the creeping feeling that maybe Darby is the one who doesn't want to be alone—with her husband.

A little more than an hour later, Rhea is forced to sit and stare as Tamar Filbin picks her nose on stage. And George Hall sticks his finger in Zeke's ear. And Noelle Brandt performs the large hand motions that go with the hymn "All Is Well" to perfection. Bodhi stands watching like he forgets whether or not he's even supposed to be a part of all this.

The church pianist slows the tune way down to give the kids a fighting chance. Marcus sings softly beside her. His large hands crease Miss Ollie's face in two from where she smiles out of the glossy program. Something about that picture, maybe the perma-grin, maybe the red eye that didn't get photoshopped all the way out, gives Rhea the willies.

The chapel is hopped up on chrysanthemums and gladioli. She scans the crowd, made up entirely of Little Academy families. Her phone vibrates. She checks the number, recognizes it. Her investment advisor calling. And her heart skips. Two days she's been waiting for this call to find out which, if any, of the angel investors the advisor reached out to have chosen to invest in this round of funding and here it comes now. She watches it ring, ring, ring, wondering if there's a socially acceptable exit plan.

Then it stops. She can't believe she missed it. Now what happens? What if her advisor doesn't answer when she calls back because she's at back-to-back children's birthday parties or something awful like that? Rhea chews her lip. She pored over those profit and loss statements, those projections, those slides on growth opportunities and target demographics. How much longer is this service going to last anyway? This fake funeral business.

A slideshow plays. On the projector screen, pictures of Miss Ollie dressing up on Dr. Seuss's birthday, of her posing at the teacher appreciation luncheon, of her doing shaving cream paintings with the kids. Marcus pulls out his handkerchief.

Three staccato pulses from her phone: a voice mail. Chill. Be cool.

She slowly reaches her hand into her bag and slides out a white capsule. The slideshow ends. During the prayer, she bows her head, slips earbuds out from the case, and nestles them into her ears.

Distracted by her movement, Marcus glances over and real-quick registers the earbuds. He tilts his chin like, *Are you kidding me.*

"Just checking a voice mail," she whispers, maybe too loud given that a few heads turn in her direction, it's hard to tell with these things in.

She presses the "play" icon on her phone even though it's hard to focus, what with Marcus trying to stare her into an early grave of her own.

The voice of her investment advisor, Margot, comes through: "Sorry not to reach out with better news, but I heard back from one of the angel investors from our last meeting and I think they still want to see a slightly broader reach before committing to financing. We'll circle up and get back to the drawing board next week. Again, sorry not to have a more positive update. Have a great weekend!"

Even once she's capped the earbuds, Rhea's ears feel clogged. She swallows, her insides smarting. Nothing to do but look straight ahead. Pretend it's all good. But disappointment pumps into her bloodstream. Negative energy for days.

Think, Rhea, she wills herself. She wants this, wants this so badly she could scream and that's what's scary, wanting something so badly it forces the insides of herself out into the wide-open world.

Eyes glazed, she listens to the rest of the ceremony. Erin Ollie was a beautiful soul. Erin Ollie was a light that touched every person she met. Erin Ollie is in a better place. *Erin Ollie was a fraud,* she thinks darkly.

Only once they step into the sun outside the chapel does she notice how the air-conditioned cold has been seeping into her bones, and she tilts her face to the sky to let the rays in. She tries dialing Margot.

"Well, that just about ripped my heart out of my chest and stomped on it, how about yours?" Darby rejoins her, Griff having run off somewhere.

Little does she know how fucking true that is for Rhea. She's mourning, all right. If she would have been able to answer her phone, maybe she would have gotten some answers, some context, a goddamn workaround. Maybe she could have convinced Margot to fix this with the angel investor. Get her the money, some way, some how. Now Margot's not answering her phone.

Mary Beth's charm bracelet jangles on her wrist as she joins their little clump. "Hi, Marcus." Her eyes are soupy and her mouth, when she smiles, is a pathetic squiggle, but she's holding it together, just like everyone else.

"Sorry for your loss." He bows his head, looking sharp in his navy blue suit and fresh haircut. "She was a good teacher. We were lucky to have her."

Rhea feels the weight of both of her friends' gazes moving over to her. "Marcus, why don't you go find our son?" she says, even though she can see Bodhi and the other children on the side of the chapel, near the reflective pond, milling together with freshly cut, long-stemmed yellow roses.

Marcus squeezes her hand when he leaves and, yep, Darby and Mary Beth clock that, too.

"Guess you two didn't discuss how much you *loved* Miss Ollie." Darby tries to make the jab sound good-natured, but the circumstances turn it sour.

"Don't say it like that." Mary Beth swipes at her nose. Rhea would have expected Mary Beth to be buzzing about, organizing the children with their roses, delegating whatever it is they're supposed to be doing with them other than wielding them like lightsabers.

"There was nothing to discuss," says Rhea. "She wasn't my favorite. I didn't want her dead. End of story."

"I'm just saying, you might do a better job of showing it." Darby flips through the program for the service. That photo of Miss Ollie again. Staring at her accusingly.

"Darby," Mary Beth scolds. Like she's everybody's mom, not just Noelle and Angeline's.

"What? You could have come to the meetup at the park, that's all I'm saying. I'm allowed to say that, aren't I? You said so yourself."

What's that saying? Friends are the family you get to choose. Only, at a certain age, it's: Friends are the family your kids choose. Rhea wonders if she'd make the same choice under different circumstances. Maybe not, but also maybe.

"I've got a lot on my mind," says Rhea. How's that for the understatement of the year.

A uniformed police officer stands next to a Black woman in a gray pantsuit. He leans over to talk in her ear. The woman listens carefully to what the officer tells her and turns to look at something. As she does, Rhea can just make out the metal lump of a gun holstered underneath her blazer. A steely cold nestles between Rhea's shoulder blades. Then she realizes what the something is that the woman has turned to look at: Rhea.

Their eyes meet. And Rhea feels her edges crackling like a paper set on fire, the perimeter burning first, a red, uneven line, brittle ash crumbling around as it spreads.

"Yeah, I think we all do." Darby is doing her exasperated voice, the one she usually reserves for discussing Lola. "Apparently they found footprints at the scene. Did you know that?"

The woman in the gray suit breaks eye contact first and, with that, the connection she shared with Rhea severs, too. Rhea could have been imagining it. But her heart's beating faster, practically out of her chest.

Mary Beth—"Who told you that?"

"Asher's dad. The lawyer. You know the one, he wants everyone to *know* he's a lawyer. That guy. He does have very nice hair, though."

Rhea's eyes ping-pong between her friends. Heart still hammering.

"And they don't know whose?" Mary Beth's nose is running and she seems to be out of Kleenex. She keeps trying to dab in the most ladylike way possible with the back of her hand.

"They were . . . small." Whoever told Darby—an administrator, another mother, a teacher—probably did so in confidence, but that was their mistake.

Rhea glances toward the woman once more to be sure she's moved on. "But that would mean one of the children found her," she says.

Mary Beth covers her mouth with her hand. "Which one?"

All three of them turn to watch the four-year-olds gathered by the reflective pond. Bodhi picks petals off his rose and drops them into the water. Some of the parents take pictures of their children dressed up in their fancy clothes, which feels wrong, but unsurprising. Wild-haired little Bex sits on the ground and starts to cry.

"Exactly." Darby watches with a frown as Lola lowers herself to her stomach in front of the pond—her skirt lifting to show a sliver of white bloomers—and sticks her fingers into the water, then splashes. "That's exactly what I'm afraid of—what it will take to figure out who saw what."

Mary Beth's face buckles, as though the scaffolding in it was never quite structurally sound.

"You okay?" asks Rhea.

Mary Beth gives a teary nod. "I think I should go get Noelle. I feel like she probably needs me."

Darby and Rhea stay put while Mary Beth toddles away, a tad bit unsteady on her feet. "And then there were two." Darby shrugs. Despite Rhea's best efforts and her most prickly loner instincts, she still manages to get glued together with certain people. With Marcus, with Mary Beth, with Darby, perhaps now, even, to some degree, with Miss Ollie.

When she's around Darby, she feels like a better mother in comparison; she knows that's mean to think, but it's true. If Mary Beth were still standing here, she probably would keep her mouth shut. Because Mary Beth would say, *How do you know Erin Ollie wasn't her real name? Why were you looking into her background? What were you doing there?* Darby's a safer choice.

"Darby," Rhea begins, because it all comes down to karma and her chakras, those mysterious spinning wheels of power located along her spine that have been thrown completely out of alignment.

But Darby has started talking at the exact same time and, as usual, her words spill out faster and louder. "What would you do if Marcus went behind your back?" she says.

"What—what do you mean?"

"Like, I don't know." She seems frustrated to have to explain herself. "Something to do with Bodhi maybe. For example. What would you do? How would you handle it?"

Rhea rears back. Does Darby know? Has she somehow found out that Rhea has indeed gone behind Marcus's back about Bodhi—worse than that even? She bristles. "I—"

"Shh, shhhh." Darby pats Rhea's hand and she stops talking.

"You ready to go?" Griff skulks up out of nowhere, doesn't even acknowledge Rhea's presence.

"Yeah, sure." Darby pats her bag and her pockets, checking for her cell phone, her wallet, absentmindedly. "We can head out. Let us just grab the kids, okay?" She shoots Rhea a meaningful look.

Apparently Rhea gets no say in the matter.

Five minutes later, the adults ride home in oppressive silence while Lola and Bodhi point out an ambulance, a motorcycle, an old-timey truck. Lola is hungry. Bodhi is hot. Rhea wants out of the car before there are meltdowns. When she waves goodbye to the Mortons, she feels worn out, clear down to her bones.

At least, she's learned one thing, all credit to her strong sense of womanly intuition, and that's that Griff Morton is lying about something. She'd bet her life on it.

"Go change out of those clothes," she tells Bodhi, once inside. "And make sure you put them back on hangers. Those are new."

She crosses the kitchen and tips a ceramic vase. A tiny bit of silver skitters along the countertop like a tooth. She slaps her hand over it to stop it from falling into the sink. There, she holds it up to the light as she's done every day since *The* Day, and on the right straight edge she checks, sure that when she looks hard enough she can still make out the orange-red hue of a few drops of sticky blood.

FIFTEEN

▼

For as long as she can remember, Mary Beth has kept up a chatty rapport with God. She's not one of those kneel-at-the-foot-of-her-bed Christians. She prefers to keep her Lord and savior up-to-date with the frippery of her daily routine:

Dear God, remind me to pick up fragrance fillers for our plug-ins at Target today while I'm in the store. Dear God, I'm struggling with whether to allow Angeline to get the Bratz dolls. I pray that you'll speak to my heart and help me to make the right decision. Dear God, this weekend's episode of SNL made me laugh out loud, thank you. Jesus as a best friend is actually true for Mary Beth.

But the conversation has dried up.

For the past week, it's been radio silence and she can't exactly blame God. It's been five days since anyone set foot in Little Academy. What she hopes—if she dares to—is that a return to school might herald normalcy and a restoration of her silent blabber. She has a lot to catch God up on and it's not all good, she's afraid.

Today, the school issued an oblique message regarding the returning class of fours:

Parents,
If your children have exhibited biting behaviors, we ask that you please plan accordingly. The front office is available for questions and guidance. Don't hesitate to reach out.
Welcome back in this time of grief and healing.
Yours Truly,
Mrs. Parker

On the day school reopens, she arrives early by design, clasping Noelle's hand tightly on her way into the building. Today will be difficult, yes, but not insurmountable with the right mental outlook. *I can do all things through Christ, who strengthens me.* Look! It's coming back already.

"Do you remember what we talked about?" she asks as the door to the academy swishes shut behind them.

The most striking thing is how nothing's changed, really. Children's artwork has been left untampered with on the walls. There are all the usual signs to wash your hands before entering the class. Sneeze into your elbow. As if the scariest thing that could happen here is catching a cold.

"It's not polite to speak about what happened to Miss Ollie," Noelle recites with impatience.

"That's right. Miss Ollie questions are Big Feelings questions and they should be handled by mommies and daddies only. Got it?"

"I know."

Still, Mary Beth wants to hear her say it again. "Noelle—"

Mary Beth stops, not dead, nothing so dramatic as that, but she just sort of peters out along with all the words that were flowing right along with her.

"What, Mommy? What?" Tug. Tug. Tug. Will Noelle ever stop tugging?

Directly in front of Mary Beth, the door to the supply room stays closed. It's almost as if she expected it to have vanished. Like the school would have demolished the place with a wrecking ball.

That would have been nice.

The industrial paper cutter sliced clear through the bone of two of Miss Ollie's fingers, just like they always warned the children it could. Mary Beth tries to picture how this could have possibly unfolded. Why would two fingers have borne the brunt?

Something must have happened. Miss Ollie must have been startled into bumping the open paper cutter. Or there was a struggle. She might have reached back behind her, to the counter, where the cutter sat, for support and—

But of course that's not what killed her. Two fingers gone does not a dead teacher make. For the parents, the students, the rest remains a mystery. Maybe it's better that way. Or maybe it's worse.

Mary Beth stretches her hand out and touches the door handle. Twists. Locked. "Oh." She hesitates. Her heart jumps rope.

"I think it's *so* important—" Mary Beth swears her skin jumps a millimeter off her skeleton at a voice mere inches behind her. "—that we're coming back to school sooner rather than later. Sorry, it's just me," says Megan Tolbert. Zeke and Noelle immediately latch on to one another, and Mary Beth tries to act happy to see them.

"Sorry," says Mary Beth. "Jumpy today, I guess."

"Same here. Zeke has been so needy ever since—well, you know."

Mary Beth reads between the lines. Five days of being nibbled at and slurped from has left her feeling like a human vending machine. The only moments in those days that she managed to feel like a discrete person were, paradoxically, the ones during which her husband was inside of her. She remains determined not to miss a day in bed with Doug. When she isn't careful, when she doesn't stay focused, it feels like she's sliding uncontrollably this way and that around her slippery life. It makes her practically seasick. But the 30-Day Challenge presents achievable goals. Fixed points on the horizon. See? Everything's okay; everything's fine. She's having sex.

"Well, today will be good," says Megan. "The kids need routine."

Routine, yes. They just need to get through the days. Check them off, one by one, the way she and Doug are doing, but also not at all the same way, naturally.

Noelle and the other children at Little *will* grow out of it, this disgusting blood habit. As far as she can tell, the trajectory of a child with the syndrome is roughly the same as that of a more run-of-the-mill biter. Twelve months. Eighteen, tops. That's not forever. It'll just feel that way.

One day the tooth fairy will arrive for the fours of Little Academy and pluck their vicious peewee teeth out from beneath pillows and then maybe this will all be over and it will feel like something the parents collectively made up, like the tooth fairy herself.

"*We* need routine." Darby joins them. Five days without childcare and look at them, all knocking at the gates, murder be damned. They're supposed to be *enjoying* their children. Are they all really so eager to be rid of them? Mary Beth prefers not to answer that.

Instead, she thinks about the small footprints found at the scene, what they might mean for her, for all of them.

"Is everyone returning?" Megan asks.

"I think so," answers Mary Beth. There seems to be little choice. Parents work. Parents have lives and custody agreements and other children. These are all things that must go on and so must the school.

"How does that saying go?" asks Darby. "If you stop traveling and doing normal routines, you let the terrorists win. That's how I'm thinking about it. We can't let the killer control our minds."

Megan pales at that. A killer on the loose. A murderer. Haven't they all been trying not to think about that? Haven't they agreed not to say it out loud?

"It's like marriages," Darby continues, oblivious to the way she's marched into a dark room and conjured Bloody Mary for them in the mirror. "In the face of tragedy, they either pull together or fall apart." She flicks her fingers to sign an explosion. "We need to pull together."

Mary Beth's throat feels parched. She's second-guessing whether this is a good idea. Perhaps she shouldn't leave Noelle after all.

"Mary Beth, you're always so good at that." Megan's medical badge swings from the pocket of her scrubs. "Please, tell us what you need. Anything. We're there."

Mary Beth needs a damp cloth. She feels hot and that swimming sense of seasickness again. "Not me," she croaks out. "We just need to worry about the kids."

One by one, each of the mothers in attendance hangs a backpack on a peg and sends their kid into a new classroom, off to a new, not-dead teacher, each trying to ignore the alarm bells ringing in their ears, trying to employ the same steadfastness they've previously reserved to tune out children's questions while trying to carry on adult conversation, the same bullheaded fixity required to neglect their own needs. Somewhere Miss Ollie's killer is on the loose and that somewhere may, indeed, very well be here.

Mary Beth scales the two flights of steps to Pastor Ben's office on the church campus. The ministers' offices are located on the third floor of a stone building off the beaten path. It's an old structure, barely renovated, with window air-conditioning units and floors that still smell faintly of pine. She knocks on a white door on which gummy old paint drips have long since dried, one coat done over another without taking the time to sand in between.

"Just a moment." The cast-iron knob turns noisily in the joint and then Pastor Ben is there right in front of her in all his Pastor Ben glory. She thinks: *You can't think Pastor Ben's attractive after Miss Ollie's been murdered.* Only she can and she does. She remembers the way Erin mooned after him, asking her, the older woman, the sexless mother, what she thought of Ben. A lot, she should have replied. She thinks a lot about Ben.

He greets her wearing a clean undershirt and jeans, ushering her in as he moves for his own chair across the way.

The seat beneath her is an old schoolhouse chair with metal legs and a curved wooden back, designed to be stacked. Her bottom feels slippery on it. "I wanted to talk to you about—about what happened to Miss Ollie," she says.

He drops back into his chair, his intense green eyes fastened on her. "I'm listening."

"I want to make sure you're prepared to protect the children." She tries not to sound overly dramatic, but it feels important. They're a community, after all, they need to act like it. "I probably shouldn't be telling you this, but a child's footprints were found beside the body." She can't bring herself to mention Miss Ollie by name.

"A *child's* footprints?"

She nods. "We have to think one of them might have . . . found the body and been too afraid to say anything." A four-year-old witness. More than one person will be after these children. To say nothing of their . . . condition, which, in truth, only seems to be getting more pronounced.

She's begun spotting the signs before Noelle has a craving. She gets this yucky collection of saliva at the corners of her mouth, a bit like a dog. Mary Beth is disgusted by it. She would never admit that to anyone, but every time she sees that pool of spit shining on either side of her daughter's lips, she feels repulsed, revolted by her own child. She mentally quashes the image in order to continue without gagging.

"I was thinking it wouldn't look good for the church, the class unsupervised, doesn't feel safe. They'll need an advocate," she says. "Someone to make sure that nothing's blown out of proportion by the press. Or the police. This syndrome that many of the kids are exhibiting. It's harmless. Rare but there are other cases, not just ours."

Harmless, so long as you don't put too much stock in the bruising track marks that can now be seen running up the length of some of the parents' arms. Innocuous so long as you don't mind a few muscle cramps and a touch of lethargy, but honestly show her a parent who doesn't experience both regularly.

Ben's eyes are kind and his voice gentle. He'll be a father someday. "I hate to think that this is affecting them. They're so pure of heart at that age. I have a nephew. He turned one a couple weeks ago. I got to help him smash his cake."

"With your work on the youth center and your commitment to children, knowing we have your support for our class would be incredibly meaningful." A morale boost, really. She can share with the other parents. Maybe in an email blast. That feels very on brand for her. She likes it already. "You might even come to talk to the children. Help them to process their grief, spiritually, I mean. Heaven!" She exclaims too loudly, the idea just occurring to her.

Oh god, she sounds deranged. It seems that ever since that day, her moods have been swinging wildly this way and that. She can't get a proper grip. Then again, that's more or less what she's doing here. Why she's assembling the skills of Darby and the support of Ben and the co-operation of the other moms and dads. She'll get a grip and then they'll all move beyond this terrible, no good, very awful day, just like in that picture book Angeline loved so much at Noelle's age.

"You could talk about heaven, I mean. And guardian angels. I think the kids would really like that. I think," she says, the emotion building in her throat, "we all would."

SIXTEEN

▼

Rhea could have sworn she dropped Bodhi off at school two minutes ago when suddenly the alarm blares on her phone, signaling the time for pickup. She isn't ready. She should have more to show for her free hours. And yet, they've come and gone.

They started with a call from Margot, phoning her back. *No, there was nothing to do about the angel investor. Yes, they would think of something. Don't worry, it would all work out. Rhea would see.* But Margot was just saying shit, going through the motions. Rhea is one client on a roster of many.

After that defeating call, she sat amidst the detritus of packing boxes and customer service emails and new products and, not for the first time, couldn't move, or didn't want to. She felt mulish. Didn't care that the wallet she was punishing would not be some big-dollar corporation, but her own puny time bank. Still, she didn't want the moment she dropped off her son at school to feel like the starting gun of a sprint race, one she would be required to run, at that breakneck speed, for more than the length of a whole Iron Man competition.

So what did she do? Did she, at least, jog? Move in the general direction of the finish line? Surely, help would arrive somewhere along the way. No. She wasted entirely too much time staring at a financial statement that wasn't even hers, that, in fact, had nothing to do with her.

It was like a Wikipedia rabbit hole, once she started she couldn't stop clicking and clicking and clicking. Rhea isn't one for rabbit holes. That's more Darby's domain. Darby, who listens to podcasts about serial killers and, occasionally, regales Rhea with stories of women (always "upper-middle class," which just means plain old rich) who've gone missing and kids—always white—who've been kidnapped from their beds.

Were it not for the fact that she had been required to prepare and pore over the very same forms for Terrene to show to the angel investors, the documents she found open on Miss Ollie's laptop computer might not have caught her eye. They would have seemed written in a foreign language. But now she translates the pluses and minuses, the dollars and cents, the transfers and deposits, and keeps coming to the same conclusion: Either she's not reading it correctly or the columns don't add up.

From her seat on the floor, she stretches her back. She could ask Marcus. He'd know the answer straightaway. But if she tells anyone where she got the forms and when, there will be questions no one but her could answer and she's afraid she's not ready to.

The moment she steps back on campus, she feels it again: an intense wave of déjà vu.

Her vision swims. She's overcome with the bizarre impression that she's a former version of herself. The version that sat trembly-handed behind her car steering wheel, shaken from what she'd just done. It's all there, shimmering at the edges of the pristine campus underneath the same baby-blue sky that portended disaster just over a week earlier.

The other mothers mill about in front of the entrance and she thinks: *Not today. Please.* She doesn't want to parent by committee ever, but definitely not today. They might like to cluck and fuss and flap their mama-bird wings, but that's not Rhea's bag, sorry not sorry.

"Rhea." Darby lifts onto her tippy-toes, pushing her head into Rhea's line of sight. "Did you hear me? Are you even listening?"

Rhea blinks, unsure of how long Darby has been trotting beside her.

"I said, did you see Lena's shoulder?"

"Why would I have seen Lena's shoulder?"

"You have to see it. You just have to. Lena, come here." Darby raises her hand and beckons her over. Lena is quick to oblige.

"Rhea, oh my god, Rhea, do you want to see something?" Lena's got those crunchy curls from too much supermarket gel and it smells like expired nail polish when she leans over and peels a bandage from her shoulder, all before Rhea can answer yes or no. She would have answered no, for the record.

"Lena!" Rhea exclaims on impulse.

The skin on her shoulder is so swollen, shiny, and red that it looks like her arm's made of plastic. There are six puncture wounds, four of which are a deep purple-black and a yellow pus-like mound curves around one of the other wounds. The sight makes Rhea's teeth ache. "That's infected. You need to do something about that. Pronto."

How she let it get to that point in the first place, Rhea has not one clue. These mothers are out here caring about the strangest things like matching bows and monograms and middle school wait lists when they're still serving their kids up full doses of animal growth hormones in their sippy cups. It doesn't make sense and, when Rhea has pointed this out—she's entitled to express her own opinion—they either lie and say they don't or act like they're too busy to worry about every little thing.

"It isn't Bex's fault." Lena replaces the bandage. "I took too long with the blood draw. But, you know, it's not exactly paint by numbers. I'm kind of funny about needles."

"Yeah. Of course," says Rhea. "I know." She doesn't.

"Just don't mention anything to Maggie's mom, Roxy. She's *anti*." Darby leans in. "She sent Megan this long email about the potential long-lasting behavioral consequences of indulging *cravings*. Apparently Maggie is still pure as the driven snow and Roxy is very proud of it."

"Well, I'd put some aloe vera on that if you have some," Rhea says to Lena. "And I can bring you some turmeric milk to drink tomorrow."

Lena looks awash with relief. "Remind me to come to you when I have questions, Rhea." She contorts her body to examine her wound again.

"It's nothing," replies Rhea. Though, it's not nothing. Rhea knows what she's talking about. Sure, she knows the thoughts that go through people's heads when they meet her and Bodhi together. *Oh, poor thing, I can't imagine being a single parent. Does she work two jobs? How does she make ends meet?* But with natural parenting, Rhea feels in control. 'Cause you know she's doing all the stuff that good, two-parent homes are doing, plus some. Which means she belongs here even more than some of the other mothers who "belong here." "You know, maybe it's worth consulting a naturopathic doctor to offer some advice about what's going on with the kids." Rhea is feeling generous. "I could suggest someone."

"Do you really think our kids biting is *natural?*" Darby says. "You know, come to think of it, I don't think I've ever really understood your preoccupation with natural, Rhea. Aging is natural and I am deeply uninterested in it."

Yes, well, that's obvious, thinks Rhea a little less generously. She looks at Lena and Darby and at the other squawking mothers and it occurs to her: *No wonder this biting epidemic is getting out of control.* The mothers are handling it the same way they handle everything else with their children, fighting against the organic order of things. "I think our bodies are made to be listened to, including those of our children," Rhea answers smoothly.

Oh, she knows that look, the one she's getting from Darby right now, the one like *here comes the crazy attachment-parenting bitch.*

"The way I see it, there's nothing wrong with nurturing. Fostering the connection through bodily closeness to raise secure children." She speaks slowly and uses soothing tones, knowing this might not be what they want to hear. She remembers there had been a reaction when she pushed for a chemical-free brand of hand soap in the classroom. "Maximal parental empathy and responsiveness, that's the way I deal with Bodhi."

One of the reasons Rhea gets along with Darby more than the other moms is that she's not defensive or threatened by Rhea's parenting. She always looks kind of awestruck.

"God," Darby whines. Her expressions often land comically close to Lola's. "You make it sound so *simple.*" As if this is the worst thing it could be and then—and then, too late, probably way too late—Rhea hears what she's said.

That's how I deal with Bodhi. They don't think—do they think—?

"Excuse me." A woman approaches, interrupting before Rhea can. She looks like one of the "corporate mommies." The type who clickety-clacks through the halls in pencil skirts and silk blouses and looks Very Busy. "I'm Gabriella Becker with KNT News." Rhea's spine stiffens. "And we're covering a story about the tragic murder of Erin Ollie."

Darby rushes to fill a potentially awkward silence, like potentially awkward silences are the leading cause of death in women over thirty. "Hi, I'm Darby. I think the administrative staff would likely be better positioned to answer any of your questions and I'm sure the family—" What family? "—would appreciate privacy at this time." Darby sounds like a cruise director, but a friendly and competent one, so there's that.

"Understood, but we're interested in hearing from *parents* because of the firsthand experience with the reported spate of juvenile vampirism at Little."

"I'm sorry, the what now?" Lena's go-to move is that hard-blinking thing.

"*Vampirism,*" Darby enunciates. "Like vampires. Some of the other parents at school are calling our kids the Little Vampires, apparently. It's not very kind," she tells the woman.

"And they're not vampires." Rhea keeps her face expressionless. "I thought you said you were doing a story on Miss Ollie."

"We are. But the situation in your class is highly unusual and the timing—we'd like to interview some of the mothers of the affected—"

"Did she say 'infected'?" Lena directs the question to Rhea and Darby like Gabriella's not even there.

"*Affected* children." Rhea sees right through that tone. "Have any of your children shown signs of vampirism?"

"We're not answering that." That's one difference between Rhea and the other parents at Little; they're all so deferent to authority, every last one of them. "Who called you?" Rhea asks.

"I'm sorry, I always protect my sources." Gabriella's smile is a tightrope wire. "Listen. We're going to run a story on the school with or without parental involvement, so the only question is whether you, as the mothers, will have a voice." Gabriella Becker hands them each a business card, along with the implied threat, before she clicks away.

They watch her go. No one can even muster a comeback. So that's how it's going to play.

"Rhea should be the one to give the interview," says Lena.

"Me? Why me?"

"*Because,*" Lena continues, as though this isn't the most she and Rhea have spoken all year, which Rhea hasn't minded. "Because of what you said. Empathy and secure connections. You have such a peaceful attitude about it. You'll make this look—like you said—natural."

"I didn't mean . . ." Rhea begins. "As a single mother . . ." She veers off in this direction automatically because there are times pulling the card is useful. When she said that's how she dealt with Bodhi, she meant *in general.* Bodhi isn't a biter. *Bodhi would never.* The thought snaps into her head.

But another is occurring to her. A deep, dark, niggling thought.

"She's right." Darby reenters the conversation like a small bulldozer. "You're so laid-back about this whole thing. And. And!" She claps. "You could promote your business. It's perfect. You could promote Terrene. It could be really good for you, Rhea. It's like the whole organic, granola lifestyle. If you package these diagnoses up like that, then that would be so much better. For the kids. And you. Don't you think? You're the perfect poster child."

"I don't know." Free advertising for Terrene. On television. Her investment advisor's voice mail rings in her head. *A broader reach.* People do worse to get ahead.

"That's free PR advice from a formerly very well-paid publicity executive," says Darby, clearly proud of herself, as she should be, because maybe Darby built a career and it had taken a hit after having a child, sure, but she had a job that people recognized and respected. Not to mention the financial support of a husband, even one who is kind of a dick. And Rhea has debt and a dream and a desire for a life for herself and her son bigger than the one she came from.

She'll never know if she would have suggested the same thing had Darby not stolen the words out of her first. If the last two weeks have reminded her of anything, it's that you can never know what would have happened had you chosen differently.

That night, Rhea paces the kitchen of her duplex, her body tense and restless.

Bodhi barks and sniffs at the floor, pretending to lick his hands. He twists around her ankles. "Bodhi," she says, feeling guilty for her tone. "Bodhi, can you stop that? I can't walk."

He pants and pretends to sit obediently. Then he howls.

"You're going to make me trip." Her fingertips hook into the back of her neck and she tilts her face up to look at the popcorn ceiling. The day is heavy on her. She's got too much on her mind. Doesn't know what she's going to do about any of it.

"Baby?" she asks. "Can I ask you something?"

He nods, still half in character.

"Are you having certain cravings? Impulses, I mean, like . . ." She searches for a better word. "Are you hungry for anything special? Something like that?" She scoops him up and straddles his legs around her stomach. He squirms, but she holds him fast with her sinewy muscles. "Some of the kids in your class, their bodies have been talking to them, telling them that they need to—to take a drink from their mommies and daddies. Their arms or legs, for instance. Are you feeling like that's something you might be wanting to do?" Rhea keeps her spirit open and accepting. She concentrates on radiating warmth and beaming light toward her son. "I want you to know, it's okay. You can bite mommy. It's okay this time. If that's what your heart is telling you to do."

"No." Bodhi pulls a face, like someone's held a camera in front of him and said, *Now a silly one.* He thrusts back against her and she wobbles. "That would hurt you. Biting is bad."

"Right, usually, that's exactly right. But if you need blood, if that sounds good to you, I understand."

Bodhi sticks out his pink little tongue. "That's disgusting. Gross."

"But." She strokes his head. "Maybe you'd feel better if you tried."

"Yuck! Yuck! Yuck! *Blech!*" He spits, cheeks puffing out. Droplets spot her forehead and she grimaces.

He isn't going to bite. He doesn't want to. He is still her precious little koala boy, wrapped around her body. Her miracle son. Her moon and sky.

And yet there are seventy-five shipments that needed to go out today still sitting in her living room, tinctures that should have been mixed, a backlog of customer emails that require responses.

She lets her son slide down the length of her so that she can rummage through her purse and there, buried deep in her satchel, she finds what she's looking for—Gabriella Becker's business card.

SEVENTEEN

▼

"Go ahead and fire me now," Darby exclaims, tossing her hands up in the air. "I'm no good. Mine don't look anything like the pictures." She winces as she kneels on the hard-tile floor of room 401, squinting between her makeshift attempt at an egg carton creature and the Pinterest printouts provided by Mary Beth. It's strange being in a new classroom, almost worse than if they'd remained in Miss Ollie's original.

"Read the instructions." Mrs. Tokem, the class's new permanent substitute, patrols the tables, dipping to untwist the caps off glue and scoop glitter into neat piles.

Nothing has made the students and parents alike miss Erin Ollie quite like the presence of Mrs. Tokem, an older, cropped-haired woman and frequent poster to political threads on her neighborhood's Nextdoor forum.

"Are you sure you want a sloth, Zeke?" Darby dots the back of two googly eyes with Elmer's glue. "How about a crab? I think I could probably have some success with a crab."

But Zeke doesn't want a crab. In fact, none of the children assigned to Darby want crabs or turtles or snails or hatching chicks or anything else that might remotely be in her wheelhouse.

Darby's knees crackle like that old brand of children's cereal when she stands. She saunters over to Mary Beth, who is busy stockpiling materials at the craft counter. "Tough crowd out there," she says, glancing over her shoulder. "So far my best attempt has been the walrus. Looks like you got a nice caterpillar. A caterpillar makes sense for egg carton animals. I need more egg cartons, by the way." She leans her elbow on the surface like she's waiting for her drink order at a bar. "But can you please be careful with that thing?" She points to the box cutter. "It looks lethal. Also, I'm probably not cut out for this."

"We all have to pitch in," Mary Beth murmurs. They glance over at Mrs. Tokem. The parents agreed—or at least no one publicly objected—when the school director issued a call for "parental supervision" in the fours classroom.

And so she is doing the thing where she pretends to be at her desk in her home office when she is really here doing arts and crafts while surreptitiously answering emails from her phone just quickly enough to keep from pissing off anyone important. She's trying to avoid giving all mother-employees a bad name, but she's just one mother and she has only her own children and it is really hard to worry about all those other mothers with their faceless children and tricky jobs and so, for the most part, she forgets about them and allows people at the office to whisper about how this is the problem with hiring moms.

Trust her. She's had a corporate job in a fancy office. And there is more online shopping while sipping a fresh cup of coffee uninterrupted than anyone cares to admit.

Mrs. Tokem comes over to collect a new assortment of pipe cleaners and they fall silent until she's passed.

"Did Lola pick a science fair project?" asks Mary Beth, as if Miss Ollie didn't die.

"I can't even believe we're still doing science fair projects," says Darby. She's been feeling protective of Lola's now-dead preschool teacher. She's been struck by the frequent urge to jump around and wave her hands and say, *Hello, what are we doing exactly?* Are they just, like, accepting this? Miss Ollie is dead. Oh well. Take it in stride. Life moves on.

Darby isn't sure she's ready to move on. She has questions. So many questions that keep her up at night, staring at the ceiling fan, staring at her husband.

"They still have to learn. They have to be prepared for kindergarten."

"I guess," Darby grumbles. "Lola's doing octopus. I haven't bought the poster board yet." Because poster board requires a trip to an actual real-life store, and yet for some reason she is expected to acquire poster board on top of dealing with an eighteen-month-old and a four-year-old and a job and a murder and the provision of a steady supply of her own blood. Pause for applause. Anyone, anyone? She didn't think so.

"Octopus what?" Mary Beth clicks open an X-Acto knife.

"She wants to learn about octopi—*what*? She's very into marine life. I thought it was good. What's yours?"

"Noelle's doing a storm in a glass. It's just a small demonstration, nothing fancy."

Darby shrugs because, in her opinion, storm in a glass doesn't sound any better or worse than octopus. It does, however, sound less native to a four-year-old. "Hey, why aren't Lola and Noelle sitting together, do you think?" Darby asks.

The one positive is that Lola was thrilled to see Darby in the classroom. It was like being a celebrity, for both mother and daughter. All of Lola's classmates shouted things like, "Lola, your mommy is here!" and "Where's my mommy? Is she coming?" And Lola wanted to hold her mother's hand and show her activity centers all the way up until it was time for everyone to take their seats for craft time.

"Hm. Not sure," Mary Beth says distractedly.

"I keep wondering what that meeting would have been about," Darby says. "So strange. I think it's going to bug me forever. Like an unfinished sneeze."

"I've been trying not to think about it."

So has Darby, but no use. It was one of the only things she could think about, in fact. Why didn't Miss Ollie show up to their meeting? Was she already dead by then? Did something come up and she changed course to deal with something or someone somewhere she shouldn't have been?

There are extra security features in place. Parents and staff wear badges. Kids have wristbands. The parents are paying for an off-duty officer to stand outside the building during school hours. But the parents are talking. What if the killer has a badge? Darby shudders at the thought, at what it could mean.

So far none of the children have come forward with any new revelation. The image of tiny footprints in blood feels more and more like a product of the rumor mill than genuine news.

"Do you have any idea, though?" Darby asks about the meeting.

"Not really."

Darby watches her friend. "Miss Ollie didn't give you any kind of *hint* when you picked up Noelle?"

"*No.*" Mary Beth looks up from the cartons and out the window. It's a nice view over the garden from here. Beyond it, the iron-cross steeple of the church's independent chapel cuts into the sky.

"What came up?" Darby asks without agenda. Or without *much* of one. "I mean, why'd you have to cancel?"

Again, Darby pictures her feet on the cream-colored sidewalk, her winding path through the campus, through the church building, faster and faster she went until she had nearly broken into a run. By the time she returned to the classroom, sweating and disoriented, there was no adult present, just a lingering scent of something that Darby remembered distinctly smelling like eucalyptus.

"I had a doctor's appointment I forgot about," says Mary Beth. "And my head, you know, not cooperating."

"Oh," Darby says. Though Mary Beth keeps a calendar. A pretty, floral day planner. Not just the impersonal one on her iPhone. "Is everything okay?"

Mary Beth sighs, as though for the first time ever Darby has finally succeeded in cracking her nice-lady exterior, as though Darby has *annoyed* her. "Everything's the same," she says.

Darby bites her tongue for a full five seconds, but it's no use, she has more to say, Darby always has more to say. She's what's referred to as a *verbal processor.* A therapist once told her, so she knows it's true. "It just, it makes you wonder, though, doesn't it? Do you think she'd still be alive?"

Mary Beth fiddles with getting the X-Acto knife through a pulpy section of the carton. "I don't know. I can't think that way." Her eyes glisten.

Fantastic. She's upset Mary Beth. She's a monster. Because Mary Beth actually is this nice, deep down, underneath it all. Darby has run tests.

"You know, I think I'll go ask the girls why they're not sitting together," offers Darby.

Technically speaking, she's abandoning Zeke, but his sloth truly is beyond all hope. "It's kind of fun being part of the class," she says as she makes her way over to Lola when, out of the blue—

"SHIT!"

Darby stiffens and a mere foot away Mrs. Tokem snaps to attention. The fact that Mary Beth was the one to utter—no—*shout* an obscenity seems to have short-circuited the hardwiring in Darby's brain.

"What's wrong? What happened?" Darby can't take one more bad thing.

"Shit," Asher parrots, followed by a few of the other boys in class. "Shit, shit, shit."

"That's not a kind—" Mrs. Tokem scolds.

Mary Beth holds up her trembling hands. She's cradling her right with her left, thumb pressed into the webbing of her opposite. Two thick streams of blood dribble out over her nail and slide down her wrist.

Darby's molars press hard together. "You poor thing."

Mary Beth's nose wrinkles as she squeezes her eyes shut. "Is it bad?" she asks, turning her chin. "I can't look."

The whole scene unfolds in the most eerie silence save for the sound of Mary Beth sucking in air through her teeth like a beached fish. Darby won't know how to describe it when she tries telling Griff later this evening—*Creepy, menacing, my actual spine tingled.* Absolutely one of those had-to-be-there situations.

Mary Beth seems to be exhibiting a gravitational pull on the children, so drawn are they, these small bodies, to her. Bex wears light-up sneakers that blink purple with each step; the peach fuzz around Asher's lips glistens with fresh saliva; Zeke squirms.

Darby clocks the moment Mary Beth opens her eyes enough to register what's happening before her. She pulls her elbows in, making her body into a tight package.

When Darby pushes inelegantly through to her dear friend, she takes her hands in hers, cupping the pulsating wound, and glances out at the gathered children. Their pupils are their own black holes. Lola's breaths are shallow. Noelle's nostrils flare.

"Class—it's just a little boo-boo." Mrs. Tokem's voice strains. "Ms. Darby and Ms. Mary Beth have it under control. They are grown-ups."

Darby surveys the kids—the straight edges of their Chiclet teeth—and tries to remember how many baby teeth are in a child's mouth. Eighteen? Twenty? Now, there would be a useful science fair project. Multiply by ten. Two hundred little teeth.

She puts her arm around Mary Beth's shoulder. "I think we better get you out of here," she murmurs into her ear.

Mrs. Tokem taps shoulders and brusquely demands kids return to their seats or else lose Privileges.

Mary Beth nods once. Brushstrokes of artificial blush stand out on her blanched cheeks.

"We'll just pop out," Darby says, already hightailing with Mary Beth to the door amidst at least one or two howls of protest from the class.

In the hallway outside the room, the air feels at least three degrees cooler.

"Shhhh, it's okay." Darby hasn't had a look at the hand yet, but chances are it will be okay. Between the two of them, it's rare for Darby to be the one in charge. Once at a gymnastics birthday party, Lola threw up in Darby's lap and Mary Beth jumped into action. She threw away Darby's cell phone case and went to fetch paper towels from the bathroom before Darby even came out of shock. But this time, Darby's pleased to find she's rising to the occasion. She leads Mary Beth down the hall and tests a knob. It gives.

"That's the—" Mary Beth protests, but they both fall silent. "It was locked before . . ."

The supply room is as clean as if nothing ever happened. A rainbow of construction paper, stacked bins of glue sticks, primary-colored finger paints, Popsicle sticks, ziplock baggies, latex gloves, and hand sanitizer await.

"I think it's okay. We'll just be a minute." Darby eyes a bucket of gleaming grown-up scissor blades behind Mary Beth. "Here, let me take a peek."

Mary Beth's fingers are chilly to the touch.

"Oh, it's not even that deep." Darby leans down for a better look, turning Mary Beth's hand this way and that.

"Ouch, that hurts." Mary Beth retracts her hand, reproachful.

"Sorry. I did tell you to be careful. I think you can get away without stitches. I bet the nurse has some of that surgical glue or maybe a butterfly bandage. It's in a tricky spot." Darby turns to search the cabinets for a first aid kit, trying not to think about Miss Ollie, *only* able to think about Miss Ollie. Where was her body? Is she standing in the same spot?

"I'm an idiot," Mary Beth groans.

"You're not an idiot." Darby's voice is muffled within one of the cabinets, which has the comforting but tickly smell of dust. "You're a distracted mother."

"That's a terrible thing to say."

"It is?" Darby's fingers close around the shiny red-and-white plastic of a first aid kit and she hauls it up. "Why?" Inside, she finds a coil of gauze. "Hold still," she commands.

"Distracted mother means *bad* mother. They're the same thing. Synonyms. Distracted mothers are the ones too busy playing Candy Crush and having affairs with their pool boys and popping Vicodin to notice her kid's just wandered into oncoming traffic. Watch it." She glances down to where Darby is sloppily wrapping her hand up in the white gauze, crissing and crossing with no particular pattern, displaying exactly the same level of skill as she had with the egg carton creatures. If nothing else, she's consistent. "Is that me?"

"That's a bit harsh, don't you think? Our eyes are supposed to be laser-focused on our kids at all times? No texting while mothering, is that it? I don't mean the Vicodin part, but distraction just means not giving something your full attention. Do my kids really need my full attention or can I have some of it, too?" Darby finishes up her terrible bandaging handiwork.

"Did you see the way they looked at me?" Mary Beth's white shirt has several dark smears of blood across the front that might not come out. "Even Noelle."

"Maybe especially Noelle. But that's to be expected. You're her mom."

Mary Beth examines her fat, clumsy hand. "You don't think they would have . . ."

"No. Of course not. I mean, they're four."

The color is returning to Mary Beth's face. She smooths her hair into place. "That's true," she says, her voice still weak. "I mean, they still get put in time-out."

Excuse me, but do you mind telling me why the kids are lined up like they're expecting a firing squad?" Darby has just led Mary Beth back to the classroom to gather their giant mom purses, it being the end of the school day anyway.

"Darby." Mary Beth tuts.

Well, they are.

Mrs. Tokem glares back at them. "There's a situation. Someone *defecated*." The way she says it gives Darby goose bumps. *Defecated*.

"Yikes." Mary Beth cradles her injured hand. "Who?"

"Just what we need," says Darby, who actually does smell something funky now that she's had a moment to process.

"That's what we're trying to figure out," says Mrs. Tokem. "It's disgusting."

"God," Darby mutters as she scans the room. "I hope it wasn't Lola."

Mary Beth points. "Oh dear." A fresh, steaming pile of you-know-what is in the cubby beside Mrs. Tokem's polka-dotted lunch box.

"What's going on now?" Lena Feinstein is the first to arrive for pickup and Mary Beth does the honors of finding a polite, non-shaming way to catch her up.

"Oh my *god*. There has to have been *witnesses*," says Lena. Wait. How is Lena so confident that it's not her daughter? It feels unfairly presumptuous. Does Bex have a bulletproof anus? The Arnold Schwarzenegger of sphincters?

"But how did a child pull down his or her pants and complete his or her business without a single person noticing?" Mary Beth muses.

The same way a teacher got killed, probably, Darby thinks darkly. One thing after another after another after another.

"It was an *accident*," Darby assures anyone who is bothering to listen. She senses another crisis coming on. She reviews where they are in the process. Mitigation, preparedness, response, recovery. Best to skip straight to step three, as it stands. "Not the end of the world." She tries to sound chipper while watching Lola, who is busy scratching a bug bite on her knee. Darby's 99 percent sure that her daughter would *not* mistake a cubby for the toilet, but it pays to be vocally kind in the unlikely event that 1 percent doesn't work out in her favor. "Just so long," she says, circling back to mitigation and preparedness, "as it doesn't happen again."

Mommy," says Lola, "did you know octopuses eat their arms when they're bored?" She's been in good spirits ever since the unsettling incident in the classroom, which wasn't even that unsettling—probably.

At the changing table, Darby wrestles Jack's arm into a onesie while he attempts to crocodile roll out of her grip. "Is that true?" She breathes heavily.

"It's true." Lola beams. The fringe of her bangs has grown too long and keeps getting caught in her dark fan of eyelashes.

"Then that's definitely going on the science fair board." Darby tugs the zipper from Jack's big toe up to the base of his throat. "There." He squeals as she scoops him up. He feels like a sausage busting out of its casing—is she feeding him too much? His chubby arms wrap around her neck and his hand pats her back slowly.

Her heart swells with a fierce love, written in the marrow of her bones and preserved and reinforced through billions of years of evolution. She thinks: *My life without these two small, small people wouldn't be worth living.* Maybe it's the intensity of that feeling itself that's so terribly exhausting—will science ever know?

"Is Noelle's mommy still hurt?" Lola can be so attuned to other people's feelings, so kind. Once Lola told Darby that when she thought about her little brother she felt like she might cry and Darby had to explain the phenomenon of happy tears. She wishes other people had a window into the Morton house to witness these moments with Lola, but then maybe everyone wishes for that because whose children ever perform on command? Child actors, she supposes.

"She'll be fine." Darby sets Jack down on the floor, but Jack has other ideas. He wants up, up, up. His fingers pinch and he begins to whine. "Just a scratch," Darby reassures her daughter. She groans with the effort of retrieving Jack again. "Thanks for asking."

From outside, she hears the welcome rumble of the garage door opening and out of habit, counts the seconds until she hears footsteps mount the stairs and the door open behind her. "Daddy!" Darby cries with unveiled joy, having promised herself years ago she would never refer to her husband as *Dad* or *Daddy*.

Lola's look unexpectedly darkens. She tucks her chin into her chest and glares out from behind her curtain of hair, mood changing as if by an unseasonable gale. "Daddy, go away," she says.

"That's not very nice, Lola," Darby chides. "We don't tell people to *go away.*" Not that Lola's harsh words are altogether a surprise, since Lola does this, shifts her alliances, her temperament, her favorite ice-cream flavor, with no warning. But it can still sting. "You're late," Darby says.

Griff takes off his backpack and shoves it onto the kitchen counter. "I know, I know, and I'm only home for a minute, sorry. I have to get back to the salt mines." As though he's a 1940s movie star. "I came to say hi and bye."

She pulls a face. "Why come home at all?" They follow Griff back into the master bedroom, a parade of Mortons.

"Why the third degree?" His belt buckle clinks as he slips out of his pants. "I wanted to change into more comfortable clothes and I wanted to see you all." She gives him a look. Sometimes she feels like his mother, too. Or maybe not just sometimes. "Nobody's going to be in the office this late at night."

Griff crosses the room to the dresser and Lola hisses when he gets too close while Jack claps—people, like art, really are subjective.

"What's gotten into *her*?" Griff wrestles his arms and head through a T-shirt. "Has she been fed?"

"We ate dinner before you got home. It's in the fridge." Darby's a terrible cook; Griff's much better.

He glowers without any real heat behind it. He looks like Lola. "That's not what I mean."

Lola's eyes flit between her parents.

"No," Darby says coolly.

"No?"

"*No.* I'm not a vending machine. And it's not like it's life or death— Why are you doing hair pomade if no one's going to be at the office?— she'll be fine."

"I don't understand why you don't want things to run smoothly."

"I do," Darby protests. "I just have different ideas about how to get there."

The bulb of understanding lights up in Lola's eyes. "I'm thirsty, Mommy. Please. Please, I'm thirsty now."

"Fantastic." Darby smacks her thigh. "If you just hadn't mentioned it, it wouldn't be an issue."

Griff even smells good. He checks his watch. "We can't just starve her."

"*Starve* her? I thought we agreed we were going to be more strict with her, stick to the rules?" Though she's not sure they've been able to reach any agreement at all when it comes to Lola. Still. They're at least supposed to pretend to be on the same page. She would have liked to hear Rhea's answer to her question. What *would* Rhea do if Marcus went behind her back about Bodhi?

"I—" His eyes flick up as if she's taking a long time to understand a simple concept. "You know how it is. Sometimes there's no good answer. We're quick to give her an iPad on the airplane. I've seen you give her a cookie before dinner just to keep the peace. We've gone months with you letting her sleep in our room even when it was driving me insane."

"I see someone's been burning up the dad text chain again."

"They have *wives*, Darby. It's not like they're unilaterally making all the decisions in their households. I'm just saying—"

"I'm thirsty!" Lola has the floor and she knows it. Jack does, too, which is why he climbs up from his knees, using Darby's waist to sway unsteadily on his porky little feet. "Please!" Lola shrieks—not a five-alarm bell, but certainly the smoke alarm is starting to beep. "I said *please!*"

Everything was not terrible just a few minutes ago, right? That was this house? She's not mistaken?

"You brought it up, you deal with it," she says, disappearing only to return moments later to her unruly brood.

She shoves the cardboard box of supplies recommended by Megan the nurse into his arms. She's used them twice, but both times gave her a serious case of the creeps.

"I don't know how to use these."

She rolls her eyes and digs through the box until she has her assortment of instruments laid out.

He waits in his short-sleeved T-shirt, his forearm facing upward. "Hold still." She should put her reading glasses on for this, but her reading glasses have been abandoned upstairs and does anyone understand how unappealing it is to have to retrieve things from all the way upstairs? She cleans the surface and unsheathes the needle. Then—

"That was violent." Griff's upper lip curls on one side.

"I have no medical training," she says. "And yet somehow everyone thinks this is still a great idea. The *best*." Fucking Rhea and her attachment parenting. Wielding words with positive connotations: *empathy* and *compassion* and *secure connection*. Darby feels as if she is giving so much of herself, her body, her mind, and yet the frightening thing is, everyone else seems to be giving more. It scares her. Literally horrifies her. She wants to scream.

She pokes him again and the most she notices is a clench of his abdominals; like, where is this sudden stoicism when he comes down with a cold, hm?

Lola—and Darby swears this is true—sniffs the air. Sniffs it. Like a dog or a rabbit. And says, "I want Mommy."

"Mommy's not on the menu this evening," says Darby.

The storm returns to the little girl's face.

"Oh my god, what's the point?" The needle stays stuck in Griff's arm as he swipes his fingers through his beautiful head of hair.

"Don't look at me," Darby says. "Jack, shoot, what do you have in your mouth?" She bends, turning her finger into a fishing hook, and scoops around in Jack's mouth until she comes out with a feather from a pillow. Lucky again.

Griff, noticing the floppy needle stuck in his skin, does the honors. "If she'd let *me* be the one to feed her, don't you think I'd be more than happy to do it?"

"Not really, no. You weren't really itching to wear condoms when we were trying to prevent pregnancy if I recall, which seems like sort of the same thing."

You would think Darby had spoken in a made-up language.

"I'm sorry, I really have to go," Griff says.

The parade of Mortons exits the bedroom. Griff finds his keys, his phone, his wallet.

"Are you going to worry about Lola or not?" He points at their daughter. "You can't just let her cry."

"I'm always worried about Lola." There it is again, this idea that *good mother* means worrying, constant, expert worrying. The energy in her house is combustible.

"How can you be late anyways?" she asks Griff as he lurks by the back door. "I thought you said nobody was going to be up at the office."

"It's work, Darby. Someone's expecting me." He picks up Jack and gives him a perfunctory kiss on the cheek.

"Did you know that in France it's illegal to contact an employee with work communication outside of work hours? People need distance and off-hours, that's the point. People need to disconnect."

"This isn't France." He pushes Jack back into her arms. She feels like a docking station for a Roomba, her children occasionally leaving her, but never for long, always called back home, and it makes her inexplicably sad that the most apt description of herself is in the form of a vacuum cleaner.

She can't even imagine what she might accomplish with two free hands.

"I was talking about *me*."

There he goes. She turns back, the Mortons now minus one, and when she does, she startles to find how close by Lola is standing. An arm's length at most and staring, there, with the flat black-hole pupils and the flaring nostrils and the glistening lips that Darby felt times ten in the classroom today, and Mary Beth's question from earlier that day returns to her: *You don't think they would have . . .*

"Come on." She rolls up her sleeve and prepares a new syringe, fresh cotton swabs, and all the other accoutrements. She thinks: *How is anyone supposed to lose weight, go to the gynecologist, clean her closet, and parent gently? How does any mother do anything?* "Tell me something else about the octopus," she says.

Minutes later, Lola's expression has cleared, leaving behind the precious daughter who gives clammy hugs and counts bouncing her knees as dancing. "After a girl octopus lays eggs," Lola says, voice husky, "she quits eating and just lays there and gets real skinny until her babies hatch and then she dies."

"That's terrible," Darby says, inching back against the sofa cushion. She cuddles her daughter. "Poor mommy octopus."

TRANSCRIPT OF INTERVIEW OF WITNESS, LINCOLN SAWYER

APPEARANCES:
Detective Wanda Bright

PROCEEDINGS

DET. BRIGHT: Lincoln, did you like Miss Ollie? Was she a nice teacher?

LINCOLN SAWYER: Most of the time.

DET. BRIGHT: Most of the time, okay. So sometimes you didn't like Miss Ollie?

LINCOLN SAWYER: Yeah, because sometimes she was mean.

DET. BRIGHT: What did she do that was mean?

LINCOLN SAWYER: She took away my scissors privileges.

DET. BRIGHT: Ah. Your scissors privileges. Just yours? Or the whole class's?

LINCOLN SAWYER: Mine and Tamar's.

DET. BRIGHT: Why'd she do that?

LINCOLN SAWYER: Because I got in trouble for cutting Tamar's clothes.

MRS. CHELSEA SAWYER: When was this?

LINCOLN SAWYER: Um. Yesterday or last year?

MRS. CHELSEA SAWYER: Why would you cut up Tamar's clothes?

LINCOLN SAWYER: We were just trying to be werewolves!

MRS. CHELSEA SAWYER: Lincoln, you know—

DET. BRIGHT: Which one, Lincoln? Was it last year?

LINCOLN SAWYER: Tomorrow I think? But after Christmas.

DET. BRIGHT: I see. How did that make you feel, Lincoln, when Miss Ollie took away your scissors?

LINCOLN SAWYER: Mad. Real, real mad.

DET. BRIGHT: I'll bet. And what do you do when you're mad?

MRS. CHELSEA SAWYER: Now, wait a minute. What are you imply—

LINCOLN SAWYER: I growl. Like this. *Rawwwrrrgrrrrr.*

DET. BRIGHT: Oh, wow, that is scary. You do that a lot, Lincoln?

MRS. CHELSEA SAWYER: Like he said, he's into werewolves. He howls at the moon before bed. That kind of thing. Kids go through these phases, you know—

DET. BRIGHT: Let's try to let Lincoln answer, okay?

MRS. CHELSEA SAWYER: Not necessarily *okay*, no.

DET. BRIGHT: Did you want to hurt Miss Ollie, Lincoln?

LINCOLN SAWYER: No. I like Miss Ollie.

MRS. CHELSEA SAWYER: See! This is what I'm saying.

DET. BRIGHT: Lincoln, I'm going to ask you a question that you might know the answer to and if you do, you might think you need to keep it a secret, but I'm going to ask you to be honest with me, okay? Can you do that? Do you know who hurt Miss Ollie?

LINCOLN SAWYER: Yes.

DET. BRIGHT: You do? You know who hurt your teacher?

LINCOLN SAWYER: Wait, no. Sorry. I thought you said something else.

DET. BRIGHT: What did you think I said?

LINCOLN SAWYER: I thought you asked if I know who the Poop Bandit is. 'Cause that's the secret I know the answer to.

EIGHTEEN

▼

This is a bad idea.

Rhea's concern over the merits of this particular idea comes way too late. The studio comprises two red chairs, angled slightly toward each other, stationed atop a raised platform. Box lights point down at her from the ceiling, making the T-zone of her face go shiny. Behind her, a flat-screen TV mounted to the flimsy temporary wall displays the orange-and-white logo for KNT News.

She pulls out a small tube of roll-on oil she's stashed in the pocket of her skirt, glides it across her wrist, and inhales the healing scent of eucalyptus.

"Five minutes," the producer warns, and still Rhea stays fixed to her seat.

Gabriella Becker joins her on the chair directly across from Rhea, pulling notes into her lap and leaning on one arm, all comfortable, like she lives there. "The interview," she says, without looking up from those notes, "will go exactly as discussed, so no need to worry about a thing."

"And you'll mention Terrene? You'll . . . give me a chance to talk about it, right?"

Gabriella's big brown eyes flit up and Rhea holds them like, *Yeah, I said it.* "Exactly as discussed."

The night before, Darby prepped her. Get in front of this story, control the narrative. Humanize their children.

Rhea almost told her then. She could have said: *Darby, it's not true, Bodhi isn't a biter.* She thought if anyone would take it in stride, surely it'd be Darby. But then she noticed the tissue-paper-thin skin below Darby's eyes and how it had purpled. A little bruise seeped along the crook of her elbow, surrounding a pinprick. And Rhea changed her mind.

For the first time, she researched Renfield's syndrome online, picking at the scab of the internet until it bled out the information she needed. A graveyard of adult sites, grown men and women doing little more than playing pretend, wishing there were such things as vampires and hobbits. There were pictures of pentagrams, a graphic image of a goat with its throat slit and a naked man posing with his tongue out next to it, and Rhea thought: *Well, do it then, drink it already.*

The children were different. Of course they were different. Without agenda. *A benign but disturbing medical condition,* one author wrote. An obscure Christian organization Rhea never heard of referred to one group of five-year-olds' urge to drink blood as a biblical temptation, a precursor to masturbation and women's menstrual cycles.

Rhea, who has never had a healthy fear of computer viruses, clicked through her search engine indiscriminately, unafraid to visit the hits on pages five and six and seven, which was where she found an abandoned Reddit thread, the last entry dated five years earlier.

Parents. Offering advice, tips, and tricks for raising children with pediatric Renfield's as though this is the popular breastfeeding website KellyMom.

Rhea read about parents developing Pavlovian responses, wincing whenever they had to brush their child's teeth or wipe their noses or feed them applesauce. She skimmed casual stories of otherwise precious, normal children with bloodstained teeth, picking scabs, foraging for maxi pads, and sneaking into mommies' bedrooms for a late-night nip.

She noticed something about the final entry, the one that was written five years ago. It wasn't written in the same back-and-forth style as the others. It was posted eleven months later than the original flurry. No one responded to the late post, which read simply: *They will get blood, one way or another. Let this be a warning.*

In the studio, Rhea squints into the spotlights. "About how many people watch, do you think?"

Gabriella bends the papers on her lap, then folds her hands over them. She has a helmet of shiny hair and fake eyelashes that look like spider legs up close. "Considering this will be aired straight through on our parent affiliate, it'll be roughly two million." The corners of her lips twitch. So this isn't a big deal *just* for Rhea, then; good to know.

Rhea wriggles now, trying to find a comfortable position for her back. Seven minutes, that's all she has to get through. Seven minutes without screwing anything up.

This is about risk and reward. If she can get through this, she'll have scored free promotion to literally millions of viewers, and this promotion is about to be buzzy as hell. Watch out; those investors are going to be lined up around the block.

"Three . . . two . . ." The producer with the headset holds up his fingers; there's one more chance to change her mind, to do the right thing. But do the right thing for whom? "One." Before it's gone.

"I'm Gabriella Becker sitting down today with the mother of one of the students at Little Academy, the preschool where a young teacher's brutal murder on campus has rocked the nation and brought to light a mysterious medical condition that's been plaguing the student body. Meanwhile, a killer remains at large. Rhea Anderson, welcome."

"Thank you for having me, Gabriella."

"Rhea, as the mother of one of Erin Ollie's students, maybe you can start by telling us a little about your and your son's experience with her as a teacher. What was she like?"

"Wonderful." There goes Rhea's first lie. "She had an infectious smile. She loved the kids . . . like they were her own. I miss her already." Followed swiftly by the second.

"I'm sure you do. I'm hoping, then, that you can also shed some light on the strange set of circumstances that led up to her death. There's something of a phenomenon affecting a number of the children in Erin Ollie's class, isn't that right? Some are calling it a vampire syndrome. What can you tell us about that?"

"I can tell you it's not referred to as a vampire syndrome—"

"But the children drink blood. Correct?" Gabriella's maple, artificially curled hair slides over a silk jewel-toned blouse perfect for TV as she tilts her head.

They will get blood, one way or another.

"Some of them have certain cravings for blood." Rhea won't give her the satisfaction of coming off as defensive; this will not be that kind of interview. "Or maybe just what's in blood, like some sort of vitamin deficiency, or something like that we don't—"

"You mean like maybe they're anemic and this is their reaction?" Gabriella cuts her off again.

"Not anemic per se." Rhea aims for thoughtful. "We tell children in lots of different contexts to listen to their bodies. When we're potty training or trying to instill healthy eating habits, for example. When we nurse babies. And this is no different. It's all very natural and should, we believe, be normalized."

"I'm sorry? You think that drinking *blood* should be—did you say normalized?"

"I think lots of aspects of parenthood can feel foreign and even scary at first," says Rhea, feeling the seconds of the interview slip by, wondering when and if Gabriella is going to get to Terrene. "But then you realize how beautifully and organically designed the whole process of becoming a mother or father to these children is and you think it's not just worth it, it's incredibly rewarding." That was the line she practiced. Stay on message.

"Incredibly painful, I imagine, too."

Rhea lets a beat pass.

"How have you handled your son's condition at home?" Gabriella tries.

She knows then. Call it intuition, call it a vision, call it whatever you like, but Rhea understands all at once that she was a fool to think Gabriella had any intention of segueing into talk of Terrene. She isn't even here to give her side of the story, not if Gabriella can help it. She's here to fuel more headlines, and, once the camera has stopped rolling, Gabriella Becker will apologize, not particularly profusely, for running out of time and make hand waves at how KNT News should have her on again sometime, only they'll both know that sometime will never get there.

So Rhea lets the moment stretch another uncomfortable second before she puts Gabriella Becker out of her misery by answering, "With love." She smiles, and not that TV dinner smile straight out of the frozen section that Gabriella holds so dear, but one pulled from her heart when it faces toward the sun. "In fact, I have based a whole company on love. Love for our natural bodies and our natural universe. It's called Terrene; that's T-E-R-R-E-N-E." Rhea keeps going, no pause, careful not to leave so much as a breath in which Gabriella can jump in. "And if you go to the website"—Rhea then makes sure to enunciate each letter of the web address—"you can find all sorts of natural, accessible, easy-to-use homeopathic remedies that embrace pure, organic restoratives. We are not trying to cure. We want to help find balance in a natural state. That's our philosophy at Terrene. And," she adds, "at Little Academy."

The tendons in Gabriella's neck are guitar strings, but then the camera probably won't pick up on that, just as it doesn't yet reveal the way Gabriella's lipstick bleeds into the emerging creases around her lips or the crusting concealer beneath her eyes and in the crevices beside each nostril, but someday in the not too distant future it will. For now, what's done is done and Rhea's the one who's seen to it.

"But someone *killed* your child's preschool teacher. Aren't you worried that this natural state you speak of could actually be . . . deadly?"

"Deadly?" Rhea's voice flatlines. The words from the message board surface—*one way or another.*

"Yes, deadly. That's the question."

Rhea pictures Bodhi's face and the mound of his tummy over pull-ups at night and the downy hair just starting to grow on his legs. The way he still calls TV *TB* and pronounces except as *expect.* And then she laughs. The laugh of a second-rate daytime talk show host. Ha, ha, ha. "They are four years old, Gabriella. Four. Tell me what four-year-old could overpower a grown woman. That's what I'm trying to get through here. These are normal children. They weren't bitten by radioactive spiders. They're just our kids."

"Well, you can certainly at least understand the public's fascination. Did your son's pediatrician offer any kind of prognosis? How long do medical professionals expect something like this to last?"

"He didn't offer a prognosis," Rhea answers carefully. "No one can know for sure when the children will grow out of this stage, but one thing I do know is that as far as I'm concerned, there's no rush. We have to support them. That's not just our duty, but our honor as parents. We are joyfully available to meet their needs, all of them, whoever our children turn out or desire to be. Anyone who would think to do otherwise isn't fit to be a parent, end of story."

Rhea's ears ring on the way home from the interview, the end of which she can hardly remember, and Bodhi's with Marcus until who knows when, for as long as she wants, maybe. How long might that be?

Her palms are sweating on the steering wheel. She still has so much left to do. Today, she set the wheels in motion. Terrene in front of two million people. Time to get to work.

No sooner has she had this thought than her stomach growls. When'd she last eat? She groans, remembering the curbside groceries she was supposed to pick up yesterday. Only she never made it. And those groceries are long gone by now. She'll be lucky if they refunded her money.

Her phone rings—*brrr, brrrr, brrrrrr.* "What's up?" she asks Marcus.

"Why didn't you tell me Bodhi has this—whatever this—this thing is—this syndrome? How come this is the first I'm hearing about it?"

"You watched the interview." A cacophony of honks sounds up ahead.

"Of course I did. You were on TV."

"Don't freak out," she tells him. "It's all good."

"I'm not freaking out, Rhea. But medical stuff, that stuff I get to know, too. You can't shut me out. His pediatrician wasn't concerned about anything specific?" It's not that Marcus wouldn't go to the doctor appointments, it's just that Rhea's two ears work perfectly fine and she doesn't need two more.

She crawls past an exit-sign billboard, one she'd usually ignore except that today those golden arches seem like some kind of sign from the universe. A beacon atop a slippery-sloped hill.

"Bodhi's doing fine," she reassures him. "Just fine. Now, you know I know what I'm doing when it comes to Bodhi."

"I don't get it. With me, he hasn't asked for any—you know—he wasn't showing any signs he needed—"

"Blood," Rhea supplies. "Marcus, I'm sorry. But I really can't be doing this right now."

"I know you're busy."

"I am. I really am. We can talk about this later." Or never, that'd be cool, too. "Sorry. I've got to go. I'm getting another call—" She punches the "hang up" button on her touch screen, pulse thumping, and points all the air-conditioning vents at her face. Marcus. Why didn't she factor in Marcus? As if she doesn't know the answer to that perfectly well.

Breathe, Rhea, breathe. She is a force. She is not a reaction to a force. And she can deal with Marcus.

She veers onto the exit ramp and before she knows it she's looking up and down the giant, light-up menu filled with dollar deals and Big Macs. Rhea pulls on her big sunglasses. She keeps looking around like somebody might be tailing her—she is something. It's not like this is an actual thing. Not something she does.

It only takes one more thought of her mounting to-do list, her shrinking time, and her empty refrigerator to work up the courage when the lady's voice crackles through the speaker box, "Welcome to McDonald's, may I take your order?"

By the time she gets home, she's already destroyed the evidence, but she's still startled by the three thudding knocks that sound on her door. For one stupid second, she thinks: *They know.* But who and what exactly would they have found out? At this point, she could make that particular question a multiple-choice quiz. Whoever it is pounds with the side of his or her fist, not knuckles. *Bang, bang, bang.*

"Rhea Anderson?" a woman's voice calls from the other side. *Bang. Bang.*

Rhea tiptoes across the rug to peer through the peephole. On the other side of the door stands the woman in the gray suit.

NINETEEN

▼

Earlier, Mary Beth sat in her pajamas and powered off Rhea's KNT News interview with a heavy feeling in the pit of her stomach. *Normalize children drinking blood*, Rhea said on national television. And Mary Beth thought: *Normalize?* Is that really where they've landed?

It does seem in vogue to normalize things these days. Mental health. The conversation around STIs. Body hair. Which all sound well and good, but Mary Beth feels like a fuddy-duddy when she finds herself still on the fence about others and finds still more examples completely absurd. Normalize talking about money. Normalize consensual incest. Normalize walking on all fours! Normalize sharp-toothed vampire children. Where does it end? She wonders as much later, when the sky has been spitting down all morning and on through half the afternoon, when the news reaches the mothers of Little Academy that Asher's mother, Katia, has been sent to the hospital for a blood transfusion.

It goes without saying that this is very bad news.

She can still taste the butter from her bagel this morning. It might have gone a little rancid on the dish. She still ate it, though. That's where she's at, by the way, should anyone want to know her whole mental state. Rancid, but only a little, and down the hatch it goes.

Actually, minutes before that, she'd begun to feel kind of pleased with herself in a vague, non-self-congratulatory way because the turnout for "Who Feels Sad?" with Pastor Ben Sarpezze is good, exactly as she expected it would be. Ten families from Little, and not just Miss Ollie's class, have arrived and taken a seat in the school's multipurpose room, which is basically just a big, empty room with blue carpet and a wall of full of mirrors.

There's Marcus with Bodhi, and both of Lincoln's moms are in attendance. Of course Megan has brought Zeke and Roxy scrolls Instagram next to her daughter, Maggie.

"Can I please sit here?" She watches Noelle ask George's mom, polite and proper as if she were one of Kate Middleton's kids, though not the oldest, who Mary Beth thinks she remembers throwing a tantrum in public—poor Kate.

Noelle is wearing a navy-blue T-shirt dress with a cat appliqué that Mary Beth had purchased online just this week. One of Mary Beth's favorite relaxation activities is putting items in her digital cart. Knee-high socks for the girls. Straw purses that will go with anything. Sunglasses. Vintage knickknacks for that weird open spot on the built-in shelves. Bamboo-thread throw blankets. Half-zip pullovers for Doug. She debates and debates, adding them one by one only to leave them there hanging in the ether until they sell out or disappear or she forgets about them entirely. It soothes her, thinking about all those things she could own.

But this week, she hit "order." Window after window, she scrolled through her tabs on her browser and confirmed purchases. Each time, she felt a rush of adrenaline charging her up. Again and again and again. The boxes started arriving on her porch this week. Anyway, she thinks it's good for Noelle to have a new outfit for today, for a time like this, something to make her feel spiffy.

"That one's mine," Mary Beth pointed out proudly to Pastor Ben when he arrived. The adorable little girl in the brand-new dress. *Isn't she pretty? Isn't she well-mannered and clean?* she wanted to say.

And then came the news about Katia. A mother in the hospital, a school of other mothers doing the math. *She's going to be okay. She's going to survive* feels like thin consolation, especially when some say she refused a feeding. Didn't offer a vein. Listened to her child scream and cry and wail for her and responded like a father who pretended not to hear his baby wake up in the wee dark-thirty hours of the morning. She didn't make herself—What were Rhea's exact words?—*joyfully available.*

"Doesn't your heart hurt when you hear your child crying for you?" they used to ask each other at the beginning when their littles were all much littler. "Can't you just not stand it?"

Apparently, Katia had withstood. The attack happened in the middle of the night, when Asher snuck down from his bedroom, the way another child might go in search of a glass of water. His mother's screams must have startled them both because he latched on to the edge of her armpit and wouldn't let go. Likely nicked an artery with his canine. Her husband thought she was being murdered—which was nearly true.

The vocabulary was undeniable—an *attack*. A child attacked a grown-up and now all the adults in the room seem to be unsteadily attempting to catch their balance.

Pastor Ben pulls up a flimsy folding chair in front of the small semi-circle of kids. "Who here is sad?" he asks with a frown.

Several of the parents tentatively raise their hands along with the children.

A year ago, she sat in this exact same spot, part of the three-year-old curriculum to celebrate Dr. Seuss's birthday. (*Mud, crud, dud, flood, blood*, she rhymes in her head.) Now she listens to Ben describe angels and beautiful songs and a white-fluffy-cloud version of the kingdom of heaven.

"Have any of your families ever moved to a new house? Or maybe when your grandmother comes to stay, she has to go home to somewhere far away? You can think of it like that," he suggests. "Miss Ollie came to visit and then it was time for her to return home to heaven."

"Do you mean Miss Ollie *moved* to heaven?" Maggie crawls onto her knees.

What Mary Beth likes about Ben is how seriously he's taking the children's questions, as though they are brilliant, insightful questions from esteemed theology professors, not four-year-olds. He trains his entire being on Maggie and her Instagram-scrolling mother. "She did. You can think of it as her new home address."

Ah, that's perfect, thinks Mary Beth. Very palatable. Just what they need.

When she floated the idea of the counseling session to the other parents, she endeavored to be thoughtful and respectful. She used a very inviting font in her email. *All faiths welcome, please come if you believe your child may benefit from processing the pain with a trained professional.* No pressure. That was her other motto. It's just that kids listen to strangers far better than they listen to their parents; it's a scientifically proven fact.

"Will she send us postcards?" asks Zeke. "Because my grandma sends us postcards from Boca sometimes."

"Great question," answers Ben, all Johnny-on-the-spot. "She will, she definitely will, but they'll be heaven postcards. Like when a bird sings an extra-pretty song or a flower blooms or a butterfly flutters by, those are heaven postcards and you can bet some of those are from Miss Ollie when she's thinking of you."

This morning, as she was walking onto campus, Mary Beth saw a bright red cardinal perched on the playground fence. *Did you send that, Miss Ollie? Was that your doing?* Mary Beth uses the gauze still wrapped around her poor hand from the X-Acto knife incident to dab at her misty eyes.

"But—but— If Miss Ollie moved, how come she didn't say goodbye? How come we didn't have a party with pizza and cake?" Sweet Bodhi. He might have developed a bit of a crush on Miss Ollie.

"Miss Ollie would have loved that, wouldn't she have? She probably loved cake. But she loved all of you even more. The truth is, some people know way ahead of time that they'll be leaving to go to heaven. They can pack their bags and talk to their family and write letters, but others don't get any warning at all. They have to go right away. They have no choice. But you know what? She told me to tell you all goodbye and to keep an eye on each and every one of you so that I can let her know how you're doing."

"But how will you do that?" She can tell Bodhi is on the verge of tears. He is slurping his air. The heave of his slender back gives him away—he really is so skinny. His shoulder blades stick out from underneath his T-shirt like discarded chicken wings.

"I'll pray. That's why I'm a pastor at the church. It's my job."

She doesn't envy Ben. Does anyone really want to explain to a room of complete innocents that life isn't just unfair, it ends? And yet here he is, assuming the mantle, volunteering as tribute. Ten young faces gather round at an event that, in less capable hands, could usher in the end of their youth and he says, *Not today, not on my watch. I've got you.*

So there you go. Once again, Mary Beth is proven right: People are nice. People are good. She can remember that, even in the midst of murder. In fact, she must.

Ben asks the kids to get up off their bottoms and follow his lead. First, he slumps his shoulders and takes a walk around the group looking dejected. He looks like a sad, mopey mime. Then, the very next moment, he does a ridiculous jig, his elbows and knees jutting up and down like he's on a marionette string. The kids laugh and then stop short and he catches them—aha!—it's okay to be sad one minute and silly the next. It's okay to feel their feelings. They should normalize big emotions.

Mary Beth is feeling a feeling right now, this very instant. She is seeing Ben in a new light. Not as just some sexy sausage, but a man, a man who is good with kids. And the beauty of it, the perfection of him, hurts her. A lump forms in her throat.

"Excuse me," she announces at the end once the lump has cleared. "Would anyone like to take this opportunity to donate to the new youth center? We're planning a bronze plaque on the front of the building in honor of our dearly departed Miss Ollie."

Every parent raises hands.

I just got off the phone with Asher's dad, Bill," Mary Beth tells Doug at home. "I'm thinking about baking some cookies for Katia, but . . ." She trails off.

It was only last semester that a girl a year below Noelle had developed leukemia and Mary Beth sprang into action, organizing a blood drive and a fundraising effort for medical bills. She baked cookies to offer blood donors after their contribution. But now the thought of more of those delicious sugar cookies feels grotesque. Completely the wrong thing. "I'll think of something else," she finishes half-heartedly, as if Doug cares what she does or doesn't make Katia Brazle.

It's a Friday evening and Doug tips his head back onto an armchair, resting his eyes. The soles of their daughters' shoes squeak as Noelle and Angeline kick them off against the wall of the hallway and jockey for position toward their bedrooms. Usually, they'd be busy arguing their cases for which movie to watch. But for the first time in as long as Mary Beth can remember, no one's mentioned movie night. Instead, the weekend is a hollow stretch yawning out before them, all of their typical plans having vanished in the wake of what happened at Little.

She and Doug used to *live* for weekends, waking to their internal alarm clocks only when it was already light out—can she even imagine? They had dinner plans at restaurants where they didn't have to ask for the check the second the food arrived while still tipping extra to make up for the buffet left on the floor. They were spontaneous. They flew to Vancouver on a Friday night and took a redeye back on Monday. They saw live music and weren't terrified of drinking too much for fear of payback the next morning. There was a thing called brunch and on Saturdays it was the ultimate, that sliver of time before the dread of the weekday slog set in, while Sunday nights were depressing. Five whole days stretched ahead before another taste of freedom. Now the whole construct's been flip-flopped. The weekend stretches long before them. All that unstructured time that had seemed so luxurious in their twenties is a barren wasteland in their late thirties.

All this is to say that the shriek coming from Angeline's room was really just a matter of time, but it still comes sooner than Mary Beth expected. "NoNo! I told you never to do that *again*." Angeline stomps out of her bedroom.

Though the two look like sisters, Angeline's personality is a hard left turn from Noelle's. Angeline is sporty and dominant. When she plays soccer, she runs headlong at the offensive player even when she knows she'll get kicked hard in the shin or elbowed in the stomach. At petting zoos, she gravitates toward all the animals with scales and feathers that Mary Beth herself is a little afraid of.

"I didn't!" Noelle is already crying because Noelle cries as a reflex, never the tough one.

"You did and now it's not working and that's your fault!" Angeline whirls on her sister and points like a prosecutor in the Salem witch trials. *You.* People did warn her what it would be like to raise two girls. "Mom! NoNo used my charger to plug in her tablet and now the charger doesn't remember my tablet and now it won't work and my tablet is dead and I can't practice my reading."

Mary Beth tries to recall whatever invisible protective layer she often musters to make herself impermeable to the girls' antics.

"I didn't touch it." Noelle shrinks into the wall.

Doug peels open his eyelids and drags himself off the cushions to investigate.

"Then how come your tablet is plugged into *my* charger?" Angeline's hands are on her hips. She has serious big-sister energy. Mary Beth can relate. She once had it, too. Maybe still does. "*Your* case is purple. *Mine* is lime green."

"I *said* I didn't do it!" Noelle sticks out her tongue.

"Noelle," Mary Beth warns. "We don't make ugly faces."

"Noelle." Detective Dad returns. "I have to say that it looks like you've been caught red-handed." He holds up Angeline's charger connected to a purple tablet. Aha! "What do you have to say for yourself?" He's teasing. Sort of.

Noelle takes the tablet from her dad and sinks down to the ground with it hugged tightly to her chest. *Here we go.* "My hands aren't red, Daddy, they're pink," she screams.

"Then I'm taking *yours*." Angeline snatches the top edge of the tablet cover and pulls, but Noelle clings to it. "Let go, NoNo. It's not fair."

"It's mine." Noelle yanks back.

"Let goooo." Angeline goes for her sister's fingers and tries to bend them backward.

"Hey!" Mary Beth or Doug says this. She really can't tell anymore;

they've been here before and everyone knows the drill. *"Hey!"* The girls do not care if their parents have had a hard week, if their parents are exhausted to their brittle, calcium-deprived bones. It's not their job to.

"Stop it!" Noelle shrieks.

"You stop it!"

"You're going to break it. It's mine!"

"Ahhhhh!! Ahhhh!!!"

"Ahhhhhhh!"

"You *bit* me!" Angeline howls.

Mary Beth rockets up. "Noelle! No! No, Noelle!" She streaks across the room and yanks her youngest by the elbow so hard her adult fingers leave red welts on the skin. "What are you *thinking*?"

Her heart pounds. A bite. Blood. Red blooms behind her eyes. The picture of Noelle's tongue bright red and how quickly this can all get out of hand.

Angeline's big blue eyes are round saucers. Mary Beth turns her daughter's arms over and back, over and back. "Are you okay?" she demands like she's angry, which she's not.

A slick of saliva smears across her forearm, which Angeline wipes across her cotton dress. But that's it. Nothing else. Just spit.

Mary Beth kneads the spot between her eyebrows, letting her pulse calm. She feels the familiar swelling inside her skull.

"Are you okay, Mary Beth?" Doug is watching her like she's lost her mind.

"Did Noelle bite you?" Mary Beth ignores him.

"Her teeth were on me. I felt it. She was biting down. Grrr." Angeline demonstrates by baring her own teeth; she's missing three.

Noelle doesn't deny it, which is telling given that she denies virtually everything.

Doug kneels in front of Noelle, brushing his thumbs gently over the red marks Mary Beth left, which makes her feel sick with guilt. "We can't bite unless Mommy or Daddy says it's okay, do you understand?" He sounds so reasonable in comparison.

But Noelle's face is already a storm of rain. She scampers off, barefoot, and slams the door. The sound ricochets in Mary Beth's fragile skull. She clutches her head, praying it won't trigger another episode. It's not Noelle's fault. She's a perfectionist, every teacher has said so. Criticism is her kryptonite.

"Suppose we should go in there," Doug says.

Mary Beth sighs. On her worst days, parenting feels like one big "supposed to."

Together, they find Noelle rolling around on the pink gingham bedspread, her cries sputtering like an engine running out of gas. Fat tears dribble down the sides of her face. Noelle's room looks like a French countryside picnic moments after a cargo plane carrying a shipment of toys crashed into it.

She sits down on the bed. "Enough of that." Not her best pep talk, but she's not really at her best. She forces herself to recite the fruits of the spirit: kindness, patience, self-control . . .

But Noelle bicycles her legs against the comforter and arches her back.

Annoyance walks a ladder up the knobs of Mary Beth's spine. She keeps it to herself, perhaps the only thing of hers—her bed, her privacy, her dinner, her ice cream—that the family is perfectly fine with her not sharing. "It's okay. Mommy is sorry for overreacting. I just don't want anyone to get hurt."

Noelle is, as a point of fact, very cute, like cute enough that Mary Beth worries on a regular basis that she'll attract child predators.

Doug stands in the doorway, using the frame to stretch his bad shoulder. "Maybe it would help if we—if she—you know . . ."

She thinks of pitiful Katia in her hospital bed with tubes coming out her arms.

"Sure," she says. "Okay." And then she waits.

"I thought we kept some extra in the fridge?" Doug says.

Extra. Does she have extra? Did she make too much, does she have leftovers? She thinks of all the hours in her life she's spent coaxing her

141

girls to try new foods at the dinner table. *Just one bite*, she says. *Never again*, she thinks. She will never say those words.

"We're out," she informs her husband, "actually." She figures there might be some debate about who should do the honors, but he makes no move to volunteer, which would have been gallant. A bit of a turn-on, really.

"I'll do it," she surrenders, as if it were an open discussion. Her knees pop as she rises from the bed.

"Where are you going?" Doug turns as she exits.

She returns with a sewing kit and a book of matches. She doesn't have it in her to get together all the professional-grade medical equipment a feeding would normally require, she simply doesn't.

She extracts a straight pin and holds the end between her lips as she lights a match and holds the sharp point in the flame, counting in her head to ten. She waves the match into a wisp of smoke and sets it aside before steadying herself. Noelle has quieted, curled in an upright ball against the headboard, her blue eyes watchful over the pink mounds of her knees.

On the second stab, Mary Beth gets a quivering bead of bright red blood. She squeezes it between two fingers until the bubble collapses and a rivulet weaves down her wrist.

Noelle scoots closer until her hip is pressed against her mother's. She waits, fingers in her mouth.

"Go ahead." Mary Beth offers her bleeding hand and with her other, pets the blond mass of wavy hair that falls down her daughter's back. Noelle's lips are soft as an angel's kiss and Mary Beth considers all of the gross, unsexy things motherhood has required of her and tries to figure out where this one falls on the list.

At the sound of a soft grunt, she looks up to see Doug with his eyes closed taking deep breaths in through his nose, out through his mouth—heave-ho, heave-ho.

"What's wrong with *you?*"

"Blood." He swallows hard. "I'm not good with blood. It makes my stomach—"

"That's not true," she says. "You're fine with blood." She thinks she would know if her husband of twelve years had a problem with blood.

He barely shakes his head.

"We've got two children, Doug. You were in the delivery room with both. Blood. Lots of blood."

He opens his eyes but trains them at the ceiling. "I knew I needed to be brave for you," he says with such a dollop of pride.

He does look pale.

Noelle looks up, wiping her mouth with the back of her hand. A smear of pink washes down her chin. Mary Beth is about to blot her own hand on her jeans when Noelle touches her gently. "Mommy," she says. "Can I have some more, please?"

Doug lets out a small gag.

Doug's feet are already on the ottoman when she returns, the remote pointed at the television screen. The girls are in bed. The dishes are close enough to the sink and, as long as you don't squint too hard at the Brandts' floors, they can pass for clean.

"All good?" He looks nervous, but she nods. She's taken care of it. "It seems like we should be doing a victory dance."

She tumbles onto the couch beside him, resting her head on his shoulder. "What's your victory dance like?"

"I twerk."

"Hm. Yeah. I can see it."

He flips through the channels. His breathing is so familiar to her. "Good thing they're cute," he says.

"We're cute. Aren't we?"

"Very."

"I mean not just cute. We've still got it. We're sexy." She recoils. "Sorry. It's impossible to say the word 'sexy' and still sound *sexy*, I guess."

Doug grins. The screen's blue reflections bounce in his eyes. "And to think you nearly got away with it."

"So." She shifts. "Speaking of. Are you ready?"

"For what?"

"Before we get too comfortable." She pushes upright. Post-bedtime sex is a stunt with a high starting difficulty value; one wrong move and either she or Doug could lose their concentration and wreck the whole thing. Every precaution must be taken. "You know? Oh, don't make me say the word again, that'll ruin it all."

His eyes pull away from the screen and he catches her expectant look. Turns out the light is still on downstairs, she's pleased to find. Single vacancy.

Could they do it here? Now? On the sofa? Dare they?

"Oh. Honey." He lowers the remote. "Do you think we could take the night off?"

"But . . ." She sputters. "It's day *fourteen*. We have momentum."

"But I mean, aren't you kind of drained? I know I am. I almost threw up back there."

She bristles. "Yes. Yes. But that's the point. I'm tired of feeling drained, Doug." He's missing it. "We're doing so *well* at the Sexy Back Challenge." She laces her fingers through his.

"There's that word again." Barely a smile this time, definitely no teeth. "Mary Beth, it's arbitrary. We don't have to. There's no prize. Nobody's checking up on us."

"I know."

A long pause.

"I'm sorry." He gives her hand a little shake. "We can. We totally can."

"*No.*" She shakes him off. "I mean, no means no. I'm not going to *force* you." Mary Beth is already leaving him behind on the couch. It's not even that this time she feels silly. She feels irritated. She does not feel *celebrated*, which is one of the phrases Pastor Ben used. She feels like a mom, a mom who doesn't have time to have sex.

"It's not a matter of forcing." Poor Doug is trying and it's not his fault. Not really. "Tomorrow," he says. "For sure, tomorrow."

As if tomorrow is anytime soon.

"I'm going to go take my bath," she tells him.

She is, after all, a self-sufficient woman of the twenty-first century who builds her own Ikea furniture and is in charge of the family's taxes and kills cockroaches with her shoe. Upstairs, she turns on the faucet of the bathtub and undresses. There will be a day fourteen for Mary Beth all right, even if she has to take care of it herself.

TWENTY

▼

My name is Detective Wanda Bright from the police department. I need to ask you a few questions."

Miss Gray Suit and a uniformed officer are scrunched shoulder to shoulder on the tiny porch of Rhea Anderson's duplex.

"Can we come inside?" The man, the one whose name tag reads *Princep*, requests, like he's asking for permission to use her bathroom.

Rhea recognizes the other one from the memorial service—Detective Bright—the one who'd locked eyes with her, scoping her up and down and inside out if she could.

"Can I see your badges, please?" Rhea asks. She imagines Darby or Mary Beth in her same situation, how they would invite the police officers in and offer them tea—sweetened or un-?—and apologize for not picking up the house before they stopped by.

"Of course." Detective Bright keeps it neutral as she pulls out hers to show. Princep taps the insignia pinned over his chest. He's got the piercing blue eyes of Zac Efron and she can tell he's used to smoldering them to get his way.

"Hang on." Rhea grabs a pen and the pad of paper, on which she usually writes her grocery list. She takes down the numbers on each of their badges. "All right. Come on in. What can I help you with?"

They take their places in the living room, like two pieces of bulky furniture that don't match her taste. "We're here to ask you a few questions related to the murder of Erin Ollie."

"I figured." Rhea worries that with her on-air interview she's gone and made herself the spokeswoman and that the next thing she knows, she'll be called as the chief witness for the state, like she doesn't have shit to deal with already. And now add these two with their messy auras junking up her nice, cozy home.

From her perch on the sofa, Bright plants both her feet flat, shoulder-width apart, and leans her elbows on her knees as though she and Rhea are about to talk strategy for the big game. Rhea notices pale white patches of skin on the woman's hands, the beginnings of vitiligo. "So far during our investigation, we've heard nothing but glowing praise about Miss Ollie as a teacher."

"I'm not surprised," answers Rhea.

"But I guess that's not the whole picture," continues Bright. "Because we understand that on the day she was murdered, you lodged an official complaint with the administration seeking her immediate termination."

Rhea feels as though the oxygen is being sucked from the room. *Of course they know,* she tells herself. They were always going to know. There was not going to be a future in which the police didn't find out. She prepared for this. At least that's what she thought.

"I did, yes."

"Why's that?" Bright cocks her head.

Rhea unglues her tongue from the roof of her mouth. "She wasn't the right fit for my son, Bodhi, and the school wouldn't honor my request for a transfer."

"So you tried to get her fired?" Bright feigns shock. Like that makes Rhea the bad guy.

"It was nothing personal. But there's a line she didn't seem to understand existed. She forgot she wasn't the kids' mother. Mothers should have the final say over how their children are raised, not teachers."

Bright nods thoughtfully. "What about fathers?"

"What about them?" The question comes out sharp.

"Should they not get a say?"

"Parents. You know what I mean. *Parents* should get the final say. I'm a single mom, so that's the way I think." She eyes Princep.

Rhea's mind cycles through her options, trying to decide just how much is prudent to say. The way Mary Beth had looked at her in the café the day that Bodhi was bitten, like she was being rash, too quick to jump to conclusions. But now she doesn't have much of a choice. She's got to make a move, now or never. "I found something out about Erin," she says. "Just before she died."

Bright gives Rhea the floor, as in *great, tell us*. In her own goddamn home.

"Erin's name wasn't really Erin Ollie. It was Erin Nierling. She changed it a year ago. No marriage, no divorce, no reason."

Rhea waits.

"We know," Bright says at last.

"You do?" Not that Rhea is altogether surprised. She wasn't entirely sure whether it was common practice to run a background check on a victim; the internet seemed to give two different stories, especially about a victim like Erin Ollie. After all, Erin wasn't the one being accused of a crime. But then, if they knew, shouldn't they be following that lead, tracking down the reason why a twentysomething preschool teacher who looked like a former pageant queen would up and change her entire identity?

"We had to contact the family and we pulled her application at the school. The name change was listed. She handled the whole thing by the book, Rhea. To the letter. There've been no indications of domestic abuse or a stalker or anything of the sort in her past. She may just not have liked the name Nierling. We've been down that road. The question I have is, why have you?"

"I told you. I didn't think she was a good teacher for Bodhi and the school wasn't listening to me. I'm sure she was a kind, well-meaning young lady, but maybe she wasn't meant to be a teacher at all, or not at this school."

"Bad timing, though, wasn't it?" Princep tuts.

"Terrible," Rhea agrees.

"Especially," Bright continues, "because Erin had already put in her notice."

"What?" Rhea's heart is wide-awake now, thumping around her insides.

"Erin informed the school that she'd be quitting," Detective Bright lays out the facts in simple words that don't make any sense to Rhea. "She wasn't planning to finish out the school year."

"You think that had something to do with me? I had no idea she was thinking about leaving. We didn't have some big blowup. I never yelled at her; it wasn't like that. I can promise you, if she were thinking about quitting, it wouldn't have been because of anything I said."

Would it? Rhea has replayed that day over and over again and now she's learning she was missing one of the most crucial pieces of the puzzle this entire time. It's unnerving to think of herself blowing into the school administration office—*Mrs. Parker's with a student right now*—feeling like she was being given the runaround, feeling like she was being treated as less than. Would they have kept Darby waiting? How about Mary Beth? *Do you want to leave a message with me? I can give it to her as soon as she's finished, or you can wait?*

You can tell her I want to meet with her about having Miss Ollie fired, by tomorrow, Rhea told her. And then because she's a real woman who handles her own affairs, she left to tell Miss Ollie the same.

"I didn't know she had one foot out the door." Rhea tries to regain her equilibrium, but her mouth's got other ideas. "I mean, obviously. Or else I never would have—"

"Do you have a history of violence, Ms. Anderson?" She watches Princep pinch his mouth around the question. And she fears the tendrils of heat that have begun to claw their way up her neck. White, hot, familiar.

Detective Bright clears her throat. "Rhea, we ran our own background check. On you."

TRANSCRIPT OF INTERVIEW OF WITNESS, ZEKE TOLBERT

APPEARANCES:
Detective Wanda Bright

PROCEEDINGS

DET. BRIGHT: Zeke, I'm curious, what kinds of activities do you do at school?

ZEKE TOLBERT: Wash hands, journal, playground, wash hands, snack, centers, clean up, circle time, lunch, activities, then the mommies come.

DET. BRIGHT: Is that the order that you do your activities every day?

ZEKE TOLBERT: What's *order* mean?

DET. BRIGHT: Like a schedule. Do you always do wash hands then journal then playground or do you sometimes do playground then journal?

ZEKE TOLBERT: We always do wash hands first and then journal then playground. But I wasn't the calendar helper.

DET. BRIGHT: Okay, so, then, let me make sure I get this straight. You washed hands, then did journal, then went to the playground, then washed your hands again, had a snack, did centers, cleaned up, circle time, lunch, activities.

ZEKE TOLBERT: No.

DET. BRIGHT: No what?

ZEKE TOLBERT: No, it was picture day. That's different.

DET. BRIGHT: Oh, picture day. When was that?

ZEKE TOLBERT: Before chapel.

DET. BRIGHT: I'm sorry, so that day, you had picture day and chapel?

ZEKE TOLBERT: Yes.

DET. BRIGHT: Okay, got it. And during that busy day, when was the last time you remember seeing Miss Ollie?

ZEKE TOLBERT: When she took Lola to see Mrs. Parker.

DET. BRIGHT: Who is Mrs. Parker?

ZEKE TOLBERT: She's the boss of us.

DET. BRIGHT: Why did Miss Ollie take Lola to see Mrs. Parker?

ZEKE TOLBERT: Because that's where you go when you get in trouble.

TWENTY-ONE

▼

The parents of Little Academy four-year-olds are completely fine. As in, they couldn't *be* more fine. And that's on the record. Yes, this year is presenting a new set of challenges, but that's also fine. Because isn't the primary role of a parent to equip a child to *deal* with new challenges? To *model* appropriate emotional responses? To *label* their feelings in order to better deal with them?

"I feel bad," murmurs Mary Beth, who, prior to leaving home this morning, acted as a human buffet for her daughter, triggering the start of another horrific headache episode, if anyone cares. No? No one? Well, okay then.

With a terse smile and without removing her oversized sunglasses, Mary Beth hands the school parking attendant, in his snazzy bright yellow sash, her photo ID. A new protocol. *Fine*, but new. Only a precaution to avoid media stepping foot on campus unannounced; nothing to be alarmed about, but there are a lot of sickos and perverts in the world so *be vigilant*.

Mary Beth glances up to the rearview. Her daughter's ocean-blue eyes stare calmly out the window, her hand resting gently on the head of her stuffed duck, Chicky, who travels shotgun in the car seat's cup holder. A big pink bow rides high on her loose blond curls.

Meanwhile, Mary Beth's own eyes water from the pain radiating out of her stupid, defective eye socket. By night, Mary Beth grows her spreadsheet, collecting any small scrap of information she can find like a mother bird building her nest. She's outlined a few schools of thought currently gaining traction within the Little community.

First are the parents who are certain the problem must be nutrition based, that the children must not be producing enough hemoglobin on their own. However, so far no luck in getting insurance to cover the suite of lab tests required to confirm. Therefore, popular amongst these theorists is a push for a diet high in iron and folate, but as anyone who's encountered a picky four-year-old knows, spinach isn't exactly high on their preferred menu. Others have suggested that pediatric Renfield's must somehow be related to the children's teeth. Mothers compare notes: Did your child use a pacifier as a baby and for how long? Maybe a strong physical urge to clamp down, the way some babies have stronger urges to suck or like how it sometimes feels good to bite on a towel. But no dentist has heard of such a thing. There's an open debate as to the safety of offering kids rawhide chew toys meant for dogs. Then there are the parents—namely those of George, Maggie, and Tamar—who believe that if their child hasn't caught the syndrome, it must be evidence that they themselves know better; that they're doing something right. Of course, they're too polite to say so in public, but the notion is there, floating in the air.

The morning draws Mary Beth to a previously scheduled doctor's appointment, as though it's an inevitable conclusion to the events spinning around her orbit. The gravity of it all.

The clinic doctor's words have been ringing in the hollowed-out shell of her skull: *If you're serious about this, I would suggest being evaluated by a psychologist.* She is serious about it. Deadly. Dramatic measures may be warranted.

In the waiting room, she collects every pamphlet on every condition from seasonal depression to general anxiety disorder to schizophrenia and stuffs them into her purse. She then sits down with the excessive paperwork and begins answering the questions methodically, although she has to wonder if she really is the most credible witness when it comes to her own mental health.

How often do you exercise? That's a tricky one. When the girls were babies, Mary Beth could stroll for an hour, often more than once a day. Nothing stopped the infant tears more quickly than "outside." But "Exercise" is not the current life phase she's in.

Do you drink alcohol? Yes. *How many times per week?* She grimaces. It occurs to her that over time, her answer to this question has gone up instead of down. She would have thought the natural trajectory of her drinking habits would follow the opposite curve, but then when she was twenty-five, she had no idea how long the time between dinner and the girls' bedtime could last. A glass of wine or a breezy gin and tonic is an easy enough way to bring a spot of joy to an otherwise barren wasteland of a two-hour stretch. Just one. Always just one. But when she adds the week up, her answer of five suddenly feels damning.

Are you often irritable? No. Well. Only when her children are irritating or when she's stuck in really bad traffic. Because raising kids does require a lot of driving during rush hour, so she's not sure the question is fair on its face.

Are you ever irrationally angry? Define irrationally, she thinks, pen hovering. Like, she knows she shouldn't get so annoyed when Noelle refuses to get in her car seat until she's buckled Chicky. Also, it should be sweet when Angeline still crawls into bed in the middle of the night at least three or four times a week. And yet . . . and yet. More often than not, both of these things evoke rage. The kind of rage that makes her yell. Her dirty little secret. No one would suspect it but she is a mother who yells now. Even if she doesn't think of herself that way. Even if to her own ear she sounds ridiculous.

Do you cry without warning? Now Mary Beth sighs. Show her a mother who doesn't cry at the news or because she had to give the last half of her chocolate bar to a seven-year-old.

She scans her answers. If anything, they feel like symptoms of motherhood. There's a line where Mary Beth is invited to describe her reason for the visit. She scrawls: *Migraines; am I depressed???* Then hands it back to the receptionist behind the sliding window.

Mary Beth opens up an artsy magazine and tries to focus her aching eyes on the photographs of models wearing clothes no one would ever buy. She feels like she might throw up. The door to the inner office opens and she hears, "Mary Beth?"

She flips the magazine closed and stands up to see that the female nurse waiting to usher her inside is Zeke's mother, Megan Tolbert. Even from here, Mary Beth can make out her neat writing in the "Reason for Today's Visit" section.

"I—I didn't know you worked here," she stammers.

TWENTY-TWO

▼

"M ission accomplished?" Darby asks her husband upon his return from putting Lola down for bed, now looking about an inch shorter than when he'd left to head upstairs.

Well, don't look at me that way, she thinks defensively. It's not her fault *she* had the wherewithal to call dibs on Jack this evening because everyone knows Jack is the easier one to get to bed—much less time spent on negotiations that go nowhere—and yet she does feel a little at fault. Like, as the mother, it's always her sworn duty and hers alone to take care of the hardest bits, the way the Secret Service has to take a bullet for the president. Where did that stupid feature come from, anyway? It seems hardwired into her, but who programmed it there? That's what she would like to know. Whether this bug might be one that's fixed for future versions of mothers. She has her doubts.

Darby leans down to try to stuff another dinner plate into the dishwasher, never a method to her madness, dishes face this way and that. It used to drive Griff bonkers, but now they've got bigger problems, so that's nice.

He shrugs. "She kept trying to tell me this story about this photograph in her picture frame. It's that woman. You know the one? On her dresser. I don't recognize who it is—"

"Oh, shoot." Darby pauses to switch on the garbage disposal. She lets the rattle die. "That's the one that comes in the frame when you buy it. The stock image. I haven't changed it out yet." She's not nearly as embarrassed about this as she should be. She's been meaning to replace it with the photo of Lola petting a stingray for her birthday at the aquarium, but then never got the picture printed. She used to get pictures printed *all* the time. She took disposable cameras to sleepaway camps and college parties. Such a surprise to get the photographs back, opening the flap of the envelope and sliding the glossy pictures out to flip through, careful to avoid fingerprints. It feels sort of pointless now. She has gobs of pictures on her phone. It runs out of memory space at an alarming rate. She's the queen of pulling out her camera right after her kids do something particularly cute or precocious, Darby's voice in the background, *What were you saying about your bear? Tell me again that thing about your brother? Could you sing that song for Mommy, just one more time, please?* Her children stare blankly at the camera, or worse, pick their noses. Darby can't imagine not taking this detailed record of her kids. She can't imagine how it would look if she had a lock screen on her phone depicting a background other than Jack and Lola looking adorable. It's like wearing a wedding ring out in public. You don't have to, but you really should if you don't want to invite questions about your commitment. And so it is: Her phone, like her brain, is running out of mental space thanks to her to children.

"How long's it been in there?" he asks, more amused than accusatory. He looks different in a way she can't quite put her finger on. More grown-up? Less Griff-like? No, that can't be it, but she has the strangest feeling she hasn't gotten a proper look at him in a while. That day, that day on which Miss Ollie died, seems to have permanently messed with her mind.

She rips a paper towel off the roll and begins swiping it over the glass-top stove. She made a chicken and quinoa concoction she learned about on TikTok that didn't come out right or, if it did, wasn't very good. "About a year so far," she says. "I'm thinking of making that my next New Year's resolution. What do you think?"

"I think it's prudent not to try to take on too much, yeah," he teases, though, truth be told, she can't guarantee the next eight months will proceed any differently from the last twelve, so it's entirely possible that stock photo image will still be there, waiting for her, come January.

"She had this whole backstory about the woman," Griff says. "She has a mean little daughter who steals things from Lola and won't give them back. She was getting really worked up about it. I had to take the picture down and put it on our dresser."

"She's pretending." Darby considers. "And stalling."

"I don't know. It's weirder than that, though. It's like she doesn't know the difference sometimes between real and imaginary. It's just—"

She stops wiping the stove. "What?" Her heart stomps around in her rib cage.

"I don't want to say it." He shakes his head.

"Say it," she insists. The not saying it is worse, obviously.

"Creepy," he mumbles.

"Don't say *that*," she snaps at him, and he gives her this look like, *Have you lost your mind, woman?* "We're her parents." As if that settles it. Game over. Sorry, she just doesn't understand what he's after, what point he needs to prove.

Lola is quirky, maybe even a tiny bit weird. So what if she makes up elaborate histories for strange photographs. And has tantrums that are maybe on the more aggressive end of the spectrum. And fibs on occasion. You know who else was probably a tiny bit weird? Mozart. Picasso. Bobby Fischer, if he's even real. Though so far no signs point to Lola being a genius. Jeffrey Dahmer probably wasn't the most normal four-year-old either and he likely hadn't even started eating people yet, so in that regard, Lola does happen to have a head start.

Oh god, here they go again. He hasn't gotten on his soapbox about the counselor evaluation for Lola in a while and it's not as if she hasn't noticed. She has certainly, certainly noticed. But she's not up to the challenge tonight. She needs to change the subject before they spiral.

"I've been meaning to ask you." She picks up the broom and begins to sweep, gently, keeping her eyes diverted. "Does my vagina feel different to you?"

Griff guffaws as if the question is hilarious, as if Darby is being Darby again. *Oh, Darby.* "You've been *meaning* to ask me? That sounds like you've been meaning to ask me if we could have lunch with your parents this weekend. Not your . . . vagina." He half mouths the word, half says it out loud.

She smiles benevolently at her husband. At just over forty, she's never been confident that he has a firm grasp on female anatomy. Not the parts that matter for satisfying sex, those he gets, but ovaries and menstrual cycles and what have you. She once asked him how he thought a woman went to the bathroom when wearing a sanitary pad and after considering it with the concentration he might dedicate to an eighth-grade math problem, he answered that he imagined they just peed on it. Like a small dog.

"That's not an answer. I want to know for real. Like, you know, is it looser? We've never truly discussed it."

"I'm not sure it's something that really requires discussion."

"I'm just curious," she persists. Doesn't she have a right to know about her own vagina? It's just—well, it's just this thing that she's been having with her body lately. She doesn't have words for it other than that she hates it. Only, haven't you heard? Women aren't allowed to hate their bodies anymore, so she knows there must be another, better word for it. If she's being honest, it's not just the diastasis recti situation and the tummy that will not be tamed. It's the whole kit and caboodle, all of it. She is constantly sore from carrying twenty-five to thirty pounds of extra weight on her hip or in front of her when her children decide their legs don't work, which is pretty much always, unless there's a moving vehicle available to run in front of. She feels slimy and touched the way she does after getting off an airplane, except somehow it's become her permanent state. People wipe boogers on her. And now her daughter wants to wrap her mouth around her skin and feed and, maybe, perhaps, Darby thinks it's time to take a survey, assess the extent of the damage. *How bad is it?*

Griff leans his annoyingly flat stomach against the countertop. "It's hard to remember a time before kids. I don't know. It feels a little different. I guess. Wider, maybe?"

"Oh." She pauses over the sink. "Is it less, you know, tactile for you?"

"No. Darby. It's plenty *tactile.*"

Darby glances down at her fully dressed crotch as if she might be able to discern some visible difference there. "Do you know what I think? I think penises—or is it penii?—should have to change after kids." She can never decide what to call his penis. None of the words she knows seem to fit. Penis sounds too scientific for something with such a personality. *Dick* sounds rude and *cock* pornographic. "I know. Right after a man has a baby, *that's* when he should get circumcised."

"For the love of—you want to *cut* the skin off a grown man's penis? That's horrifying. We would remember that. People do it to babies so that they won't know better. Otherwise, it'd be too traumatic."

Darby wipes her hands on a dish towel and tosses it aside. "I had a third-degree tear when I gave birth to Lola and nobody thought twice about that." Except for Darby. She thought about it every time she felt the stitches pull even when she sat on soft cushions. She thought about it every time she visited the toilet with a trusty squirt bottle to spray up into her nether regions just to keep her own urine from stinging her stupid. She watches her husband. "See, you don't even remember. You probably don't even know what a perineum is. I'm right. I can tell!" She huffs. "Well, that's settled. If I run for president that will be my platform."

"An eye for an eye," Griff says. "Got it."

"A touch of foreskin for a bit of labia."

They actually do have sex that night, which is a pleasant surprise given they haven't been keeping up their usual routine as of late. Not that they have a *routine*-routine. But there's a certain expectation, a rhythm they've fallen into over the years, and that rhythm has been disrupted.

It wasn't *good* sex and for that, she must admit, she was the one to blame. His hands on her body. Everywhere he touched, like he was shining a flashlight on all the parts that have been troubling her lately. Her wrecked breasts. Her dry nipples. Her butt cheeks that resemble the surface of the moon. Her stomach, didn't he know better than to touch her *stomach*? She kept thinking: *That's rude of him; he shouldn't do that.* And then she wanted to cry. Wanted to cry at her husband's touch. She couldn't think of anything more depressing. She should have showered. He shouldn't have sprung it on her. He shouldn't have looked so sexy.

The next morning she wakes up and informs Griff that she's getting a personal trainer.

"*Now?*" he asks at their side-by-side sinks. He's fresh out of the shower and standing there in a towel, no shirt. Just standing there. She can't think of the last time she would have felt comfortable standing for any amount of time in even her underwear. She's resorted to going into her closet to change, which is absurd. They have two kids together.

Right, that's her point.

"Yes, *now*. I mean, after work, yeah, but now." She shimmies on a pair of yoga leggings—look, she won't even have to change up her wardrobe—and a loose T-shirt that offers coverage. *Coverage* is such an old-lady word, fuck. "You'll have to handle school pickup and care on the days I have my . . . appointments. Sessions?" She'll work on the vocabulary once she successfully becomes a gym person.

Griff takes a handheld buzzy device from the leather Dopp kit she bought him last Father's Day and runs it along the insides of his nostrils. "Don't you think," he says, pulling his mouth down for better nose access, "we have a lot going on? I mean, we've had so much change to our routine in such a short amount of time."

"Now is the time," she declares firmly. "I'm packing my gym bag as we speak." She steps over two messy piles of clothes on her closet floor and tugs a crumpled-up duffel bag from a top shelf. Several out-of-style clutches rain down on her head and she ducks for cover. "Let's see. Tennis shoes." She scours the vicinity. "Socks . . ."

Griff pokes his head in to check on her. He looks kind of panicked. "Does it have to be today?"

"*Yes.*" Now she's annoyed. "Did you have *plans?*"

"No."

"Then what's the problem?"

"You look fine." Now he sounds annoyed. "I love you the way you are."

"Thanks." She stumbles out of her cave of a closet. Someday she *will* clean it, but one thing at a time.

He waits. As if he expects his proclamation that he likes her just the way she is will be enough to throw her off her new direction. *Okay, as long as you like me, Griff, as long as I look fine, then never mind.*

"What's gotten into you?" he asks. She might ask him the same thing. He runs his fingers through his still-damp hair, which hasn't even started to thin. Meanwhile, she is still losing thick chunks of her own hair in the shower ever since she stopped breastfeeding Jack. She has a bald spot on the hairline of her right side. She's going bald before her husband. "You're going to get hot and leave me, is that it?" he asks.

She stares at him and he tries to laugh it off, like she doesn't have a sense of humor.

"What's that supposed to mean?" she asks. She's fully aware that Griff nurses a pet fear that, without her, he would have to go out in the world and interact. Without her, he would have to call the repairman when the refrigerator breaks. He'd have to speak to the cable technicians. He would have to deal with so many people. He loves her, but he also needs her. *"Get hot,"* she repeats. "As in you don't think I am already?" She's determined to sound more angry than hurt, though the reality for her is definitely flip-flopped. It's like her "hot" just fell and dropped out her flappy, wider vagina.

"Come on. You know that's not how I meant it."

The anger comes and the burn of it is a relief. Two weeks ago, she would have sworn her husband would always be on her side, no matter what.

"You know, you're always so focused on Lola's issues. But I think you're the one with the real issues. Where's *your* evaluation from a counselor, Griff? Huh?" Darby holds herself together. "Something's seriously wrong with you." She hits below the belt and doesn't care. A touch of labia for a bit of foreskin. *How's that for coming in hot, honey?*

TWENTY-THREE

▼

I t happened again," Lincoln's mom, Chelsea, murmurs to Mary Beth at the playground.

"Again?" She feels fragile, like one of those rickety toothpick-and-marshmallow bridges built by elementary schoolers. "You're kidding," she says. "Where?"

"This time, it was in the book nook," Chelsea says, then adds darkly, "The class copy of *Dragons Love Tacos* has been permanently removed."

To date, there've been two mysterious incidents since the first, one at the bottom of the slide, one in the play kitchen. This marks the fourth incursion.

She angles her body to shield herself from the wind, which has picked up over the course of the day. Above them, the American flag flaps violently against the pole. "So who was it? Do we know?"

"Still the sixty-four-thousand-dollar question."

They watch their children play normally within the fenced border of the playground area. It feels like they're being detained. A look around at all the other adult faces in attendance and none of them suggest a parent who is having a *good* day.

Mary Beth has always been fascinated to see the way the office of president of the United States ages a man—so far only a man—in four years, but that's nothing, that's only four years. By that math, Mary Beth has already served two terms as mother and still has years and years to go. She tries to imagine what she'll look like by her kids' eighteenth birthdays and then thinks, better not.

"I don't understand how that's possible? A child can't drop trou and do . . ." She waves her hands around for effect. *"That* without anyone seeing."

"This one can," Chelsea intones ominously. "Asher's dad is over there giving Mrs. Tokem an earful."

"It's not Mrs. Tokem's fault, really."

"She called the cops."

"She what? Why? Why would she do that? It's not a crime. Or it shouldn't be when kids—when—" A creeping, sick sensation turns over her own bowels. "You know what? I'll just go investigate, at least represent the class. In an official Room Mom capacity." She pulls herself together, tucking herself in, making herself as tall as a woman who has never managed to clear five foot three inches can possibly look. She can fix this. That's what she does, that's who Mary Beth is. She's a fixer.

But, as she approaches Asher's father, Bill, and Mrs. Tokem where they stand talking over the playground fence, she's sweating in all the places you can't see.

"I was specifically asked to provide this sort of information," Mrs. Tokem is saying, and for a flash Mary Beth hates her, this stupid, old, no-fun woman in knee-length shorts. And it's an emotion that shocks her system because Mary Beth hasn't hated anyone, maybe ever. "If any became available. I've been in close contact with the detectives on the case." As though she's been given some sort of volunteer deputy sheriff star to pin to that beige cardigan of hers.

"But—" Mary Beth stammers, not waiting for an opportune moment to interject, just going for it. "But what were you *thinking?*"

Mrs. Tokem has adopted a "power stance," feet wide apart on the playground's artificial turf.

"You're also required to protect our children's privacy," Bill insists. He's always walking fast around the school with the hard soles of his dress shoes clacking too loudly, all *Look at me! Here I am!* Mary Beth can't decide whether Bill's a nice person, but right now she doesn't care because he happens to be right. Privacy *is* all the rage in parenting these days, a hex on parents who post pictures of their toddlers in the bathtub, and, well, doesn't this seem like the most extreme violation thereof?

Mary Beth thinks yes. She thinks she is not overreacting, that no one can suggest she is. She's simply reacting. That's an important distinction to remember. It's the job of adults to protect kids. It's more than that. It's her moral obligation.

"I was thinking that a teacher is dead and that I am a teacher," replies Mrs. Tokem. "They're just finishing up collecting the sample from the classroom and then they'll be on their way." Mrs. Tokem swishes her palms together, done and dusted.

"Think about it. Why would the police want DNA samples from our *children*?" She can't help if she's talking too loudly; Mary Beth is naturally sort of a loud person.

"We can't interfere with the investigation." Maggie's mother, Roxy, leans over, obviously having been listening the entire time. Of course. How very helpful, Roxy. Not only is she unconcerned, if Mary Beth isn't mistaken, she might be giving off signals in the opposite direction: *Get your little monsters under control.*

"There are consent forms for saliva samples via a mouth swab. You can sign them or not, completely voluntary." The teacher hands them out to each parent, moving on from Bill and Mary Beth. Dismissed! Easy as that.

"Why the kids, though?" Mary Beth's mind is spinning.

"Isn't it obvious?" asks Tamar's mom. "The footprints. The creepy little footprints."

Bill trots after the teacher while Mary Beth watches helplessly. "There are only ten kids in the class. The police can use process of elimination," he tells her.

Word of his son's overzealous feeding on his wife had spread well beyond their classroom by now; Mary Beth understands his concern.

As a parent, Mary Beth sometimes finds that there are things her children want to do that she instinctively says no to. *You cannot play with the Scotch tape. Don't sit on the countertop. Quit playing with the faucet. Because . . .*

Because . . .

She's been a mother long enough to know when things are a bad idea, and right now her mom sirens are blaring. They can't allow this to happen because . . . because . . . because . . .

Just then the male officer and female detective who were snooping—*unchaperoned*—through their children's classroom emerge. They look overheated and unhurried, the man in his slim-fitting navy pants and bulky belt, the woman in her wool suit, the top buttons of her starched pastel-pink shirt unfastened at the neck. Each year the school invites police officers and firefighters to the school for a career day and every time she welcomes them with a box full of doughnuts, not caring if the gesture is too on the nose. Well, she might not be so quick to offer next year.

She's trying to think of what to say or do. Something. Something. She is supposed to be doing *something*.

"Stop!" she yells at the police officers, who are making their way back to the patrol car.

To her surprise, they do stop and turn.

It's best if she doesn't conjure too vividly an image of what they must see walking toward them, but if she had to, it would be a woman with a messy mom bun, frizzed where the tail of her hair sticks out of its rubber band, a pudge of fat and skin hiding not very well beneath the waistband of her black yoga pants, the control-top band of which she can never decide whether to wear over the lump, under it, or strangling it down, and sporting flip-flops. A mom of the first order.

"Can we help you, ma'am?" Detective Wanda Bright nudges her Oakley sunglasses over the bridge of her nose.

"Would you mind showing me your search warrant, please?" says Mary Beth.

Bright's partner, Princep, mashes gum between his teeth. "It's a crime scene. We don't need a search warrant."

There's a small brown bag in Bright's hand that Mary Beth can't keep her eyes off of. "No crime occurred in *that* classroom," she says hastily. "The kids have moved classes after . . . after what happened."

Is she really doing this? Is she really going to stand in the way of two uniformed officers and their job?

She sees no other choice. So the question, really, is *can* she? Can she stop them? It might sound crazy to believe that she can, but then again, Mary Beth once talked her way into the Bahamas even after forgetting her passport.

"The school is a crime scene, ma'am," Bright repeats.

"That doesn't mean you can just *take* things." Even though, for all she knows, it means that precisely. All she has to do is sound right enough that they question things first. Buy time. As much of it as she can afford. She thinks of Bodhi and Zeke and Bex and the others, and, of course, even Noelle, and she musters her nerve.

"A teacher gave us permission." Bright pushes up her iridescently mirrored glasses with the hand not holding a bag of poop.

Mary Beth is going to have a few more choice words for Mrs. Tokem, but for now—"She doesn't own the school. It's a 501(c)(3) organization. It's not for profit. It's for us. *We* own the school. *We* pay her. That's right. Hand it over." She twitches her fingers at them.

"Ma'am." Bright doesn't move.

None of the other parents have come to join her, not even Asher's father, Bill.

"The school can't disclose medical information without parental consent." She tries another angle. There's got to be one that will do. "I xeroxed the forms. Hundreds of them. I should know."

"Please step aside." Princep holds out his hand like he works as an armed guard protecting the queen's crown jewels instead of, well, what it is. "This is an active investigation. We're working within our authority," he rattles off.

Bright frowns and tries to pass her. Instinctively, Mary Beth reaches for the stool sample bag. "I'm acting within *my* authority to protect the students." She makes no mention of the fact that she was not *elected* to her position, but instead was the sole volunteer on an empty sign-up sheet.

"Did you just reach for my gun?" Bright lurches back. "Did she just reach for my gun? Did you see that?"

Princep's hand goes to his holster. "Ma'am. Ma'am. Back. Way. Up."

"I didn't—" Mary Beth looks around a little wildly for support.

"I can have you arrested for obstructing an open investigation *and* assaulting a police officer." Princep has not taken his hand off of the gun. His thumb rests lightly on the hammer.

"This is fucking ridiculous," Mary Beth says. She slaps her hand over her mouth. She almost never curses.

"You need to keep a respectful tone, miss," Bright warns. "I felt her reach for the gun."

"I didn't reach for your gun. Why would I reach for your gun? I'm a mom!"

"I'm going to need you to quiet your voice." Princep stands between her and Detective Bright, physically separating her from that brown paper bag.

A searing pain lances her directly through the right side of her skull. She pulls an ugly face and falls a small step forward before catching herself.

"I've warned you." Princep moves into her space. The pain is not yet all-consuming, but she knows what's coming and she tries to think. Her daughter is probably not the Little Shitter. But Lola could be. And Darby is a dear friend. And . . . and . . . and . . . She wouldn't even have to get away with the bag. She could just contaminate it, render it useless to the police. That's a possibility, isn't it?

Mary Beth considers the next couple minutes of her life before they happen, minutes in which she may become a person with an arrest record on a day in which she isn't 100 percent sure she put on deodorant.

And then God intervenes.

Or at least his envoy. Pastor Ben is at Mary Beth's elbow before she's even heard him approach. "Are you okay?" He touches her so lightly a rash of goose bumps races up the back of her arm and underneath the sleeve of her T-shirt.

"I'm fine. Mostly," she adds. "They're not listening to me." She grips her forehead in her palm. The sudden pain is dissipating, but behind it, she notices a smudge of blurry light cast in rainbow colors just over the spot where Officer Princep stood two minutes ago. She blinks, but that hardly makes it better. Somewhere behind her, Mary Beth feels her daughter's eyes on her, waiting. Questioning. "We have to do whatever we can to protect the children. The children. Just like you said," Mary Beth insists.

Pastor Ben straightens. "I see. Detective. Officer. I'm afraid you're not welcome on this campus without a personal escort from me. Do you understand?"

"That's a matter to take up with the police chief." Detective Bright plants her feet.

"Great. I believe he attends church here on occasion, so I'm sure he'll know right where to find me."

"We would be well within our rights to arrest her." Princep nods to Mary Beth. But he makes no move to do it. Detective Bright tilts her head and the standoff ends. Shame and embarrassment rush in, leaving Mary Beth wishing deeply that there were a place she could sit down.

The smell of fruity shampoo overwhelms her nostrils as she finds that Zeke's mother, Megan, is now by her side wearing her nurse scrubs. "Mary Beth." Megan throws her arm around her. "Oh god, Mary Beth, are you okay? It's okay, I can handle her," she announces. Through her watery vision, Mary Beth can just make out the embroidered patch on Megan's scrub pocket: *Mindpath Psychiatry & Psychology*. "She's one of my patients."

TWENTY-FOUR

▼

This is probably a mistake, thinks Darby as she enters the gym, one of those big-box franchises with no personality. It smells like a combination of Lola's laundry hamper and the wet-floored locker room of the old YMCA pool.

A man with shiny hair and biceps the size of her thighs stops her and asks if she wants to try a sample of the protein powder he's selling in fat, squatty jugs, or how about an energy bar. He sits behind a folding table that's been dressed up with a bright purple cloth, his brochures neatly stacked in front of him, like he's presenting a fourth-grade science fair project. Nobody stops, not even Darby, who can often be guilted into these kinds of things.

The front desk manager takes a long sip from a bendy straw dug half into a gallon-sized water bottle with motivational words marking off the ounces. *Good Morning! Remember Your Goal! Keep Chugging!* "How can I help you?" the woman asks with a satisfied little *ah* to demonstrate her thirst has been properly quenched.

Beyond the manager's vestibule is a sea of young people, many of whom dress like Kardashians. The women are wearing spandex pulled up far past their belly buttons to accentuate their voluminous asses and itty-bitty sports bras. She spots several girls filming themselves with their phones as they perform squats with a stunning amount of weight stacked on either end of a metal bar.

"I'd like to work with a personal trainer, please." She avoids her usual chitter-chatter and knocks straight to the point.

The truth is, she might not have gone through with the whole trainer idea were it not for the conversation with Griff this morning. All afternoon, she found herself aggressively tapping away at her keyboard, anger simmering like a low-grade fever. *Tap, tap, tappety-tap*, as if her computer had been the one to insult her this morning and not her husband.

She kept thinking: *How dare he?* But, really, if she's honest, there's a lot more to this whole Griff thing, a lot she's been tamping down over the last couple of weeks. And it all comes down to that terrible, unusual day on which Miss Ollie was murdered. The axis on which it hinges. She can feel it. She has *been* feeling it, the horrible mix of anxiety and inertia. Around they keep spinning, faster and faster, but if anyone in the Little Academy community is whirling most tightly, getting the most dizzy, Darby suspects it could be her.

For if she'd known, if she'd had any inkling that gorgeous afternoon while sitting in the school parking lot scrolling absentmindedly on her phone that by walking into the school she would be marching into a horror movie, she'd never have gone in there. Always she has harbored the belief that she would survive a scary movie for exactly this reason, not that she ever watches them; she covers her eyes. In this instance, she might have settled for that.

Instead, she saw.

She should tell someone. See something, say something, that's patriotic, right? She might have told Rhea about it. She'd been building up to it, mustering her resolve after the memorial service, but then Griff had clomped over, wrecking the opportunity, sending her yo-yoing back and forth with indecision ever since. She's still waiting for her moment of clarity to show up. Maybe at the gym.

"Absolutely," says the front desk manager, who doesn't look like one of the Kardashian girls now that Darby's paying better attention. Her teeth are big and the two front ones overlap and she has a beautiful figure, as Darby's mother would say, and thick auburn hair that does not look like it falls out in the shower. "We would love to connect you with someone to talk about your fitness goals." She smiles widely, not like someone who is self-conscious of her crooked teeth. "I'll just—" The manager picks up the handset phone on her desk and presses a button.

"Personal trainer to the front. Personal trainer to the front." Her voice booms throughout the entire gym, as though she's a cashier at Target.

Darby feels her face get hot and her palms begin to sweat and she hasn't even begun to exercise. She takes a deep breath, tucking her husband and Little Academy and Lola and Miss Ollie away in her mind for now.

"Someone will be right with you," the manager informs her, and Darby is shuffled off to the side to wait with her droopy duffel bag and dirty sneakers, out of the way of the regular gym goers.

The someone who arrives is a fellow named Cannon. She shakes his calloused hand. She can't be sure from this vantage, but she's pretty sure she's an inch or two taller than Cannon, who has a military haircut and veiny forearms and informs her that fitness is not just his career, it's his *life*.

"Tell me about your goals," he says.

This one she knows. "I want to get my body back."

"Okay . . ." The corners of his mouth tug downward.

"I'm a mom," she explains.

"Ah, I get lots of mothers in here. Mommy makeovers."

She doesn't like the sound of that. She doesn't feel vain. She feels reasonable. More like something belonged to her, she loaned it out, and now she would like it back, please. That's all.

"For this initial consultation . . ." He presses his fingertips together, ready to talk strategy. "We'll start by doing a physical assessment, just as a benchmark to see where you are today."

"Oh. Okay. Fair warning. I may be a little out of shape."

"No warning needed. Trust me, I've seen it all." How old is Cannon? Twenty-two, maybe twenty-four? So she highly doubts he's seen it all.

However, she's pleased when he starts by leading her in a series of walking stretches that feel doable; not just doable, but—and this is surprising—enjoyable. She follows his lead, lifting her knee and pulling it across her body, swinging her arms across her chest, lunging and stretching off to the side. Is this what it feels like to stretch? She can't imagine why she's been avoiding it so stubbornly. By the end of the walking stretches, she's feeling downright limber. When she was a kid she could do splits. She won't try that now, but maybe someday.

Just then, her phone starts ringing at full volume where she left it next to her car keys.

"Sorry," she says. "I should have turned the ringer off. One second—" She jogs over to her phone to demonstrate some hustle. Griff is calling. The nerve. He hasn't reached out all day and he chooses now. She sends him to voice mail, returning slightly out of breath and righteously pissed off.

Perhaps it's that energy that's the reason she's able to perform twenty-five passable push-ups from her knees when Cannon asks, marking the result down on some kind of chart she's not privy to. "Were you an athlete?" he says earnestly.

Darby pushes back onto her heels and swipes sticky hair from her forehead. "Volleyball. In college actually."

"Thought so. I can tell. You have the muscle tone."

She tries not to look too pleased with herself. Darby Morton doesn't just look like a mom; she looks like a former athlete. She completes her lunges without complaint. When—

Her phone bursts into sound again. People turn to look. It's very passé to have a phone ring these days. "I'm so sorry," she says. Cannon looks at her sternly. This isn't just his career, it's his life, after all!

She scurries to turn off the ringer once more. It's Griff. She remembers now that she has him on a special setting, so that his call always rings through. It's supposed to be in case of emergency, but they usually use it so that they can help each other find their phones between couch cushions. Darby turns off her phone entirely. Good riddance.

"All set," she reports, and hopes that Cannon won't make the workout harder in retaliation.

She returns to a plank position, and Cannon asks her if she has diastasis recti—which she confirms sheepishly—as well as any other considerations he should be cognizant of, and she very nearly laughs when he looks at her with such gravitas and says, "I don't allow injuries on my watch," like he's Batman. But also, she's comforted. She thinks maybe all personal trainers would make excellent partners if they know this sort of thing.

Darby is sweating through her vacation T-shirt when Cannon announces, "How about we wrap things up with a mile run?"

She stares at him. "Cannon," she says. "If you make me run, I'll go home and never return."

"Roger that," he replies cheerily. She's allowed to sub in jumping jacks instead, which make her pee a little, but she decides not to report this to the trainer.

The funny thing is that by the end of the session, Darby feels like she's positively glowing, the way people said she would during pregnancy but never managed to. It's as though her body has been there waiting for her all along, just waiting for someone to dust it off and carry it down from the attic. She remembers suddenly how it felt to run with her teammates, the good hurt of her thighs burning, not the nagging pain of her back when she tightens the buckles of a car seat.

She returns to the front desk manager. "I'd like to book more sessions, please. With Cannon, if possible." Who would have thought?

"Wonderful," says the woman. "I'll just get you entered here in the computer. What's your name?"

"Darby Morton." She pulls out a credit card from her wallet. "M-O-R-T-O-N."

The woman types as she talks. "No relation to Griff Morton, I'm sure?"

Darby tilts her head. "Griff. How do you know—" She almost says *my husband*. "Griff?"

No one—and this is an actual fact—ever knows Griff. Not even if they've met him at a party or something. It's just not possible that Griff, her husband, Griff, has an acquaintance she doesn't know about.

"Oh, we first met online," she says, taking Darby's credit card from between her fingers. "Through UCB."

Online. Griff met a woman online. Darby is trying to process. She reads the woman's name tag. Sarah. Sarah with an *h*. Sarah and Griff met online.

"And then later we connected at Hideout," Sarah continues. "When we got serious, though, I had to move on, it just wasn't a good fit for me. No hard feelings." She hands Darby back her credit card.

"Right." She presses her lips together. "UCB." What on earth is UCB? She's sure she's never heard of it. And Hideout? Is that a bar? She could ask, but then, she's Griff's wife and she doesn't want to show anyone, especially not some floozy with great auburn hair and a figure that won't quit, that she doesn't know what her husband is doing with his free time, not even a little bit. Not one clue. (Also, she should note that she does regret that first bit. Sarah is probably not a floozy.)

"Well, you're all set." Sarah smiles. "Plan to arrive fifteen minutes early each time and bring plenty of water." She lifts her motivational water bottle. "Look forward to seeing you around the gym."

Darby thanks her. *Thanks for the information. Thanks so much for cracking open my happy marriage, Sarah.*

For the first time in as long as she can remember, Darby doesn't turn on Spotify or a podcast or the radio on the way home. She drives in deafening silence while the thoughts racing through her head roar loud, louder, and louder still.

How has she been so stupid? Of course she's known that something's been going on with Griff lately. Or has she? On some subliminal level. At least. She can't actually decide. It's like she's looking back on the last several weeks with a different-colored lens and it's definitely not rosy. The late nights at work. The primping. Wearing black sweaters back to the "office." Definitely shady behavior, but she thought his weirdness, his coolness toward her, must have something to do with Lola and how they couldn't agree on how to parent her. She thought somehow her husband discussed their daughter with Miss Ollie behind her back, against her wishes. Now she doesn't know what to think.

Liar. The word is sharp in her mind. *Liar, liar, liar, you are such a big, fat liar.*

When she enters her front door, she's prepared to confront the issue—to confront Griff—head-on, come what may. She will demand answers. Right now.

"Griff!" She barrels through the door. "Gri-iff!"

Her eyes pass right over the couch and then—and then back again.

"Darby." There, in lieu of her husband, is calm, serene, at peace Rhea. Except not her usual Rhea. This Rhea looks like garbage.

"The kids," Darby whispers. Fear wraps around her body and she simultaneously feels frozen inside it and as though she could leap out of her skin to get away. "What's happened to them?"

"Everyone's okay," Rhea says softly.

"Jesus, Rhea." Darby sniffles. "You scared me."

"The police have brought Lola in for questioning."

TWENTY-FIVE

▼

R hea could have sworn she heard Darby hiss the word *liar* as she unlocked the door. Really. That's what it sounded like. But then again, maybe Rhea's ears are simply primed to hear it. *Liar.* Playing it back in her head, she can't be sure anymore. Like one of those viral memes where different people hear different words: *Yanny-Laurel* or something equally ridiculous.

She feels like a home invader. It's obvious Darby had no idea Rhea would be waiting inside and here she is, shoved into Darby's space. Rhea would hate that if it were the other way around. She doesn't believe in friends dropping in uninvited. It's aggressive.

Why didn't Darby check her phone, though? Darby is glued to her phone. *Edward Phonehands*, she's been known to call herself. She has a very self-deprecating sense of humor that Rhea doesn't share.

There was a certain stage in their shared lives when Rhea and Darby used to text regularly in the middle of the night during the time Bodhi and Lola were both boycotting sleep on principle. Back then, Darby's phone obsession was something of a welcomed feature of their relationship. Rhea would get a small jolt of energy and joy when a text came through at 2:00 A.M. and she was already up. *Nothing good ever happens after midnight*, Darby would text. *My mother was right.* They played a game called "You wanna know what?" sending weird facts back and forth, each trying to outdo the other, each trying to keep the other awake. Looking at her friend, she realizes she doesn't know when the last one of those texts was sent. Just that one of them was the last and that was it, they were gone forever, the game ended, without anything to mark the occasion, just as, one day, it will be the last time Bodhi sits on her lap or calls her Mommy or asks her to sleep next to him. It all will come crashing down eventually.

"Where's Jack?" Darby asks after the immediacies have been pushed out of the way.

"He's in his room playing Star Wars toys with Bodhi," she says. "I heard your car pull up and figured I better catch you alone."

Darby's house is eerily quiet with the boys tucked away. There are spiderweb scratches on the hardwood from where somebody's moved furniture around. A damp hooded towel has been dropped beside the rug. Obviously, the Mortons weren't expecting company today.

"So you think Lola and, uh, Griff, you think they're still at—at what? At the police station? Is that where they take children? Or is there some other place more suitable for kids maybe, with blocks and stuffed toys and crayons? That seems like a long time, doesn't it?" She seems overheated. The splotches on her neck and cheeks look rash-like, as though she's having an allergic reaction to the news.

"I don't know," Rhea tells her. "I don't know how long it's supposed to take." Did Darby ask because she thought Rhea would have the inside track, because she'd be able to speak from experience? Probably not. She's being paranoid. News travels fast, but not that fast.

Darby goes to the kitchen and pours herself a large glass of water. "Are they questioning all the kids or just Lola?" Her eyes close as she takes a long pull from the glass while still standing beside the refrigerator.

"I don't know that either. Sorry. They took a DNA sample from the school today and I don't know what to think." Except she does. She for sure does because it's what they're all thinking. Bex's mom was walking around with an open wound. Zeke attacked her son. Asher's mom landed in the hospital. And before today, parents were whispering about how kids could get belligerent if they weren't "fed" properly. It felt like the children at Little had latched on to the wrong end of the Little Red Riding Hood story. *My, what big teeth you have . . .* the parents thought. *The better to eat you with, Mommy!*

"I don't get it." Darby sinks down on the sofa beside Rhea instead of the chair across, which Rhea would have preferred. "Do they think she saw something? I've asked her. I've definitely asked her. She won't tell me anything." Darby looks miserable. "Unless it's about marine life."

Rhea stops herself before she can say *I don't know* one more time. "It feels like maybe they're not just treating the kids like witnesses anymore. It feels like they could be suspects."

Darby looks at her sharply, then, dropping her eyes, she pinches the bridge of her nose. "Fuck, Rhea." The force of her words surprises them both. "I know you're speaking words, but it's like I literally don't understand what you're telling me. Is this about those little footprints? Because the kids are all over that place. No one locks the door the way you're supposed to. I mean, mistakes happen."

Rhea doesn't know what she means by that. Not if the footprints were *in* the blood. If that's how it went down, then the footprints had to have been put there after.

"I don't understand it either," Rhea agrees. Two police officers came to *her* house to ask *her* questions about *her* past. And now those same officers are stomping around *her* child's school. Are they grasping for straws or are they on to something? "The police are probably trying to throw us off-balance. Force someone to make a misstep."

She imagines Miss Ollie's eyes still and glazed as a taxidermied animal's, trained at the ceiling. A creeping pool of dark red. A child hunched inside the supply room. A trail of imprints marking the path.

"Sorry," Rhea says. "Poor choice of words."

"But not Lola. They can't think that Lola would have . . ."

Rhea doesn't know what to do with her hands. She wonders how she looks to Darby in this moment. She hopes Darby isn't paying attention too closely to her; better not to leave a lasting impression after she goes.

But no sooner has Rhea thought this than Darby turns her full, wide-eyed gaze back onto her. Like a cartoon character. "I know you had it out for her," she says solemnly. "Miss Ollie. But, well, I'm telling you now: I didn't agree with you. Not at the school. Not at the café. I was just being supportive. Like when a friend goes through a breakup and you say, 'Oh yeah, that guy was a total asshole. You can do so much better. He's going nowhere in life.'"

"Darby, about that, Miss Ollie wasn't who you think she was—"

Darby squeezes her eyelids shut. "Enough. No, Rhea. No. I let you have your hissy fit or whatever." Rhea feels branches of cold steel fan out in her lungs. "But Lola loved her. She pulled special books for Lola every week. And they sat and had special cuddle time and Lola has really needed that lately. Miss Ollie called it 'filling her love cup.' She was so good to Lola. Not everyone is. Not everyone"—she swallows—"appreciates Lola. She was a great teacher, Rhea, and I'm sorry. I know you have a chip on your shoulder about everything and everyone, but now . . ." Darby looks at the ceiling and Rhea spots tears teetering precariously on her lower lid.

A surge of anger strikes Rhea and she wants to slap those silly, perfectly perched tears out of Darby's head. Of course Darby's going to side with Miss Wholesome Polly Perfect. Just like she's always suspected, Rhea's never been one of them.

"Is that what your husband thought, too?" Rhea shoots back. "That she was *such* a great teacher?" She's not about to take the entire blame for this. No way. Just because she died doesn't turn Miss Ollie into some kind of discount saint. Darby thinks she's been too hard on Miss Ollie? If she only knew how much Rhea held back, well, she might be singing a different tune.

After all, it was Rhea who was sitting in her car when she saw Miss Ollie talking to a man through the windshield. At the time, she could feel the tension building in the back of the man's neck from clear over there. He was hulking over Miss Ollie. Her face obscured. Rhea watched the teacher retreat a couple of steps. He pointed a finger at her. Like, really pointed it. A purposeful shake. At the time, Rhea imagined what her friends might do in a situation like that. Would they intervene? Would they check to make sure the woman was okay?

Not Rhea. She didn't do a damn thing to help that woman. Instead, she smugly sat back and thought to herself that she wasn't the only one who didn't care for Miss Ollie.

But the man looked familiar. Chestnut hair, physically fit—and then she realized: Wait a second, she knew him, like actually *knew* him. *Darby, come get your man.*

"What's that supposed to mean?" Darby's chin snaps back as if she didn't start this. "I *talked* to Griff. He didn't know what you were talking about." But Darby's pupils tell a different story. She was listening that day at the café. Not just listening, she followed up. She took action.

And flash forward to today, in the aftermath of the Poop Bandit's second strike, Griff looking like some prick, surfing on his phone like that.

You're in charge of pickup today then, huh? Rhea asked him just to prove she's not like him.

Just today, he practically grunted.

Okay, excuse me.

And she did until half an hour later when the dust settled on Mary Beth's near arrest and a set of cops came over holding little Lola Morton's hand. Griff tapped Rhea on the shoulder and asked if she could take Jack home. He might have said please, and that's a big might. Darby wasn't answering and he had to go down to the police station and Rhea said, *Yeah. That's fine.*

Darby blinks at her expectantly.

"And I guess you believe him over me." Rhea shrugs. It doesn't settle anything. "Bodhi!" she hollers. "We've got to get going anyway."

Bodhi comes obediently at the sound of his name, effectively ending the conversation for them. Doesn't matter. Things work out fine for people like Darby, just wait and see.

Rhea peels open the door and the stress she has been holding back breaks open, too. "Call me if you need anything," she says, when they both know Darby won't.

"Wait, Rhea!" Darby shouts too loudly, Rhea hasn't even managed to get out the door yet.

Rhea hesitates. "*What?*" she asks.

Were Darby and Mary Beth talking behind her back about how they had to humor Rhea so she didn't explode? Like she's some trashy redneck fixing to get loud and run her mouth with no filter because she never attended cotillion? Is that how it was? It's not the first time Rhea's been made out to be the bad guy, but she's upset with herself for expecting more from Darby.

"Never mind." Darby sounds exasperated.

Join the club.

But on the way home, Rhea continues to try to piece it all together. Just in case. Just if she needs it. The detective knew she tried to get Erin fired. She knew about Rhea's criminal record. She did not know that Rhea hadn't just been on campus, she'd been in Miss Ollie's classroom, or else she'd have said so. She did not know about the little silver *A* because that's rattling in Rhea's cup holder. She did not know about the strange set of financial documents Rhea had found and . . . stolen. And that means Rhea knows something that Detective Bright doesn't. Reveal it and she'll wind up tipping her hand. Her only choice then is to figure out what it means before she has to.

She drives on autopilot, her mind so preoccupied with the puzzle she's trying to work out, she won't remember taking an early exit off the highway, she won't recall seeing the sign or reading the menu, she will feel such a schism between mind and body that when she finds a greasy sack of hamburgers and french fries plus a Happy Meal for Bodhi in her lap, she will feel hardly any guilt at all. She will not recognize herself and so she'll feel, in this instance as on other recent occasions, plausible deniability: She wasn't the one who committed the crime; you must be thinking of somebody else.

TWENTY-SIX

▼

"They struck again."

Most days, Mary Beth calls her younger sister, Blythe, on the way home from school as something of a coping mechanism. Blythe and her husband, Jerry, don't have kids. They have restaurant week and trips to Napa and even though they frequent über-pricey places like the French Laundry, it turns out you can eat a lot of über-pricey food for a whole lot less than the über-pricey cost of having kids.

"Who?" Blythe asks from her downtown office clear across the country. Mary Beth visited once and felt the slick, oily hand of envy slide its fingers around her heart at the floor-to-ceiling smudge-free glass, the plant kept alive as if by night fairies, the receptionist who offered coffee, tea, or sparkling.

"The Poop Bandit," Mary Beth says, glancing back to ensure that Noelle's headphones are on. She's listening to a children's audiobook and staring out the window.

"Is that a new superhero? Ugh. I hate children's marketing departments. Like those gross emoji pillows. Does Noelle have those?" Blythe does marketing for a major movie studio. She claims the move to LA had nothing to do with the reason she stopped attending church, but Mary Beth thinks it's quite the coincidence otherwise.

"It's not a superhero." Anyway, it's not, like, an official name, just something one of the dads said offhand. "Remember, I told you a few days ago how a kid in Noelle's class had . . . *relieved* . . . themselves on the playground without anyone knowing." Once is an accident. Twice is targeted. Three is serial and four, well, four's a spree.

"Oh yeah, that was you?" Blythe says. "Okay, right, I'm with you now."

"Yes that was *me*. How many stories about children's bowel movements are you currently juggling?"

"Honestly?" Blythe sighs. "A lot. No offense, but every time I ask about a friend's baby—and I'm just being polite, mind you, I don't actually care, except about my nieces, calm down—they tell me about their baby's poop. How often, the sounds, the consistency, the blowouts. And it doesn't get that much better when the kids get older. Exhibit A."

Mary Beth's fingers clench around the steering wheel. Blythe is an okay aunt. When the girls were babies she was always buying them beautiful clothes in the wrong sizes—designer peacoats, size eighteen months, only obviously at eighteen months it'd be mid-July. That kind of thing. And she has never, ever offered to watch them overnight. Or for an evening so that Mary Beth and Doug could go out for dinner. As an aunt, Blythe enjoys tea parties and going down waterslides and reading bedtime stories in roughly half-hour increments.

"Nobody mentioned what a large percentage of my life would be focused on feces when I had kids." Mary Beth tries to bite back her natural inclination to seethe. *Sisters.* "I never have enough battery on my phone anymore because Noelle has to watch something when she goes potty. Seriously, the amount of time I spend worrying about the frequency of Noelle's and Angeline's toilet visits is startling."

That's right, Blythe, it's not all waterslides and *Goodnight Moon* over here.

"Are you trying to prove my point or . . . ?"

"No," says Mary Beth. "I'm trying to tell you about the Bandit. Because it's actually gotten kind of serious." Mary Beth tries to sound suitably ominous. She feels like she could use some perspective from an outsider.

"Got it. So it's a boy in Noelle's class."

"No." Mary Beth swears it's like her sister isn't even listening. She keeps track of her sister's inside jokes about her new boss and who wasn't invited to which dinner party and offers thoughtful suggestions for adult birthday gifts. And none of that is inherently more interesting because it doesn't involve kids. In fact, the second you mention kids, people act like you're such a snooze. Where is the great American novel about motherhood? Is it really so much less fascinating than middle-aged men with alcoholism and angsty affairs? And anyway, what Mary Beth is detailing is actually a compelling mystery, if anyone would pay attention. "That's the unsettling thing," she stresses. "Nobody has any clue who it is."

"A regular Houdini—no, no, wait—" Blythe snaps her fingers. "*Poo-dini.*"

"Oh. That's good. Do you mind if I steal that?"

"Be my guest. I saw that interview of the mother in your class on TV, by the way," says Blythe. It seems that everyone has seen that damn interview.

"Rhea," Mary Beth says. "She's my friend."

"She made this whole bloodsucking thing—I can't remember what you called it—sound not all that bad. Maybe you're letting it get into your head too much."

Into her head too much? Mary Beth could laugh. Into *her* head? There are four-year-olds toting thermos cups containing multiple ounces of their parents' blood into class because it's been decided, collectively, that's what's best for the children. Robin checked into a hotel while on her period.

"I know what happened to that teacher—" Blythe continues.

"Noelle's teacher."

"It was horrific. Tragic. Really just *ick*. But, and I say this with love, you sound kind of nutty. I think maybe you need to get a life *outside* of the kids. Something for you, you know?" Mary Beth suspects that she does not say this with all that much love. "Have you thought about that? It can't be your whole identity. Look at Mom. She's sixty-five."

"What about her?"

"Well, she's going on that cruise, for one."

"What cruise?"

"The one she's leaving for this weekend. She's going to be gone for a month. I'm sure she was going to tell you. She's been busy packing. It's with one of her online groups."

"That's . . . fantastic," Mary Beth answers flatly. It's not fantastic. It's so not fantastic that her eyes are leaking tears completely against her will. How could her mother, who lives ten minutes down the road, leave for a month without telling her? She can't express any of this to Blythe. Blythe thinks that between the two of them, Mary Beth gets the upper hand with Mom because Mary Beth's kids get gifts and babysitting time and Blythe has expressed, jokingly only obviously not, that these "extras" should be accounted for when it comes time for her birthday, Christmas, and, eventually, inheritance.

But a life! An identity! And now she's supposed to find those things while juggling a meager sex life, a four-year-old with a penchant for blood, and a murder investigation without free babysitting. She squeezes her eyes shut to keep from screaming and then suddenly remembers what she's doing—driving—just as a horn from an oncoming car blares her back into her own body.

"I'm sorry, Blythe," she says, breathless. "I have to go before I kill someone."

TWENTY-SEVEN

▼

C hildren, like show business, simply must go on, Darby thinks. Try having them in a catastrophe, just try. They still need dinner and baths and bedtime stories. She can't sit on the couch and stare into space and cry and think properly. She must tend to Jack. She must heat up leftovers and tell him, "Just one more bite, just one more bite for Mommy." She does it all according to routine. One foot in front of the other. On second thought, that's probably the best thing about having children, too.

She's developed a peculiar skill as a mother. She can read an entire picture book out loud, cover to cover, while thinking about something else entirely. She'll reach the end of the book and literally have no idea what she's just read. Nothing. It's kind of amazing. So there she is, splitting her brain in two as she reads *The Pigeon Wants a Puppy*, complete with funny voices and a theatrical performance, and all the while she is thinking, thinking how she cut her leg shaving a couple days ago and used toilet paper to stop the bleeding. She threw the bloodied wads in the wastebasket and about half an hour later she passed back through and found Lola had pulled them out and was licking the dried spots of blood.

The first bite on her hand was scary. Such a terrible shock to her system. Her daughter meaning to hurt her like that. But that wasn't even the truly frightening part. The frightening part was how Darby had loathed Lola in that moment, detested her, abhorred her. Whatever you wanted to call it, Darby felt it. There's no way around it. She couldn't stand her daughter then. It was like an out-of-body experience. The canine teeth sank through her skin and she might have thought: *I don't want to be her mother.* The words felt familiar in her head, like an echo. What kind of terrible person thinks that about their child?

She wonders if Rhea even remembers those late-night texts they used to send to each other. Facts swapped back and forth to pass the time. Darby always had a penchant for true-crime tidbits, killing time by looking up the horrific deeds of notorious murderers. *You wanna know what?* She would text Rhea now if they were on texting terms at the moment, which she suspects they're not. Murderers always became murderers because they had bad mothers. Watch a few episodes of *Criminal Minds* and her analysis will be proved unassailably true. Unloving, negligent, no-good mothers. Like Darby.

Darby went to do one little thing for herself—go to the gym—and look what happened. Just look! It's like she's being dragged back by her hair to be taught a lesson. She might feel like she's giving so much, but somehow it's still less than the other mothers. She wasn't *joyfully available* or *responding intuitively* or whatever the fuck it's called. Sometimes—or often—she responds to Lola's myriad requests with a tense jaw and a barely concealed quiver of annoyance. She thinks guiltily of the sappy posts she puts on Facebook each Mother's Day—*Feel so lucky to be these two's mom*—and feels like an imposter even though it's true. Absolutely, fundamentally, unequivocally true.

She's thinking herself in circles. At some point, she's moved on to reading *Chicka Chicka Boom Boom*. Jack fidgets in her lap, trying to push to the next page, when she hears the back door *beep-beep* and her heart leaps. They're home!

She lets Jack push past the remaining pages and she hurries to get him settled in bed. She wants to see Lola, to give her a big hug and tell her, *I love you and I know you had nothing to do with Miss Ollie, I know it, I know it, a mother always knows.* Even mothers like Darby.

She scuttles down the stairs—*skit skat skoodle doot*, the picture book words stick in her mind like an earworm—and nearly runs headlong into Griff as he rounds the banister. Lola's head rests on his shoulder, open-mouthed, her legs wrapped boa constrictor style around his waist.

"She fell asleep on the drive home," he whispers.

Darby's body throbs with longing. The little girl she created looks so peaceful. She has such a nice, sweet, perfect nose and long fingers and shiny hair like a Pixar character. *Is it supposed to hurt this much?* Darby wonders. Even when her kids aren't trying to hurt her, sometimes it's their beauty that does it.

Once again, she's relegated to waiting, *more* waiting, while Griff carries Lola up to her room and deposits her gently in bed.

It's not until he reappears without their darling daughter nestled in his arms that it hits her all over again, like the second point of impact in a one-two punch: Griff's role in all this. It's her least-favorite kind of argument to have with her husband, the kind where he doesn't know they're in one.

Of course she believes Rhea. Darby may not exactly be Miss Corporate America any longer, but she's still a modern woman and so *Of course I believe you* has to be her go-to response even if every cell in her body vibrates in the opposite direction, telling her, *No. No. No. Not Griff.* But the evidence is not in his favor. Not now, when there is a Sarah Met-Online. And if there is a Sarah Met-Online, who is to say there aren't more women, more possibilities, more terrible truths waiting to be discovered.

She only has one shot at this. *Darby, you cannot fuck this up,* she cautions herself. So she waits, waits to talk through the day, the interrogation—*no, it wasn't just Lola, other kids are being questioned, too; no, he doesn't know what they're after; yes, Lola was polite; no, he doesn't think they should be worried, not really, not yet.* She has to read his face or she'll always wonder.

"We need to talk," she says when he goes to the kitchen to get his vitamins, the element of surprise on her side.

"Isn't that what we've been doing?" He looks like Griff again. Just the regular old Griff she's known for eight years, not the glimpses of some alternate-universe version she's been seeing parading around and out of their house at odd times of day.

"Who is Sarah?"

"Sarah?" he asks. "Sarah who?"

It didn't occur to her to ask for a last name. "Sarah-Sarah. I don't know. How many Sarahs do you know, and we'll work backward."

"Well . . ." He looks up, squinting. "One, I guess." And then she clocks the moment he knows he's been caught.

"I can't believe you met a woman online. Don't try to deny it. She told me. She didn't even seem to know you were married."

"Yes, she does," he insists like that makes it better. "She definitely knows I'm married."

Darby stares at him for a long beat. "Well, then she's a bitch." Darby was right the first time. This Sarah woman is a hussy and this time she's not taking it back.

"Sarah isn't a *bitch*," he emphasizes. "She's nice. She's funny."

"Why are you defending her to me?" Darby shouts because this warrants shouting even if she risks waking up both of their children, and that is saying something. "Is Sarah the only one? Is she even the first?"

But Darby suddenly feels like she knows the answer, like the pieces are falling into place.

"The only what? Friend I've met online?"

"Yeah. 'Friend.'" Darby uses air quotes.

"No." Griff shifts on his feet. He looks uncertain how to proceed, like he's waiting for her to tell him, as always. He looks like that nervous man with no self-assurance who couldn't order his own drink at the bar she met so many years ago. "This isn't how this conversation is supposed to be going." He gives his hair a little tug. "I had a way I was going to do this."

"Oh! You had a way you were going to do this, did you? Well, too bad!" Her thoughts are spinning so fast they form a dust devil in her head. Around and around and around. She has to hold her temples like she's just gotten off a teacup ride. She is totally disoriented. Where is she? Whose house is this? Who does he think he is? "Listen," she growls. "I'm going to ask you again because now Lola's involved. Did you or did you not have some sort of a private disagreement—an argument—with Miss Ollie a couple days before she died? At Little."

"No," he says, and he doesn't even sound defensive. Is that good or bad? *Should* he sound defensive? Which way would be better? She doesn't know. Maybe it would help if she were writing these observations down for later review. "We already went over this and it's simply not true."

"Which part?" she asks.

"All of it. Well, the part about Sarah. That's true. But that—I think—"

There's something about staying utterly still that makes Darby feel just the right amount formidable.

"You never mentioned going by the school, Griff. Not once," she tells him. She wants to get all of her stuff in first. He should know the extent of the case against him. She isn't going to be pushed around, especially by the least pushy person she knows. No, Griff. Not happening. "I can't understand why you wouldn't mention it."

"Because I didn't," he implores her.

"Rhea *saw* you."

All the signs were there.

"No, she didn't."

At times like these, Darby really does not recommend having a good-looking husband. Harder to stay mad at a face like that, but she's managing. A *Sarah* will do that for you. "You know, Griff, it's really not cool to gaslight women anymore."

"I'm not."

There it is, that smooth calm. That irritating calm? That creepy calm? God, how come Darby never considered that Griff's steady demeanor might be a cover for all sorts of mistruths? *Nothing to see here*, Griff Morton would lead one to believe and, oh, how she was led.

"Do you even know what gaslighting means?" she asks. Darby's not so sure she could offer a firm definition herself if pressed.

"Yes, Darby, I know what gaslighting means. I've been on Reddit. I'm an IT *professional*, remember?"

"Right. But—" Her lip quivers. She can't look at him another second, can't bear to. "I went to go talk to Miss Ollie." She's been so careful, so unbelievably careful to hold this in, but it doesn't matter. Because Rhea's onto something. It's already out. "I'm not *stupid*, Griff. I'm not that kind of woman. You should know that by now. I was supposed to have a meeting with Mary Beth about the girls, but when she canceled, I went to go talk to Erin myself. And I was going to ask her, ask, you know, about why you came to speak with her. Go straight to the source. I figured it was about Lola. I know we don't always see eye to eye about her." This. She wants to tap her finger on that last bit for emphasis. The reason she jumped to the initial conclusion that her husband had headed her off, gone to get the first word in about Lola, perhaps requested the counselor evaluation without consulting Darby—which would have been bad enough, by the way—was not because she's a naive twit; no, the reason she had ignored the late nights at work, the new emphasis on his appearance, all that, was because her mind was already circling around Lola. She was primed to ignore her husband. He was usually so ignorable in social settings.

So she believed the best-case scenario, gave the benefit of the doubt, and even that wasn't a particularly great one because when it comes to their daughter, they're supposed to tell each other things.

He lifts his eyebrows with seemingly boyish hope. "And what did she say? I'm sure she backed me up. She would have had to."

She swallows. Is this it? He's so confident that Miss Ollie would back him up, that she would have had to, why? What would give him that confidence?

Her hands are shaking now. She's not well. "I didn't get to talk to her, Griff."

"Why not?"

"Why do you think?" He must know the ending. "She was dead."

She can see the mental math written on his face as he calculates it in his head. Darby was on campus on the day of the murder. She was looking for Erin.

"That's not all." She keeps her voice low. "I saw something, I mean someone. I saw someone leaving, right when I showed up. I swear I had no idea Miss Ollie was dead."

"Who?"

She frowns. Never mind, it doesn't matter whether she stays still. "You," she says. "I saw you."

His mouth twists. She doesn't recognize his eyes. "You didn't. This is insane. I wasn't at school that day."

"Which day?"

"Either! Why would I lie about it?" He swipes his hand across the counter, knocking a heavy Ralph Lauren glass from a set they'd received from their wedding registry. It cracks open on the floor. They stare at it together. Never once has either of them reacted like that in their marriage. An unspoken line crossed.

"The same reason you never told me about *Sarah.*" She can't help saying the name with a schoolgirl teasing singsong.

"This is insane," he says.

"I agree."

"I didn't even know Miss Ollie."

"All the men *knew* Miss Ollie." She can't believe she was so la-di-da about the dads at Little ogling Miss Ollie. Worse, she was *cavalier.* Ugh. She hates her past self.

Griff rolls his eyes, but he doesn't pretend that he doesn't know what she's talking about.

"I saw you," she repeats. "You were leaving. You didn't look back to see me, but you were."

She was so surprised to spot him from a distance across campus, sort of delighted at first, the way it was a pleasant coincidence to bump into a friend at the airport. She yelled, "*Griff!*" And when he didn't turn, she yelled it louder. Nothing. "*Gri-iiff!*" Again. Only this time a spike of irritation wiggled under her skin. He was ignoring her. Well, no thank you. That didn't sit right. So Darby did what Darby would do: She gave chase.

Her feet against the cream-colored path. Through the church campus, she set off at a brisk pace, but he kept walking faster. Faster and faster. It took incredible self-control not to break into a run. And then somewhere between the unfamiliar church buildings, she's disappointed to say, she lost him. Griff vanished, as if he were a ghost. Or a figment of her imagination.

At that point, she was sweltering with both anger and effort and she thought, *Enough of these games. I'll ask Miss Ollie directly what my husband is doing here, what secret opinions about Lola he's shilling.*

The rest is history, as they say. Almost. Because now she knows about Sarah.

"And—" She gathers steam. "—by the way, it's not just that. You've been acting weird lately. I've been fine to go along because you are, you know, kind of weird. But now. Now I can't believe I've been so stupid. Disappearing on me. Just vanishing on these late-night work shifts that never existed before. And smiling at your phone. What's so funny, huh?"

Nothing. That's the answer. All of a sudden nothing is funny at all. Her husband looks grim.

"What are you accusing me of exactly?" He asks the question very slowly.

She thought that was obvious. "I'm asking a very simple question and I think it demands a very simple answer."

"Are you asking if I've been cheating on you? Because it sounds like you're asking if I've been cheating on you."

At last, anguish from her husband, and it soaks every square inch of familiar terrain on his face and Darby doesn't like it, not one bit. A sheen of oily sweat gleams off his nose and forehead and she feels that she too is sympathy sweating. He's supposed to deny it out of hand. He's supposed to tell her she's lost her marbles. He's not supposed to lose his cool. And now, she's terrified that the next words out of his mouth will push her over a cliff so steep she can't possibly scrabble her way back up.

TWENTY-EIGHT

▼

R hea slides into a chair across from Marcus at the coffee shop near his office, one of the cool spots with baristas who give a shit about where beans are sourced from. "Now still a good time?" she asks, accepting the mug of coffee he's already thought to order her.

"I've always got time for you." Rhea isn't "establishment," but she can admit she likes a man in work clothes. Marcus does his gray slacks and pale blue button-down proud. "You don't have to ask."

"Yeah I do," she reminds him, and tries not to feel too badly when she spots him deflate. She just means they have boundaries. Boundaries are good. And they don't need to know everything about each other, do they? Until they do. Unfortunately, that might be now.

She should be thrilled. In the last two days alone, orders for Terrene have quadrupled. A freshly verified Instagram account. A shining city on a hill. An example of a self-sacrificing mother doing everything in her child's best interest.

She *is* all those things, she insists, as if someone has argued the point. At least in spirit, where it counts. And when she lays her head down at night, she sleeps just fine, thanks. Better, even, given how her advisor's been fielding investor calls left and right. There may even be a wait list for different rounds, who knows. Well, Rhea knew, as a matter of fact.

If Rhea were listening closely, she might hear her dreams falling into place—*click, click, click*—like music. Instead, she hears the creaking of the joints as the ground shifts beneath her house of cards. A single detail from her early twenties could change everything. There is music there, all right, music she's got to face. In the form of Marcus.

"Is this about the—the biting, because Rhea, I swear, I'm not denying him. He just doesn't want to do it with me. I offer, just like you said. I don't know, maybe I'm not doing it right, but I *am* trying."

The number of opaque Yeti tumblers sent to school with the children has multiplied. *My nine-year-old thought it was Spaghetti-Os in there and took a sip without me knowing it and threw up,* Chelsea told them one day in abject horror, *and I thought: My god, we've got to take him to the hospital, he's vomiting blood. And then I realized, that was my blood. And I almost threw up, too.* Rows of the discreet containers line up in the new in-class mini fridge, masking tape labels stuck to each. Mamas measure out the milliliters, the way they once did in ounces with breast milk. Here and there, a child will run to his or her mommy at the end of the day with a faint red-orange mustache still smudged across his or her upper lip and the mother will lick her thumb and try to smear it away while the kid whines, "Yuck." It's like they're walking on glass. She can feel it in the fragile, baby-bird way the mothers carry themselves, as if they've regressed, gone back in time to those frangible newborn days when mothers pulled on outside clothes and rubbed in a bit of foundation, swiped mascara, and tried to look like real people, not crumbly scones destined to fall apart the moment one accidentally bumped her elbow too hard on the edge of the car door.

Rhea never intended to outright lie on-air, but then the day before, she opened up a vein and siphoned a hundred milliliters into a brand-new tumbler. *Just in case,* she told Bodhi, who didn't really care as long as he got to play. The tumbler comes back, and every day since she sends the same hundred milliliters; back and forth it goes. She's afraid to open the lid and find out what it looks like in there. And so she doesn't. No need.

She shakes her head. "Don't worry about it. I think we've got Bodhi under control."

He puffs his cheeks out and exhales. He's so scared of doing the wrong thing and she doesn't exactly do anything to alleviate that fear. Some fears are healthy.

"You know Terrene is growing, and this is a critical time," she says, fingers tightening around her warm cup. She studies the soft green leaves of the willow on her arm and reminds herself how the tree's supple branches allow it to withstand strong winds.

One of the beauties of working for herself is that she hasn't had anyone run a background check in years. Her mug shot's out there. But it's not *out there*, out there.

Still, sometimes she looks it up out of a masochistic need to keep it fresh in her mind.

She majored in bioethics at a college she hated but could go to for free. Her father warned her against wasting her time studying *liberal arts*, a term he learned from one of her brochures and used like a swear word. After college, she moved back to Austin, took a job in public health where she earned $35,000 a year organizing files in a horrible brown office with moldy carpet, playing waitress on the side for cash. She hated her father most on the days when it felt like he was right.

That was before. Because after, it turns out you can't have an assault record and work for the state. Really, you can't have an assault record and work much of anywhere these days.

But Rhea made do. She spent most of her time working as a personal executive assistant for a man who asked in the interview: *Do you mind if I run a background check?* To which Rhea answered very confidently that she wouldn't mind at all and then obviously he was too lazy to run it. She even landed her job as a nanny that way. Oddly enough, Marcus didn't think to ask for her arrest record before they jumped into bed together either.

"Yeah, I'm here." He nods. "Whatever you need. I'm so proud of you. You're such a role model for Bodhi."

"Thanks." But there's heat behind her eyes.

"Just like my mother was for me," he adds. "I feel really lucky that somehow we wound up with you."

"I guess that's my point." She blows on her coffee. "You do think I'm a good mother, right?" For the record, Rhea hasn't spent many moments questioning the morals of her past choices. She's not making excuses for them. She should never have laid hands, she knows that. But what's done is done. Only, once you become a mom and a *female* business owner, that stuff doesn't fly. Oh sure, people love a good redemptive arc for fathers, just watch a few comedies from the 2000s and you'll see what she means. The dad that gets his shit together. Stops drinking. Stops smoking. Starts showing up in his kid's life ten years too late. But mothers? No. There's no redemption for mothers. Mothers better be born perfect. Pure and virgin white.

"Of course."

"And you trust me and you trust my judgment?"

He glances over at a man and a woman at the next table clearly involved in some sort of casual job interview that's not going that well. "Yeah. I mean, I want to be involved . . ." He uses his knuckle to scratch beneath his nose. "I'm his father."

"You are involved."

"Okay."

"What's that supposed to mean?"

"Only that you're kind of a solo artist, you know? Looking out for Number One." He keeps his eyes trained on the floundering man with the résumé. "Not in a bad way."

"Number One?" She lifts her eyebrows. "I make every meal, do laundry, do pickup and drop-off ninety percent of the week, and I'm looking out for Number One?"

"I didn't mean it like that." Marcus slouches, hunching in that fancy shirt of his.

"How *did* you mean it, then?" Rhea wants to give Bodhi everything. She kind of wants to give Terrene everything, too. Last time she checked, they're not the same everythings.

He rolls his eyes. "I mean, you need help. Your job—your career, your business—it takes up a lot of space. As it should. But maybe you need to let some stuff go, let people in."

"My job takes up space? *Space?* I think I've got plenty of space. I don't think anyone's suffering—least of all Bodhi, if that's what you're implying—from a lack of *space*." She can't help comparing herself to him, can't help worrying that someday he might up and start to believe Bodhi would benefit more from living with him in his grown-up condo, being driven around in his luxury SUV. "Nobody's claustrophobic here, Marcus." She feels the mercury in her barometer sliding up. Same as it did that night at the Roosevelt Room. A little bubble of memory rises to the surface and pops: *How many times do I have to explain myself?*

She'd pressed the palms of her hands against the metal table to cool them, and when she brought them to her lap, they had left oily palm prints. She and the white, male, twentysomething John Doe officer both stared at them as they talked, so much that Rhea eventually moved her hands back, refitting them to the spot she left, even when her fingers got cold, even when they started to lose circulation. It was a long night, the smell of secondhand smoke and stale coffee, the ghost of body odor.

Rhea was a cocktail waitress and usually it was a good time. She made friends. She listened to the regulars' problems. She even helped some people. And she felt good doing it.

She knew that guy was going to be an issue; she'd waited on him before, but tonight he was edgy with alcohol and in the mood to show off for his buddies, which is the worst mood for any man, as far as Rhea's concerned. He was the type of guy who wore flashy bald eagle swim trunks on the Fourth of July and shitty sunglasses owned by his father in the eighties, who favored penny loafers and yacht rock that he was too young for. A former frat boy, he nurtured the paunch growing over his khaki shorts as a status symbol, as though to broadcast, *I don't have to look good to attract women, that's what the money is for.* And when a Jay-Z song came on, he sang all the lyrics—*all* of them.

You look like the kind of girl who could use a big tip.

It felt like she'd been caught smiling, not knowing she had food in her teeth. She understood: She'd been to college. She'd moved away from home. She worked in an ugly office, but in an office nonetheless. She dressed business casual and still a guy like him could smell her white trash from a mile away and he wanted to make sure she knew she wasn't fooling anyone.

Her face burned, her pulse bulging in the tender spot at her throat.

He asked if she'd ever had a nice meal. When she said she had, he asked her if she knew what *omakase* was and said it was so cute when she didn't. He'd fix that, he said. He could *Pretty Woman* her, he said. She felt like someone had poured fire down the front of her shirt and her job was to stay chill.

And then, as she was walking by, balancing a tray of fancy drinks on her shoulder for her largest party over there in the corner, what'd he do? He *touched* her ass cheek. Like it was one of the many things he owned. Like it was nothing. Like her ass was for sale.

She can still remember the sound of cascading glass as the tray tipped and they all hit the floor one after the other after the other, too late to save. The eyes of an entire bar turned on her and he laughed. He fucking laughed.

Right up until she whirled around and clocked him with the one highball glass that had somehow stayed on her tray. The son of a female state senator. Four stitches through the eyebrow. Charges pressed. She had *assaulted*-assaulted him. What he did was "different." There was never any excuse for physical violence, don't they teach that in public schools? And that was the end of that. Her mother said she always knew this would happen. At thirteen, Rhea dented the side of her mother's car with a travel mug, so obviously this whole thing was inevitable.

Before that day, she wouldn't even have thought of herself as a woman with a temper, but there it has been ever since, coiled in the basket like she's keeping a wild animal for a pet. The world keeps it fed and she keeps it contained in case she ever needs it again.

"I'm not trying to argue with you." Marcus puts up his palms as though he can sense it there, too. "Let's reset. What'd you want to talk about anyway?"

She pushes her nails into the fleshy meat below her thumb. *I am the rising sun on the ocean horizon. I am light through the still trees. I am the lasting snow at the top of the mountain.* She breathes her affirmations in and out. "Nothing really," she says. "I just wanted to see if I could get you to take a look at some financial statements for me and tell me what they might mean."

He grins as she slides Miss Ollie's documents across the table and decides, once again, that what Marcus doesn't know won't hurt her.

TWENTY-NINE

▼

W"ait," Darby commands her husband as he opens his mouth to speak. "Maybe I should be standing up for this."

"I think the advice is usually the other way around," he says.

"Well, I think *I* should be standing." She removes herself from the sofa they spent eight hours deciding on, popping between Crate & Barrel and Pottery Barn and back again until they finally collapsed on this exact floor model and cried out together, "We'll take it!" before erupting into a fit of stupid giggles. That was seven years ago. She still likes this couch.

She feels much better standing. *Assume an athletic stance*, her volleyball coach always told her, *so you're ready for the strike*.

Griff looks twice as uncomfortable as he did before. Good. He stares down at his shoes. "What I was going to say is—" He coughs. She hates unnecessary coughing because that's marriage, hating someone's peculiar, obnoxious noises; marriage is not an affair with their children's preschool teacher or a lady at the gym. "I'm sorry." And she can tell that whatever he says next, he really is. Sorry. "I didn't want to tell you this way. I haven't been working late." *Oh no.* Her stomach climbs to a sickening elevation, waiting for it. "I've been taking an improv class."

She stares at him. Like she's watching a movie and the sound and video display aren't totally synced.

"An . . . improv class."

"Yes." He shakes his head as though even he can't believe it. "Yes, I can show you the receipts and everything. And as far as the phone thing, we're on a group text chain. It's funny. *I'm* funny. On it, I mean." He shrugs one shoulder.

"I know you're funny," she snaps. "I'm married to you."

"I'm sorry." Can he please stop saying that? "I set a goal to get over my—my social anxiety disorder, that's what the therapist called it." Darby feels, of all things, a spark of anger. For how many years has she been encouraging him to seek professional help and always she was made out to be the pushy bad guy. But now, Griff's done it. He's not only looked up a therapist, but made an appointment and seen one. Probably more than once from the sound of things. Without telling her. *Why* didn't he tell her? "I saw an Instagram ad for an online therapist and I thought, why not? His name's Rahul. I should have told you about Rahul," he says, as if reading her mind. "But I had this idea that it would be a surprise. A good surprise."

Bullshit. The thought comes to her so briskly that she flushes crimson. Sure, maybe he took the classes, but he didn't care about surprising her. He wanted something to himself.

"Also . . ." he falters. "I was embarrassed and not sure if I would chicken out. Plus I knew you'd want to come to one of my shows."

"You have *shows*?"

"Showcases, more like. They're not a big deal. Nothing fancy."

"Who are you?" It's the most articulate thing she can manage on short notice. Therapist. Improv. *Shows.* A whole world about which Darby knows nothing.

"There was that Christmas party at the end of last year. Do you remember it? You told me it was a girls' night. But I found the invitation in the trash and it wasn't. It wasn't women only. There was *karaoke*."

Darby does remember. She sang "Come On Eileen" and she missed Griff in that moment because he loves that song, but she didn't feel guilty. "I was doing you a favor," she says. A small fib. He should be thanking her. She's always making casual excuses for him. *Oh, he does like you, he's just an introvert. No, no, he clams up sometimes, sorry. Really, he's so wonderful, just not a big group person, you know?* She can think of a dozen of these conversations she's had with friends over the years. Eventually, she got desensitized, though, and stopped feeling the need to explain Griff.

"At first I was mad. It was almost worse than if *you* were having an affair. I mean, that's how much you didn't want to have me around? It was awful, Darby."

Hold on a minute, the conversation is moving entirely in the wrong direction, she's swimming upside down. How is she the bad guy here? What's going on?

He grins sheepishly, asking her to understand something he's never even bothered to explain to her. "But it was a wake-up call. I get it now. It's frustrating for you to have to babysit me at parties and whatnot and, well, believe it or not, I don't love it myself." He chuckles. "Rahul says it's a real thing. There are symptoms. Excessive sweating, trembling, nausea, difficulty speaking, a rapid heart rate. An actual diagnosable syndrome and I have it. I know it's not like I'm a social anxiety disorder *survivor* or anything." Though it sounds to her like that's exactly what he thinks, like she should make him some colorful supportive wristband. "So I knew I had to treat it like a disease, to do something drastic. Dive into the deep end, so to speak."

"Well, you did it," she manages weakly. Her husband. A comedy troupe member. It's so important that she look happy for him, that she perform this happiness convincingly. She has no time to consider how she actually feels.

"I'm not totally cured yet, but Rahul says maybe by Christmas we could try having a dinner party or something? The point is I'm getting there. It's a start. See, at first, I just did an online class, like with Rahul. That's where I met Sarah. She was in my class at Upright Citizens Brigade. Level One Improv. Kind of neat that they offer it. It's a very *safe space*." U-C-B, Darby thinks. *He met Sarah at UCB and then, and then* . . . "And then I was finally ready to try it in person. I go to this theater near my office. I'll show you sometime, now that you know."

"Hideout?" she asks, feebly.

"You know it?" He grins like this is all the best news ever.

He stretches out his arms. A hug. The man is expecting a hug. From her. The pallor has retreated from his face, now rosy with pride. He's thrilled. It's all out in the open. As though this couldn't have worked out better if he planned it. He's a changed man. Or at least a changing one.

Darby allows whatever sense of forward momentum that carried her this far in the conversation to send her gently floating into his arms, as if that were where she intended to land all along.

"Thank you, Darby," he says into the top of her hair.

"You're . . . welcome?"

She's relieved, isn't she? Or mostly relieved.

At least until it's the middle of the night and she can't sleep, but her spinning head has slowed enough to consider how two things can be true at once. Griff can be doing improv. Griff could have also been at the school. One has virtually no power to negate the other and yet she let the conversation end right then and there. Griff truly could not have planned it any better, which of course he didn't. He improvised.

THIRTY

▼

This morning, when Mary Beth woke up, she felt like her old self again. Squeaky clean, not even a glimmer of headache on the horizon. It was marvelous. She had a desire to make Mickey Mouse pancakes. *Vintage Mary Beth,* she thought fondly. She is a woman who can make crabs out of a croissant and cucumbers and form Sponge-Bob SquarePants from spaghetti. She goes the extra mile. That's who she is as a mother, as a person.

"Good morning," she sang to her little family like she was Julie Andrews in *The Sound of Music.*

The faces of her daughters glowed with youthful radiance. They were beautiful, a stunning feat of nature like a national park. "Breakfast with a view." She smiled, looking at them, really looking for what felt like the first time in weeks.

Only a year ago, Noelle had slept with an alligator blanket named Alli and was deathly afraid of the snow monster in *Frozen* and greeted everyone she saw with "Hello, guys," like a vaudeville actress. Now she's four and a whole new person who sleeps with a bear and gets embarrassed when she passes gas and still the beauty remains the same.

She thinks about those national parks, those stretches of untouched land, and believes her daughters truly are a lot like those splendid views; they must be protected.

An hour or two later, still in her chipper, can-do Mary Beth mood, she knocks on the office door of Pastor Ben. "Now still a good time?" she asks in the creaky hallway.

The hotter the temperature climbs, the less capable it seems the window air units are of fending off the creeping humidity. A hint of mildew mixes with the smell of a microwaved breakfast sandwich. On the bathroom door hangs a typed sign that reads *Sensitive Plumbing,* and

Mary Beth thinks maybe for her next project she'll tackle getting these offices renovated properly.

Today, she arrives as her most presentable self. The Bible is full of redemption stories—see the Prodigal Son, and Jonah, and, of course, Job. Hers involves a ladylike dress and some judiciously applied argan oil. Though perhaps presenting a self who has not almost assaulted a police officer in front of a pastor is all the improvement she really needs.

She just has this sense that everything is going to be okay.

"Hey, hey." Pastor Ben looks up from where he was writing in a journal. There's no product in his hair today and a wavy lock falls over his forehead, which he swipes back as his eyes meet hers. He sets down his pen and ushers her inside with a big, hospitable gesture. To her surprise, instead of staying where he is, he comes around to occupy the guest chair beside her. "Do you mind?" he asks, hovering over the cushioned chair. "Easier to focus without my computer screen beckoning."

"By all means."

He nestles his back into the support. "Thanks for coming," he says. "I wanted to go ahead and check in again about those fundraising efforts for the youth center." When he hikes his ankle over his knee, she notices a small tribal sun tattooed on the inside bone. "The coffers, you know, seem to be sort of, you know." He flattens his hand. "On a plateau."

"I think it's paused, mostly," she says. She did imagine this was coming and yet still doesn't like the feeling of not being in a position to *wow*. "We did ask for contributions at the counseling session you led with the children, which was fantastic, by the way, but wanted to let the families regroup given the circumstances."

"Paused isn't stopped, though, right?" He toys with his chin.

"Of course not. I check the office regularly for any new slips. And, you know, a few of the parents thought it would be nice to earmark a portion of the money for Erin's funeral expenses. We could give it to the family as a gift." She doesn't mention that "some of the parents" were just her, actually. "I need to deal with that paperwork, but—"

"How much do they want to earmark?"

"Oh. I don't know exactly. A couple thousand dollars might be appropriate. I can get you hard numbers." She grabs a pen and planner from her purse and makes a note.

He sits forward, elbows on knees, his shirt pulling tight across his broad shoulders. She remembers when Doug's shirts used to do that. Now they just sort of bunch up around the love handles. Not that she's complaining. Just noticing. A woman's allowed to notice, isn't she? Especially given—given that their 30-Day Challenge has hit the skids. There, she said it.

"I understand the school is going through a really difficult time," he's saying gently. "But I also find that's one of the reasons we should pull together now more than ever. As a community."

"As a community," she echoes. Gosh, she loves that word. "Right. True. Give them an outlet, something positive in the future." She mulls it over. "So, you'd like me to restart the efforts in earnest then?"

He considers. "I think that would be what Erin would have wanted."

She makes another note and frowns at it. Her handwriting looks sloppy. "It might not be tomorrow," she says, still staring at her shaky cursive. "But I'll get the wheels moving. We've all had a lot on our plates." She clicks her pen and, with a note of finality, snaps her planner shut. Gung-ho Mary Beth to the rescue. Just one more task to tick, but tick she shall.

"Of course, no problem. I'm curious actually. Tell me about that. Have those two officers—what were their names?"

"Detective Bright and Officer Princep," Mary Beth recites, the set of her mouth wavering. Bright and Princep have both been recurring characters in her dreams the last several nights. Stress dreams. Like the ones she used to have in college when she would realize at the end of a semester that there was a class she'd forgotten to attend all year. Only now her stress dreams are these two police officers. They're never *doing* anything. Sometimes she might show up to a dinner party and find them seated across the table from her. Or get coffee only to find one is her barista and yet also somehow still a cop. Always she knows on a subconscious level that it's a dream, but she can never wake herself out of it and so she has slept fitfully, their presence haunting her.

"That's right," Ben says, as if the answer had been on the tip of his tongue. She doesn't think it was. "Have they stayed out of your way since I had a word with them?" There's a small puff of pride: *Oh, you know how men get.* However, the way he came in was gallant, she must admit. And he absolutely deserved credit for smoothing things over. She doesn't know what might have happened otherwise. She could have been in handcuffs. Then she would not have had a nice Mary Beth morning with her nice girls in her nice house. It's like everything is balancing precariously. She wants to do her Mom-Voice: *Step back, just a smidge, please, you're too close to the edge.*

"Thank you." She puts feeling into it and hopes he knows how much she means it, truly. "They're very . . . persistent." She rubs her palms over the skirt of her dress.

"There are good and bad types in every profession, unfortunately." He shakes his head dolefully.

"I guess that's true." Though she wasn't assuming that Bright or Princep were bad necessarily.

"And the—the stool sample—did they ever even, you know, bother to test that?"

Oh good, she loves when she can impart useful information. "They did," she says with authority. Part of the reason for her improved disposition. "They compared the stool sample collected from Poodini—sorry, that's just a name that some of the parents are calling the child in question, I actually started it, not that that's important at all, but it's a little funny, not funny ha-ha, but you do have to find the humor in these situations. So yes, they compared the cells or DNA or whatever they do in labs against all of the DNA and follicle samples and what have you found at the scene of the—" She always trips at this part. "—the murder, and there was no match." She feigns wiping her brow. "So that's one worry crossed off."

"Interesting." He rubs his fingers and thumb hard into the socket of his eyes. He looks like he has a lot on his plate himself. "So, sorry, I'm in the dark. What's crossed off?"

"Well." She lets her eyes drift to the ceiling as she puffs her cheeks. "I guess the logic is if the Poodini sample had been a match, then the police would have thought that there was a really good chance that—that one of the kids was *involved*. A child acting out one way might act out another and so on."

"Except for those children's footprints you mentioned. So they still must think one of the kids might have seen something, right?"

She feels the eleven between her eyes deepen. "I don't know. I can't even get my daughter to tell me who she played with at school, so if any of the kids saw anything, they haven't bothered mentioning it."

Lola had been brought in for questioning and she hears other students will be, too.

"Anyway." She lightly steers the conversation. "Our hope is that the fact that this fishing expedition they went on was a complete dead end will encourage the police to keep casting a wider net. Look around. Think of the broader reach of the school and people around."

"How are the parents feeling, though? What are people saying? What do people *think* happened?"

She tries to suppress the small surge of dread she's felt at every mention of Miss Ollie's murder, of which there have been many, unavoidable instances over the last couple of weeks. She feels the impact once again flood her nervous system like two hair dryers plugged into an old electrical outlet, threatening to break her circuit.

The memory swims through the filter of the incredible pain she was in that day. The mere mention is enough to conjure a phantom version of it. She can feel the outline, the physical shape of it, throbbing right there in her right eye socket, drilling through to her brain. She wanted to hurl. The entire morning, through the awful psychologist appointment, in her car, every instant, she fought down vomiting.

What she most wanted to do that day was crawl into her bed or sink into a hot bath or do both simultaneously somehow. She thought: *Can we please get this day over with already?*

That was her intent. She went to school for the meeting, but then decided it would be better to pick Noelle up early and reschedule for a time she felt more like herself. Like today! Today would have been an excellent day for the meeting with Miss Ollie. Today, she could have looked Darby right in the eye and said, *I'm sorry, I adore you as a friend, but the girls don't get along anymore because Lola has issues, something you might want to have looked into.* And then Mary Beth could have pulled out a few websites and phone numbers as resources to help Darby process the information and Miss Ollie would have been there to back her up and together, they could have gotten through to Darby before it was too late. But it was not today. She made her decision to pick up Noelle early and now she thanks God she did, for who knows what would have happened otherwise.

"What do people think happened?" she reflects, at the same time clocking a faint throb of pain that has begun pressing against the nerve behind her right eye. *Oh no.* She wants to believe it's a phantom pain again. From the memory. However, it's the stupid, little, nothing pain— not the agony of a cracked bone or the spasming strain of childbirth— that starts to break her heart. And doesn't the very fact that the ghostly pain returns at the memory of that day lend credence to the doctors' infuriating suggestion of anxiety? "Someone in the congregation, a vagrant even, staff, a friend who knew where she worked." Her voice cracks. "Not a lot of great answers."

He studies her, trains the full intensity of those evergreen eyes on her. "Come on," he nudges, coming to the edge of his seat. "You must have some inside beat. You're the go-to, aren't you? Room Mom? Pastors have to keep things confidential." He's teasing. She thinks he's teasing. She laughs, but there's nothing to fill it after, so maybe he really was expecting her to tell him something substantial.

She's heard gossip, of course. The kinds of things one would expect. Someone saw a weird guy hanging around the school the week before and never reported it. Miss Ollie had a secret life. She killed herself and the family refuses to accept it. Some are more realistic than others, but Mary Beth makes sure to remind everyone: They're just rumors.

Ben clears his throat. "You know," he says, "I've been meaning to check in with you about your husband. You said you took on my Sexy Back Challenge?" He grins.

"Did. Yes. We fell off the wagon. There are more important things going on at the moment." She doesn't bother to hide her resignation. It doesn't matter that it's correct. There are far more important things going on than whether she and her husband of a decade can fornicate for fun every day, but, then, that's kind of the point. There are always more important things going on because everything is more important than sex, really.

Half the time, Mary Beth doesn't even know what she's after. It's not as though she's a sixteen-year-old boy or a Yorkshire terrier, walking around with an uncontrollable urge to hump things. And she already feels connected in her marriage, so it's not that. Sex to Mary Beth is a thing she wants to cut out of the world and drape herself in because it looks pretty on her.

And in exactly the way an expensive dress would be spliced from the family budget when times are tight, so too is romance when *time* is tight.

Pastor Ben looks as if he might have something to say about that. Might view himself the way, say, a doctor does, prescribing exercise as a preventative measure.

He rests his chin on his palm and looks up at her and, as he does, she experiences a very specific déjà vu in the way her teenage heart had felt staring at the back of Andrew Wohlensky's head during algebra. And just like back then, a piece of her thinks, improbably, *If only I could have him, just for a very short time, that would put my slightly broken heart back together again.* She swallows as her head pings her, bopping her with the little pain signal. *Remember me?*

"I heard what you said," Ben murmurs, like he knows she'd be embarrassed if someone else were to overhear. "I listened. About how you always feel like you're the one, you know, pushing the agenda. Initiating sex. And I just want to say, Mary Beth, I think your husband is crazy."

The graze of his fingers is so light on her calf it could almost be an accident. But Mary Beth's whole body wakes up—*zip, hello*—finding that she's been transported into a scene from her dreams, one in which she indulged a small fantasy that had involved This. Exact. Scenario. She sighs a long, deep sigh. That was a good dream. She'll miss it. Because in reality, it turns out, Pastor Ben is kind of a creep.

THIRTY-ONE

▼

Darby absolutely, positively does not feel like herself. She wants to call out sick from work, but, of course, you can't really call out sick when you work from home. It's like an unwritten rule.

It's her husband, Griff. He's given her an illness. An awful, soggy malaise. This morning, she relied heavily on inertia—an object in motion stays in motion—to combat the problem, buzzing around the kitchen, packing lunches and getting kids dressed and applying sunscreen like the house was on fire and she needed to get the family out, out, out the door. *Sorry, no time to chat*, she tried to telegraph to him.

"Everything okay?" Griff asked as he poured his first cup of coffee. "Need a hand?"

Under different circumstances, she might have replied something like *"Ha!"* Because that did sound like her when she got into a mood with him.

"Someone's stompy this morning." The crack of the refrigerator door sounded somewhere behind her.

"Busy morning," she told him. "You know. Like always." Her muscles were sore from the workout with Cannon, which should have been satisfying, but instead kept annoying her each time she bent down for a sippy cup or reached into a cabinet overhead.

It was a relief when Griff finally left for work and she no longer had to go to the trouble of avoiding him. She never avoids her husband, not even when it comes to sex, which she knows is a thing wives do, at least according to TV, but not Darby.

It's just, no matter how she slices it, Griff lied to her. And he's acting as though the special rules for surprise parties apply when they definitely don't, do they? She could maybe understand that he wanted privacy around going to therapy. She could reluctantly concede that. And maybe the therapist suggested the improv and then . . . and then she gets turned around in her own logic the way she has so many times over the last twenty-four hours. Because if Griff could lie to her once, what's stopping him from doing it again?

By the end of the day, she still hasn't managed to kick the Griff-induced sickness.

"I missed you," he says when he returns home. He's got this new way about him. Self-confidence or something. She's not sure whether she likes it.

She lets him kiss her on the cheek. "I need to take a quick shower," she says. "I feel gross. Can you watch the kids?"

Both children have plastered themselves to a Netflix show about rainbow unicorn puppies. They look so happy, their little necks arched out, exposing their throats, colors bouncing off their faces. She doesn't have the heart to turn it off and insist they do something that won't turn their brains to mush. Like crafts. They should do more crafts.

She doesn't really have any intention of taking a *quick* shower; she lied. See, two can tango.

She locks the door and turns the water to extra hot so the steam billows and the glass clouds and her lungs loosen.

Lola hadn't asked to be fed today, hadn't requested a single bite or sip of blood. Darby thinks this is a good sign. Some of the other children are greedier than ever. Bex is up to something like 500 milliliters a day. George's mom looked horrified by that tidbit and Darby is inclined to agree, it's a little too much information. But today, nothing. A sign, maybe, that this whole parasitical, leechlike behavior is drawing to a close. Just a phase! Just like old Dr. Meckler had said.

From inside the shower, she hears the doorbell ring—*Who could that be?* She freezes, soapy fingertips dug hard into her scalp. Unable to hear anything else, she returns to scrubbing. Just an Amazon delivery. Let Griff get it.

"Darby!" There's a rattle on the locked door. "Darby!" Another rattle, then silence.

She switches off the shower and pulls the not-fresh towel from where it hangs over the top of the glass. Scrunching her sopping-wet hair in the towel, she hears voices in the living room.

Darby finishes drying off and grabs the first items of clothing she finds cast slipshod on the bathroom counter—a loose pair of gym shorts and one of Griff's big college tees.

"Griff?" she calls as she pads into the family area to investigate. She's always being called to referee things between the kids. "Griff—oh." She hesitates, trying to process the scene as she comes across it in her living room. "I'm sorry." She steps back, sinking toward the door to her master bedroom. "I'll just be—"

"Stay. Please, Mrs. Morton."

Darby's eyes flick to the two bulky pairs of tactical zip boots digging dirt into her rug.

"Is everything okay?" She directs the question not to the two police officers—one male, one female—but to Griff, whose hand rests firmly on Lola's shoulder. The TV is off, happy little faces no more. Lola loops a strand of hair between her teeth and chews while Jack scoots toy cars around the foyer on his knees.

The first officer—Princep, according to the name tag—isn't more handsome than her Griff, but he's up there. "We just had a few follow-up questions for your daughter related to the incident at school."

"She—she already went in to answer—answer questions," Griff stammers, looking to the woman—middle-aged, Black, natural hair, and nice, shapely eyebrows.

Darby nods in solidarity and her hair drips heavy droplets onto her bare toes. She looks at Griff, knowing instantly what this means: She has to call a stalemate. Whatever misgivings she may have about her feelings surrounding Griff, they end here. Whatever he did, whatever he said, whatever she saw, they will stand together.

"A few more," says the female officer, whose tag reads simply: *Det. Bright.* She has a line of piercings up the cartilage of her left ear and yet she's still got that "in charge" aura.

"That seems . . . excessive for a child." Darby doesn't even offer them a seat.

"We're simply following up based on new information and subsequent interviews." Princep flashes his dimples like all this is a good thing. Lucky them, they've been selected out of a hundred participants for a grand prize.

"I'm sorry, what are you trying to say?" She looks to Griff, who has clammed up; she knows that look. The hunched shoulders, the nervous rub of his lower lip. Hello, where is his new outgoing attitude now? It would be lovely if someone, anyone, could swoop in and tell them what to do in this perplexing situation. Where *are the grown-ups?* she finds herself thinking. Or rather, when did *they* become them?

One time, the house alarm sounded in the middle of the night in error and when she and Griff woke up, they both just sat in bed for about thirty seconds, waiting for their own respective parents to swoop in and take care of the problem. What a rude awakening it was to discover the parents were them.

"When we investigate a murder—" Detective Bright is a hand talker, something Darby usually likes in a person because it's often an indication that this person can carry a conversation, but this is one conversation Darby would much prefer to be over. "—we're primarily looking for two things: motive and opportunity. When we last spoke your husband confirmed that Lola is one of the children afflicted with this—this Renfield's syndrome, I think you're calling it."

Darby glances sidelong at her husband, who has now apparently developed an itchy nose.

"A very mild case. We have clear boundaries. It's—you know—it's not a big deal," Darby says, her voice tipping up. "Actually, I think Lola is one of the first kids to be outgrowing it. I'm not even feeding her anymore." Darby embellishes, but it could be true.

Princep has withdrawn a flimsy notebook and is jotting down what she's said, creating a record—an official record! "I understand that when parents don't offer a blood supply on demand, you know, that the kids can get, er, agitated?" He gives her the smoldering look of a movie star cop. Where does he believe the cameras are? "Is that the kind of boundary you're referring to?"

"Are you implying that I'm falling down on the job as a mother somehow?" Better question: Is this because of Rhea's interview? All of that "joyously available" nonsense, the body knows what it needs. Because Darby would like a word, please. A small addendum. Last she checked, intensive parenting was a relatively new trend, but now it's—*what?*—the norm, the expectation, the baseline standard? Baby-enrichment classes, oven-baked sweet potatoes, and patient, positive, lobotomized directives to sit in a child's feelings with the—it takes a lot of time and money. Has anyone checked the temperature of the water recently? Have the princesses from the storybooks they all diligently read aloud to their kids swooped in and somehow turned the parents into sad, boiling frogs?

Beside her, she feels her husband's full body cringe even before he says the word. "Darby."

"Has Lola exhibited any behavioral issues recently?" asks Princep, clearly trying to lower the temperature on the conversation by trading on those soulful blue eyes, but no thanks, hard pass. "Ones that maybe you witnessed, but your husband hasn't?"

"Who told you that?"

"We will, of course, be confirming and corroborating any answers you give us here." That's the female detective. Who is the good cop and who's the bad one here? Darby's getting turned around.

"She's four," Darby says. "Do you know a four-year-old without behavioral issues? They're like—I don't know—tiny little dictators at this age. But all of them, even the bad ones, *not* that Lola is one of the bad ones, are almost definitely going to turn out fine and not be serial killers or whatever."

"Okay." Detective Bright nods neutrally. "I agree with you there. But we still have to ask the questions. Speaking of, we've already had the chance to ask your husband this, but where were you in the hour before school pickup that day? Do you remember?"

Darby freezes. She purposefully doesn't look at Griff. Where did he say he'd been?

"Waiting in my car," she answers.

Detective Bright tilts her head. "You didn't go into the school early?"

"Why would I?" Darby asks.

The image of herself as she pursued Griff through the campus, never catching him, always too many steps behind.

"Because there was a calendar meeting on Erin's schedule. I think you were supposed to have a conference with her, weren't you?"

When Darby arrived back at the class that afternoon for the meeting that no longer seemed likely to happen even without Mary Beth, she could have chosen to collect Lola then, signed her out on the sheet, and brought her home safely. Instead, she couldn't bring herself to give up even one of those last few delicious minutes of alone time.

There it is. Her great, mortal sin. Why can't she be a good mom for once? Does she really prefer her phone to her living, breathing children? And now she can't even bring herself to consider what those extra minutes might have cost her daughter, what might have happened as a direct result.

"Not just me," Darby clarifies quickly. "Mary Beth was supposed to come and she had to cancel."

"Did you consider going anyway?" Detective Bright lifts her nice eyebrows.

Darby looks over to Griff, who looks pale beside her. "No," she replies. "Listen, I know you're doing your jobs and you have to be thorough. But do you know what I think?" She believes it's time to steer the conversation. "I think the odds are really good that Miss Ollie had an angry lover. A boyfriend, I mean. It's always the boyfriend. You're the police officers, I know—"

"Detective," says Bright.

"So surely you of all people know this. Though I realize you didn't know Miss Ollie personally like we did."

Lola squirms out of her dad's grip and, in her periphery, Darby can already feel the Lola Morton plane flying into turbulence.

"Erin Ollie," says Detective Bright, "was gay."

"Gay?" Darby stares at them slack-jawed. *"Gay?"*

"She didn't have a boyfriend," adds the detective. "She had a girl-friend."

"Yes, I know what gay means, thank you."

Miss Ollie was a lesbian? It feels strange that Darby had no idea, but then, why would she?

"We understand from friends and family that they were in a very committed relationship," Princep's saying. "They'd been living together for about three years and were talking about buying their first home."

Darby is nodding along, but hardly listening until she realizes that everyone seems to be waiting for her response. "That's great!" she exclaims.

"Great?" Bright repeats.

Darby rolls her eyes. "Not great. Obviously it's very tragic. I'm just trying to communicate that I'm supportive. I'm sorry that I automatically assumed she was—you know—*straight*, that is very, I guess, heterocentric of me, but then it sounds like everyone is trying to leap to certain conclusions here. Like, just because she doesn't have an abusive prick of a boyfriend or something convenient like that doesn't mean you should be interrogating *our* children. In their homes."

Princep motions with his hand to slow down, making him resemble a run-of-the-mill traffic cop. "We're simply following up on a few pieces of the narrative, that's all."

"Well, I—" Her mouth twists. She feels a small, unpleasant gush in her underwear that reminds her, for a split second, of being in middle school. "Oh." Now. Of all times, really? As if there's such a thing as a convenient period, but its arrival does explain a few things.

She swallows, hating the feeling of blood soaking through to the shorts she's wearing.

"Darbs?" Griff uses his concerned voice. The one he employed when she was in labor.

On the floor, Lola has been pedaling her legs, scrunching up the rug by digging her heels into it, back and forth, highly annoying, but low-priority behavior on their particular daughter's seismic scale. Lola stops and stiffens.

"I was saying—" She restarts, only she doesn't actually remember what she was saying. *No further questions*, is that something that real people say or just lawyers on TV?

Lola crawls over the inches of carpet to her ankles, peering up at her with big, concerned eyes. "Everything's fine," Darby assures her. "Just fine."

"Mommy!" Lola paws at her ankle. "But Mommy!"

"Okay." Detective Bright's eyes dart between Darby and Griff. "Lola's name came up in a number of the other interviews and she may have information that could be useful."

"Mommy—"

"Don't interrupt when grown-ups are talking," Griff says.

Darby pushes Lola's prying fingers off her thighs. "Surely this isn't what they're teaching in the academy." Let it be stated for the record that it is difficult to muster the right amount of wherewithal and intimidation without a tampon. "If your best witnesses are four-year-olds—I, uh, I'll go to the media. You want to be on the news for this?"

"We're just doing our job," Detective Bright replies, no fucks given.

"I didn't think so." Darby shifts her weight self-consciously.

"Mommy!" Lola's chin is pressing into Darby's hip. "I have something to tell you. Mom. Mom."

"Hold on, Lola."

Jack has reached his limits of independent play and he, too, has begun to whine, lying on the ground and arching his back. Bright and Princep are watching the kids without trying to seem like they're watching them, like they're the King's Guard and won't be distracted from their station.

"Have you tried asking Lola any more about that day—the day Erin was found?" Bright's eyes flick to Lola. "Since she's been home?"

"What exactly have you wanted us to ask her?"

"We wondered if she might have volunteered anything." Princep shifts his feet, hip-width apart. "After we spoke. It might have triggered something, a memory."

"Mom. Mom. Mommy!"

"Again: Like what?" Her temper is getting shorter. "She didn't see anything. She doesn't know any—" A blast of searing pain shoots out of Darby's left buttock. "Jesus Christ, are you kidding me?" Darby feels herself bare her teeth, squinting her eyes shut tight. She latches on to Lola's ponytail and yanks her daughter hard.

Griff, a man of action, few words, springs into it and she thinks, in a full body throb of love that feels as if it must be centered somewhere around the open wound on her ass, how perhaps all really is forgiven, or at least eventually will be, because she could not possibly be more attracted to him than she is in this very moment when he swoops, tucking Lola under his arm, absorbing the blows from her kicks silently, stoically, and carries her down the hall to their bedroom.

Darby is reasonably certain that only she—and not the two cops present—noticed the red outline of blood freshly wet around her daughter's lips. In the meantime, Darby has been working to refashion her face into a look other than one of surprised agony, and in record time.

"Did she bite you?" Princep stares at the spot where Darby was indeed bitten, which is her ass, and so she stares back with fierce white-lady judgment.

"Barely a nip. Didn't even break the skin."

She presses her hand over the small tear in her gym shorts. Already she can feel it wet and leaking. *Oh god.* She feels like she's oozing everywhere.

"I don't think we have anything else to add," she says stiffly. "At this moment. But we will definitely be sure to call if Lola thinks of anything useful."

The Mortons pile into Griff's SUV and Griff drives her to urgent care, where five stitches are sewn into the not-particularly-firm meat of her rear end.

On the way home, they stop at Walgreens for Neosporin and her prescribed wound care ointment. The cashier behind the counter is an older, gray-haired lady who peers over at Darby and her husband and children with a gleam in her eye, as if she's in on a secret. "How precious." She grins, showing her yellowed teeth. "They look just like you," the woman says. "I have two grandchildren, both in middle school now. Gosh, I miss that stage. Enjoy it. It goes by so fast."

Does it? Darby takes the bag of supplies. A marathon is over in roughly four hours. Four hours probably does seem like a pretty short amount of time to anyone who is not the marathon runner.

That night she stands with Griff over the sleeping lump of their daughter in bed.

"I don't understand. She looks so innocent," Griff whispers, and Darby hears the implication and knows that he's worrying about the flip side of that word: *guilty.*

A jolly seahorse night-light glows in the corner of the room, casting shadows. Darby uses her toe to pick at a dried spot of toothpaste on the carpet.

"You don't think—?" Darby has tipped her head onto his shoulder and together they stand fused, Lola's parents.

"No." He shakes his head. "I mean, of course not. She's just a little kid."

Below them, Lola breathes heavily through her nose, her little body somehow at a forty-five-degree angle on the mattress, legs twisted in the covers.

"She gets so mad," Darby says.

"Yeah, but."

"You think she's a freak."

"I think we've both thought that," he murmurs into her hair.

"She's scared of the pink elephants in *Dumbo*," adds Darby. "She couldn't—"

"Not without telling us, right?"

"I don't know." She exhales. "She didn't tell us when she wrote on our leather chair with her fingernail. She didn't break even when we confronted her with the letters that had been written there: *LM*."

Griff's skin is warm against her ear. She listens to his voice hum through as a vibration. "She was very strong in the face of damning evidence."

"But she's a good kid."

"She loves us," he agrees. They're arguing the same stance. Convincing each other of the same point. Preaching to the choir. "She loves Jack. You see her with him."

"She would never bite Jack," says Darby.

"I mean," he murmurs. "Would she?"

Tears prick her eyes. She swipes them away before Griff notices them dampen his shirt. She remembers staring for hours at Lola as an infant, how she and Griff talked out loud about how beautiful she was, how much more symmetrical her face was than other babies, about her eyes, her length, all so obviously superior to the rest of the dumb babies. Now when she looks back at pictures of those early days, she sees Lola for who she was, a misshapen, quivering bundle with baby acne, and still she thinks now Lola is truly beautiful, now her face is so symmetrical, now her hair is gorgeous, now she is so much prettier than Darby ever was and Darby is so much happier for it. And yet, what if her eyes are playing tricks on her all over again? How can she ever know for sure?

TRANSCRIPT OF INTERVIEW OF WITNESS, MAGGIE CHAPARRO

APPEARANCES:

Detective Wanda Bright

PROCEEDINGS

DET. BRIGHT: Do you like your school, Maggie?

MAGGIE CHAPARRO: My mom said school, well, she said it's really been going downhill for a while.

DET. BRIGHT: I see.

MRS. ROXY CHAPARRO: I didn't say—I'm sorry, I was just sending an email—Maggie, that's not—

DET. BRIGHT: It's fine. We want to encourage honesty and I don't want you to feel like you're being questioned here, Mrs. Chaparro. Earlier, though, you were saying something about the school photographer, Maggie?

MAGGIE CHAPARRO: Mr. Smiley was sick so I didn't know him. Mommy said he looked like a pedal.

DET. BRIGHT: A pedal. Can you translate?

MRS. ROXY CHAPARRO: Kids. They hear everything. I just said to Miss Ollie, in passing, that he looked like—that he looked like a pedophile. I was being—

DET. BRIGHT: What made him look like a pedophile?

MRS. ROXY CHAPARRO: I don't know. Some people just do, you know? Like doughy. Pale. Puffy lips and out-of-date glasses.

DET. BRIGHT: What time did you have pictures taken?

MAGGIE CHAPARRO: After Zeke got in trouble for potty talk and Bodhi told everyone he was going to marry Miss Ollie.

MRS. ROXY CHAPARRO: Let's see. It was around 2:30, I think.

DET. BRIGHT: It sounds like you were there.

MRS. ROXY CHAPARRO: Just for a second. I forgot Maggie's bow and

I don't like her looking like a ragamuffin. It reflects badly on me and it bothers my husband when we get the photographs back. Plus, she does better with a bit of coaching.

DET. BRIGHT: Mrs. Chaparro, why didn't you mention you were on campus?

THIRTY-TWO

▼

Rhea has stopped looking both ways before entering the Chick-fil-A drive-through. For breakfast, she orders her usual chicken biscuit and hash browns and then the same, but with milk, for Bodhi, to his delight. She reminds him not to get used to it and the two of them devour their meals while listening to a "Songs to Sing in the Shower" playlist on Spotify. Bodhi's put on two and a half pounds in the last week and a half while Rhea has lost six on fast food and root beer. Only a matter of time before the other moms at school start sniffing around asking what *is* her secret.

By Rhea's calculations this will last another two weeks, three tops, and then she'll be through the worst of it. Six investors have signed their letters of intent following her interview. And with that money, she can rent space in a warehouse. She can get an assistant. She can give herself a raise. She can get a cat. She can get a life. And she'll look back on this time and be like, *Who? What? Oh, that was me?*

Yesterday, they'd called Bodhi in for questioning and he'd surprised them all when he insisted Rhea was in the classroom the day of Miss Ollie's murder. But no, she assured the detective, he was remembering that wrong. She was in the classroom the day Bodhi was *bitten*, not the day of the murder, ask anyone, ask Mary Beth, ask Darby even. This is the problem with kids. Unreliable witnesses.

Well, he didn't mean any harm. As soon as she pointed out that she was there on the day Zeke attacked him, he was able to correct his memory. Of course mama was right. Mama's always right.

She smiles at her son through the rearview mirror. "So, Mr. Bodhi. What are our positive affirmations today?" He swings his legs, the rest of his body pinned in by the three-point harness of the car seat.

He chews his food slowly and with his lips shut tight—it's the little things—and then swallows. "I'm brave," he says. "And I'm true. I'm quick. I'm strong. I'm kind. I got *good* hair."

"Oh yeah, you do."

Of all the tinctures Rhea concocts, the thing she most wishes she could bottle up is Bodhi. His essence. His comedic timing. His curiosity. His inherent politeness. None of which she can take responsibility for. Bodhi at four years old is a magic of her own making but none of her design.

So what if he doesn't have the syndrome? Details. The point remains. She's a conscientious mother, which is more than she can say for many of the other parents.

She stares at him for too long until he says, "Mom, why're you staring at me like that?" He giggles and lifts his chin, exposing that little-boy neck she nuzzled when he was seven pounds eight ounces.

Through her windshield, there are all the makings of a weekday morning going on. Cars stuck behind school buses. Moms rapping behind steering wheels after drop-off like windows aren't see-through, and that Starbucks line's still maddeningly long.

"You're right, you're right." She reverses out of their parking space and turns down the volume on the speakers. "We should go to school. How's school going?" she asks. Bodhi hasn't said much about Miss Ollie. In fact, Rhea hasn't been able to get a firm sense of how much he understands about what happened to her. In some ways, he's such an old soul, but in others, he's slow on the uptake.

"It's all right."

"What do you mean it's all right?" She exaggerates his ho-hum tone. "I thought you loved school. I thought you wanted to be a teacher when you grow up. Isn't that right?" Did it bother her that this new future occurred to him only after having Miss Ollie? A little, but that was before. Situations change. *Rhea* has changed.

It's a less-than-five-minute drive from the shopping center to school. She goes the speed limit, braking at a stoplight. Rhea gives Bodhi his time to answer because that's what the positive-parenting YouTube channels encourage. Bodhi doesn't have to like school. He doesn't have to like any of the same things she does. That's okay. He's his own person. She is her own person. And Rhea can be cool about that.

"It was me," he says when she's pulling into the school parking lot.

Rhea goes cold. She chooses the first spot she sees, one far away from the entrance where no other parents have been desperate enough to park yet, and brakes too hard at the median. Their bodies sway forward before being pressed back into the seats with an irritating jolt.

"It was . . . you?"

No, no, no what no no no.

Of all things her mind chooses to dredge up, it's the memory of the day Bodhi was born. The first thing she recalls after she woke up from the sedatives is that he was clean. She had a clean baby. No gunk or slippery goo, no sign that he'd been swimming around her insides earlier that day. She stared at Bodhi's closed eyelids and felt the world both expand and contract simultaneously.

The aftermath of the anesthesia was still giving her the shakes and she held her sleeping son to her chest as she clenched her teeth to keep from chattering him awake. Later that day, the female doctor who delivered Bodhi came by to check on Rhea during her rounds. Marcus, who arrived and was biting his tongue about not getting the call sooner, thanked the doctor for keeping Rhea and Bodhi safe. Rhea looked away.

She hated the doctor like it was her God-given right to. The doctor paused.

"There are no perfect decisions when it comes to becoming a parent, that's true at every stage," said the doctor. It was the closest thing to an apology Rhea would ever get. "I should know. I've got three kids of my own. Welcome to the club."

And Rhea thought that maybe with three kids, this doctor could afford to make mistakes, but for Rhea, there would only be one Bodhi, she knew that from the start, and so she would do it perfectly from then on.

But now, her eyes frantically search around her tin box of a car for a solution, something to stop the train. She might even wish that doctor back if it meant someone could put her to sleep, anesthetize her against what her son is about to say next. Wake her up when it's over. Her heart hammers at her breast.

"What is?" she asks tentatively, praying she misheard.

"It was *me*." Bodhi starts smudging lines onto the window glass with the tip of his finger, enthralled in the shapes he's creating.

"What do you mean? What's you?" She unbuckles her seatbelt and twists to look at him full-on.

"You know." He glances over at her, ducking his head to prompt her. "The one who went Number Two at school."

Her fingers fly to her mouth. She's on the verge of either laughing with relief—did she *really* think her son could have killed his preschool teacher?—or crying because what the fuck. *Okay. Okay* . . . She recalibrates. This is bad, but it could have been worse. The sun floods through her windshield and the whole car smells like grease now that the engine's been cut. Start over. Did Bodhi just—did he say—"When?" she asks.

"Every time." This in the same sweet boy's voice that wakes her up in the mornings. So. Like, no. Uh-uh. Rhea doesn't think so. She kneads her forehead with her fingertips. She's going to get to the bottom of this. Just no, no way.

"You went in the cubby next to Mrs. Tokem's purse?"

He nods.

"You went at the bottom of the slide?"

"And in the book nook and the block station." His lower lip puckers thoughtfully. "And in the flowerbed next to the playhouse but nobody knows about that one."

"Bodhi Anderson." *Whooooaaakkkkkayyyy.* Her eyes are rolling around in her head like that triangle in a Magic 8 Ball. She is feeling a whole heap of feelings, she knows that. A fresh, steaming heap of them. "You did not do that." She points her finger at him. Points it. Rhea doesn't point her finger at her son. So, you know, things are happening. "Why are you telling me this now?"

"Miss Ollie says we are never supposed to keep secrets from our parents. Only surprises. Surprises are different because they're secrets set on snooze." He lifts his shoulders to his ears.

Is her child an alien? Was he body snatched? Is that a possibility she should explore?

"When'd she tell you that?" Rhea demands.

"When she taught us about stranger danger." Bodhi goes back to his smudge drawings, like crude, oily-palmed cave art.

"So you were just . . . waiting to tell me?" Rhea kneads her forehead, trying to make herself come to terms with reality the way a woman might be forced to accept her husband has a secret family or is an accused sexual harasser. She's been living with the Little Shitter. Poodini. The Bowel Movement Bandit. In her house. Her son. "Oh my god, I don't understand why you would do this." She explodes and the crumpled remains of her fast-food breakfast scatter onto the passenger seat. "Were you not able to make it to a toilet?"

"I could."

"Was it an accident?" She has never seen a positive-parenting YouTube video about this.

"No."

"Were you mad?"

"I don't think so."

"Well, fuck."

"Fuck," Bodhi repeats solemnly.

"Bodhi." She shoots eyes. "I did not—" But please, someone finish that sentence for her because all she can think to do is drop her head on the steering wheel. What's she supposed to do? Does she really think kids—heck, not just kids, parents—are going to be nice once they find out her son has been excreting all over their precious school? It might have been better if he *did* kill somebody. Nicknames are no joke. And that's if they *don't* kick him out, and her schedule cannot afford him getting kicked out of school right now.

Rhea hasn't even started to google, but, hey, that's coming. And Marcus. Shit, Marcus. Maybe she should call Bodhi in sick today.

The thought makes her to-do list weep. *Terrene, my other precious baby, you need to crawl over and take the back seat—again.* Because this Bodhi Thing is a *thing*-thing and she's going to have to figure it out one way or another. She doesn't get it. How did she screw this up? She still breast-feeds. She doesn't yell. She *bathes* with Bodhi.

A knock on her window startles her. "Jesus!" She peels her forehead from the steering wheel to find Mary Beth peering in at her. She waves, her charm bracelet jangling down her forearm. "I saw your car," Mary Beth calls through the glass. "It's distinctive!"

"I can hear you fine." Rhea pushes the "down" button on the window controls and Mary Beth scoots clear of the moving glass.

"We need you," says Mary Beth.

Rhea would laugh—like, who does Mary Beth think she is, an actress on *Chicago Fire*?—but she's finding it hard to find the humor in anything at the moment. "There's a situation. I'll fill you in." Mary Beth beckons her to hurry, hurry, hurry.

"*Okay*, give us one second."

"I am," Mary Beth says. "Hey, is that Chick-fil-A?"

W hat's all this?" Rhea enters the hallway for the upper fours, un-sure of what she's walking into or what *she's* supposed to do about it. It all looks pretty business as usual. Sneakers squeak against the tile floors. A finger-paint masterpiece comes loose from its thumbtack and the construction paper sails to the floor; someone sticks it back up on the wall. A chorus of voices in another class sings the morning "God Our Father" prayer, echoing the verses back and forth. What's every-body freaking out about?

Bodhi hurries ahead of her, slipping through the other parents who are milling and murmuring like a herd of cows. He ducks out of his backpack and, after he greets Mrs. Tokem, Rhea watches him disappear through the pony door and into the classroom without a backward glance.

"It's a huge problem is what it is." Mary Beth crosses herself: Father,

Son, Holy Ghost. "Look, you can't see him from here, but." She tugs on Rhea's sleeve, which Rhea doesn't love, but she allows it. She pulls Rhea to the other side of the hall and presses her closer to the wall. "That man. Right there. He's a forensic podiatrist, apparently."

Rhea can only make out half of this man, who is wearing a gray polo and black slacks, as he kneels down doing—well, she doesn't know what he's doing. "What's he doing?" she asks, tilting her head for the angle.

One of Lincoln's mothers, Robin, sidles over to them, hugging her chest tightly. "He's using clear acetate sheets to take impressions of the children's shoe- and footprints."

Rhea sees a flash of her son as he darts across the room toward the forensic podiatrist, disappearing out of view. In the soft, fleshy part under her jawline, she has begun to feel her pulse pump. All around her, the parents talk amongst themselves—*What does this mean? Are we back to those footprints again? But I thought—what about—they brought Asher in for questioning and Bex and George, who's next? They wouldn't be focused on the kids at all if it weren't for this biting business, let's just be honest. Actually, if I can be honest, maybe they should be looking at the biters. . . .* It's hard to hear herself think.

"I tried going to Pastor Ben, but he's not in the office yet." Mary Beth paces a small circle. "And I don't think I have a leg to stand on after the Poodini sample incident." Rhea wills herself not to react at the mention of *her son.* "We need to think. What can we do?" She looks at Rhea with big, hopeful eyes and way too much mascara.

"What can we do about what?" Darby shows up before Rhea can find a place to hide. Not that she would, but she might slink.

They haven't spoken since Rhea watched Jack during Lola's interrogation and Darby acted as though Rhea not liking Miss Ollie was the same as if she said she hated puppies, though, frankly, Rhea's not much of a dog person either.

Mary Beth runs down the whole state of affairs once more and Rhea avoids eye contact at the same time Darby tries to make it. Static ripples over her skin.

"Why are some of the kids over there and others not?" Rhea nods at the kids playing over in the Home Living center. "Are they already done?" Less than five minutes earlier, Rhea was trying to work out how she was going to deal with the unfortunate news that her son is the Poop Bandit and now . . . and now what's she supposed to be doing again?

"They're only doing the kids with the syndrome," Robin explains, glancing around the other worried faces.

"But that's—that's—" Rhea searches.

Nearby, Asher's dad removes his cupped hand from around his cell. "Completely legit," he says. "I'm on my phone with my criminal defense attorney buddy." Robin nods at this, as though they've all been waiting for him to report back. "Apparently they can do it. The more invasive the search, the more justification the police need to have—so that's why they're not doing everybody, see, they're tailoring it. But—yeah?" He waits to listen to advice from his friend before returning his focus to the moms. "It's a big misconception. They can search backpacks, cubbies, anything. The school has no duty. The kids can even answer questions without a parent present. He says they probably already have done all of that and we're just now hearing about it."

To Rhea's relief, Darby gets momentarily roped into another group's tittering. Mary Beth hooks her hand around the back of her neck and stretches it, looking up at the ceiling. "So now we're trying to figure out what to do. Because we don't want to make things worse," Mary Beth says.

Rhea's mind feels like an object spinning so fast that it doesn't appear to be moving at all. She's suspended in motion, unable to break loose of her spiral. She's made no progress by the time she feels Darby's reentry—*Get over it*, Rhea tells herself silently, she knows she should get over it, but while Rhea has a lot of strengths, that isn't one of them.

"I feel like I'm not doing the best job crisis managing right now," Darby says diffidently. "But I'm sorry. It's very hard to form a plan when I have no idea what the hell's going on." Her voice rises. "We don't know what they already have—Robin over there swears the children did artwork in which they did footprints using finger paint and now where are those pictures? Where are they?" Darby looks like a mother who's lost sight of her child in the mall. It's this reaction, this appalled, panicky, how-is-this-happening-to-*me* knee jerk that kicks Rhea out of orbit, plummeting her back down to Earth, because in the entirety of their four-year friendship, which may, after all this, in fact be its entirety, Rhea can't think of a time she's seen Darby take anything so seriously.

Asher's dad hangs up the phone. "We need to be strategic. What are our options and how will it look if we don't cooperate?"

"So. I don't understand," Rhea says. "What's this mean? This means that our kids are—our kids are officially, like, suspects? What about Griff?" The thought just springs out. It's not premeditated, not like murder.

"What about him?" Darby spins on her.

Rhea shrugs it off. "I don't know. He had beef with Miss Ollie, that's all I'm saying."

"*You* had beef with Miss Ollie," says Darby, her neck turning a deep shade of garnet.

"It's different," Rhea replies, and it is, in some way she can't fully articulate that probably has a lot to do with the fact that she's a woman and women don't slice off a lady's fingers and let her bleed to death. Women aren't violent.

Except that's not true. Because Rhea apparently is.

Watching her two friends bicker, Mary Beth looks like she's developed a very painful cavity. "Let's stop and show each other some grace. Please," she begs.

Darby and Rhea both look like they're fresh out of grace.

Asher's father clears his throat. "We don't know if the kids are suspects or if one specific kid is a suspect or what."

Rhea's mind is in free fall and she's starting to think somebody cut the bungee. They're taking the kids' footprints. They tried to get a DNA sample—oh god, that sample belonged to *Bodhi*. The realization smacks her with such force she feels unsteady on her feet. Rhea, for better or worse, has been here, seen that. She's done the whole arrest thing. And if anyone's naive enough to think cops will ask questions first and make decisions later, they better think twice. The thought of Bodhi mixed up in all this, the chances of that on the rise.

Screw deep breaths. Rhea is *not* okay.

"Not all the kids anyway," adds Maggie's mom, Roxy, who has clearly been listening in. "Remember! Only the biters!"

"But Bodhi isn't," Rhea blurts.

"Isn't what?" Mary Beth asks. "What are you talking about?"

"Excuse me. *Excuse me.*" Rhea begins pushing through the parents. For starters, Rhea has lost her mind. And when you lose something, what's the one thing you're supposed to do? Go back and find out where you last had it. Only problem is Rhea has no idea when or where that was. Did she have it when Bodhi told her over Chick-fil-A this morning how he'd been defiling the school? Did she have it when she talked to those two officers in her house? Did she have it when she went on air and gave an interview implying she had Bodhi's syndrome under control? Did she have it when she tried to get Miss Ollie fired?

Wherever it is, wherever she lost it, it's long gone by now.

"Bodhi, Bodhi, get out of this line." She is through those doors so fast that sorry Mrs. Tokem can't stop her. Rhea hooks her hands under Bodhi's armpits and lifts him onto her hip.

"Ma'am, it's a simple footprint. We're getting them for all of the children," says the forensic podiatrist, whose mannerisms and golf-ready haircut suggest that he's the equivalent of an accountant in the world of cool CSI jobs.

"No. You're not, actually." She draws herself up to her full height and tries to pay no mind to the many eyes now looking on. Rhea's heart is trying to escape from her chest. "Bodhi isn't a biter, okay? So, this—" She gestures widely. "—isn't applicable to him. He shouldn't be in the pool of suspects."

"What do you mean he's not a biter?" Darby calls from outside the door.

Rhea's upper lip is sweating. Bodhi's small for his age, but at four and a half, he's still getting heavy. "I mean, he's not interested. He's never bitten me or craved blood or wanted any part of it."

"You went on national television." Robin summarizes the obvious.

"Yeah, I did. Because y'all asked me to. And I never confirmed or denied that he had it. I never specifically did," Rhea replies.

"I think you know what you led people to believe." Robin is backed up by many, many grumblings of assent. "You told everyone to be empathetic and available and—"

"Okay. Then I led them to believe wrong."

"Wow." Asher's dad says *wow* exactly the way she'd expect Asher's dad to say *wow*. "And why should we believe you now?"

There's probably a whole lot of psychological shit—okay, bad word choice—that she's going to have to unpack in order to sort through why her son's been defecating all over school, and chances are some of that baggage is going to belong to her. Maybe her son's dead teacher did know something about something after all. But one thing Rhea doesn't have wrong is that she loves Bodhi. And she's not going to permanently screw him up. Not for the world.

She looks frantically around, feeling trapped.

"I'm sorry." Robin doesn't sound even a little bit sorry. "You want us to just take your word for this?" Rhea doesn't need anyone to translate: The currency exchange rate between her word and theirs isn't favorable.

She slides Bodhi off her hip, onto the ground. A shiny pair of grown-up scissors sits in a cup too high for the children to reach. Rhea crosses the room and flips the scissors open to as close to 180 degrees as she can manage. Nobody stops her and she might think about that for a minute later, might wonder if, were it one of the other mothers, like Darby or Mary Beth, would they have all rushed to scream *No!* Either way, once she's begun the gesture, with no objections, she has little choice but to go through with it.

The blades are a cloudy gray color and not that sharp. It takes four times, sawing over the same spot on her arm, before she gets a solid trickle of blood—bright and red enough that she can make a presentation of it. She knows better than to baby the arm, although it does sting. She brings it over to Bodhi. "Here. I got this for you." She crouches down beside him. His chin jerks in the opposite direction. "Bodhi," she says, loudly enough so that the gawking parents can hear. "Take a drink. It's okay. I'm saying it's okay."

Bodhi sticks out his tongue. "Disgusting!" He sounds like such a little kid. "Blech! Get it away, Mommy!"

"Are you thirsty?" She tries again patiently. There was some small risk that Bodhi would have changed his mind, but no, he's still her Bodhi. She doesn't recognize the shift in the room's chemistry, spreading out like a gas leak between the children. There are no carbon monoxide alarms for this sort of thing, no warning bells, and Rhea has been so divorced from the reality of the situation for so long that maybe the most genuine evidence that Bodhi has never exhibited any sign of being a biter is the way her back stays turned from the side of the classroom where the forensic podiatrist continues to ask children to step on clear, sticky sheets, one by one by one.

"So what?" Robin presses. "You're in the habit of acting like an expert about things you know nothing about? I think that really says something about you and your brand, Rhea."

Rhea opens her mouth to respond and thinks for an insane second, *Did I scream?* before she realizes the actual scream has come from just behind her in the moment before she is toppled to the ground by the force of tiny, insistent hands where the aroma of sweet, hot breath fills her nostrils and a knee with a tattered Star Wars Band-Aid clocks her hard in the eye.

THIRTY-THREE

▼

Darby's phone buzzes.

"My buddy got a tip from one of his courthouse friends. The judge issued a search warrant for *your* house," Asher's father, Bill Brazle, informs her.

"My house? Just my house?"

"They're on their way there now." Bill has become a bit of a team player since his Asher put Katia in the hospital.

The funny thing is that Darby continues buckling Jack into his high chair like this is a routine call that she can take one-handed. "For who?" she asks. "Like, which one of us are they coming for?"

She thinks of Rhea and the way she so carelessly—no, callously—tossed out Griff's name and it has since occurred to Darby, more than once over the last few hours, that she is done with Rhea Anderson. For good.

"Uh, Morton," Bill says. "All he said was Morton. I'm hearing that one of the pastors at the church had a change of heart about the kids or something. He's talking. I don't know what exactly he's saying, but I think it's fair to assume it's not good."

"A *pastor*? What, like he's saying they're the devil or something? What is this, Salem?"

"I don't know the extent of it," Bill is saying as her remaining time ticks by. "Just, you know, try to act surprised. I don't want to get my buddy in trouble." In trouble. *In* trouble. The police are coming to search her house. Pretty sure if anyone is in trouble it's the Mortons.

"What should we do?" asks Griff once she's hung up and filled him in.

Darby stares at the pantry, looking for something suitable to feed Jack, only she's not really comprehending what she's seeing or how she might turn it into a meal. She keeps thinking as she rummages for food:

When am I ever going to make it back to the gym? Which is obviously all wrong and completely beside the point.

"I don't know," she says, picking up a bag of dried lentils and setting it back down. Her pantry is so disorganized, it's a travesty. "Do you have anything to hide?"

"No," he says. "No, of course I don't have anything to hide."

"I don't know then. How should I know?" She shoulders through the pantry doorway past him. Lola's turned on the television without asking. This entire afternoon, every time Darby lays eyes on her daughter she thinks, *At least she wasn't the first to attack Rhea.* She has a palpable sense of relief about that. That honor went to Bex Feinstein.

"Nobody tells you what to do in this situation," Darby says. "I have literally no idea what's going on."

"I'll google," Griff offers.

"Oh great, you'll google."

The pounding on the door, when it comes, still feels utterly shocking. They may as well be bullets fired through the hardwood. "I'll get it," says Griff grimly.

"Mr. and Mrs. Morton." It's Detective Bright on the other side. She appears friendly, sharply dressed, and with a note of: She really doesn't want to make this any harder than has to be. "We're going to need you all to step outside the house."

Darby appears next to her husband. "My son, Jack, is eating dinner." Or more accurately, crying over an empty tray. She doesn't know why she tries telling Wanda Bright this. It's not as if she expects her to say, *Oh, sure, fine, we'll wait,* but it's like Darby needs to push on the bruise, needs to confirm: Yes, they are kicking you out of your home. *That's* how serious this is.

"The whole family," she says. "I apologize for the inconvenience, but it's standard protocol."

Exactly that serious, then. Darby scribbles down a couple of phone numbers on a Post-it and, after that, she is allowed to take less than she would save in a fire.

This time it's not just Bright and Princep who arrive. Two hulking black SUVs block her mailbox and pebble driveway. Darby tries to tell herself it's okay, the neighbors will think the cars are here for some soccer team's carpool or something. Who would notice such a thing? But then a whole uniformed squad descends on her house, spilling out of every Suburban door like industrious little ants, wearing what look like shower caps on their feet as they disappear through the gaping entrance.

She has the overwhelming urge to explain to the team of investigators: *Oh, we're still planning to pick out new light fixtures for the hallway, we do actually know that one is hideous, and see that bathroom? Imagine it with some really cool wallpaper from Anthropologie.*

Instead, she keeps switching Jack from one hip to the next each time her arm gets tired. There's no good place for him. She's forgotten to call the lawn guy back for weeks and the grass is ankle-high and itchy. Her son usually runs straight for the curb anyway. Lola tries to do a cartwheel. Lola has no idea how to do a cartwheel.

"What are they looking for?" Darby asks. "What could they possibly be looking for?"

"Are they going to take my stuffed animals?" Lola asks from the ground where her very unladylike posture puts her cotton underwear on full display.

"No, Lola. Of course not." Griff watches the front of the house as if he's watching it burn. "I mean, I don't think so."

"I think they're in our room, Griff. Look, the shadows in the windows."

He doesn't. He turns his back on the house and walks over to the mailbox, where he rests his elbow on the top because he's that tall and jabs his fingers through the roots of his hair. "We should call a lawyer."

Darby bounces Jack on her hip. There are two patrol cars and a van parked out front. The neighbors are bound to think someone's been murdered. Someone *has*.

"Right," she says bleakly. "We should."

"We don't know any lawyers." Griff looks stricken. She's never seen her husband like this before and she could do without seeing it now. One of the main reasons she got married in the first place was so that she had someone to pick up cockroaches with toilet paper and so that if there was a bump in the night, she could send him out with a baseball bat. Right now, Darby feels as though she's being unfairly expected to wield the proverbial baseball bat.

"Griff." She lowers her voice and makes sure none of the investigators are within earshot. "Remember what I said? I—I saw you . . . at the school that day. I'm not—" She closes her eyes and balances herself. "—I'm not going to say anything. But you have to tell me so that I can be on your side."

He looks at her with such despondent misery, as though the only wish he has in the world is for her not to ask this again. *What did you do? What aren't you telling me?* her brain screams.

"I told you," he says. "I wasn't there."

To have someone she loves so much unable to trust her with the truth, a truth she saw with her own eyes, is to be untethered from all the things about her family, her life, *she* has known to be true. She can see them drifting apart after this, floating away from one another, but it won't be her that untied the rope. That will be on Griff's shoulders.

She hands Jack to Griff, which evokes a round of wailing. Then she goes to knock on the neighbor's door. She asks to use their cell phone and dials Bill Brazle back, one of the numbers she thought to collect on her Post-it, and, surprise, surprise, she's connected with one of his buddies. She has mixed feelings, but at least she's in possession of a name and a number.

"Okay," she says when she returns. "We've got somebody lined up. Just in case. Jack, don't pull the flowers. Those are Mommy's special flowers. Why'd you let him down?" she asks.

"Who cares about the flowers, Darby?" Griff snaps.

"I do. Or I will after this is over. I will be super sad that all the flowers that I planted are destroyed. You know what, I didn't put sunscreen on the kids."

Darby looks longingly back at her house, where all of her things—
like sunscreen and bug spray—are shoved into drawers.

"Now where do you think they are?" Griff asks.

"I can't tell." She cranes her neck. "They must be toward the back, the
laundry room or— Oh god, he's coming. He's coming. Look normal."

Princep's boots swish through the grass to where the family waits.
Can they go back in? Was that it?

"Where is this pair of shoes?" Princep holds up a class photo and
points. In it, Lola stands in the second row, body angled parallel with the
other students, next to Zeke and Noelle.

Cautiously, Darby takes the picture from him and holds it up to her
face. The shoes are a pair of hot-pink sparkly Crocs, hard to miss.

"I don't know." She shakes her head. "Did you check the laundry
room? There's a cubby in the laundry room where we throw everyone's
shoes," she says. But she hasn't seen those shoes in a while. For how
long? A few days? A few weeks?

Princep pulls a radio on his shoulder over to his mouth. "Did we
check the laundry room?" He waits for the answer. "We checked the
laundry room. Is there anywhere else these shoes may be?"

"Lola's room? Under her bed? Beneath the couch?" Darby ticks off
places.

"All checked," he says.

"Well, I don't know, then." Not that this is the time to worry about
keeping up appearances, but Darby isn't someone who likes to have people
over unannounced. She requires a forty-five-minute window to get her
home from total train wreck to livable conditions and that's just the tip
of the iceberg. Things are constantly going missing in her household.
She builds it into the price of purchase. Those shoes? They'll probably
show up, but there's a 75 percent chance it will be after Lola's already
grown out of them. Can Officer Princep wait until then? If so, great.
Sooner or later, one of her disorganized linen closets is bound to spit
them up.

"Mrs. Morton, are you the primary caregiver for Lola?" he asks, and she has the distinct feeling she's been called into the school principal's office.

"Yes. I mean, what does that mean? I'm the mother, you do the math. Sorry, that came out sassy."

"And did you pick Lola up from school on picture day, the day she was wearing these shoes?"

"Yes."

"I'm going to be up front with you all. We're going to make an arrest tonight." Princep tucks the photograph into his breast pocket. Darby reaches for Griff. Oh my god. Oh *my* god. She can't breathe. "And I want to explain to you what's happening so that you understand. The investigators were able to take footprints of the students, Lola being one of them. The soles, however, did not match the footprints found at the crime scene. They do match the brand Crocs, specifically the ones the investigators were able to source from the photograph taken during class pictures. The same day Miss Ollie died."

"What's your point?" Griff's nose twitches.

"Prints from these shoes were found at the crime scene in Erin Ollie's blood. And now they're missing."

Jack nuzzles into Darby's neck, his fingers toying with her earlobe. Her ears ring. She forces herself not to side-eye Griff. Choices made now may be permanent.

"Darby Morton, you're under arrest for intent to interfere with evidence." Officer Princep delivers the news calmly. "I'm going to have to ask you to come down to the station with us for processing and questioning."

"What? *What?* Why me?"

"You can't be serious." Griff is still soft-spoken and she wants to scream at him to buck up, do something. "You're not taking my wife," he says. But he takes Jack from her anyway. "This is just a ploy to get more information. You're using her. What does this have to do with Darby?"

Princep has already asked her to hold out her hands. She feels the cold metal bracelets click onto her wrists. The phrase *standard procedure* is thrown around some more and she feels how bizarrely unsurprising it is that she will make it to jail before she ever makes it back to the gym.

"That can't be necessary," Griff says. "These are scare tactics."

"It's for everyone's safety. We'll make sure she's comfortable."

Lola's arms are around her legs, making it difficult to walk naturally in step with Princep. "Mommy!" Darby can't look at her face. She won't accept that her daughter will remember the sight of her mother getting arrested. No. She simply won't. But so quietly, so only Darby can hear, Lola whispers, "Mommy? Should I bite him?"

Just as quietly, Darby breathes, "Maybe later."

THIRTY-FOUR

▼

"C an they do that?" asks Mary Beth from her kitchen. She opens the refrigerator, looking around for a suitable option to stress-eat.

Darby got one phone call, and since both her new lawyer and her husband knew where she was, she called Mary Beth to relay the terrible news.

Darby's voice sounds tinny through the line. "They've got forty-eight hours before they have to formally charge me with anything. This is kind of a freebie, I guess. But they can question me."

"What are you going to say?" Realizing that nothing in the refrigerator is going to cut it, Mary Beth goes for one of the three pints of Blue Bell ice cream stashed in the freezer door.

"Nothing. I don't know anything. I wish I did. What do you know about the pastors at the church?" she asks. "Are they stodgy? Are they Satanic Panic types? Is Communion a thing? It's not real blood or anything, is it?"

"What? No. It's not even wine. It's Welch's grape juice. Why?" Mary Beth's stomach feels like a sponge being wrung dry.

"I guess one of them has been talking about the kids, implying that there's really something *wrong*-wrong with them." So this is about the children, then. Rhea surprised them all with the mention of Griff and, Mary Beth is sad to say, she felt a flutter of hope. It would be awful for Darby. She would not abandon Darby under any circumstances. But Griff Morton is exactly the kind of guy who you might hear is a murderer and say, *Oh, he was always so quiet, he kept to himself, but now that you mention it, there was something funny about him around the eyes.* Griff Morton would make sense. Mary Beth wishes she could hug her friend right now.

"That's not good." Her knuckles whiten around the spoon.

Ben. It has to be Ben. But why? Why would he do a 180 like that? Because she didn't welcome his advances? She's almost forty years old, what did he expect? But then also, what had she expected? What had any of them expected? She asked him to look out for the children. And now this. She won't stand for it.

"I'll look into it," she promises Darby. "I'll get to the bottom of it."

"This is my fault." Darby sounds miserable, like her nose might be drippy. "I could have picked Lola up early. I could have spent time with my child. Extra time. I mean, why not?" Mary Beth can't answer that. "I will never forgive myself, Mary Beth. Never."

"Darby—" she begins.

"People listen to you, Mary Beth. Just please don't let everyone go poisoning the well before anything's, like, official. That's all I'm asking." Darby sounds panicked and small, like a mouse with her tail caught in a trap.

Mary Beth spoons cookies-and-cream ice cream into her mouth straight from the carton. She feels a connective tissue with other mothers, something biological joining herself to them, and so *of course* she's having an emotional reaction to the news that Darby's family is going through this. Of course.

Her hand trembles and a drop of ice cream quickly melts on the countertop.

"She's a child," Darby says just before her time's up.

After, she paces in front of the door to the backyard, looking out at her two girls bouncing together on the trampoline. Her spoon scrapes the cardboard bottom of the carton. "Darby's in jail," she tells Doug, who sits on the couch reading his phone. "Like actual jail."

"Lord, why?" He looks at her over the top of the phone. He doesn't remark on the fact that she's eating ice cream standing up. She supposes it's not actually that unusual for her.

"Lola."

He frowns. "I always liked Lola. She always said, 'I had so much fun, thank you for inviting me' without her mother asking her to."

"Lola Morton? The girl with the bangs?"

"Yes, Lola Morton. Noelle's best friend."

"They're not really *best* anymore. I mean, don't you think Lola's kind of wild?" She watches Noelle rolled up in a ball on the trampoline while Angeline jumps around and tries to get her to break form.

"You're around her more."

She turns her attention back to her husband to see the thinning patch of hair at the top of his head as he bows to read his phone again. "She could have done this, don't you think? Lola?"

Doug always wears socks in the house. His feet get cold easily, a point that tends to remind Mary Beth at moments like this that he's fragile in ways she isn't. "If that's what the police are saying, then they probably have good reason."

"That's exactly what I was thinking. The police aren't reckless. They wouldn't just arrest anybody." She chews a jagged piece of nail.

She waits for Doug to say more, but, then, he doesn't know anything, really.

"Pastor Ben came on to me," she says. Doug looks up. He sets his phone down beside him on the couch. "What are you doing?" she asks.

"Putting down my phone," he tells her.

"Why? It's not a big deal. I'm just relaying more information." She takes a seat on the beige overstuffed armchair that looks exactly like the more expensive one in the Arhaus catalogue.

"Putting the phone down feels about right. Probably a little old for kicking people's asses."

"Plus, he's in good shape," she says.

Doug shrugs at his belly—why do men's bellies get so hard with age? She should look it up. He plants his socked feet on the rug and rests an elbow on each knee. "Why are you telling me this?"

"I don't know. It just felt like something I should tell you." Amongst other things, maybe, but it's a start. "He touched my calf." He watches her until she feels silly. "I know you trust me." She rolls her eyes.

"I don't." Doug's jaw goes slack, eyes serious.

"You don't—what—trust me? What's that supposed to mean?"

"It means I don't trust you, not entirely."

Is she supposed to be offended? Can he do that? They've already been married such a long time. Isn't trust the foundational principle of a relationship? "I don't take your fidelity for granted," Doug continues. "I don't think that if I sit on my butt and ignore you and scratch my own balls that you won't make eyes at another man."

Mary Beth touches her cheek to feel that it's warm. She's blushing. Physically blushing. Her husband made her do that. "Do you think I made eyes at another man?"

"I'm picking up my phone now," he says.

That night, the girls have filed out of the bathroom to their respective rooms with wet, combed-through hair. Noelle accepts a half-full sippy cup of her mother's blood from the refrigerator, saving them all a lot of trouble.

She asks Noelle, "Where is the dress with the apples on it that Grandma Raines and Grandpa G gave you? They want to get a picture of you in it." This is a common problem in the Brandt household, the need to supply photographic evidence of their children in various gifts sent by relatives.

She's been maintaining a low-grade level of alert for the missing dress, checking casually in all the usual places, some of which aren't that usual—bottom of the hamper, game closet, underneath the girls' beds—but now it's officially starting to drive her crazy.

"You must have seen it somewhere." The news of Darby's arrest has left her with a brittle edge. She keeps looking around, waiting for someone else to notice. Like it's all an outrageous joke that only she is getting. Here she is still performing her own motherhood. The calm. The mind-numbing tedium. The supposedly bottomless well of patience. Has anyone considered—has *she* considered even—that there might, in fact, be a bottom to it?

Noelle is busy soaking in her thirty allotted minutes of iPad time on the bed.

Mary Beth revisits Noelle's closet. She scoots out the bookcase cubbies, examining the back. She finds a dead cockroach, but no dress. On the floor of the closet are discarded dust jackets from picture books that wind up ripped anyways. She moves the stuffed animals, which don't even belong in the closet in the first place, when out of a giant plush cat pillow falls a bracelet that Mary Beth doesn't recognize—a pretty little bracelet with a manatee dangling off it. She bends to pick it up. "Where'd you get this?" she asks Noelle, who shrugs.

And then a yo-yo falls out of the cat. Mary Beth turns the giant cat pillow over and sees that it has been ripped apart at the back seam, much of the stuffing removed. She sticks her hand in and out she shovels a deluge of trinkets—children's sunglasses, a new water bottle with whales on it, a hair clip, a bow, a notepad, another bracelet, a keychain, hand sanitizer, a plastic octopus.

"Noelle, where did you get all these?"

Her daughter shrugs.

"*Noelle?*" Mary Beth snatches the iPad out of her hands and switches it off. There. Noelle tucks her chin into her shoulder and squirms. "Noelle, I asked you a question."

"I took it," she whines.

"Took it from whom?" Mary Beth feels around in the cat and comes out with a gel pen. The Brandts don't own gel pens.

"Lola, mainly."

Noelle is going to cry. Mary Beth senses it, like a drop in air pressure. It's coming. It's happening. She can't let that sway her.

"These things belonged to *Lola*? Why are they here? Why would you take them from her?"

"Because I can." Her daughter sniffles, but there's something in the performance that today, for once, Mary Beth isn't entirely convinced by. "She lets me."

"That's not very nice." Mary Beth stares down at the pile of odds and ends. What are the chances Lola Morton gave these to Noelle, let her have all this stuff for keeps? She bites her lip, unsure of whether she wants to know the answer. Normally she could call Darby and ask, but Darby's in jail.

"Noelle, how long have you been taking things from Lola?"

No actual tears have fallen. Her face is red and her eyes squinted together, but where are the tears? She's in big trouble. She does know that, doesn't she?

"Since . . . since school started . . . I'm sorry, Mommy. I didn't mean to."

Oh my god. Mary Beth sinks down onto the foot of the mattress.

"Mommy, please don't be mad. It was an accident."

There's a layer of ice crystallizing over Mary Beth's heart. She will admit to wishful thinking. Fine, yes, she thought her prayers were answered, that she had faith the size of a mustard seed that could move mountains. When Darby called and said it was Lola's footprints that were found at the scene of the crime, Mary Beth breathed the deepest sigh of relief. Because she was wrong. Slowly, she turns to face her daughter, who looks back at her with clear, dry eyes.

"Noelle," she says. "Whose shoes are in the Target dumpster?"

TRANSCRIPT OF INTERVIEW OF WITNESS, ASHER BRAZLE

APPEARANCES:

Detective Wanda Bright

PROCEEDINGS

DET. BRIGHT: Asher, I'm hoping you can help me figure out what some of your friends have been trying to tell me. Do you think you could help me out?

ASHER BRAZLE: My dad says never commit to a timeline.

MR. BRAZLE: That's my boy.

DET. BRIGHT: Okay. Well. Thank you for that honesty. Something I'm sure we both value. Asher, I want you to look at these two pictures and tell me what about the two pictures is different. It's a game. Can you do that for me?

ASHER BRAZLE: Okay . . .

DET BRIGHT: Okay . . . Do you need help getting started?

ASHER BRAZLE: Yeah.

DET. BRIGHT: Well, see, in this picture, the turtle is wearing a red hat. In this other picture the turtle's wearing a blue one. That's different.

ASHER BRAZLE: That's funny. Oh! Look! Here the squirrel is eating a hot dog and in the other one he's not eating anything.

DET. BRIGHT: Exactly!

ASHER BRAZLE: And in this one the dog is riding a unicycle and in the other, that's a motorcycle. Dogs can't ride motorcycles.

DET. BRIGHT: Very good. That's exactly what I mean. You get it. Now pretend that day, the last day you saw Miss Ollie, pretend that day is like one of these pictures. I'm trying to understand what about that day was different from your normal days. Make sense? What can you tell me, Asher?

ASHER BRAZLE: Lots of things. It was a crazy day! That's what Miss Ollie said.

DET. BRIGHT: Tell me about that. What made it crazy?

ASHER BRAZLE: Mr. Smiley wasn't there to take our pictures. That was one thing. And then, in chapel, we learned about David and Goliath and that's when Lola got in trouble.

DET. BRIGHT: Why did Lola get in trouble?

ASHER BRAZLE: Because she threw a pebble at Noelle and it hit her in the eye. Just like in the story.

DET. BRIGHT: Where was this?

ASHER BRAZLE: In chapel. Lola had a rock stuck in the bottom of her shoe and she took it out and she threw it.

DET. BRIGHT: Then what?

ASHER BRAZLE: Then we stopped chapel so that Miss Ollie could take Lola to Mrs. Parker's office for a talking-to.

DET. BRIGHT: Did you stay in the sanctuary during that time?

ASHER BRAZLE: No. We got walked back. Oh. That was another different thing about that day. Instead of Ms. Neary doing our story, we had a special guest.

DET. BRIGHT: Who was the special guest, Asher?

ASHER BRAZLE: His name is Pastor Ben.

THIRTY-FIVE

▼

Darby wasn't strip-searched; she really wishes she could announce that to everyone at once— *Hi, I didn't have to bend over and cough, thank you so much for your attention, carry on.* But so far she hasn't found a natural way to work that into conversation.

She met the custody sergeant, went over the reasons for her arrest, handed over the things in her pockets, which he placed gingerly in a plastic bag for safekeeping; she spoke with her new lawyer, she sat in a cell for hours, she went over again with the police how, yes, she did pick up Lola, and no, she did not know where those shoes were and, no, she did not purposefully get rid of them. The first release review came six hours after her admission into the station, right on schedule, as her lawyer had warned her. And then the next, nine hours after that one, when they announced they did not have enough to justify continuing to hold her.

After fifteen hours at the police station, Darby was a free woman. Griff was sheet white when he came to collect her. He looked worse off than she was. "What did you tell them?" he asked.

There was nothing much to discuss. They both knew what he was really asking, whether she told the police officers she saw him at school that day, whether she believes their daughter could have killed her teacher.

A private email arrived from the school administrator the very next day: *We think it might be best if you kept Lola home for the foreseeable future, considering recent developments in the case of Erin Ollie.*

And Darby thought: *Who is "we"?* Is the Queen of England speaking or was an entire committee elected while Darby's back was turned? Either way, she didn't care for the tone. It implied her daughter was a menace, a danger, and, most horribly of all, guilty.

"We are not going to hide ourselves away." Darby pulls up to the school with both of her children buckled into the back seat, prisoners to their mother's monologue. She feels like a whole new person. Less self-deprecating, less compliant, maybe she *has* been hardened by the system. "We're not going to lay low until things have *blown over*. You're not Typhoid Mary. We pay tuition. On time. Most of the time."

"Is Noelle going to be there?" Lola shakes her bangs, which are in desperate need of a trim, out of her eyes.

"Of course, sweetie. Okay, just remember to keep your head held high. *I* know you didn't do anything wrong. And *you* know you didn't do anything wrong." Though Darby's conviction on this point has wobbled over the last couple of days. The thing is, Darby bought those Crocs for Lola's birthday. They're her favorite shoes because of the hideous sparkles. And now they've vanished into thin air. There has to be a logical explanation except, for the life of her, she can't think of one. She can't remember which shoes Lola wore on which day.

Lola nods, all business. Darby goes around the sides of the car and gets her kids out. She and Lola high-five and she feels a little braver, a little more justified. The Morton ladies have got this covered. Lola is Lola. And Darby will make every single person at this school look her in the eye before condemning her or her child. So there.

"Mom." Lola skips alongside the stroller. "What's Daddy doing here?"

"Daddy's not here. Daddy's at work." Darby is power walking to make up for her jumpy stomach.

"No, he's right there." Lola drags on Darby's arm. "Mom, right there. I promise. See!"

Despite herself, Darby follows her daughter's finger across the campus to a nook on the side of the church sanctuary where, to her surprise, Griff—tall, dark, lean, unfairly defined rear end—is standing with his back to them, talking to a woman dressed in all black.

"You're right," Darby says, amazed. "That *is* Daddy."

"I told you." Lola pouts. "I don't tell you guys things because you never believe me but I wasn't lying about my nice new water bottle and I wasn't lying about this."

"We do believe you. We always believe you." Darby isn't paying enough attention to sound convincing about it. "What's Daddy doing?" She weaves her head, trying for a better angle.

He could do drop-off. She would gladly let him. It'd be more convenient for her anyway. She might actually log on to work on time for once. So, fine, if he's so keen to come to school, have at it.

Griff turns to gesture. Only Griff's not Griff. He's tall like Griff and dark haired like Griff and lean and from the back anyone, even his wife, could easily mistake him for Griff, but that's not Griff.

THIRTY-SIX

▼

Beneath the safety of her cool, linen sheets, Rhea curls herself into a ball on top of her mattress and thinks about what she's become: the most hated woman in America. Or at least this zip code.

She worried she might have forgotten how to wallow—like, who is this person in her pajamas at 2:00 P.M.? Twenty-three-year-old Rhea would know. But it's coming back to her. Hour by hour, the longer she stays put.

She feels herself coming undone, moving backward through time. Into the dark again, to the moments before she was put to sleep, and this time it feels like she wakes up in reverse, childless, not a mother. Who would she be? Who would she become without Bodhi?

She once read that as early as the second week of pregnancy, there is a two-way flow of cells and DNA between the fetus and the mother. Having a baby literally changes who you are at the most basic level, but not always for the better. Gather all the famous mothers—fairy godmothers and Mother Earth and Mother Teresa—and you might think those baby cells have some sort of magical powers that transform women into benevolent entities instead of regular bag-of-bones people with the same reserves of patience and honesty and self-control as everybody else.

Alone without her son, Rhea must come face-to-face with all the ways motherhood has brought out the worst in her. Nobody likes that story.

Seconds, minutes, or hours later, Rhea doesn't kick off the covers when the lock on the front door turns and she hears, "Rhea! Rhea, it's just us, Marcus and Bodhi. Don't shoot."

She rolls her eyes as Marcus laughs at his own joke. Over in the kitchen, she hears the refrigerator door crack open. "What are you still doing in bed? Don't you have work to do?" Marcus leans against the doorframe wearing real pants and a real shirt like he's trying to rub it in.

"What are you doing in my bedroom?" She keeps her head on the pillow.

"You weren't answering your door. Or your phone. And I've got a spare key, remember?" He holds it up with a big grin. She rolls over. She doesn't even know where her phone is. Last time she saw it there were six missed calls from her investment advisor, not to mention a couple texts—*a phony, a fraud, untrustworthy, false pretenses, pulling letters of intent, not all but some*—and that was enough for her to go off the grid. Little Academy parents sure do talk quick. "Come on," he groans. "You're better than this, Rhea."

"Actually, Marcus." She listens to Bodhi rummage around the kitchen for snacks. Can she even pretend to care what he gets into anymore? "Maybe I'm not. Maybe I kind of suck."

She knows she must be in it bad because she lets Marcus, her ex-nothing, sit on her mattress and rest his hand over the lump of her feet.

"Bodhi isn't a bloodsucking little biter. That's a good thing, whichever way you slice it."

Speaking of which, that slice on her arm? It's angry, red, and infected, so who knows when was the last time the school had bothered to sanitize. Not to mention the nasty bite on her right tricep that still feels tender and swollen to the touch.

She flips onto her back and stares up at the ceiling. "That's not really the point."

"I don't know why you hold yourself to these crazy standards, Rhea. You're doing just fine."

She knew what it would mean sending her son to a school like Little Academy. She wouldn't just have to keep up with the Joneses, she'd have to beat them. A philosophy like free-range parenting is all well and progressive when it's adopted by parents with money, but for people like her, that same logic can look negligent. So she played their game and whose fault is that?

"Do you know," Rhea says, ignoring Marcus, "that Jessica Alba turned her natural lifestyle brand into a billion-dollar company and she's got three kids. How'd she do that?"

He sighs. It's dark in here. The last time the two of them were together in a dark room, they made Bodhi. "I don't know if I'd go modeling your professional business off the *Honest* Company right now."

Rhea takes the pillow from the other side of the bed and whacks him over the head with it. He makes a big thing out of ducking for cover. He would.

"What's really going on?" he asks, turning serious. "Is Terrene underwater, is that it?"

"Why do you have to go there?" She folds her arms over her chest, which probably does not have the intended effect from her horizontal position. She feels like a kid.

He strokes the stubble on his chin. "Those documents you showed me at coffee the other day, all the money flowing out, not enough in, they didn't add up and I thought—I thought maybe that's what you needed to talk to me about, but you chickened out." He gives her a mischievous side-eye.

With great effort, she heaves herself up to a sitting position. "Why are you doing this?" She tilts her head. "Acting like we're friends."

"We are friends, Rhea. You're my best friend." He stares at her with those deep brown eyes, the ones her son inherited, if she's being honest, and reaches in to pluck at her heartstrings. She can't help it. She busts out laughing, shooting spit every which way, probably.

"What?" He throws up his big hands. "We made a little man together. I see you at least four times a week, more than I see anybody else, and I look forward to it. When I come get Bodhi, I always think, *Oh good, I get to see Rhea, too.*"

She quits her giggling and wipes her eyes where tiny tears have gathered at the corners. He shakes his head like he always knew she was nuts. She shakes hers right back at him and says, "God. You know what, I think you're right."

She and Marcus make a pretty good team and here she's been acting like she's been doing it all alone. She may be a single mom, but she's got people.

"So?" he says. "Are you going to let me help you or what?"

"It's not me." She can tell he still doesn't believe her, but then she probably deserves that. "They belonged to Miss Ollie. I think she was stealing money from the church."

"No shit? Wow." He nods, processing. "Why didn't you say anything?"

"It's complicated. There are . . . factors," she says carefully. She thinks she might have told Darby about the documents; she was going to try to, but then Darby went and eulogized the woman popularly known as Miss Erin Ollie and made Rhea out to be the bad guy and, call it intuition, but Rhea could see no good would come from exposing her vendetta any further. But things change, people change, for the worse, for the better, and everything in between.

"There's a parent meeting at the school. I found out at pickup." Marcus rubs his head.

"Then you should go," she says. "You're Bodhi's father." It sounds so simple saying it now. Half of Bodhi belongs to Marcus and there's nothing she can do to change that; she wouldn't want to if she could. She can admit that, now that everyone's being honest.

She thinks back on the Rhea that existed several weeks ago, how desperate she was to keep him out after the failed meeting with Mrs. Parker, when she went to Bodhi's class that day. It was stupid. She wanted to pull Bodhi out, to make a big thing of it because she could, because she is Bodhi's mother. But Miss Ollie wasn't there. Her computer was open and an idea jumped into her brain, pure and simple. Change Marcus's email address in the system. That was it. That was all she had to do to keep control. She went into the class contacts, and she entered the wrong email address for Marcus. A fake account. So whatever Miss Ollie sent, Marcus wouldn't receive. Easy as that. She wanted so badly to avoid being held accountable to him; she was willing to do anything. And now, come to find out, Miss Ollie was quitting anyway. Why? Why would she do that?

She would do that if she were stealing money from the church and trying to get away with it.

He reaches over to her nightstand and turns on the table lamp—the nerve. "If I go to the meeting," he says, "I'll be fielding questions that only you can answer and I'm not doing that. This could be a good opportunity to get over with whatever needs getting over."

"I can't tell the other parents about Miss Ollie stealing money." It'd be too much of a risk, too high a possibility of getting mixed up in a bad situation, the way she had back at the Roosevelt Room when no one wanted to hear her side of things. She feels like she's got a few pieces of a jigsaw puzzle, but some of the most important ones seem to have gone missing, like Lola's shoes.

The thing she never appreciated enough about Marcus until now is he knows enough not to ask why.

"Okay," he says.

"You think I should go to the meeting with all those other parents who hate me?" She looks at him like he's someone whose opinion she cares about because he is.

"My theory is that parenting is sort of like a horror movie," he says. "Like one of those really bad eighties slasher flicks. You don't know what the hell's going to jump out at you next. And the worst thing you can do is split up."

Since the moment Bodhi was born, she's been performing motherhood, her version of it, in a one-woman act with the worst critic in town sitting front row—herself. She's tired, though. And Bodhi's only four. Four years is long enough to get pretty exhausted, even with yoga and crystals and essential oils and all of the extremely worthwhile and valid self-care things she's been cheerleading for.

"Here's the thing," Rhea says, pushing her sheets past her hips. "Lola didn't kill Miss Ollie." She doesn't know what the missing pieces of the jigsaw puzzle will reveal, but she does know that.

She's kept the silver *A* close by, trying in vain to wait for a clear sign from the universe that never came. The only thing she knows is that there must be some connection to the murder and this silver trinket, and that connection isn't Lola. Rhea has been shutting everybody out, convincing herself that she didn't need them. When Darby said all those nice things about Lola and Miss Ollie's relationship, a part of Rhea had felt relieved. She'd thought: *Good, I can put you outside, too.* Maybe deep down she thought that the more people she let in, the greater chance they had of finding out she was a fraud, but turns out she went and exposed that all by herself, just the way she liked it. She does need her people and, if she's lucky, they need her. If anyone's going to hear her who matters, Rhea knows she's going to have to go down to the school and face them.

"I'll go to the meeting," she says. "But I need you to do something for me in the meantime."

Marcus smiles back at her with big, white teeth. "Anything you need." He winks at her. "You name it."

This is going to take some getting used to.

THIRTY-SEVEN

▼

Ben Sarpezze. Ben Sarpezze. *Ben Sarpezze.*

Darby couldn't wait until she got back to the car to pull out her trusty phone and start googling.

Down two children, who are now safely—ha!—at school, she cracks her knuckles, preparing to knock out some of her best internet sleuthing to date. It's like she's been training for this for years.

Darby hates her phone, but only because she loves it so. Naturally, she would be irritated with—maybe even fire—any babysitter who dared look at her phone while watching the children. They need to be engaged. On the kids' level. Not liking pictures.

But Darby can't seem to hold herself to the same standard. Some mothers may need a glass of wine to ease them through dinner or bath time, but if asked to make a choice—alcohol or iPhone—Darby would pick Apple every day of the week. She doesn't even know when it got so bad, this love affair with the small black rectangle in her palm, only that at some point she began to need this intimate time with her eyes glued to her screen the same way she used to crave chocolate or sex or really good weed.

Even when she intends to set the phone down and focus, she often finds herself picking it right back up again to look up just one more thing. Before she forgets. And so it goes. Reading articles about the dangers of screen time while ignoring her own children, wondering if every mother is doing the same or whether she truly does have a problem.

But this is different. She really must look into this one thing—just one.

She pulls up the church website and anxiously waits for it to load.

She recognized that guy. Sort of. The handsome new pastor, the one trying to raise money for the youth center, but now Darby needs to know who he really is.

She scrolls the church staff bios until she finds him. Ben. Associate pastor.

He's young, like, way young. Probably his first job out of seminary, if she needs to guess, and not that Darby is some kind of expert in this arena, but she imagines a position at RiverRock Church is a pretty big score right off the bat. How'd he manage that?

He came to the church six months ago and "has a heart for addiction and rehabilitation ministry." That sounds noble, Darby concedes. Other than that, his biography is scant, just another note about how he digs the outdoors and experimental restaurants.

Okay, so that's Ben Sarpezze in a nutshell. A man who looks exactly like her husband from the back. So freaking what? It's probably nothing. But then is there any such thing as "probably nothing" when her daughter is suspected of murder?

Darby opens up a new browser window on her phone and enters his information into the search. She scrolls past a few fruitless Yellowbook entries and linked ads for Ancestry and 23andMe, unsure of exactly what she's hoping to find. *Nose to the ground*, she thinks, her eyes traveling lightning fast across the screen. And then, just like that, she spots a KNTV news story from nine years back and feels a corresponding pitter-patter in her chest as she taps it with her finger and waits for her slow, old iPhone to load. It's like driving behind an elderly lady. Her patience, which was not so impressive to begin with, shrinks.

"Come on . . ." She taps again, but that might only make it worse. "Aha!"

Here we go. It loads.

FAMILY OF TEEN KILLED IN BOATING ACCIDENT SEEKS JUSTICE

Last summer, the Lake Travis community was rocked when a collegiate soccer player was killed in a horrific boating accident.

"He had his whole life ahead of him," said his mother, Gina Nierling.

"I spoke to him before he went out for the night and I said, 'Be careful.' He promised he would be."

On board at the time of the crash were three boys, Benjamin Sarpezze, whose family owned the boat, Maxwell Johns, and the deceased, Oliver Nierling.

Sarpezze and Johns both confirmed that Nierling was behind the wheel and had been drinking heavily that night, but his family questions the timeline of events. "Ollie had combine training for the under-twenty-one youth national soccer team in a few days and he wouldn't have been drinking, let alone heavily," Gina Nierling went on to say.

Prior to leaving on the boat, twenty-year-old Benjamin Sarpezze was seen on surveillance video using his older brother's ID at a local gas station to buy alcohol. No charges were pursued.

The boat hit the pylons of a bridge at roughly 10:00 P.M. before beaching on shore. After swimming to safety, Sarpezze and Johns noticed Nierling was missing.

Local personal injury lawyer Rick Sarpezze arrived on the scene promptly, having been notified of an accident involving his boat. He volunteered to contact the families, but the Nierlings claim they weren't called until four hours after their son was discovered missing.

A civil lawsuit has been filed in county court by the Nierling family against the Sarpezzes. Oliver Nierling is survived by his parents, Gina and Bob, and his younger sister, Erin Nierling.

Darby stops reading. Erin Nierling. Something Rhea said the last time they spoke, before Darby cut her off, now floats back to her. *Miss Ollie isn't who you think she is . . .*

Darby thought Rhea was being petty again. But what if she was being literal?

She pulls up Facebook and struggles mightily to remember her password before finally successfully resetting it. "Erin Nierling," she murmurs as she types the name. And there, staring back at her, is the woman *she* knows as Miss Erin Ollie.

Her phone buzzes, startling her half to death. She groans as her boss's number pops up and she slides her finger across the screen, prepared to do damage control. "This is Darby," she says in her work voice. Her boss—such a dated term, but, then, he *is* dated—is a white-haired man named Carl who looks like he's been squashed in one of those aluminum can compactors, everything but his earlobes that is, which get longer and longer each time Darby has to meet with him over Zoom.

"Why aren't you at your desk?" he asks. The man always sounds like he has a frog in his throat. He's a grandfather now, but probably not a favorite one. He would never pull a quarter out from behind a child's ear, which is a shame in Darby's book.

She bites the inside of her cheek, hedging. "How do you know I'm not?"

She really doesn't have time for this. She has to get to the police station. The image of those investigators traipsing all over her house like they owned the place, looking for a pair of sparkly pink Crocs when this hard evidence was just waiting on the internet, sends shockwaves of anger down her limbs. They should pay her for doing their job.

"Because," Carl drones, "if you were, you'd be answering my emails. You're supposed to be at your desk by nine thirty. That's the agreement. You can work from home if you can be trusted to *work*." Carl's emails? She can't remember the last time Carl sent a truly time-sensitive email. She gets real emails from team members—the twentysomething and the tired dad of a newborn and the single fiftysomething-year-old who loves salsa dancing and her pug. They have a good rhythm. They sort things out together. But never from Carl. Carl is the butt of a joke, sorry to say, and she's just not in the mood to laugh at the moment.

"What did the email say, Carl? You've got me on the phone now." She's never been this direct before. She's still sitting in the parking lot of Little Academy. Normally she'd be home with her second cup of coffee by now—she really should clean out her car, but there are always more goldfish to be spilled and sippy cups to roll underneath seats.

Carl blusters and says something about how that's not really the point. *So, then, what, this is pointless, Carl?* she wants to say. *The same way I feel about cleaning my car, say?*

Every minute she worries the police are out there solidifying a case against Lola, and she's seen enough *Law & Order* reruns to know that once the police get stuck on a suspect it can be hard to pry their hands off of them. But pry she will.

"I'm managing a crisis," she says, more snappily than she intends, but she's not sorry about it. "Isn't that my job?"

"And what crisis would that be?" Carl sounds very tired with her.

"I think you know my daughter's preschool teacher was killed," she says. That should be reason enough, but there's more, there's a lot more.

He sighs. "I'm very sorry about that, Darby." Usually she's so careful about responding to his emails first, making him feel important, like he's part of the royal family—and, just like them, he's all for show. "I haven't wanted to say anything because I know you're a mother, but the amount of time you spend away from your desk, sending emails from your phone, it's becoming a problem."

"What kind of problem?"

She imagines him tugging on one of his long earlobes as he *deals* with her. Maybe that's how they've gotten so long in the first place. "It isn't fair to the other employees, who are expected to be at work."

"Right." She nods. That must have been very difficult for him to say, poor guy. He probably worried about being PC. "Fair," she repeats. "I know how important it is for the world to be *fair*. Isn't that what you Boomers are always saying? That life, it's so fair! Have I got the phrase right? I mean, you'd know better than me!"

Wow, she mouths to herself and yet—and yet—she doesn't wish it back. If Griff can go do improv, she can go do some job she actually cares about if she has to.

"Are you finished?" Carl's tone is a warning.

"I'll handle whatever needs handling when I get past this family emergency later this afternoon." She's only guessing. She has no idea how long it will take to unravel a mystery. "I can do this job in my sleep."

He scoffs so that she has to remove the phone from her ear. "Is that so?" he says.

"Yes, that is so. This job puts me to sleep, so that's how I get most of the work done. Listen, I'm sorry. I really am. But I have to go. Right now." She moves her finger to the red button at the bottom of the screen.

"Are you quitting?" He raises his voice.

"Oh no." She hesitates. "Of course not. But do feel free to fire me, the county has a very nice severance package that I've had my eye on for some time." And with that, she hangs up on her very steady job that she took four years ago to be a mom.

Darby has every intention of marching into the police station with a great deal of brass, but the thing about police stations, she learns quickly, is that they seem specifically designed to stamp out any remnant of self-assurance you may have when you walk through those doors. There's so much gray—gray carpet, gray cubicles, gray ceiling tiles, and vinyl vestibules—it feels like a "mute" button for her eyes. "I need to talk to Detective Bright." She leans over to speak to the uniformed lady sitting on a gray rolling chair behind a desk. "Right away," she adds, not wanting to betray the version of herself who was so intent on marching.

The woman pushes a clipboard sign-in sheet toward Darby and rolls back from her desk a few feet. "Hey, is Bright in?" she asks the bullpen of mostly white-shirted officers. Darby wonders if there are different uniform colors for days in the office versus days spent outside of it.

"She's at her cousin's wedding this weekend."

The woman rolls back in her direction and repeats the words that Darby had been able to hear perfectly well.

"Where's that?" Darby asks.

The woman wears too much hair gel. Darby would get a headache if she wore her hair slicked back into a bun that tightly. "Tulsa," says the woman.

"The whole *weekend*?" Darby forgets about the gray "mute" button.

"Think so. What's it about? We can get someone else to help you."

"The case of Erin Ollie. The murdered preschool teacher." Darby sounds like a middle-aged Nancy Drew, which sounds sad.

"Oh yeah." The woman lightly taps her fist on the desk. "Let me get Princep for you. Hang on."

Darby wants to object. She'd like to say, *Don't you have anyone else available?* But she can't work out what reason she'd supply. She gets a bad feeling about Officer Princep—never trust a man that good-looking— and then she remembers Griff and feels guilty for judging him, for ever suspecting her poor husband of any wrongdoing. She'll have to say sorry, but Darby's not great at apologies. Either way, Officer Princep will have to do.

She's asked to wait for him in a small meeting room where the air-conditioning vent blows directly down the back of her shirt. She scans the ceiling for any sign of a camera, but finds none. She wouldn't mind being filmed. Film away! The only thing worth seeing in here is a scantily stocked vending machine that hums softly in the corner next to a water-cooler. She rises and takes one of the cone cups, fills it up, and sucks the water straight down before Princep even arrives.

"What can I help you with, Mrs. Morton?" He looks older without the company of Detective Bright, probably closer to forty than she'd previously thought. That's comforting. No ring on his finger, as she suspected. He has the blandly attractive face of a soap opera star, not an Oscar winner.

On the way over, she thought about how she would tell her story and decided that she wouldn't oversell it. She'd stick to the facts, ask leading questions, let them draw the conclusions.

"Please," she says, "call me Darby."

He presses his lips together. "How's your—" He points to her, not wanting to say *butt*, obviously. "Hip?"

Hurts. Hurts a lot. And the bandage keeps coming loose, after which the stitches stick to her pants, and she has a big ugly bruise that's turning putrid green, but other than that— "Fine! Oh god, that was— I'm fine. Totally fine. Really."

"Glad to hear it."

Unable to hold it in any longer, Darby launches into the whole tale, pulling up the article and detailing the accident that led to the death of Oliver Nierling, who was the brother of Erin Ollie, who is actually Erin *Nierling*. Ta-da! When she finishes, she notices herself panting a little. She forgot to breathe. "Did you know about Ben's involvement in Erin's brother's death?" she asks.

She momentarily deflated when she heard that Princep and Bright were aware of Erin's true identity and that they'd run a background check on both of her names and come up with nothing, but then that would make perfect sense, wouldn't it?

He's quiet for a long moment, studying her. "Actually, no."

She exhales. "I didn't think so. I just— I had a hunch. Don't you think that's weird? The Nierlings clearly believed that their son, Ollie, wasn't really driving the boat, that he was on the straight and narrow, and the Sarpezzes *had* money."

"He's a pastor now, though?"

"Yes," she explains patiently. "At the church connected to Little Academy. I understand it's an easy thing to miss if you're not familiar with the ins and outs of the Little community. Erin's family sued Ben's for a lot of money. But unfortunately, the Nierling family attorneys were no match for the fancy whiteshoes of the Sarpezzes. I discovered that Erin's family lost." Darby is editorializing a bit because, in fact, she doesn't know whether it's unfortunate or not, but the feeling she got when she learned the end of the story was, without question, sorrow.

"That's good work," he says, and he does sound genuine.

Darby's heart blips up. It's all fitting together, or starting to. "What happens next?"

"We'll look into it." He rises from his chair.

Her mouth drops. "You'll look into it?"

He holds out his hand for her and she doesn't know whether he wants to help her out of her chair or simply shake hands. Neither seems appealing.

"Detective Bright gets back to the office on Monday. I'll brief her and we'll look into it."

"Don't you think you should *call* her?" Darby presses.

"She's at her cousin's wedding," he says as if that settles it, as if Tulsa is the motherfucking Arctic Ocean. Off Darby's look, he softens. "Darby, I understand why this is important to you and we'll take every lead seriously, you have my word. But Lola's footprints were found *in* the blood. We're being as sensitive as possible because we've never dealt with a potential perpetrator this young before, but you may have to face the facts that your daughter needs help. She's a minor. That's key. A terrible, terrible thing happened and the family needs answers. But she will have a life after this."

Darby sits motionless in her chair, unable to muster the leg strength to move when he leaves. He's wrong about Lola and her life. Wrong about her future. Right now, she's so young, so tender and impressionable. She may not rot in jail, but there are bigger, deeper consequences than that. If she grows up with a scarlet letter for murder, how will Lola ever define herself apart from it, and who would let her? Darby thinks about her daughter, with her monster tantrums and sensitive spirit. She's worried already a thousand times over that Lola will grow up to think Jack is the golden child and, as her mother, she can't let that happen. She must be sure of it. But how?

The Nierlings have lost two children without justice. Thinking about it, her own maternal heart is a tiny bit wrecked. How would she feel if every closet she checked in the middle of the night, every reading tutor she wrote checks to, every moment she stopped herself from screaming in frustration, every green vegetable bribed down, every puddle of vomit, every snotty nose, every time-out and knotted ponytail and lost retainer, every slobbery kiss and sweet-smelling forehead, every quiet hug, disappeared? In their darkest moments, sitting alone at night watching television, how pointless it must sometimes feel to the Nierlings, all of it. And that's why, no matter what, Darby can't let anything happen to Lola.

After a long moment, she summons what last scraps of brass she had when she came in to leave the police station. The sun is already on its downward curve and her stomach growls. She's missed a call and a text, both from Bodhi's father, Marcus, of all people, and her empty stomach sinks. What's happened? What could possibly have happened now? She reads the text: *Can we meet in person? I'll come to you.*

THIRTY-EIGHT

▼

Well after hours, Mary Beth enters her access code to the Little Academy building. The parking attendants and new security personnel have all gone for the night. Soon, the parents will be gathering for a state of the union meeting and she'll be expected to attend, but for the moment, she remains undecided.

The hallway lights are motion activated and they trip on as she makes her way down the hall. With every step, she feels as though she's losing altitude. Cold sweat crops up on the back of her neck.

Behind the closed door at the end of the corridor, Miss Ollie's old room sits untouched, like a shrine, the children having moved to an unused class on the other side of the building in the weeks following her death. She waits outside the door as if something might happen without her setting it in motion first. She feels Schrödinger's cat on the other side of the wall, both dead and alive. Awaiting confirmation.

On the first day of school this year, Noelle wore a smocked dress with apples embroidered on the collar, a bright blue bow pinned in her hair, and Mary Beth thought how grown-up she looked. It's the first year Noelle has helped put on her own shoes, climbed into her own car seat, carried her own backpack.

The latch emits a faint click as Mary Beth opens it, the smell of finger paints lingering in the dim air. Parent-teacher evaluations weren't set to take place until just after spring break, but Miss Ollie would have been keeping progress reports on file. Now to figure out where she stowed them.

The cubbies have been emptied and very little is left in the small teacher desk at the corner—some paper clips, dry-erase markers, and a spool of string. There's a rolling cabinet on which a TV sits. Mary Beth kneels and tugs the aluminum doors open and—bingo. A neat pile of green two-pocket folders are stacked on the middle shelf there. On each, she finds a label: *George, Tamar, Maggie, Zeke*. She shuffles through until she finds Noelle's name.

Mary Beth lets herself drop flat onto her bottom and sits cross-legged, the folder balanced on her inner thighs. She remembers one of the last things Miss Ollie ever said to her: *I think it's time that you, me, and Darby get together to discuss what's going on between the girls.* She thought she knew what that meant.

Inside the folder are the usual assessments. A few writing worksheets. Some pictures. A couple cute photos of Noelle and her classmates that Doug and Mary Beth would have found adorable in this parent-teacher meeting that will never take place. But on the back page, there's the formal evaluation, written in the handwriting of a dead woman.

And sitting right there on the floor, Mary Beth forces herself to read every last line.

THIRTY-NINE

▼

The last meeting of the Little Academy four-year-old parents begins at dusk. Without Rhea.

She imagines her absence is noticeable as much as it's noted, the other parents remarking at how they aren't surprised she's not there to show her face. She imagines them feeling better for it, savoring it like the last sip from a fine bottle of wine, imagines, too, that while they're bitching and moaning about how she's too chicken to show up, they're secretly glad she's gone—*Ha, proves them right*—a free pass to whisper about her as much as they please, to pile on a pile that's already been dumped over her good name.

Maybe she's catastrophizing. Or maybe not. She is a small speck in the universe. A single molecule of water floating through the stream. She is dust on the winds of time.

Oh god. When did she become so full of shit?

When she started believing she was a good mother. Like she had this all figured out. Rhea came up with all kinds of rules and decrees, philosophies and lines in the sand, as though that could mean she had it on lock. As though that could mean she didn't gag at the contents of a super-smelly diaper or long to blast explicit rap lyrics in the car with Bodhi riding in the back seat.

Rhea opens the double doors to the multipurpose room knowing that she's about to face some different kind of music, but what the hell—she's a tired mom just like everybody else, too tired to care any longer.

TRANSCRIPT OF INTERVIEW OF WITNESS, LOLA MORTON

APPEARANCES:

Detective Wanda Bright

PROCEEDINGS

DET. BRIGHT: Lola, what did you think of Miss Ollie?

LOLA MORTON: I loved her. She was my best friend.

DET. BRIGHT: What made her your best friend?

LOLA MORTON: She didn't yell at me for tattling and she believed me.

DET. BRIGHT: Believed you about what?

LOLA MORTON: I don't know.

DET. BRIGHT: What happened, Lola? I'm like Miss Ollie. I'll believe you, too.

LOLA MORTON: Miss Ollie said she was disappointed in me. And I pouted and got really mad. She walked me back from Mrs. Parker's and I think that's how come she's dead.

FORTY

▼

Noelle is a smart student who catches on quickly to lesson plans,

Mary Beth reads.

but her social skills leave some areas for concern and will need to be addressed as she moves toward kindergarten. Noelle can be sneaky when she isn't monitored closely. She has a quietly dominating personality that she uses to manipulate and at times strong-arm her peers. She has taken a special interest in subjugating her best friend, Lola, causing emotional distress for her and little remorse from Noelle. On several occasions, I have caught Noelle taking things that don't belong to her from her classmates, and even killing a cicada that Lola had "befriended," but it's her singular focus on Lola, one of the quirkier personalities in the class, that worries me. I have tried to deal with this in the classroom to the best of my abilities before escalating the matter; however at this point, I would recommend a full assessment by a licensed child psychologist to monitor signs of behavioral disorder for early intervention.

Mary Beth sits back, stunned, wondering if this changes everything or if it even changes anything.

Since the moment she found her daughter covered in Miss Ollie's blood, she's been haunted by the idea that Noelle may have made a terrible mistake. Never once did it cross her mind that she may not have made a terrible mistake, but might instead *be* terrible.

And yet. Here she is, face-to-face with the terrible truth, and what she will do with it next is up to her.

"Nobody's supposed to be in here outside of school hours." The voice causes Mary Beth to tense up, but so would the man standing in the doorframe.

Pastor Ben.

Without the lights on, his eyes shine, shadows sharpen the lines of his face, and she can't quite figure out what she found so handsome about him a few short days before. The scent of his bodywash—clean and decidedly male—reminds her of guys she met in college. Well before Doug.

"Sorry." She can't muster a smile for once as she climbs to her feet. "I thought my daughter forgot one of her old lunch boxes in here. I was just going through a few items. For the class. I'm Room Mom," she reminds him. It sounds rote, like she's playing a recording of herself.

He's standing such that there's no casual way to breeze past him and so she's stuck in social-nicety land, a place where she would typically consider herself a local, though today it feels as if she's somehow forgotten the language entirely.

There are only a handful of words that seem capable of pinging in her brain. *Noelle. Behavioral disorder. Manipulate.* They throb in her head, becoming something palpable. Her daughter's a bully. Mary Beth Brandt, professional nice person, has raised a sociopath. Isn't that what Miss Ollie was implying?

"The building's closed," Ben repeats.

"Right. Again, sorry about that." This time, she moves to pass him, assuming this will trigger his own social cues, but he holds up a hand to stop her.

"What did you take?"

"What do you mean?" Her temple pulsates, a warning shot of pain. She tries to take a deep breath, in through her nose, out through her—

"I saw you fold up a sheet of paper and take it. What was it?" The room behind her feels much smaller now. Ben is tall. Ben is in excellent shape.

"Nothing." She feels hatchet lines fan out around her lips as she purses her mouth tight. She doesn't know what his problem is, but she sees the tendon that runs from his neck to his shoulder tense.

"It must be something. God honors the truth and those who speak it." He smiles benevolently.

Her face reddens. "It's private." She shifts back a step, eager for some distance. Something to quiet the alarm bells sounding from inside her skull. She's not sure she's thinking straight. She's not sure she's thinking at all.

"You seemed uncomfortable last time we spoke." He looks deeply concerned and yet she's not buying it.

"I wasn't," she says. "Just tired. And busy. And married," she adds without removing the point on it.

"So, it's not me then?"

"Not you," she confirms. A swell of nausea pushes the contents of her stomach up, up, up. "I do need to go, though."

"Why are you in such a hurry?" He pushes into the room, forcing her back again.

"There's a meeting with the other parents I should attend." This time she can't steady her voice. She looks around blindly. The crude paintings still pinned to the wall. The tissue-paper caterpillar. An abandoned game of Twister on the floor.

"Why do I get the feeling that this actually has something to do with Erin Ollie?"

"It could be where we're located." Mary Beth tries to control her breathing, but it keeps managing to get away from her. She can hear the air rasping through her lungs.

"She was on the youth center committee, too, wasn't she? With you?" He must know the answer.

She falters, unsure what this has to do with anything. "Yes. She wanted to make sure the school was represented." She walks with her hands on her hips, trying to pull oxygen. The room has begun to spin. "It made sense." The familiar pain bulges behind her right eye, as if out of nowhere. It punches her brains in. It blossoms like an atom bomb detonated inside her skull.

"Did she ever mention me?"

"What?" Black spots creep around her vision on one side. "Maybe," she says. "In passing. I'm sorry. I'm feeling kind of woozy."

"Let me help you." Ben's fingers close around her upper arm.

"Ouch, that hurts." She tries to shrug off his grip, but finds herself unable to break free.

"I need to ask you to come with me," he says, like she's being placed under arrest. "We can't have people taking things off school grounds without permission. Hand it to me."

"No." She shakes her head. Saliva is tacky in her mouth. "It's got nothing to do with you," she says. Noelle. Her daughter. Her blood. Hers.

"I think—" He yanks her into his chest. "—that I'll be the judge of that."

Her cheek smacks hard against his elbow and she feels herself being flung down. A knee is on her hamstring. Fingers claw at her back pocket. The pressure of his forearm is hard against her throat. She can't breathe. She feels like someone has clasped a fist around the middle of a balloon, the pressure building, swimming up to her eyes. She gathers her energy, trying to scream, but before she can finish the thought, she has no more thoughts; the life blinks out of her.

FORTY-ONE

▼

Welcome," says the bearded man at the front of the room. "Please come in and have a seat." He beckons Rhea forward. He's wearing a white coat and she knows who he is instantly. The naturopathic doctor that *she* recommended—Dr. Fox. She didn't realize he would be here but, then, she supposes everyone is still looking for answers wherever they can find them. "We were just discussing the seven Bs of parenting—birth bonding, breastfeeding, baby-wearing, bedding close to the baby, belief in the baby's cry, balance and boundaries, and beware of baby trainers—and together, we're considering, based on this very group, adding an eighth B: bloodletting. Isn't that exciting?"

The room is large and open, with a wall of mirrors in front to facilitate the kids' creative-movement classes. Rows of folding chairs that are normally stowed on pallets in the back have been set up to accommodate the parents. The carpet smells musty. A cardboard cutout of Jesus stands in the corner like he's in time-out.

"Yeah, thrilling. Look," she tells him, "I'll take it from here." The door sinks shut behind her. She hears the seals suck together, corking her inside with these people.

"Uhhh . . ." He looks around, confused. Did he miss a memo? "Well, see, I'm providing some encouraging facts about scientific attach—"

"That's okay, I got it." She edges right in on his spot and, with no one giving him any indication about what he's supposed to do, he slinks over to sit in the front row.

At the same time, she's catching some serious heat from all those eyeballs trained on her, but at least nobody's throwing tomatoes yet. Marcus figured if they do, they'll at least be organic. She's glad someone's amused.

"Hi," she says to deafening silence. No one's about to make this eas-ier on her. She can't blame them. "I wanted to apologize to everyone for making it seem like Bodhi was dealing with—like we were handling all this, you know, pediatric Renfield's and whatnot, no problem, when we weren't having to deal with it at all, really." She twists the bracelets around her wrist and tries to keep looking up and out instead of down at her sandaled feet.

"You used us as an opportunity to help your business." She didn't expect Megan to be the first to speak up. That stings.

"We felt like we were some kind of negligent parents if we weren't totally fine with getting our blood sucked because you made it sound like we should be," adds Robin. "Like you were so cool with it. *Perfectly natural.* You walk around like you're better than us because you read the labels and don't give your son Happy Meals ever, apparently."

Rhea nods. "I know. And that definitely wasn't right." At this point, she doesn't even know which she started lying for more—her business or her reputation as a mother. They became so tightly braided along the way and Rhea has never kept fingernails long or sharp enough to untangle them. She can't miss the three or four not-so-subtle eye rolls from some of the other mothers—even Lena. *Damn.* She might swear the air-conditioning in the multipurpose room has gone on the fritz. Her kingdom for a bit of circulation. "I get it, okay?" she says. "I don't know what the hell I'm doing. I mean, for real, I've been feeding Bodhi McDonald's on a regular basis. For weeks now. I don't know."

"This from the woman who packs purple cauliflower for lunch?" Maggie's mother, Roxy, scoffs, then looks around, soaking in the approval of the other parents, for once on the inside. "That's rich."

What did that brand consultant advise Rhea to be? That's right: ef-fortless, aspirational, less folksy. Well, how about exhausted, disorga-nized, and messy as hell?

"I deserve that, I guess." Rhea shrugs. She's doing what she came here to do. and by the time she leaves, she needs to make it so that she can show her face again. And maybe, just maybe, even rebuild a shred of Terrene, but that's secondary. "Everyone wants to be seen as a good mother. I mean, seriously. Do y'all remember what they did to Britney Spears when she held a kid on her lap in the car for all of two seconds? I'm just trying to hang with all you moms who are really good at organizing playdates and coming up with cutesy party favors that say *thanks for popping by* on bubbles. That's not my bag, but it looks really grown-up from where I'm standing. So I used a different bag and made sure it was made from reusable water bottles." No one laughs. "It is what it is, but I still—"

Tamar's mother rises to her feet, making Rhea shut up. "Sometimes I'm so tired." She swipes dark bangs out of her eyes. "I don't brush my teeth at night."

Roxy snickers from a few seats over, then looks around again for some of that approval, but Megan shushes her and says, "I listen to audiobooks in my headphones while I give my kids baths. I don't even talk to them."

"My nanny is way better at playing with my kids than I am," adds Chelsea.

"Oh my god, mine, too." Tamar's mom drops back into her chair. "I tell my college-aged nanny she can't be on her phone while taking care of the kids, but the truth is when I'm with them I'm on the phone all the time. And it's not important stuff either. I'm talking Instagram and TikTok."

"At the pediatrician's office, I always circle the option that says George gets three to four servings of vegetables a day," says his mother, Charlotte. "But honestly, I'm lucky if he gets that in a week."

Robin raises her hand. "I've forgotten to give money for the last two years for the end-of-year gift, but I still put my name on it."

Chelsea gently slaps her wife on the arm and gives her the evil eye.

"I still haven't gotten my youngest swimming lessons. I mean to every summer, but I never even put him in one of those baby classes to splash around," says Lena.

"Maggie threw up in her bed in the middle of the night a few weeks ago and I just balled up the sheets and made her sleep on the bare mattress." Roxy slaps her hands over her mouth, her shoulders hiking up over her ears.

"I'm even worse. Last semester, I sent Bex to school a couple hours after she threw up because I had a lunch date with friends I didn't want to miss."

"We gave up on sleep training in two days and I'm pretty sure that's why they're all terrible sleepers," says Asher's dad about his kids.

"I feel like going to the grocery store alone is a vacation," adds Megan. "I eat every bit of mac 'n' cheese left on my kids' plates even if I've already eaten dinner."

"I let George watch a full hour of television every single morning before I even get up."

A wave of murmurs grows as everyone adds their two cents, one over the next. Someone hasn't kept a photo album of her second kid. Someone else never got around to planning a birthday party. Another one only bathes her child twice a week. The list goes on. A lock clicks open in Rhea's chest. Maybe this is what Mary Beth's been prattling on about all this time. Perhaps there's something to be said for community.

Where is Mary Beth, by the way? And Darby?

Rhea takes a deep breath and raises her hands, quieting everyone before someone confesses to feeding their child Purina Puppy Chow or something gross like that. If she were going to admit that she also solved the mystery of Poodini now would be the time. She hesitates.

The silver *A* is the weight of a pebble at the bottom of her pocket. Somebody else in here hasn't been telling the truth either. And now it's time to figure out who that is, no matter what it means for Rhea. The truth's got to come out sometime.

With the charm halfway out of her pocket, she stops. "Does anyone else hear that? Listen." They do. They listen—the sound of sirens rolling up on Little Academy after dark.

FORTY-TWO

▼

D arby's phone battery was at 3 percent when she arrived at school with the intention of joining the meeting in the multipurpose room and revealing to everyone what she learned.

Only an hour ago, she sat across from Marcus at a round coffee shop table not quite meant for two and asked with grave seriousness, "Are you sure?"

Earlier, she told Griff—she did not ask—to pick up the kids from Little at the end of the day. She'd fill him in later; it's been a day and it's not even over.

"I'm sure," Marcus told her, but he went through it again, explaining the numbers slowly, the profits and losses and what they meant. He told her that he was reasonably certain that someone, based on the figures, was embezzling money from the church and that Rhea had a strong suspicion that someone was Erin Ollie, née Nierling. "She thought, given everything with Lola, that you should be the first to know."

Darby got a sticky lump in her throat. "I'm really not a crier," she said, which is a bald-faced lie.

Darby sat back and thought about what to do. When Erin, a young, vibrant woman with a PhD, took the job at Little Academy, the parents all thought it was something of a miracle. Preschool Poppins had appeared out of the clear blue sky, not with an umbrella, but a rainbow-colored maxi skirt, and who were they to look a gift horse in the mouth? But here lies the reason. Erin Nierling changed her name to Erin Ollie to conceal her identity from a pastor at the RiverRock church. It made sense. He wouldn't recognize Erin even if she used a name that would honor her dead brother. He might not even know Ollie Nierling had a sister. He wouldn't put the pieces together until it was too late.

"It's for the youth center," Darby told Marcus. It felt like she was turning a camera lens, turning it and turning it and she was finally finding the right focus. "Which means Erin wasn't stealing money from the church, really. I think she was taking it from Ben, that it was *Ben* who was siphoning it off already."

Now what? She half expected confetti to rain down from the ceiling as if she were on a game show—you've done it, Darby Morton! Achievement unlocked. But she finds instead that the ends are still loose and floppy and her fingers are too thick and clumsy to tie them together into a bow. Detective Bright is apparently unreachable in Tulsa and Officer Princep still carries the firm belief that a child—most likely Lola—killed Erin. Will Marcus's evidence be enough to sway him?

It will, she thinks, if she can recruit backup.

Golden hour sinks over the empty playground and the climbing stalks of wildflowers in the garden and the handprint path and its stone steps, and the whole place has the smell of freshly cut grass. Somebody's left a basketball out on the court, where it sits still and forgotten, and she thinks she hears the faint voices of a choir practicing inside one of the church buildings. So when she climbs out of her car, she experiences a silly, inexplicable little moment in which she's filled with warm, gooey, heartrending love, the kind that strikes her every so often and without warning and which she always watches and appreciates, like a particularly impressive bubble blown by one of her children that either floats off or pops immediately.

She hasn't prayed since she was a teenager, but she gives it a try, channeling her inner Mary Beth. She asks God (if he's up there) to help her discredit Ben Sarpezze, the pastor who—she's now 100 percent sure—has had every reason to turn on not just her child, but all the children affected. When Darby thinks about the way that man used four-year-olds, with their terrible teeth and bloody tongues, sure, but also their sweet questions about whether ghosts are real and what kind of animals make bacon and whether people can be pets, all the love built up in her heart drops like a stone.

Just then, a tall, shadowy figure crosses the buildings before her eyes.

"Was that—?" She looks around as if someone else might be around to confirm, but she's alone. Alone with her thoughts and her decisions. He disappears into the preschool building and she holds her breath, thinking: *What do I do next?*

Does God answer prayers this quickly? Are they expedited when sent from church grounds?

If only she didn't hesitate, she will think. If only she charged after him like a superhero. Her mind will run through the scenario.

She tries Griff. Maybe he'll know what to do. She tries Mary Beth. Those four minutes will stretch to an eternity when she replays them later, and later, and later.

Because by the time she follows Pastor Ben into the hall, she knows where Mary Beth is—*9–1–1, what is your emergency*—and it's already too late.

FORTY-THREE

▼

On the other side of this life, Mary Beth Brandt would tell you that you don't walk toward a bright light or cross over a rainbow or even hear the voice of God. But you do see your children.

Time works differently during the last few moments of consciousness, she'd let you know. Of course, in those remaining heartbeats, there couldn't have been more than a few seconds, but she felt the weight of each of her daughters on her chest, their smooth backs, softer than peaches underneath her palms, the smell of their toothless breath. She sang to them in the middle of the night, small heads in the crook of her elbow, the world asleep around them. She patted their freshly diapered bottoms. And gradually they grew into toddlers and she counted each new word—*Mama, Dada, ball, bear, turtle, duck.* She saved locks of hair. They were frightened of Halloween decorations. They learned to share and then forgot. Soon, they were little girls, a stage that for Mary Beth's youngest, she hadn't yet seen. But there it was. Jean shorts and camp T-shirts. One loved art, the other karate. They fought and cut their own hair so badly Mary Beth cried. The family had cake when each started their period and Doug tried to play it cool. There were training bras and electric razors and soon enough she had young women with the stress of grades and choices of colleges. There were disappointments and friend fallouts that sank craters into their hearts only to be filled back up again by trips to the movies and secret sister hugs. They made bad fashion choices and left home, broke up with significant others who would have made good partners. They started jobs first doing things they hated and one of them would grow up to do something she loved. Doug saved newspaper clippings. Mary Beth saw her daughters grow up inside her eyes in the time it took her to blink—it all went by in a flash—in the time before she lost it all. Those moments taken from her seemingly forever, never to be returned.

Now sounds filter in slowly, like an AM/FM radio searching for a station. She has no sense of whether she's hearing the sounds with her ears or whether she even has ears—lobes and ear-piercing holes stretched with age, as they were. She waits, listens, until there's a sense of gravity and with that the sense of a blanket beneath her fingertips, her body sinking on a mattress.

"I can't believe she had a stroke," says a voice. "Can she talk?"

Mary Beth listens in part because it doesn't occur to her that she can do anything else.

"The doctors think it could take up to a week before she fully recovers normal speech." Doug. Her Doug. She has so much to tell him, but can't quite work out how. "We can't thank you enough. You saved her life."

Somebody *saved* Mary Beth's life? When? Who? She listens with interest, all news to her. She would like to do something to be part of the conversation, but what?

She attempts to move her fingers but finds it extraordinarily difficult. Not impossible, just probably not worth the effort. She opens her mouth and finds that it's in working order. Up, down, tongue side to side. Okay, then, that's a relief.

"Does she know?" a third voice asks.

"We're not sure," answers Doug. "We've explained to her the extent, but it's hard to tell what all has stuck. We're taking things slowly."

"Oh gosh. I— If there's anyone who can handle it, it's Mary Beth."

What a nice thing to say, thinks Mary Beth from within the cave of her mind. Even though she doesn't have the faintest idea what "it" refers to. Still, she should say a proper thank-you. It's not right to lose one's manners even under trying circumstances, maybe especially so. It occurs to her that the best way to join in would be to open her eyes and let everyone know that she is, in fact, awake, so she's not just eavesdropping.

There. Open!

But wait. Did she? Are they? She tries pinching her eyelids shut. And then—*open*. Nothing happens.

"Look," says the third familiar voice, low and throaty. "She's waking up."

"Oh good. I'll leave you to it. This will give me a chance to go find something to eat real quick." Doug again. She even recognizes the sound of his footsteps as he leaves what must be a hospital room, leading her to believe that she's been awake before, in this room. He doesn't seem surprised, relieved mainly. And now that she thinks about it, this all does feel vaguely familiar. Like if someone told her about a dream she had when she was a child.

It's strange. Very, very strange.

"Mary Beth?" The first thing she senses about Darby Morton is the smell of her floral hand cream. She scoots Mary Beth's legs over and sits on the bed alongside her—yep, that's her. "It's me, Darby. And Rhea's here, too. We were so worried about you."

She blinks. The faintest hint of silhouettes form in the darkness as if she's looking at her friends underwater at night. Where are they? Where is she? Why hasn't anyone turned on the lights?

She thinks about what she should say, how she should ask it. "Dead?" She could have sworn she meant to say more words than that, but *dead* is what comes out, so *dead* it is.

"Ben?" Darby says. "Ben Sarpezze? No, unfortunately not."

Okay, she thinks. That's something to process. Mary Beth meant herself. *She* is supposed to be the one who's dead. Though no one's crying and, not to brag, but Mary Beth has always believed that if she dies—no, when, obviously—there will be a lot of people crying. She thinks about this sometimes when she brings over one of her casseroles. It's a nice bonus. Here's a casserole and now you'll cry at my funeral.

But Darby said *stroke*. Old people suffer strokes. Her grandmother died after one several years earlier. Mary Beth isn't old. Not that old anyway.

"What—what happened?" Her words come out slurred, like she's had two too many glasses of wine. Better this attempt than last, though. And will somebody please turn on the freaking lights? She's getting frustrated.

She feels Rhea hovering nearby, a nice calming force to counterbalance Darby, who can frankly be a bit stressful.

"I—" Darby stutters as though she's the one who suffered the stroke.

"She might not remember anything," says Rhea.

"Not sure we should be the ones delivering the news," Darby replies.

Mary Beth, alarmed that she may be kept in the proverbial dark and not just the actual dark until Doug returns (whenever that may be) manages to walk her fingers over to Darby and squeeze her wrist. Softly is all she can manage, but it's enough. Darby clasps her hand, hot against her own ice-cold fingers. "Okay, well, uh, Ben tried to kill you. We think. But then you had a stroke. Those headaches you were having, they were apparently not caused by stress or whatever, but were due to your birth control. That vaginal ring thing you use? Yeah, that one. It was causing blood clots and one was traveling up through your brain and eventually you had a stroke and passed out. I'm pretty sure Doug mentioned all of this? Anyway, I think Ben thought he killed you very quickly. He started to strangle you and I guess your brain went haywire and that was the final straw: You had a stroke. The thing is, I saw him go in and had a bad feeling—had no idea you were already there or else I would have—" Darby stops talking abruptly. "Oh god, I'm so sorry, Mary Beth. I promised I wouldn't get weepy—I thought you were dead, too. Then Ben was already running and—"

"Why?" Mary Beth doesn't know if it's the aftermath of the stroke or if Darby truly is being confusing. A cloudy memory of Pastor Ben in Miss Ollie's old classroom bubbles to the surface. She was frightened. Wasn't she? Uncomfortable. Something was off and she didn't quite understand why or what was happening, and then—

"Because he murdered Miss Ollie." Darby sounds like a true-crime podcaster.

But no, Mary Beth thinks. *Not right. That's not right.* That day—the day that Miss Ollie died—her head was wreaking havoc. Every step was agony. She was in constant danger of dry heaving. "There was some kind of struggle, and he stabbed her. You must have figured it out at the same time I did and once he realized you knew, then he thought he had to get rid of you, too," Darby concludes.

Mary Beth shakes her head, her mouth working at words that won't quite come. Ben killed Miss Ollie? No. But Mary Beth already knows that's not true. Does he believe it is? Just as he believed he killed Mary Beth herself? Tears drip from her eyes.

Mistakes were made.

"You don't need to be afraid," Darby soothes. "He's in police custody. I called the cops and that handsome officer—Princep—he ran Ben down while he was trying to escape. He thought he was going to be on the hook for murdering you, too, caught red-handed."

"He confessed, Mary Beth," Rhea adds softly. "In exchange for taking the death penalty off the table."

"Why?" Mary Beth croaks, and she hopes they can all chalk it up to her traumatic brush with death. She wants to see her friends' faces, to make sure this is all real.

"He was embezzling the money from the youth center and using it to fund a pretty lavish lifestyle. For a pastor, anyway. Miss Ollie's family had a history with him. Erin had it out for him and was blackmailing him, maybe to help her parents, who live in Alaska now—did you know that?—with the legal fees he cost them," Darby explains. "Sorry, that's a lot of information."

"No." Mary Beth uses every ounce of remaining kinetic energy at her disposal. "Why . . . is it . . . *dark?*"

FORTY-FOUR

▼

Rhea makes a promise to herself: Her last lie will be a small one. "I forgot Mary Beth's things in my car," she tells Darby. "I'm going to go grab them and run back up."

"Want me to come with you?" Darby offers outside Mary Beth's hospital room. She's been overly deferent and cautious around Rhea since their reunion and, frankly, it's freaking Rhea out.

"No, no, you go ahead. You have to get Jack."

The two women hug. It's been three days since Darby texted the terrible news to Rhea from the back of an ambulance, asking her to pick up Mary Beth's personal effects. Hours after that, Rhea was finally escorted into the classroom and allowed to collect Mary Beth's things. The shreds of a white T-shirt lay like a chalk outline on the scratchy carpeting of their children's former classroom; the paramedics cut it off. It seemed like an entire trip around the sun since she had crawled across to pull Bodhi from Zeke's teeth. All the things she didn't know then, she couldn't even count them.

The world was different. The space rang with an impermeable silence, the kind of silence that felt blasphemous to break. Rhea breathed deep, in and out, in and out. She tilted her palms away from her body and she made a slow, deliberate rotation. She didn't know what the hell she was doing, but whatever it was, she needed to do it. This room, this school, this chapter of her life during which she didn't recognize her own main character—her.

A plastic bag slouched across the tile, beside the classroom sink. She picked it up. And slowly, stiffly, as if nursing a forgotten injury, began collecting the items jettisoned in the chaos of stabilizing Mary Beth. A turquoise necklace. Her phone—screen cracked. A sandal. Three bobby pins. A bracelet.

Rhea picked up the familiar charm bracelet and tested the weight in her hand. The entire chain was stuffed with little souvenirs, gifts from family members. A miniature Eiffel Tower to commemorate a trip to Paris. A moose for when they went to Jackson Hole. A cross. A longhorn. A Texas flag. A wiener dog. A birthstone. Rhea could write the short version of Mary Beth's biography with the help of James Avery alone. The rhythmic clink of them was a Mary Beth signature; Rhea shuddered to imagine a world where they sat still forever, locked tight in a box for her daughters to split amongst themselves when they're old enough. How Mary Beth loved those girls.

She came across a silver N dangling from the bracelet for Noelle.

Rhea's fingers traveled the rest of the bracelet quickly. Around the entire loop she went, three times. Again. Again. Again.

Back to the N. She brought the charm to eye level, examined the link. There. The link beside it. A broken metal hook.

Rhea glanced over her shoulder and reached into her pocket.

I brought your stuff." Rhea moves slowly into the room. Doug still hasn't returned. Before she left, Darby pushed back the curtains on the window at Mary Beth's insistence.

Darby said, "Better?" But, of course, it wasn't for Mary Beth. The question only made it worse. The view is nothing but a flat, graveled rooftop where pigeons hop around with pieces of french fries in their beaks.

Mary Beth stares quietly up at the ceiling, unmoved. A toiletry bag has tipped over on the couch where Doug must be sleeping. Rhea isn't used to seeing Mary Beth without makeup. Her mouth turns down. The blue veins running from both corners of it are prominent because of either the lighting or the lack of tinted foundation.

Rhea won't act like she knows a thing about what it feels like to lose your eyesight, but her mind goes to Bodhi, to his face, to his hair, to his little-boy body; does she have a clear enough picture in her head that it could last her the rest of her life if it had to?

"Are you okay?" Rhea asks.

Mary Beth turns her face to her. Her mouth works too hard, searching for words. "Jesus . . . said." Mary Beth takes a deep, laborious breath. Her words are mushy. It's *Jee-shush* and *shed*. "I came . . . so those . . . who do not see . . ." Rhea watches her give up on the rest and a pang of sorrow hits her where she lives.

"May see," she finishes because, believe it or not, Rhea used to watch church on TV on Sunday mornings with her bowl of milky Cocoa Puffs in her lap just to feel like she had a grown-up taking care of her. "Mary Beth?" Rhea says, taking a seat at the chair beside her bed. "I'm afraid I need to talk to you and I'm coming to you because we're—" Rhea feels like she has to search for the word, too, a word that's, embarrassingly, not all that familiar in her world. "—friends."

Mary Beth's nose wrinkles. A smile? Something else?

"I found something." Rhea pulls out the small silver *A*. Gently, she turns Mary Beth's hand over where it rests at her side and presses the *A* into her palm.

She swallows. With her right fingertip, she prods the charm, feeling the angles, pinching it, bottom to top. "Ange . . . line," she says as if learning the name for the first time.

"Yeah," agrees Rhea. "Angeline." Together with the *N* on Mary Beth's charm bracelet, it creates a perfect matching pair. The Brandts' two daughters: Noelle and Angeline.

"I found it outside of Miss Ollie's class." Rhea keeps her voice low. "Because I was there the day she was killed. Too." She lets the final word land. Mary Beth's eyes search aimlessly. "Look," Rhea says. "I know you were there. I know you were involved somehow because there was blood on the charm."

There's a man who's confessed to murder because his back is against the wall, but Rhea knows all too well about police jumping to the first, the easiest conclusion, happy to let the chips fall.

"So." Rhea speaks low and slow. "I'm going to tell you how I see it. You were involved somehow and you haven't told nothing to no one." For once Rhea doesn't care how she sounds, doesn't bother to hide where she comes from. "Which means you let Darby, your best friend, spend the night in jail. You let Lola, a four-year-old, take the fall. What kind of horrible, spineless person would do that?"

A tear leaks out and rolls onto the pillow beside Mary Beth.

Rhea stares down at her own sandaled feet. "Only a person who has literal blood on their hands. Because if there wasn't blood on your hands, there wouldn't be any on your bracelet."

Rhea's played it over and over, trying to solve the logic puzzle. Was it weird when Mary Beth called every single mother in Erin's class to organize a meal train? Not for Mary Beth. It was stranger when she didn't help with the memorial service. And then her confrontation with the police officers still felt like standard Mary Beth fare, a woman who looked out for everyone, who fostered community, a woman who was, above all things, *nice.*

Here Rhea has been walking around like a social pariah because *she's* fake? Well, if that final school meeting showed her anything it's that everyone's hiding something in one way or another.

There's a long, long pause. Rhea makes no move to break it. She pictures a struggle, imagines the charm broken and flung off, skittering down the hall where Rhea would find it maybe only minutes later. "I'm . . . sorry . . ." it sounds like.

Rhea wants to shake her to force the words loose. "For what? Help me understand." The emotion in her own voice catches her off guard. For Mary Beth's bracelet to break like that and for it to be stained, this is no small thing, not something Rhea can discount.

Mary Beth says nothing, whether by choice or because she can't physically muster the words, Rhea doesn't know.

"Are you honestly saying you . . . are you trying to tell me *you* killed Miss Ollie?"

With painful, stilted effort, Mary Beth attempts to nod.

"That poor girl," Rhea says. "That poor, poor girl."

"What . . . are you . . . going to do?" Mary Beth slurs so badly it takes Rhea a beat to translate.

Rhea sinks her head into her hands and kneads the base of her skull with her thumbs. "I don't know." All this time Rhea's spent hating Miss Ollie, wanting to see her ruined, she feels like she owes her something. She feels like she owes Miss Ollie at least the truth. "I should probably tell somebody," Rhea says.

This isn't the movies. Mary Beth's a grown woman. And Rhea should have stood up for Miss Ollie when she saw Griff, who she now knows was actually Ben Sarpezze, yelling at her. The memory feels like a screw, just poking through the sole of her shoe. What kind of person has Mary Beth been? Rhea could ask herself the same thing. Whatever the answer to that is, she's a different one now and she can do things differently.

Now Rhea—and the world—knows why Miss Ollie put in her two weeks' notice. No one had ever believed the Nierlings about what Ben and his family were capable of, and when Miss Ollie realized Ben Sarpezze was taking funds from his pet youth center project, Miss Ollie knew the odds of her winning against a family like that again were slim. *If you can't beat 'em, join 'em*, as the saying goes. Rhea tries to imagine their final confrontation, what must have happened to spur Ben into resorting to murder. Cocooned in the supply room, it could have been that she was bleeding him dry. Maybe she told him she was leaving the school before she got caught, and he understood that without skin in the game, she would have everything she needed to destroy him. Or maybe it was the more personal revelation of her true identity, the sister of a friend he'd killed, and that if she hadn't let it go after these years, she wasn't likely to ever.

All along, Rhea's been collecting her little pieces and, with Darby's help, she thought they found them all. But Rhea thinks she was wrong. Mary Beth held pieces, too.

"Okay," Mary Beth mumbles out.

"*Okay?*"

Mary Beth nods. This time it looks like she's warmed up, like the motion's easier to come by.

Rhea stares at her. Something about Mary Beth is changing. She looks better, less pale. Her eyes, unseeing, gaze determinedly back at Rhea. "Okay," Mary Beth repeats.

Rhea crosses her arms. No. She doesn't get it. How can it be *okay*? Rhea is accusing her of murder. And Mary Beth is *fine* with it?

Rhea pulls out the charm bracelet and coils it into Mary Beth's hand, so that the *A* and the *N* are reunited. The last pieces should be clicking together.

"Why'd you do it?" That's what Rhea has been wanting to know. Rhea couldn't *stand* Erin Ollie. Darby *might* have thought Griff was having an affair. But Mary Beth?

Mary Beth's shoulders rise by a hair. The suggestion of a shrug. A shrug. Rhea nearly wants to claw the woman's eyes out, but the effort would seem redundant. And cruel. And then all at once it's like the answer is written right there on Mary Beth's face. Because the answer is a miniature of the mother lying before her.

"Noelle," Rhea whispers.

Mary Beth's throat tenses, the lines on her neck rising into cords. "No."

"It was *Noelle*," Rhea insists, feeling the truth of those words in her soul.

"It wasn't." Mary Beth is crying and the tears pool on her face, where she's incapable of wiping them away.

Rhea feels sick. Was the public right? Were the children a danger? Were they bloodsucking monsters all along?

She looks at Mary Beth and the answer seems obvious. Yes. And Rhea went on national television and said it was natural, but maybe it wasn't. Maybe it was deadly.

"Mary Beth, is Noelle a threat to the other children? Is she a threat to Angeline?" What does Rhea think she'll say to this? Does she really believe Mary Beth is a reliable judge in this case? But Rhea can't help herself from wanting to know what's going through Mary Beth's head.

Mary Beth's chest rises and falls and Rhea lets her collect her energy.

"I thought she was . . . found her there . . . the blood. But . . . I don't know." The words peter out.

Oh god, so Mary Beth found her daughter like that. And now Rhea has a choice. A difficult choice, but still, one for her to make. For all she knows, Ben Sarpezze did attack Miss Ollie. After all, he admitted it. He left her for dead just like he left Mary Beth. He's a bad man. And Noelle is a kid. If Mary Beth found her daughter near Miss Ollie's body, she would have jumped to conclusions. But if Ben had already attacked her, it probably wasn't anything to do with Noelle. Probably. She would have been drawn by the stench of the blood. She would have walked through it on her way to Miss Ollie. Mary Beth should have told the cops they were there. Just like Rhea should have. But they didn't.

Darby would bring Mary Beth a tissue, would dab at Mary Beth's sweet face, but Rhea isn't that guy. Her heart loses altitude as Mary Beth reaches for her wrist and holds her there.

"Would you . . . not . . . do anything for—" She swallows down the spit that's collecting in the corners of her mouth. "—your child?"

Would she? Relief hits her body like a tidal wave when she passes the threshold of the sliding glass doors of the hospital out into the baking sun. For the first time in years, she feels tears slide down her cheeks and she sits down next to a pack of medical technicians smoking beside a cement barrier. No one glances her way. This is where people come to cry and Rhea's not crying, not truly. But something is leaking out of her body, some long-held source of tension oozing from her like a toxin.

She looks down at the folded paper she surreptitiously slid free from Mary Beth's other belongings before she left the hospital room and re-reads it with fresh eyes:

She has taken a special interest in subjugating her best friend, Lola . . .

She could have told Mary Beth she'd read the evaluation. That she had wondered briefly if it might be a motive. But tomorrow she will leave the evaluation in Darby's mailbox and put the whole thing behind her.

Rhea wipes her cheeks with a bent wrist and stares out at the glare of sunshine bouncing off of car windshields, for once not particularly eager to be anywhere.

Is Mary Beth saying that when it comes to her children there is no line too far afield to cross, or even more, that there is no line at all? Rhea's made her own choices, after all, ones sometimes even she can hardly understand. She once believed she had it down, but now she considers that maybe she never will be fully qualified for a career in motherhood. If she saw a job posting, she might not even understand the description or what, exactly, she was meant to accomplish within the company.

Does she give and parent and love to make herself happy? That can't be, because so often the choices she makes for the sake of her child drive her away from her own joy.

Then is it to make her kid happy? That can't be true either, for there's no surer way of ruining a child than relentlessly guaranteeing his or her happiness.

The point of parenthood must then be that it is its own point and parents each get to choose every day from here on out to ensure it will be one worth making.

FORTY-FIVE

▼

Mary Beth's cane clicks along the tile floor as she sweeps it back and forth before each step. *Click-clack-click.*

"Come on, Mommy." The sound of Noelle's skipping feet nearby. She finds that just two months later, she can recognize them anywhere, along with the sound of her daughter's breaths, the creases of her palms, the candied tang of her sweat, as clearly as she knew her face. In many ways, the picture of her daughter has become more complete, a three-dimensional portrait. And though she suspects Doug has *not* been clipping bows into her hair like she instructs him to do, she pretends not to care.

"I'm coming," Mary Beth says gently. It's slow going, but she's getting out more. Last month, Darby gifted her with a collapsible ID cane in hot pink. It makes her feel like a visually impaired Elle Woods and she has heard the life stories of more Uber drivers than she ever thought possible, and yet she has this new idea that perhaps ministering to them is part of her life's purpose. God works in mysterious ways and all, but, you know, transparency is nice sometimes, too, isn't it, Lord? Asking for a friend!

"Can you find the numbers four, zero, zero, one?" she asks Noelle. They're both having to learn new things, new responsibilities.

Noelle hums when she's thinking hard. "Yes, Mommy, it's this one."

Mary Beth holds out her hand and allows her daughter to lead her into a psychologist's office for the second time this year. The waiting room smells pleasantly of dried rose. A John Mayer song plays in the background. The paperwork has all been completed beforehand.

"How are you?" asks Dr. Beggs. They've spoken once over the phone; the circumstances seemed to necessitate some provision of context.

"I'm okay. My doctor says if more of my vision were coming back, it probably would have started to by now." It's been three months since her stroke and though she's recovered some of her eyesight, it feels mostly as if she's trying to squint through pinholes. "Settling in to my new normal."

"You look great."

"Thanks." One remarkable thing is that Mary Beth can choose to believe her, why not?

A moment later, she listens to the sounds of her daughter fade, disappearing with the nice woman who came highly recommended on one of her mom Facebook groups.

The acute, empty sensation of being hopelessly, irreparably lost crashes over her, the way it does whenever she has the occasion to be left alone now, but already, the tide goes out more quickly and the sensation leaves her and she finds she's still standing, knowing she's right where she's supposed to be. She paces the waiting room floor as she waits for news with the same gut churning with which she might await a child's oncology results.

"She's not a sociopath," Doug assured her this morning, but there's the question of why Noelle didn't run for help when she saw her teacher injured and bleeding, there's that.

Small hands covered in blood. A red tongue licking her fingers. It's easy enough to dwell on these vivid images, burned into her pupils in this shadowy new world in which she now lives.

That day, Mary Beth went to pick up Noelle and found a classroom with no teacher and no daughter. Panic drilled through her, a panic that overtook her soul like a demon when she found them. Miss Ollie and Noelle. Together. Noelle's shoes surrounded by the lake of blood, her hands and mouth crimson. And Mary Beth had been sure that Noelle had stabbed Miss Ollie too much, too hard in order to get a drink—is that not what anyone would think in her situation?

Over and over, since the revelation of Ben's involvement in Erin Ollie's death, her mind has raced to rearrange the events in her memory. The meeting when Mary Beth had seen the two of them interact, were there signs she missed, could she have picked up on something critical? When she asked about the lock screen picture on Erin's phone, should she have asked her brother's name? Would she have if she weren't so preoccupied with her embarrassing crush on Ben? And then Erin had alluded to a love of data points, and was it not her attention to the new youth center's financial numbers that had been her and Ben's very undoing? It was.

The seed planted—the possibility that Noelle wasn't the one to hurt Miss Ollie—has at last begun to sprout, blossoming for the first time fully into what that truly means for Mary Beth.

It's demolishing her digestive system and, far more times than she would like, Mary Beth must race to the bathroom to unload her bowels in a sudden, violent onset of diarrhea.

The sense of urgency strikes again. She knocks on the plate glass window of the receptionist. "Which way to the bathroom?" She's already clenching, already terrified she won't make it.

The receptionist kindly leads her around the corner and Mary Beth escapes into the private restroom, where she sinks down onto the toilet seat, clutching her head in her hands.

She finishes, washes with soap, and fishes from her purse a glass bottle of toilet spray she's begun carrying. Poodini—*Make bad smells disappear.*

Three spritzes. She still has no idea what gave Rhea the inspiration to discover that her aromatherapy oil tinctures would actually make the most effective toilet spray on the market, but Darby helped with reworking Rhea's messaging and now she's the "From one shitty mom to the next" lady. Apparently Mila Kunis even posted about her last week on Instagram.

When Noelle's session has ended, the psychologist, Dr. Beggs, finds Mary Beth sitting in the waiting room trying to look Totally Normal.

"Done so soon?" She manages to sound like a hyperactive Chihuahua.

Dr. Beggs takes a seat next to Mary Beth and touches her forearm; people touch her more often now and it's not such a bad thing. "I told

Noelle she could keep coloring while we chatted for a few minutes." The waiting room feels empty save for the two of them, but Mary Beth still wishes for something more private. She's not sure she can properly fall apart in a public area filled with what she's sure are celebrity magazines. Maybe that's the point.

"It's good you came in," Dr. Beggs begins. "It shows that you're a very attentive mother."

Whatever it is, Mary Beth will love her daughter and help her through it and if she wanted easy she should never have become a mother to begin with. Because perhaps that's the big lie. That things will get easier. That easy is just around the corner. When there are sharp corners everywhere.

"So, I've done an assessment on Noelle. We've spoken and I want to tell you a little bit about what I've discovered."

"Okay." Mary Beth's mouth goes dry. "Yes, please."

"She's an extremely bright girl. You don't have to tell her anything twice. She's observant. She perceives emotions in others."

A thin string somewhere inside Mary Beth's chest snaps off. "Yes, of *course*, I know all of that," she says with an impatience that's atypical of her. As though it's come from a whole new person. "Sorry. I just mean that you don't need to sugarcoat it. I want to know what—I want to know who—does she have a conscience? *That's* what I need to know."

Over the last couple of months, she has observed her daughter and it seems that as she does so, she's been able to put on any number of lenses. When she's suspicious, she can find the peculiar way Noelle sometimes whispers orders to her dolls as a clear sign of sociopathy. When she's overwhelmed by love, which happens just as often, she will latch on to the way her daughter holds on to her arm as she's falling asleep to try to keep her from slipping out of the room.

"What do you think?" Dr. Beggs asks. "Do you see signs at home that she doesn't?"

Mary Beth's hands drop onto her lap. "She's always been loving to us.

And to her sister." Doesn't this woman understand that this very issue is the source of the confusion? "She's worried for characters in movies. Like Olaf. She doesn't want him to melt or anything. I always thought that was very emotionally intelligent. She likes puppies. She's *very* gentle with them." Mary Beth has already vaguely begun researching the possibility of getting a Seeing Eye dog, a cute one, something to help them, or maybe just her, move past this experience toward something positive. But that would be another responsibility on their plates.

Dr. Beggs murmurs her understanding.

"But I don't know. I don't feel like I can trust myself anymore. Maybe I'm not seeing her clearly. Poor choice of words, I know, but her teacher wrote—"

"She is *your* child," Dr. Beggs cuts her off. "I don't think you're deluding yourself into believing she's a good kid. Has she gone a little power mad? Yes, I think she probably has at school. Is that a problem? It can be. And there may even be a diagnosis to be had, but I have to tell you that my professional opinion, in which I am very confident, is that Noelle is experiencing a childhood phase that, with the proper guidance, she'll outgrow in record time."

"You're . . . sure?"

"I'm sure. In fact, in a few years, you will look back at this stage of Noelle's and laugh. It will feel like a blip on the radar. A small hurdle in the grand scheme of things."

Mary Beth tries to picture herself a few years in the future. A few years back is, after all, a lifetime. Because a few years back, she wasn't even a mother. She couldn't picture her daughters' faces. She didn't know their names or the way they smelled or the dimples on their bottoms. And so, as she tries to imagine a world that exists a few years from now, she finds she can't, that her imagination never has been or could be that vivid.

If it were, she would know that in a few years, the vampiric phase of the children at Little Academy will have been reduced to just another novelty case study in a textbook on children's psychology and one poorly written true-crime account. All the affected children will have lost the urge to bite with the loss of their first baby tooth—there will be several parents who speed this process up with a trip to the dentist and no one, at least no one within the community, will offer opinions or judgments on the matter. In a few years, Mary Beth will have a three-year-old. Having managed to improve her sex life considerably through the truncated 30-Day Sexy Back Challenge (courtesy of the now-incarcerated Pastor Ben Sarpezze), coupled with a break in her birth control regimen following a well-timed stroke, she will have gotten pregnant for a third time. Unexpectedly. Another girl. Therefore, in a few years, much to her chagrin, she will still be buying Pull-Ups and changing bedsheets. A never-ending stream of mushy food pouches and Legos on the stairs. She will be celebrating her eighteenth wedding anniversary, but at least that will still somehow feel closer to her fifth. She will never fully recover her eyesight, but she will get a retired guide dog named Bart and he will slobber and smell and she will feel God's love beaming through him. Along the way, she will have lost touch with Rhea, their kids no longer going to the same school and their painful secret being easier kept when kept apart. She will take hand-me-downs from Darby, who, incidentally, will have opened a popular gym for middle-aged folks with a comically buff man called Cannon. She will still go to church, albeit a different one. She and Doug won't save nearly enough for college because that problem feels too far away and thus, when Angeline gets into a good private, Christian college without a scholarship, they will suddenly wish they had viewed time and their money a little bit differently. She will be alarmed when her youngest goes through a biting phase, but it will pass, as will the worst of Noelle's disruptive behavioral disorder, though she will later take medication for ADHD, about which Mary Beth will become an expert and an advocate. Over those years, the Brandt family will battle bouts of talking back and tantrums, ridiculously involved homework assignments, and when it comes to Noelle, Mary Beth will never cease being skeptical of her daughter when she is involved in a disagreement with a friend, not even when she's an adult. The struggles and triumphs will ebb and flow with a feeling of both discovery and déjà vu, like they are pulled by the rhythms of the moon. Time and again as the years press on, she'll be asked to give more and more and more of herself, serving up seconds and thirds and fourths and fifths, then regenerating entire pieces of her body and soul like the poor mommy octopi Lola Morton comes to study as a marine biologist off the Hawaiian island of Kaho'olawe.

And like a good scientist, Mary Beth, too, will wonder about the mystery of it all, how in the process of raising new humans, you become a new one yourself. How love for a child can accomplish feats modern medicine and technology can still only dream of and it will do so in the blink of an eye. For that love will rewire your brain, alter your personality, modify your DNA, and explode your heart, all, somehow, without killing you. On the precipice of parenthood she once thought: *What if I change?* When the scarier question was: *What if I don't?*

Because the person she used to be could never carry thirty-three pounds of toddler around a theme park for eight hours or decipher the meaning of a single cry or roam the earth as the mythical creature known as a "morning person"; she could never have done any of the wonderful and soul-crushing and inspiring and, yes, at times terrifying things she now finds to be second nature. But one thing she will not do, not once, not ever, is look back at the year Noelle was four years old in Miss Ollie's class and laugh.

When she found them, Mary Beth's head had been pounding pain like timpani between her ears. Her temples felt as if they'd burst any moment. At first there was a disconnect. A glitch in her Matrix. She couldn't process the scene before her.

Miss Ollie was so still. Her lips pale. She looked like a waxen doll. Like a Disney princess. Noelle was frozen beside her, a tiny nightmare brought to life.

Bile coated Mary Beth's teeth, but she managed to wrestle it back into her stomach just before it was too late.

If her child had done this, Noelle would live with it forever. She would be considered a danger, never free of this single moment in time. It would define her. But Mary Beth could fix this. She could hide it. In her mind, she was already fast-forwarding, skipping to the moment when she would sign Noelle out. She'd fudge the time, but not by much. She would throw Noelle's shoes in the dumpster behind her favorite Target. She trained her mind on her children's bright futures, which she'd already done so much to secure.

She reached for her daughter, carefully, as if they were on a ledge. *One wrong move.* And then Miss Ollie breathed, a great, audible, unmistakable breath. She blinked. Her eyes searched, and that's what haunts Mary Beth the most, the way Miss Ollie's eyes found her and believed, for a second, that help had arrived.

Mary Beth should have called for it then. There was still time. The course of history could still be altered, she should have sobbed with relief.

And yet. Her heart sank deep into the pit of her soul. If Miss Ollie survived . . . If Miss Ollie survived, there'd be no escape.

Like most mothers, when it came down to it, when it came to staying up for hours rocking a screaming child through her own exhaustion or breastfeeding through tears of pain, when it came to defending her child from attack or slicing herself open to share her blood, Mary Beth would give her daughters all she had, every last drop.

Stand outside and wait for Mommy.

The scissors had begun to slide out of Miss Ollie's throat, slipping a bit further every time the teacher tried to swallow, every time her heart attempted to beat. As Mary Beth slipped her thumb and fingers through the scissors' bows, she felt, strangely, like a little girl again. How she had adored her teachers, looked forward to being a line leader, a door holder, a class helper. Being someone's child is so much simpler than being someone's mother.

There are times as a mother when it feels like too much and like she is too little, and times when she feels like she's all her children could ever need, and those when they won't need her nearly enough. She lives in the paradox of parenting, the marvel of mothering.

What if I change? What if I don't? Who am I? What have I become?

She plunged the scissors into Miss Ollie's neck and when she was certain she could no longer see the pivot point screw, she twisted.

ACKNOWLEDGMENTS

When I said I wanted to write a book about four-year-olds with a penchant for blood, there were . . . questions. Lucky for me, those questions came from the two smartest, most insightful readers I know: my agent, Dan Lazar, and my editor, Christine Kopprasch. Thank you both for your honesty and your support, and for asking even more questions during my dark night of the soul when I thought I wanted to *stop* writing this book.

I feel so at home at Flatiron Books, and that has everything to do with the wonderful team of people I get to work with there. Thank you to Nancy Trypuc, Amelia Possanza, and Katherine Turro—you are the dream team—and to Megan Lynch, Maxine Charles, and the entire sales team—I know how fortunate I am to benefit from your expertise and passion.

Thank you to Dana Spector, Olivia Blaustein, and Paige Holtzman at CAA for helping my books find homes in new mediums.

To my writing friends, Charlotte Huang (who came up with the title of this book) and Lori Goldstein—I know for a fact I wouldn't have lasted in this business this long without you. Thank you to Julia Teague and Lisa McQueen, who generously helped double-check my work (and please, rest assured any errors left behind are my own). I also have to express my undying love for my book club. It is such a delight to spend time each month with a group of women who love books—happy ten-year anniversary! And speaking of bookish friends, thank you to the Bookstagram community for championing both my work and books in general. You compose such a joyful corner of the internet and I'm happy to be a tiny part of it.

Finally, the biggest, mushiest thank-you goes to my family. While writing a book about parenting, I couldn't help feeling grateful over and over that I get to parent with my husband, Rob. And to our kids, Elliott and Colin: you are both an inspiration in every sense of the word. Thanks for being a constant presence at my writing desk.

ABOUT THE AUTHOR

CHANDLER BAKER is the *New York Times* bestselling author of *Whisper Network*, a Reese's Book Club pick, as well as the *Good Morning America* Book Club selection *The Husbands*. A former corporate lawyer, she lives in Austin, Texas, with her husband, two small children, and even smaller dog. *Cutting Teeth* is her third novel for adults.